John Farris was born in Missouri and raised in Tennessee. He wrote and directed the film *Dear, Dead Delilah* and divides his time between writing novels and making films. He lives with his wife Kathleen and their three children in Westchester County, New York.

Also by John Farris

SHARP PRACTICE

John Farris

The Fury

Futura Publications Limited
A Futura Book

A Futura Book

AUTHOR'S NOTE

The Fury is a work of fiction. I felt free to take certain liberties with actual locations in and around New York City – you won't find Sutton Mews or the Washington Heights Hospital on any map of the city. Paragon Institute is imaginary. Although my characters are as real as I can make them, fortunately none of them exists outside the pages of this book.

First published in Great Britain in 1977
by Raven Books in association with
Macdonald & Jane's Publishers.

First Futura Publications edition 1977
Reprinted 1977, 1978 (twice)

ISBN 0 8600 7566 4

Printed in Great Britain by
Hazell Watson & Viney Ltd
Aylesbury, Bucks

Futura Publications Limited
110 Warner Road
Camberwell, London SE5

1.

If the doors of
perception were
cleansed, everything
would appear to
man as it is,
infinite.
　　　—William Blake,
*The Marriage of Heaven
and Hell*

2.

On his good days
he was eerie. He
could make the rest
of the human race
feel obsolete.
　　　—Mrs. Roberta P.
　　　Edge

3.

Self-interest is the
only constant in
life, and murder
is always preferred
to impotence.
　　　—Childermass

4.

What they did would do
them in.
　　　—Anne Sexton,
The Book of Folly

For Kathy

THE FURY

One

Lately many of the girls Gillian went to school with seemed to be going through some sort of morbid crisis or startling personality change. Most had already turned fifteen, with Gillian the laggard in her class; she wouldn't be fifteen until the fourth of February, half way through the school year. Anne Wardrop, the poor klutz, had suffered a bona fide nervous breakdown precipitated by a really terrifying laughing jag during the Verdi *Requiem* at St. Bartholomew's. Gillian shuddered when she heard the details, but Anne had been through three stepfathers and a change of analyst every few months for the past two years, and everybody knew she was bound to come unwrapped. On the other hand, Carol Dommerick, she of the bright blue stare and whispering shyness, had discovered sex and was carrying on a precocious affair with a twenty-three-year-old seminarian at General Theological. After four and a half months of acute anxiety Bo Crutcher's parents had traced their daughter to Mexico and retrieved her from a hovel by the sea, strung-out, yellow as a pumpkin and full of pinworms: Bo wouldn't be returning to Bordendale this year. Sue Noyes, who had always cared a great deal about how she looked, now had to be sternly reminded to bathe and use a toothbrush, and she was letting the strong dark hair run wild over her body. Then there was Wendy Van Alexia—horse bum and free spirit—who had taken a running dive into the existentialist philosophers and the more cheerless 19th-century Scandinavian playwrights. Wendy didn't smile often any more, and Gillian missed that smile.

Bright girls, rich girls, privileged children of New York, a city that has too much of everything and is hard on tender psyches —was it the pressures of the city itself or the insupportable neuroses of their parents that was getting so many good girls down? Gillian, who had always lived on an indescribably expensive plot of ground known as Sutton Mews, loved city life, and she also knew some pretty disturbed kids who lived in Plandome and Pound Ridge. But it seemed obvious that in the city the process of natural selection was harsher, accelerated.

Gillian's father, an amateur anthropologist, had expounded on the lack of ritual, the coming-of-age rites that scarcely exist in an industrial society (except as spontaneous and frequently destructive variations on archetypal forms). In tribal cultures, regardless of the complexity of the environment, it is ritual that provides an orderly and firm sense of transition from adolescence to puberty. There is wonder in it, he said, and dignity, and a sense of fulfillment. One has lived up to the expectations of the group. One is accepted. It was quite a lot for Avery Bellaver to say, even when you got him started on a Favorite Topic.

"But in the so-called advanced civilizations, where taboo is breaking down and family groups are fragmented, acceptance and approval are concentrated in highly structured peer groups where the rules are constantly changing, dictated by fashion, by the, ah, soul-destroying perversities of our merchandisers. Except in the case of the orthodox religious among us, there are no guidelines for the young. Communication is faulty, expectations blurred. Eccentric standards of maturity are imposed on ten-year-olds by irresponsible media and disenfranchised adults. The demands change so capriciously it doesn't astonish me to see very young school children standing on street corners with bulging satchels and utter blankness in their eyes, as if they are about to scream. *What do they want? What do I do now?* There are those few, I suspect, for whom it doesn't matter, children who have the inherited stamina and self-focusing qualities necessary to survive. For the many the failure to be informed of their status is excruciating. Eventually emotional seams give way and our shamans appear unequal to the task of integrating the frail and the fallen into what is, essentially, a societal madhouse."

He blinked and was pleased with himself, but then he looked warily at his daughter.

"You're not cracking up, are you?"

Gillian was so surprised she had to laugh, which hurt his feelings. To make up for it she kissed him lightly and quickly, with a blush of sympathy and love for this aging, lonely man who could be so astute about the human condition and so totally unable to cope with the few demands that life made on him.

"I'm fine, but some of my friends aren't."

"Oh, yes. So many new faces around here. That delicate and lovely child who trembles sometimes, all over, for no apparent reason. You handle them all well. You're good to them. You listen."

Larue was the girl who trembled. She had arrived from California in October, stunned as a refugee, and Gillian immediately took her into protective custody. Larue was dismayed by the snarling city, allergic to every breath of air she took. She was accustomed to a three-hundred-acre ranch near Santa Barbara and blissful Malibu summers.

Her father was a film director, down on his luck and trying to revive his career with a Broadway musical. As a director he had the instincts of Torquemada, and he wasn't all that much fun around the house, either. Larue's mother was an actress who worked regularly in Italian co-productions on far-flung locations, a situation Gillian certainly knew by heart. The move would have been trauma enough for Larue, but the half-brother to whom she was devoted had been killed hang-gliding in the Rocky Mountains that summer. Larue had witnessed his speedy, clipped-wing collision with solid rock; thus the occasional spell of the shakes and the long-lost glaze in her eyes when she thought of him. Gillian wanted to take Larue to Acapulco with the family over Christmas, but for some dim reason Larue's father hadn't approved.

That Monday before Christmas Larue came over to spend the night. The stores were open late and both girls had shopping to

do. It was cook's night off at the Bellavers, so they ate at a
Beefsteak Charlie's on 57th, did Bloomie's and caught the eight-
thirty show at the Trans-Lux. Snow mixed with rain was falling
when the movie let out, but it was only a four-block walk to
Sutton Mews, which faced the river just south of the Queens-
boro Bridge. A freighter plowed beneath the bridge in a blaze
of running lights, making waves that smelled of the sea. Larue
was instantly homesick for the foggy Pacific.

"If you have to live in New York," she said wistfully, "this is
the place."

There were three joined, early 19th-century Adam houses on
the short stretch of cobbled mews, which had been a Bellaver
family enclave since the 1850s. The mews was reached through
an arched gateway off Sutton Square, and it was protected by a
six-man private police force. Gillian lived in the sunny brick
corner house. Twelve ample rooms, a staff of seven, most of
them day workers. Next door was Grandmother Min's house,
but for most of the year only the houseman was in residence.
The third and largest house belonged to Gillian's cousin Wade,
who like most of the Bellaver men was in the banking and invest-
ment business. They toiled in discreet offices and peopled
boardrooms across the land, tending the family's money like so
many lettuce ranchers. The family was Anglicized French, its
fortune solidly based: land grants in millions of acres dating
from the time of James II, the value of the land enhanced a
hundredfold by fossil fuels.

Two years ago, when Gillian's father had turned up alive and
well on one of the Lesser Sunda Islands after being missing for
three weeks, *Time* magazine reported that Avery Bellaver's personal worth was in the neighborhood of two hundred and seventy million dollars. It was news to Gillian, and not very interesting news; but she was ecstatic to see in print that "the
least-known member of a mighty clan has made lasting contribu-
tions to the science of anthropology." Now there was something
to be proud of.

It turned out to be one of those really great evenings that just
fall into place without any planning. After the girls changed into
around-the-house clothes—sweaters and old Levi's with wraps
and patches of vinyl tape—Gillian coaxed her father from the
depths of his ground-floor library. Avery was self-taught and

proficient on piano and bass. Larue played both classical and jazz guitar. Gillian was eclectic: harp, flute and stride piano, which she had picked up from one of the musicians who was a fixture at her mother's parties. They worked on Fats and Willie the Lion and some contemporary swinging lines until after midnight, then cooled out with an hour of recorded Shearing. The girls went to bed too exhausted to gossip, and were asleep in two minutes.

And, in the morning when Gillian woke up, her mother was home, which qualified as an event.

Gillian guessed that she had slept hard, which was a recent problem. Dreamless, muscle-clenching sleep that often left her groggy for minutes after opening her eyes, feeling as played-out as if she'd spent the night climbing mountains. A tepid needle shower usually restored her to the level of brisk efficiency, which mimed her mother's natural vitality. But this morning she had a dull headache and swollen glands in her neck, and she felt too wan to strip and go through the usual bracing routine. Anyway, there was no school and no pressing business before noon, and Laure was still sound asleep in the other bed, a pillow placed to block the sun. Gillian got up and put on her Indian mocs, drew the drapes together and went to the bathroom.

Sitting on the john she felt a little dizzy, and the headache wasn't going away. She seldom needed medicine of any kind, so there was nothing in reserve in her own bathroom. But a couple of painkillers seemed like a good idea. She walked upstairs to her parents' floor and chewed up four of the orange-flavored baby aspirin which Katharine Bellaver stored behind twenty kinds of natural vitamins.

Avery had departed early for the Museum of Pan American Culture which he had founded, and which was preparing the definitive exhibit on Toltec mythology. But Gillian heard Katharine thumping around her atelier and went up the winding iron stair to say hello.

Her mother had come in around 3 A.M. from Washington; it was now a little after seven and here she was in a leotard serenely doing the Plow. Katharine was forty-five, as long-legged as Gillian but not as tall. She was bronze-tan, with auburn hair worn in a full springy cascade of choice curls; on the girlish side but she could still get away with it. Her teeth were so good they looked unused, as if she'd been raised intravenously.

Gillian coughed glumly and looked around the studio where Katharine worked at her photography. It was one of her favorite rooms in a house she loved: vastly overblown celebrity faces looking back at her from eggshell walls, the pungent darkroom airs, the way the incoming sun joined floor and walls in brilliant geometry. Sitting here, warmed on a winter's morning, was like sitting in the shallows of an equatorial sea.

Katharine was a pretty good photo-journalist; originally she got work and magazine space because she was fabulously well-connected, but that was years ago and she had two volumes of photo essays behind her to prove she wasn't a dilettante. She had an excellent working knowledge of modern art, owned a gallery on Madison and a gallery in the Hamptons that made money, was a partner in a documentary film company and had published two short stories which Truman Capote, the grande dame of American letters, had described as "magical."

Katharine segued from the Plow into something else that looked excruciating, and smiled at Gillian.

"You didn't get accreditation for the Teheran Conference," Gillian said without thinking, and was sorry. It wasn't the time for prescience.

Katharine's smile turned a little sour.

"You *are* uncanny this morning."

"I remember you told me it was going to be a tough nut to crack."

"Oh, well, it isn't that much of a problem. The Shah will be in Switzerland this weekend. So Duff will mention me to Binnie and Binnie will mention me to his Imperial Majesty and I'll be in, and screw the goddam protocol." She moved slightly and something popped, causing her to wince in surprise. "Do you feel Christmasy yet? I don't feel very Christmasy this year."

Gillian's nose was leaking, so she nuzzled it unobtrusively against the sleeve of her robe, which had to go into the laundry anyway.

"Aren't you well?" Katharine asked.

"I feel okay."

"Your eye is really turning in this morning."

"Thanks for telling me." It was the one thing Gillian hated about herself, the slightly inward left eye that other people found charming and no distraction in a beautiful face. She'd been turning down modeling jobs since she was twelve. Well, so Katharine had scored, and they were even for now. Why it always had to be like this she didn't know. They certainly liked each other. Probably they loved each other. But they cohabitated badly, really nothing to be done about it. Gillian had too quick a tongue and her mother's obsessive sense of competition was wearing. Maybe it was something as simple as Katharine's fear that Gillian knew more about her love life than Gillian could possibly know.

"Want to join me? Rhythmic breathing is the key to——"

Gillian pressed her nose against her sleeve again.

"I'm not dressed."

"Who's watching?"

Who indeed, but Gillian was just coming into her shape and her style and she had a natural sensitivity about her body, about the last bit of baby fat and the burgeoning breasts with nipples that overwhelmed them like the noses on the faces of baby seals. She excused herself and went back to her own room.

Larue was waking up with little groans of pleasure. Gillian made room for herself on her bed beside Mr. Rudolph and Sulky Sue the house cats and explored the glands under her jaw with her fingertips. Pressure hurt. She wondered if she was about to come down with something.

"You talk in your sleep," Larue said.

"I do?"

"Loud enough to wake me up. It must have been three or four o'clock. It was still dark out, but it wasn't raining. I could see you in the light from the street. You were sitting up in bed with your eyes wide open. I thought you were talking to me, but when I said something you acted like you didn't hear. You went right on talking to somebody else. A boy, I think."

"What'd I say?"

"I couldn't catch a lot of it. You asked him if he was happy. You wanted to know—if they were treating him all right. Then you didn't say anything for a long time. You didn't move. You just—stared. You started to cry."

"God, how weird! Then what?"

"You tried to get out of bed, but you were as uncoordinated as a baby. You said, 'No, no, don't let them do that!' Then I

guess the dream was over. You just collapsed and rolled over
and pulled the covers up around your head. I had to go to the
bathroom, and when I came back you were totally zonked. Do
you know what you were dreaming about?"

"I never remember my dreams."

"I don't either, just the bad ones." Larue yawned. "What are
we going to do today?"

"Well, I have flute at one, and after that—we could go ice
skating?"

"Okay," Larue said.

Two

The Trailways bus from Newark left Peter Sandza in Atlantic City at a quarter past six in the morning. He had an hour's wait for the feeder-line bus that would take him on down to Royal Beach. The snack bar in the bus terminal wasn't open yet, so he walked three blocks, bucking the gritty salt wind off the Atlantic, and had coffee and buttered toast in the coffee shop of a hotel that looked, as most of the city looked by winter light, long-dead and archaeological.

Several rugged old men were bragging about their morning plunge into the frigid breakers. Tanya Tucker on the radio. *I believe the South is gonna rise again.* Breakfast cost Peter forty cents, so he was down to a little more than three dollars. He had his return ticket already. The coffee made his stomach hurt, a warning which he had managed to ignore for quite a while.

Royal Beach was fighting a losing battle with beach erosion. A battering storm in November had moved the tide line frighteningly close to the half mile of downtown boardwalk. Abandoned houses were crumbling into the surf. There were Corps of Engineers dredges in the harbor. Peter walked the length of the boardwalk. Shuttered shops and stalls. Pancakes. Souvenirs.

Shooting gallery. Then a fading sign over a door that looked as
if it had been padlocked for many a season. "Your fortune told
☆World-renowned psychic reader and advisor☆The Tarot in-
terpreted🖐Palmistry."

There was also part of a poster in a display case, the glass
shattered by storm or vandals. *You've read about his fantastic powers! Now let Raym   ie tell you wh   re holds!!*

Eight thirty-seven. Peter drank milk this time, in a place on the
main drag where the two waitresses were dying of boredom.
Peter's waitress had pink hair and freckles turning dark as soot
on her aging mug.

"Kind of a quiet place."

"Oh, listen, it's gory death in the winter! It'll be death in the
summer too if the Army engineers can't do something about the
beach. Worse here than it is down around Cape May. One more
good blow will do the trick. Having anything to eat? The jelly
doughnuts are fresh this morning."

"No, thanks."

"First time in Royal Beach?"

"I came down hoping to find someone. But I guess he's long
gone."

"If he's got good sense he is. You used to have to walk almost
two hundred yards to get to the water. I'm not lying! That beach
was as neat as a pin when I was a little girl, not all gobbed up
with tar from the tankers. When the oceans go, what happens
to mankind? That's the question we should be asking ourselves.
Personal friend?"

"Excuse me?"

"The one you said you were looking for."

"He's someone I heard about. His name is Raymond Dunwoodie."

The waitress looked a little more closely at him.

"Oh, yeh. People still *do* come looking for Raymond. 'Psychic
miracle worker.' I wouldn't have figured you were the type to fall
for that old wheeze."

"Just curiosity. I thought there might be a piece in it. I'm a
freelance writer."

She seemed to look too long at the frayed collar of his shirt.

"Had any success at it?"

Peter smiled, inviting sympathy.

"Not lately."

"Well—I don't think there's much to Raymond. Gypsy fortune-tellers are dime a dozen in the resorts. Raymond was just selling the same old snake oil. A little more successful at it than most. But those investigators called his bluff——"

"What investigators?"

"Oh, you know, the kind of people who are always poking around in haunted houses and exposing mediums—they got interested in Raymond when the newspapers started writing him up. Four, maybe five years ago. So Raymond went up to New York or Boston or someplace and they tested him with all kinds of machines. Sure enough, he was just a big blow-hard. A fraud. Came dragging back into town a few months later. He'd taken to drink. His mother tried to get him back on the straight and narrow, but the sheriff locked him up one night after they found him naked in a cow pasture screaming about mind-taps and government conspiracies and I don't know what. They had to send him up to Ancora for a spell."

"Ancora?"

"State hospital. The funny farm."

"Is he there now?"

"Oh, no, he calmed down and they let him go. I guess two summers ago he was back on the boardwalk reading palms, but he fell off the wagon again. He's been on and off ever since. For all I know he's out at his mother's place right now. . . . Hey, Hannah, when's the last time you saw Ray Dunwoodie?"

"Shee, who keeps up with that kook?"

"Where does his mother live?" Peter asked.

"Out the Bellbrook road. Ground floor's a bridal shop."

"Can I walk it?"

"It's maybe two miles, two and a quarter. You look like you've got stout legs."

Peter left one of his remaining dollars on the counter.

"Jingle bells."

"Have a merry," the waitress said, beaming at the buck.

For most of the way the Bellbrook road went parallel to the sound and was lined with dink cottages, boathouses, grocery stores and bait shops with old flies in the empty windows, a marina or two. It all looked tediously temporary, sandfilled, a neglected encampment. Civilization had moved on, and found something a little better. Gulls coasted above an inland dump that burned slow and soured the air.

When he saw the police car coming toward him Peter suffered a deadly moment of paranoia, cold as the point of a knife at his temple. But he kept walking briskly along, and when the car was near enough he smiled and waved. The officer didn't wave back; nor did he look Peter over too closely.

Near where the road ended in the tufted dunes he found the house, a vast salt-cured Victorian, its four stories affording enough elevation for a glimpse eastward of the sea, scintillating, blue as Old Glory. Behind the house the sound formed an inlet ringed by willows thrown together by strong winds, entangled like old mops. Peter walked up a shell drive. Someone wearing a curiously old-fashioned white dress was standing in a parlor window watching him, or so he thought, but when he was nearer the porch he saw that it was a mannequin in a satin-finish wedding gown. Otherwise Mrs. Dunwoodie didn't advertise her business.

A woman with a bulbous nose and pins in her mouth answered the bell.

"We've been sewing day and night, but it won't be ready a minute before four-thirty. I thought that was understood. Four-thirty's the best we can do."

"Mrs. Dunwoodie?"

"No. Aren't you Carolyn Oberdeck's brother-in-law?"

"No."

"What do you want then?"

"It's about Raymond."

She stared at him, mouth pursed around the pins, then opened the glass storm door.

"Good God. It's not like we haven't been expecting something, but it *would* have to come on this day of days."

She took a piece of cardboard from a pocket of her denim apron and began transferring the pins from her mouth to the cardboard, not trying to talk again until she finished. The house was overheated. The long center hall was furnished with two rubber plants. Peter heard a sewing machine somewhere back beyond the stairs.

"I hope you don't have the wrong idea about who I——"

"If it's bad you better tell me first. I'm the strong one in the family. The least little bit of added tension, and Essie will have a blowout."

The woman had two or three pairs of glasses in another pocket. She tried on one pair, couldn't make him out at all and switched to the proper lenses. She frowned at his seediness.

"What was it?" she said sharply. "Burnt himself up in bed, hey? Or was it one of those packs of ghetto kids, kicked him to death in an alley."

"Mrs.——"

"Edge. Roberta P. Edge."

"Mrs. Edge, I don't have any news about Raymond, good *or* bad. I don't even know him. I'm just trying to find him."

"Good God. Why didn't you say so? We're very busy here. We don't have time for——"

"If you could just tell me where I might find——"

"Why?" she demanded, hands on hips.

"Mrs. Edge, if I could only talk to Raymond's mother——"

"Well, you can't. She can't be bothered. She don't need the added heartache, mister."

"Mrs. Edge, I know a little about what Raymond's been through. I know why he drinks and I know that the stories he told, stories that got him locked up in a mental institution, are probably true. I believe in Raymond's powers. I have to find him, talk to him. I need his help."

She was shaking her head, but deep down she wasn't tough enough to show him the door.

"Raymond's long past being of use to anyone, including himself. And that's the truth."

"But he's not to blame."

"*I* know he isn't." She listened fiercely to the sewing machine, and fidgeted. "You didn't give your name."

"Peter."

"Peter? That it?"

"If you don't mind."

"Somehow you've got that look. Oh, I'm not talking about the way you're dressed. Don't mean a thing, it's the *eyes* and the style, how you just keep boring away quiet as you please until you've got what you're after. We've had 'em here, back when they were still interested in Raymond, still keeping watch. And you could be one of 'em, and maybe it's some kind of—trap for

Raymond, some kind of trouble he's in we don't know about. What if I told you right now to get out of here and not ever bother us again?"

"I'd go quietly, Mrs. Edge. I don't want to cause trouble. I can't afford any."

"Maybe," she said, "maybe—you could be of help to us while you're he'pin' yourself." She jerked her head toward the room behind her. "Let's sit in the parlor. Keep your voice down so Essie won't hear when she stops sewing, and wander out. We have to finish that Oberdeck gown today. We need the cash, mister."

There were two other gowned mannequins in the six-sided parlor. A plaque on a dusty desk with the legend *Complete wedding service.* Several dog-eared catalogues. Peter took off his trench coat, noting that in a matter of days one of his elbows would be through the sleeve. Mrs. Edge excused herself and was gone five minutes, long enough to worry him. He kept an eye on the drive for that police car he'd seen earlier. The sewing machine worked at random stitchings.

When she came back she had tea and a plate of cookies and a Polaroid snapshot with her.

"This was taken the Fourth of July at the Neptune's Revels Community Barbecue. Here's Essie and here's Raymond. You can see how he was off the booze for a while and started to balloon up again."

Peter studied the fat young man. He knew Raymond was just twenty-six, but he looked middle aged. High round forehead, hair long at the ears, a chipmunky grin. But there was woe beneath the brows and his hands were joined in the manner of someone accustomed to sudden fits of anxiety.

"Mrs. Edge, I know it doesn't make things any better, but there have been a lot of Raymonds."

"You know that much about it, do you?"

"I know enough."

She drew her own conclusions about his reticence and lightly touched the back of his hand.

"Maybe your stomach's in knots right now, but those are molasses and date-nut cookies. You take a handful with you when you go, they're nourishing."

"Where do I look?"

"He's in New York City, or was. That's the last we heard from him."

She showed Peter a postcard: the Statue of Liberty. The card was dated shortly after Labor Day. He couldn't read a word of the brief message. Only the signature was legible.

"Essie and me studied it together and finally made it out," Mrs. Edge said. "He was staying at a hotel called the San Marino. But that was September. He probably moved on."

"Down south?"

"No. He doesn't migrate with the other—bums. For reasons of his own he wants to stay close to that place where they half killed him. I think they pay him, why I don't know. He's hoping that a miracle will happen, that he'll get it back. All of his powers."

"How good was he?"

"Give Ray some kind of object—ball-point pen, a handkerchief—and if he never laid eyes on the person that owned it he could reel off a life history. I'm telling you, on his good days he was eerie. He could make the rest of the human race feel obsolete. But it was just a natural part of his life. He wanted to be liked, to be needed and help people. But Raymond wasn't some kind of plaster saint. He has his bad habits and his weaknesses, and they've brought him down as we know. There might be one other place you could locate him."

"Where's that?"

"Central Park. Especially sunny days in winter. He liked to sit in the sun and watch the skaters."

"I'll do my best to find him. And if I do——"

Her red-rimmed seamstress's eyes filled with tears.

"Tell him it's not the drinking that bothers us. We can put up with that. It's not knowing where he is or what's happening to him. That's what kills us."

The sewing machine was silent. "Roberta!" Mrs. Dunwoodie called. "I need a little *help* if you're not too busy."

Mrs. Edge stood up, hastily wrapping cookies in a napkin for Peter.

"Shhh, I guess you'd better go. I don't want to stir up any hope in Essie. It's too cruel."

Peter let himself silently out of the house while Mrs. Edge went back to the sewing room. As he walked down the drive he had to squint to keep the sun from blinding him. It was beautiful here, and it would be beautiful in New York. Fifty-five degrees and not too windy, a day to bring out all the pale city dwellers, perhaps even those who thought they didn't have all that much to live for any more.

With a little luck in making connections, he could be in Central Park by three o'clock.

Three

Gillian didn't believe in pampering herself, and she didn't want to ruin things for Larue, so for most of the day she rationalized her worsening symptoms, which included the swollen throat, aching joints and a slowly simmering fever that dulled her perceptions and made her session with Tynan Wells a catastrophe. If you were serious about the flute and could endure his temper then you took flute from Tynan Wells. But he had dismissed students forever for better readings than Gillian was able to provide on this occasion.

After a quarter of an hour he expressed his displeasure by leaping up from the piano bench, snatching the score from the stand in front of her (it was his own *Sonatina for flute and piano*, based on an Emily Dickinson song), ripping the score into numerous pieces and scattering them across the Persian carpet. Following that he stood for five minutes at the windows, glowering, his lower lip stuck out, while Gillian sighed inaudibly and chewed her fingernails.

"If you are ever to be any good, you must learn the things that are *not* printed on the score. You have superb technique for one your age, but I'm not looking for polish right now. I could scarcely be less concerned if you are rushed, if you miscalculate notes, if you breathe abominably; but you must never be timid. It is a *joyous* ostinato! Reveal yourself to me, Gillian. Don't bore me with mechanical repetition."

Gillian smiled bravely, but the overpowering sweetness of the roses blooming on the baby grand finally got to her. She excused herself, ran to the powder room and threw up.

When she came out Tynan was waiting for her; he put a cool hand on her forehead.

"I didn't realize you were ill. Better go home."

"I'll be all right," Gillian said, but she didn't feel any better for having heaved, just emptier.

Larue was in the library listening on headphones to Alicia de Larrocha. They made their escape and at the corner of 86th Street caught a Fifth Avenue bus going downtown.

Larue said, "All that dark, brooding fury; wow. Is he a good musician?"

"Probably the best American flutist, and one of the three best in the world."

"He wants you."

"Does he?"

"Can't you tell?"

"No."

"He'll go all to pieces one of these days, you watch. He'll fall on his knees in front of you, clutching at your skirt and begging for your love."

"Sooner or later they all do," Gillian said, getting the giggles.

"Would you if he asked?"

"I don't know, do you suppose he's that hairy all over?"

Larue whooped and leaned closer.

"Speaking of admirers, that bum back there can't take his eyes off you."

After a few moments Gillian glanced casually at the back of the bus. The bum had the bench seat to himself. He was sitting squarely in the middle. The hair that grew around his ears and clung to the back of his skull hung shoulder-length and shiny as snakes. For the moment his bald head was nodding as the bus jolted over a stretch of rough pavement. He knees were spread and his hands clutched the cord handle of the tattered Bergdorf shopping bag he'd found in a trash can somewhere. His pants were hiked up to mid-calf and his skin was dead white, which made the small sore on one shin all the more distasteful. All of his clothing looked too big for him, as if he'd suffered a drastic weight loss recently.

Pathetic, Gillian thought routinely, and at that he looked up quickly, catching her unawares.

He had one cloudy drunkard's eye and one dazzling blue eye that shocked her, held her attention. He smiled strangely at Gillian, a fawning, worshiping smile, yet there was nothing lustful about it. He hitched forward slightly in his seat as if he meant to rise and approach her, and still she couldn't look away. She was caught unawares again, but this time by something she felt rather than saw; it was like being bowled over by a strong cold wave on a beach.

Gillian jerked her head around and trembled so strongly Larue was aware of it. Larue looked at her, puzzled.

"What's the matter?"

"The damn bus fumes," Gillian explained. There were nearing 68th Street. "Could we get off and walk the rest of the way?"

"Sure," Larue said.

The bum got up too, making haste behind them. The bus doors closed on him before he could step down, and he howled in outrage. The doors reopened and the bus discharged him with a flatulent sound.

"Don't look now, but——" Larue said, taking Gillian's arm. "We've got a buddy."

"Do you want to give him money?"

"*No.*"

"Well, he probably won't bother us. Gillian, you're shaking. You're not afraid of him, are you?"

It was more like being afraid *for* him, almost dizzy with apprehension, but she couldn't explain that to Larue, or to herself. She only knew she wanted to be far, far away from this derelict who shuffled half a block behind them. Either he thought he knew her, or he urgently wanted something from her.

He didn't try to catch up, however, as they walked the short stretch down Fifth and cut through the zoo grounds. Larue forgot about him. Gillian couldn't, but they chatted about other things until they were on the crowded ice of Wollman Rink.

Gillian was a much more advanced skater than Larue; she

worked with her friend until Larue was executing turns smoothly and seemed to have the hang of skating backwards. Despite the intense sun in the hard blue sky Gillian was cold to the bone out there on the ice, and she had to grit her teeth to keep them from chattering. Great, now she had chills to go with her fired-up head. But in a little while she'd take a taxi home and crawl into bed, tomorrow she would be fine. . . .

A couple of times Gillian glanced up and saw the bum: he was just standing around, but at a reassuring distance. She was able to look calmly at him. Obviously he was still interested in her. Instead of disgust she felt empathy.

—Like most of the women in his family, who were willing to forgive Raymond almost anything.

Who? Gillian thought, startled.

"My ankles are getting weak," Larue complained.

Raymond.

She had never seen him before in her life, Gillian was sure of that. Nevertheless he *was* Raymond. Ray . . . mond Dun . . . Dunwoodie! That was as clear as if he'd come up and introduced himself, instead of furtively hanging around.

Gillian looked again for her bum, but the sun was in her eyes. And the walks and benches around the skating rink were crowded with people.

This time she couldn't locate Raymond. Maybe he'd gone for good.

"Gil, you don't have any color at all," Larue said.

Gillian smiled gently. The face of her friend, and the skaters gliding around them, were slightly out of focus. She closed her eyes and almost lost her balance, but when she looked up her vision had sharpened.

"Why don't we go up to my place and have something hot to drink?" Larue lived nearby, on Central Park South.

Gillian nodded. "I'll just take a couple of turns around the ice, and then we'll go."

She pushed off, circled smartly to avoid a gang of little boys chugging along on double runners, and found herself looking at the body of Raymond Dunwoodie sprawled a few feet away on the ice.

The contents of his shopping bag had spilled: she saw a chipped perfume decanter with a few drops of amber liquid in it. Some wilted flowers. Old magazines. There were odds and ends of clothing, including a bra; a few galvanized nails. Raymond's stony smile of terror was ear to ear; his utmost brilliant eye, pleading happenstance, peered at a sky of reciprocating blue. There was a drooling hole in his forehead an inch above the left eyebrow and a starburst pattern of blood and brains on the ice around his head. Skaters flocked obliviously past him. He was dead, but no one seemed to notice, or care.

What was left of her rational mind warned Gillian that it wasn't real, that if she was the only one who saw him then Raymond couldn't be lying there, but the taste of bile was bitter behind her locked teeth; she was already fainting as she made a clumping turn on skates and showed her ghastly face to Larue.

At the precise moment Gillian's eyes rolled back in her head and she fell, with a little murmur of apology, to the ice in front of Larue, Raymond Dunwoodie was at a telephone three hundred yards away looking for a dime. Behind him a polar bear prowled in a sunlit cage.

Raymond didn't have a dime on him. He had nothing in his pockets except a few pennies and three subway tokens.

Raymond almost sobbed. He knocked his head against the cold metal phone box and shook with outrage. But, despite his habitual lack of control over himself, his hand went instinctively to the coin return cup, and—there it was, a dime someone had forgotten! Or maybe it had dropped late because of some mechanical disorder. Never mind, Raymond had spent entire days poking into the coin return cups of public telephones without finding a cent, but now just when he most desperately needed a break. . . . No doubt in his mind at all. On this day Ray Dunwoodie had been forgiven all his sins.

For a few moments, after he'd dropped his precious dime, he was afraid his memory would betray him, and he wouldn't remember the unlisted number. His tongue dried up against the roof of his mouth. Then it came to him. He repeated the number twice before dialing to be sure he had it.

The girl picked up with the proper four-digit response and

Raymond's heart thudded as he tried to speak authoritatively.

"This is Raymond—Raymond Dunwoodie. Now don't hang up! I've got one for you this time, no mistake. I'm absolutely certain!"

"Ray-mond," she said, "we just can't put up with any more of your——"

"No, no, listen! She's just a kid, fourteen, maybe fifteen years old—just the right age—I'm telling you, she's a sensitive—hasn't come through yet, but she's on the verge—so let me talk to him, Kristen."

"Oh, Raymond, I feel for you if this is just more of your shenanigans."

"No! God, this one's amazing! As worn-out as I am, she was reading me like a newspaper. But she isn't all that aware yet, she either blocks what she doesn't want to know or lays off her reading as a hunch, the usual reaction."

Kristen hesitated. Raymond held his breath when he realized he was panting into the phone.

"All right, Raymond, he's very busy but I'll try. I'll have to put you on hold."

"Okay. But don't keep me waiting too long," Raymond said, with a touch of *amor propio* that pleased him. Then he remembered. "Hey!" he said frantically, "I'm calling from a pay phone. And I don't have another——"

"What's the number you're calling from, Raymond?"

He edged back and focused on the numbers printed on the dial, read them off.

"Very good, Raymond. Expect him to call back within five minutes."

Raymond hung up, then glanced around to see if anyone else was waiting. He was prepared to kill to keep them away from *his* telephone. He reached into the shopping bag for his last bottle of Annie Greensprings and fed himself gouts of wine.

It was cold in the shade where he waited, and the cold penetrated the layers of sweaters he wore. He waited with a hand on the receiver of the telephone. He heard the oompah music of the park carousel. He heard a siren. It seemed to Raymond that he waited much longer than five minutes.

At last the phone rang, and he snatched up the receiver.

"Yeh, this is Raymond." He listened and grew ecstatic. "All

right—right—and I promise you won't regret it." He listened longer and was cunning. "What do you want to know for? I mean, I can point her out to you when you get here, that's good enough, isn't it? Okay, I'll be on the deck that overlooks the rink. But you'd better make it soon."

Raymond hung up. He trembled from happiness. He gathered up his belongings and trudged toward the ice skating rink, taking the long way to avoid climbing all those steps by the bears' cages.

A square-backed ambulance was parked at the southeast gate to the rink, and a crowd of the curious had gathered. The ambulance crew was wheeling someone toward the opened doors. It was her. She was unconscious on the stretcher.

Raymond froze in panic. Then he ran awkwardly toward the ambulance. He pushed the people aside. The other girl, tears in her eyes, climbed into the back of the ambulance with her friend. The doors were closed just as Ray got there.

"Wait!" he cried. "Where are you taking her?"

One of the men in white looked distastefully at Raymond.

"She's—" Raymond said, and realized that anything else he might say would sound ridiculous. He panicked again and grabbed a white sleeve, smudging it. *"I said where are you taking her?"* He saw the approaching cop out of the corner of his eye. The ambulance driver shook him off and climbed in behind the wheel. Raymond tried to follow, but the cop got in his way.

"Alright, fella. Don't make trouble for yourself."

Raymond wept. "You don't understand! I have to know who she is!"

The ambulance siren whooped. It was rolling, rolling away from him.

"I said move on."

Raymond got a little push from the hickory, not much of a push but enough to set him down on his butt. By the time he got to his feet he could see it was hopeless. The ambulance was headed for the nearest park exit, that's all he knew, and he'd *lost* her, and what was he going to say this time? He'd deceived them before when he was desperate, they would never give him another chance.

The cop was still watching him, so Raymond walked slowly away, brooding. High above the rink he sat on a graffiti-covered rock. There he finished his bottle of Annie Greensprings.

"Mr. Dunwoodie?"

Raymond turned, grinning, as he always did when startled or demoralized.

A man of medium height in a trashy-looking trench coat was walking uphill toward him. The man was in his late thirties. He had a face like an anvil with skin stretched over it, untidy and prematurely silvered hair, deepset eyes the color of tarnished nickel. Raymond had never seen him before.

But the eyes told Raymond everything he cared to know about the man. He backed away, pointed west and started to babble.

"They took her a few minutes ago! In an ambulance! She had an accident or something! That's the truth! Check the hospitals, you'll find her."

The man slowed down as he approached Raymond, but Raymond continued to back away from him. He had arthritic knees, which made any sort of movement other than a straight-ahead shuffle painfully hard to manage.

"You're Raymond Dunwoodie, aren't you?"

"Sure! Sure I am. I didn't make it up, I swear! She was skating there on the rink ten minutes ago——"

A flicker of puzzlement in the secluded eyes.

"Who was?"

"The girl—the girl I called up about. The sensitive." Raymond backed into a bench and stopped. The man stood a few feet away, hands in his pockets, just looking at him.

"Oh, yes," he said softly.

Raymond breathed deeply, and it sounded like a sob of relief. He sat down involuntarily. He realized he had to go to the bathroom. He hoped that this wouldn't take long, that the man would just give him twenty dollars and go away. But he began to have doubts.

"Why didn't the Doc come himself? He said he would."

The man shrugged. "You know how it is."

"Well, I—" Raymond licked a fever blister. "He's going to pay me, isn't he? When you find the girl."

"The truth is, Raymond——" He took a seat near Raymond on the bench. "It's another sensitive we're interested in. We need to locate this one fast."

"You know better. You know I can't work long-range any

more. Why don't you use Bruckner, or Helen Tavaglini?"

Raymond found the nickel eyes unreadable. But in the last sixteen seconds of his life Raymond's powers focused accurately on the truth of the situation in which he found himself. His mind went blank from shock.

"I don't have access to them, Raymond," the man admitted. "You're the only hope I've got. It's worth at least a hundred dollars to me, more if I can get it. Tell me how much you want."

"No. I don't work any more. The girl was an exception, she was so close and so powerful——"

Raymond stood up; the man stood with him, a strong hand on Raymond's right arm, inches above the wrist. Raymond still weighed close to two hundred pounds, but his bones were light and he had no useful muscle. He sensed the man's demon, and he knew that the man would not be adverse to tearing his arm off at the shoulder if Raymond displeased him.

"I don't know you!" Raymond squeaked. "I only talk to the Doc! Nobody else!"

He tried to jerk away from the man but only succeeded in giving his captive arm a painful wrench. So he moved the other way, throwing his weight against the man; Raymond half turned, losing his balance, and found himself looking at a gray sedan idling across a stone bridge fifty yards away.

Psychically he recognized the shape of death in the nondescript sedan and automatically he grinned, a split second before the silenced revolver fired.

The heavy slug hitting the ridge of bone above Raymond's left eyebrow had the impact of a piece of reinforcing rod hurled end-first by a strong man from a distance of six feet; Peter felt a wet sting of macerated bone and tissue as the back of Raymond's head exploded and the derelict sagged down hard and to the left, losing his grip on his shopping bag.

Instinctively Peter let him go, turned and plunged downhill, getting off that bare hump of rock as fast as he could, reaching into his left coat pocket for a kleenex to wipe his bloody cheek. He headed for the biggest crowd he could find on short notice.

Twice he changed course abruptly until he was on a path with a couple of chestnut and pretzel venders between himself and the road, between himself and Raymond. He didn't look back until he was part of the larger crowd in front of the skating rink.

Then he saw, at a glance, Raymond lying on his back on the rock and a couple of kids standing a respectful distance away, staring in fascination at Raymond's tap-dancing right foot.

He also saw the gray car.

It had traveled a hundred feet beyond the place where he'd been shot at and where Raymond undoubtedly had blundered the wrong way at just the right moment for Peter's sake. The driver had turned onto an access road and was trying to get around two park maintenance vehicles.

Pressing question: how many cars did they have, and how many men on foot, and what were his chances of getting out of the park alive?

Somehow it looked hasty and ill-conceived to him, the shot from the moving car. Poor strategy; acknowledging the fact that they would go ahead and kill him if they had the chance, the method chosen indicated faulty logistics. So they had Raymond Dunwoodie under surveillance for some reason, but *his* appearance was unexpected. One car, then. Two men likely.

Peter put his hand through the right side bottomless pocket of his trench coat and grasped the .38 Baretta automatic in his suit coat pocket, trying not to shove his way through the strolling mothers with perambulators, teenagers with radios grafted to their ears, old folks with peaceful sun-warmed faces. The car was coming after him, of course, but slowly because of the people. The range was now about ninety yards, so discount the marksman trying another shot from what must be a silenced revolver. To lose the car Peter jogged down a long flight of steps and walked through an underpass, emerging near the zoo's cafeteria. They had to know that if they left their car and tried to close in on foot they were in danger of being blown away. They must already have called for backup units, but that would take a few minutes. NYPD would not be a factor.

Peter surveyed his options quickly. He had to get out of the zoo: wide-open spaces and too few people. He passed up the new 63rd Street crosstown subway station in favor of a more distant BMT station on 60th. He raced across Fifth Avenue against the light; a taxi driver was still yelling at him when he reached the subway entrance. In less than sixty seconds he was on an EE train bound for Queens.

As the cab in which Dr. Irving Roth was riding entered the park it was overtaken by two police cars going north toward Wollman Rink with sirens wide open. Up ahead two more police cars were pulled off beside the road, dome lights flashing. There seemed to be an awful lot of blue uniforms swarming over a ridge of rock that overlooked the rink. And something else. Roth had only a glimpse of the tattered man lying flung out on his back, but a glimpse was enough. Something very serious had happened to Raymond Dunwoodie.

He sat back in a corner of the seat and reached for a handkerchief; there were beads of perspiration on his balding head. The cabbie slowed the pile of junk he was driving.

"I can let you off here; can't get no closer because of all the cops, mister. Mister? Hey! This is what you wanted, isn't it? The skating rink?"

"Keep going," Roth said.

On the subway train Peter changed cars twice to make certain he hadn't been followed, and then he got off at the second stop across the river.

Only then did he feel safe enough to go into the john, where he was sick for half an hour, so sick he could scarcely hold his head up, doubly shaken by the murderous way his hopes had died. His resistance to adversity had fallen very low. Part of the trouble was fatigue, he'd been on the run and on the skids too long. But it was weakness too; he knew he'd been both weak and stupid hoping for so much, for a miracle from another victim, a burnt-out case like the world-renowned Raymond Dunwoodie.

Stupid, he thought, nourishing his anger, the only vital spark he could find. Stupid to go walking right up to him without making a thorough sweep of that area of the park. In a chance encounter they'd come so damned close. Childermass would be alerted now; after futile weeks of looking he'd be encouraged and impatient. How much had they spent so far, in pursuit of one man? A million? Childermass would spend another million if he had to. And, given his money and his manpower, he would take advantage of Peter's obsession and in the end he would win. It was just a matter of time.

Peter left the john and went upstairs to cleaner air. He waited on the elevated platform for the city-bound train to come. He ate the last of the date-nut cookies Mrs. Roberta P. Edge had provided him. The cookies had kept his stomach quiet all day. Would she blame him when she heard the news about Raymond? Of course. And that might bring the police into this, if Childermass wasn't quick to silence her with a visit and a couple of thousand dollars on the table.

Despite the shooting, it was possible that his moments with Raymond Dunwoodie hadn't been wasted. From the way Raymond had talked there was another one, somewhere. A girl, perhaps about the same age as his son.

If she was as gifted as Raymond seemed to think then he had to find her. But he was hot, dangerously hot, and to get to the girl who had been taken away to one of the city's hospitals he'd need help.

The sun was setting; it would be dark in half an hour. His train came and Peter got on.

Peter had no watch but he knew he had plenty of time to reach lower Manhattan despite the rush-hour crowds. At precisely seven o'clock in the Canal Street IRT station a public telephone would ring. For three nights in a row he hadn't been there; he'd thought seriously of never getting in touch with her again, but tonight he knew he had to answer.

And, very likely, just by lifting the receiver, he would condemn someone else to die.

Four

Larue telephoned the Bellaver house from the lobby of Roosevelt Hospital. The housekeeper, Mrs. Busk, switched her to Katharine Bellaver's secretary. Miss Chowenhill came on and asked rapid-fire questions. Where and when did it happen? How had Gillian acted prior to collapsing? Did she hit her head when she fell? And what was the name of the intern in charge? Find out, please, and have him call me in ten minutes at this number.

In the interval Miss Chowenhill made several calls, the first to Gillian's pediatrician for a fast medical history. No, she was not allergic to any of the common broad-spectrum antibiotics. The second call was to the senior partner of a very old law firm that devoted seventy percent of its time to Bellaver family business. Gillian's godfather. He cut short a partner's meeting and was driven uptown to the hospital. She called the director of Roosevelt and left a message. She called one of the half-dozen finest neurosurgeons in the world.

By then a chief medical resident at Roosevelt was on another line. Miss Chowenhill gently made him aware of the fact that he had a very important patient on his hands, and that Gillian soon would be under the scrutiny of a team of specialists, as much talent as you could pack into one room.

The resident was cooperative and candid. He didn't know what the hell it was. They couldn't rule out anything at this point, including meningitis. Her fever had spiked to nearly 106, and she was having difficulty breathing. She'd had a small convulsion. They had packed her in ice and placed her in an oxygen tent. Gillian was on fluids and Tylenol and phenobarbital to inhibit further convulsions, and he recommended 1.2 million units of ampicillin immediately, if it wouldn't disagree with her. Miss Chowenhill okayed the ampicillin.

After the resident rang off she consulted Katharine's calendar for the day, skillfully read between the lines and located Katharine at the Greenwich Village apartment of a playwright she'd been seeing a lot of lately.

Avery Bellaver was more difficult to run to ground. He had no secretary and no routine. On occasion he had departed for places like Honduras or the Kaoko Veld without telling anyone he might be gone for a month. Miss Chowenhill tried the family foundation. She tried societies, clubs and colleagues. It took her an hour and a half to ferret him out of a dim subcellar of the Museum of Natural History on Central Park West.

On Bank Street in the Village Katharine thought briefly about trying to coax Howard Wrightnour back into bed for some kind of fast windup, which she desperately needed. But one look at him, slump-shouldered and smoking a cigarette at her feet, discouraged her without turning her off.

Howard was a large man with snappish black eyes and a khan's mustache; women commonly eyed him and thought *rape*, but in truth he was a gentle and sensitive lover, perhaps cursed with too much sensitivity, because any kind of disturbance was fatal to his concentration. If one of his goldfish hiccuped at the wrong time, that was the end of it. Howard thought Katharine had taken the receiver off the telephone, and Katharine thought Howard——. He was sulking now, a little ashamed of himself.

When she was dressed she hugged and tongued him like a mother cat, bringing him out of his mood.

"I really have to run."

"I hope Gillian is okay."

"She didn't seem to be feeling well this morning. But a fever that high——"

"It's not so serious in someone her age. I mean it's not necessarily——"

"I'll call you. Don't you think Brent's reaction in the second
act would be impotent fury?"

Howard pondered the suggestion and nodded.

"I'll try it that way."

Katharine smiled tensely and left him.

There were men in her life who excited her much more than
Howard Wrightnour, but no one who needed her half as much.
Thanks to her he would finish his play, the Big One to follow
his off-Broadway critical success, the drama that would put Howard up there with O'Neill. If her own writing suffered while she
was nurturing Howard, well, there was satisfaction in being mid-
wife to a significant artistic event. She would have money in the
production, of course, not the whole shot but enough to ensure
that his play would be done in style.

Katharine drove her car, an indigo-blue Porsche with DPL
plates, uptown to 59th. Chowenhill had been guarded on the
phone. Obviously Gillian was quite ill, and the ferocity with
which she had been struck down alarmed Katharine. She left her
car where it was handy, in some strictly forbidden area of the
hospital grounds, and went in.

Five minutes later she was at the bedside of the semiconscious
Gillian, who seemed not to recognize her.

"Good God," Katherine said fervently. "What *is* it, Wally?"

The lawyer, whose name was Wallace Mockreed, put a hand
on her shoulder.

"Can't tell. If it's a virus, they'll find it in her blood. And they
need a spinal."

"As soon as possible," the resident in neurophysiology said.
"Her fever is down now, but that may be temporary."

Katharine looked at him with a wide vacant smile.

"Spinal tap? I'd prefer to have Dr. McKinstry do that. He's a
specialist. I don't want anyone else to touch her. He's coming,
isn't he, Wally?"

"Right away. Don't worry."

"And where is Avery?"

"Coming."

Katharine looked again at Gillian, at the half-open uncom-
prehending eyes flushed by the fever of unknown origin. For the

first time she felt the full impact of what might be a tragedy. She then felt a little faint, but she lingered over details that were inexpressibly precious to her. Faint smudge of Gillian's eye shadow; the tiny gold ring in one earlobe; the clean white center part of Gillian's hair. The artistic hands of her child, those fine long fingers and—nibbled nails. How often had she complained, nagged, blown her stack? "Habit portrays character. Bad habits attract bad opinions." Gillian went right on shredding her fingernails. A lot of things went through Katharine's mind in a matter of moments. That night shortly before Gillian's thirteenth birthday when Gillian crept up to her room, balled underpants in one hand. Rusty red spot the size of a half dollar on the pants. "Is this it?" she'd asked, anxious and hopeful. Katharine thought about how much trouble it was to get Gillian to dress up, and how there was always something amiss with even her most stylish clothes: a smudge or a streak or an inexplicable wrinkle, buttons gone or dangling, so that she looked set-upon, or burgled.

"I think I'd like to smoke," Katharine said in a low voice.

In the hallway of the general medical unit she took Larue's arm. "You've been so much help, I don't know how to thank you."

"It was so sudden. I know Gillian wasn't feeling all that good, but she didn't complain. I hope she——"

"Gillian's going to be all right. Larue, you look tired. Shouldn't you be getting home? Wally, would you see that Larue has a cab? Tell your father I've heard nothing but good things about his new play. We'll call just as soon as we have news about Gillian."

News was a long time coming. Specialists trooped in and out. They held conferences. A lab report came down: it was not meningitis. Nevertheless Gillian's temperature fluctuated between 103.5 and 105 degrees. She was placed on a thermal mattress. She dozed, awoke, spoke deliriously to several people, none of whom were in the room with her. Her respiration was shallow; glands in her neck remained swollen, which suggested a viral infection, despite a normal throat appearance. The hematocrit was within a normal range. Her platelet count was minimum normal, but the leukocyte, or white blood cell, count was on the low side, not uncommon with a number of diseases, including influenza.

Avery Bellaver took his wife to dinner at a place near Lincoln Center, an area filled with gimmicky restaurants that serve miserable food. This one celebrated old-time aviators. Captains of the clouds. Devil dogs of the air. A Fokker replica hung from the ceiling. There were sepia murals of exploding aircraft. The waiters wore stovepipe boots, those cunning leather helmets that fit like bathing caps, goggles and long white scarves that occasionally trailed in the meals they served.

The Bellavers concentrated on a pretty good wine list and ate sparingly.

In the past three years they had spent fewer hours together than Katharine spent at her dentist's. It would have surprised even her closest friends to know that she had any affection for Avery at all; according to their thinking she hung on to the marriage for all the correct reasons, the least of which was money. She'd won her place in the family, was tolerated by the women and respected by those Bellaver men who didn't actually covet her. Avery Bellaver was the clan anomaly, obscure, strange and unapproachable. It was admirable that she had landed him, went the smart talk, but then she'd *worked,* darling, all those *years,* getting long in the tooth while appealing to his mind and then his glands, probing, probing deftly to find a human response or two, thereafter making the most of his no-doubt feeble urges.

Katharine had heard all the gossip and thoroughly enjoyed it. She'd never made the least effort to explain her husband to anyone. His sexual urges had been and were still quite strong, thank you; the gossips seemed to have forgotten her two miscarriages a year apart. Then had come Gillian and the simultaneous tragedy nobody knew about, which decided her against further pregnancies. She still looked forward to going to bed with Avery on those occasions when mood and opportunity coincided. As for his social shortcomings, he was less shy than preoccupied. He was no good with the self-important and aggressive examples of the species, whether cab driver, maitre d', social parasite or ersatz royalty. He was not a gamesman. Politics alternately bored and frightened him. Avery's obsessions were vastly more rewarding and of some value to mankind. He wanted, for instance, to learn everything he could about the daily life of a remote Mexican Indian village he'd been visiting for twenty-five years. Once, early in the marriage, Katharine had accompanied him to Mtecla, had seen the entire village turn out to greet Avery Bellaver. He spoke their dialect and knew all their names. In this hot, dry land the hesitant bumbler disappeared; he was at ease, under no compunction to behave as a Bellaver is supposed to behave. They were not a peaceful people, they were suspicious of strangers and had stoned missionaries to death, but his respect for them inspired trust and even love.

Katharine had similar feelings for her husband, though his life was not her life and she needed the attentions of many men. She was decent about her appetite, arranging trysts so they couldn't be a source of embarrassment to him. Avery had never hurt her and she would never hurt him, the purest definition of love Katharine had to offer.

Avery studied a mural-sized portrait of a long-ago leftenant.

"I was four years old when my brother was commissioned," he said. "He looked like that. I was in awe of him."

"Did he die during the war?"

"Yes, but not in combat. He slipped on some icy stairs in Amiens and broke his neck."

"What was his name again? Oh, Charles. Mother Min wanted us to name our first-born after Charles." Katharine finished her third glass of a '64 Bordeaux. She was feeling the effect of the wine and the vodka martinis that had come before. "Do you think about him?"

"About my brother?"

"No. About *our* son. About the one who didn't live. Gillian's twin."

He shook his head. "Do you think about him?"

"Yes. Sometimes. I wonder what he'd be like if he had lived. And Gillian thinks about him, or she used to. She asked a lot of questions. I explained, as best I could, about the cord. I told her there just wasn't anything to be done. If he'd survived, he'd have been a vegetable." Katharine grimaced. "The fever. If it stays high long enough it'll just ruin Gillian's brain. Short out the synapses or something. How cruel for her to get this far, then——. She'll be——."

"Katharine."

"I know, I know. But I can't help feeling shaky. All things considered, our luck's too good. So we lose one in childbirth, but there's a bonus baby. The goddamn Bellaver luck. We're not all that charming and we've never been a national craze, but unlike the poor bedeviled Kennedys—let me see the check, please."

She took it from Avery as he was about to pay, did some quick addition.

"You've overcharged us a dollar and a half," Katharine told the waiter, who pretended to be grief-stricken. Later she said fondly to her husband, "They'll try to do it to you every time." Avery just smiled, bemused.

On their return trip to the hospital they were introduced to Dr. Hubert Tofany of the Division of Tropical Medicine at Columbia University.

"I understand you both travel a great deal. Could you give me a rundown on where you've been during the past six or eight months? You needn't bother with airport layovers."

"Do you think we could have brought back some kind of bug?" Katharine asked. "We'd have been sick ourselves."

"Not necessarily. At the Yale arbovirus lab they have a rap sheet on approximately four hundred viruses, most of them obscure, all potentially dangerous, and each has its own peculiarities. They incubate in mysterious ways. There are viruses that bother adults hardly at all, but they're devastating to children. And the reverse is true. We'll take a blood sample from each of you. What we'd like to do now is move Gillian into an isolation bed at Washington Heights. We're better equipped there to do the kind of serological analysis necessary to track down the . . . culprit. A serum may be available."

Katharine looked at her husband, who said, "We . . . my wife entertains frequently. We have visitors from all over the world. It could just as easily be someone we've had to dinner."

Dr. Tofany smiled patiently.

"I'd like as complete a list as possible. All recent house guests."

Katharine said, "Tracking them all down, that could take a lot of time."

"Yes."

"Meanwhile if you can't find out what it is—if it's something you've never seen before—"

"We'll continue the indicated protocol. Combinations of antibiotics. Sometimes, even with a new strain of virus, the patient is able to produce antibodies to destroy it. Try not to worry, Mrs. Bellaver."

They visited Gillian briefly while arrangements were made to transfer her to the hospital at 167th and Broadway.

"She's been talking again," the licensed practical nurse told them.

"Hello, darling," Katharine said. "Poor baby."

Gillian opened her eyes and looked at her through the oxygen tent.

"Ruh," she whispered.

"What did she say?" Avery asked. "Would you say that again, Gillian?"

"She hasn't been very clear," the LPN reminded them with a smile.

Gillian began screaming.

It took three of them, Katharine, Avery and Dr. Tofany, to keep her from tearing free of the IV needles, from tearing the oxygen tent apart. The seizure, and the screaming, continued for almost half a minute. Her strength was the strength of insanity, or desperation.

"Larue!" she cried, and subsided, as wet as if she'd stepped out of a shower.

"Restraints, Doctor?" the nurse said.

Tofany was checking the IV placements.

"No. Sponge her off."

Katharine retied Gillian's hospital gown, which had almost come off during her struggle. Blood throbbed in Katharine's temples and her fingers didn't work too well. There was a small cross, of gold and black onyx, on a chain around Gillian's neck. She had never seen it before.

"Shouldn't the phenobarb keep her quiet?" Katharine asked.

"Yes. What was that she was saying, do either of you——"

"She was calling Larue. That's her friend, the girl she was skating with today. Avery, where did the cross come from?"

"I've never seen it before."

"Nurse!" Dr. Tofany said harshly.

"Yes, Doctor?"

"Don't touch her!"

"But you——"

"*Have* you touched her since you came on?"

"No, sir, that was just a few minutes——"

"Go get your hand attended to. Don't you have better sense than to come into a sickroom with an open wound?"

The LPN stared at him. He nodded curtly at her right hand. She looked at the blood-soaked Band-Aid on the back of the hand and gasped.

"My Lord!"

"We're dealing with a virus here we don't know anything about. This kind of unforgivable carelessness——"

"Doctor, I don't understand. This was just a scratch. It hardly bled at all two days ago——"

"It's bleeding now. Copiously. Get out of here."

The nurse hurried out. Katharine took another look at the pale, becalmed Gillian and followed the nurse from the room. She went to a telephone, looked in her purse for a number which Larue had scribbled for her and dialed shakily. The phone rang six times before a sleepy voice answered.

"Larue?" She could hear a television playing.

"Uh-huh."

"This is Katharine Bellaver."

"Oh, *hi*, Mrs. Bellaver. Timezit?"

"A little after nine."

"I fell asleep. All that exercise—is Gil okay?"

"She's being moved to Washington Heights Hospital. There's a chance you've been exposed to something very contagious. We don't know yet."

"I feel fine."

"Are you there by yourself?" Katharine asked.

"Dad has some people in."

For the first time since Gillian had screamed Katharine was able to relax.

"Then you're all right."

She heard a stifled yawn, which was followed by a puzzled response.

"Yes, ma'am. When will I be able to see Gillian?"

"Not for a few days. She'll be in isolation until they're sure of what she has. If you notice any symptoms at all, even if you think you're just coming down with a cold, *call us.*"

"I will."

"Larue? Do you know anything about a gold and onyx cross Gillian is wearing?"

"Oh! It's mine. I know she's not into religion, but I was so upset when she passed out . . . while we were waiting for the ambulance to come I put it around her neck. The cross was blessed by a Jesuit who my mother considers to be a very holy man. I didn't think it would do any harm. I hope you don't mind."

"Of course not. That was very thoughtful, Larue. I'll keep in touch."

For a couple of minutes after she'd hung up Katharine leaned against the wall near the telephone, feeling dull and drained; a headache was coming on. Gillian's frantic screaming was too much with her; it was her daughter's agony for Larue that had sent Katharine witlessly to the telephone. It seemed almost as if Gillian had willed it, directed her to make the call. But nothing was wrong; there was no emergency. Larue was at home and safe.

Katharine knew she needed to get a little better grip on herself, because Gillian could go on like this for days. She would insist on a room at the new hospital as close to her daughter as she could get. No more thoughts of the holidays in Acapulco, and Howard Wrightnour would have to struggle along without her. Only Gillian mattered now.

Five

Robin caught the little pop fly a few feet to the right of the first-base line and sat down hard, clutching mitt and ball to his chest; while waving the first baseman away he had taken his eye off the ball for a moment and misjudged it. But he was up immediately, ready to charge the unprotected plate if Shanley, the runner on third, decided to come home. Shanley bluffed but returned to the base. Robin jogged back with the ball as he'd been taught to do at Johnny Bench's clinic; only then, with the plate covered, did he lob the ball back to his pitcher. He held up a finger.

"One more!" he yelled. "Any base!" Feast of the Assumption had the sacks loaded in the bottom of the seventh; two out and the Barksdale Baptist Little Leaguers were clinging to a 10–9 lead. The batter was a lean long-armed kid named Giffin, who had really tagged one in the 5th.

Coach was up off the bench waving the shortstop closer to third. Robin adjusted his chest protector and picked up the mask he had discarded to chase the pop fly.

"Let's hear it!" he chided the tired infielders. "Little chatter now! Stay alive, we've got 'em."

The sun was setting behind the third-base bleachers, casting an orange glow over the field. Robin hunkered down and glanced at Shanley, the biggest boy on the Assumption team.

Shanley played first base, and early in the season Robin had had a run-in with him while trying to beat out a soft roller. A bad throw had pulled Shanley a step off the bag and in trying to tag Robin he'd hit him in the mouth with his elbow; result, one shattered eyetooth and three other teeth so loosened they had to be wired. It could have been an accident, but Robin wasn't all that sure. Red Shanley was the sort who enjoyed a cheap shot if he thought he could get away with it. He looked heavy, almost fat, crouched down at third with his left foot nudging the bag, but Robin could vouch for his strength and for a big kid he could really get it into gear.

"Look who's here," Robin sneered as Giffin stepped into the box. "Hey, man, your bat's got holes in it. Wave goodbye, Giffin, wave goodbye."

"Don't you ever shut up?" Giffin muttered, glaring at the pitcher. Robin signaled for Harkaday's best pitch, a change-up, and stuck his mitt out. Giffin let one go by on the outside corner that the umpire called a strike. They were having a fit over there on the Feast of the Assumption bench. Giffin backed off looking disgusted and hit the ground with his bat.

Robin laughed. "That's what happens when you don't go to confession. Okay, Giffin, coming right at you. Show us your beautiful swing."

Ball one, and Robin had to go down to smother it in the dirt. He called time and went out to settle his pitcher down.

"Break one off," he told Harkaday.

"Coach said——"

"Break one off anyway," Robin ordered, hoping he wouldn't end up chasing the ball all the way to the backstop while Shanley sauntered home.

He went back behind the plate, and Harkaday threw his best curve in two weeks. Nevertheless Giffin got a piece of the ball, topping it to the pitcher's mound.

"'Home!" Robin yelled, crouching over the plate. The best and safest play was to first and Harkaday, who had been quick to pounce on the ball, knew it. But he was used to obeying Robin, so he hitched around and threw awkwardly as Shanley came barreling down the chalk from third.

The throw was wide but Robin knew it was going to be. He took two quick steps, grabbed the ball with his bare hand and flung himself back toward the plate, kneeling and covering it with his body. Shanley hit him and they went rolling over and over in the dirt. Robin held the ball, jumping up as the umpire called Shanley out. Shanley stayed down, open-mouthed, clutching his stomach. Robin glanced nonchalantly at him as he walked away. The knee in Shanley's solar plexus had been purely accidental, of course—but he was pleased with the results.

As the team was getting together for the after-game prayer Coach gave Robin a long look, but Robin ignored it. He was the team leader and it was up to him to make crucial decisions on the field. If either the curve ball or Harkaday's hasty throw to the plate had gone astray Robin would have accepted all the blame, and shrugged it off. Johnny Bench never made excuses, either. When Johnny blew one, which wasn't often—maybe a couple of times a season—he looked you right in the eye and owned up to his mistake. He didn't remind you of all those games he'd won practically single-handed with his bat, of the shrewdly called games that made his pitchers look like geniuses. And that was Robin's style too.

He shrugged off congratulations, praised his teammates for every good play he could remember, slapped a few palms and rumps and walked home alone, carrying the tools of the catcher's trade, limping just a little from bruises, weary but satisfied.

Robin was ten years old, and from the age of three he had lived with his aunt and a man he called sir but refused to call uncle in a pleasantly shaded old frame house that leaned decidedly to one side, like the Tower of Pisa, but somehow never fell into the pond next door, despite much groaning and popping of rafters in a windstorm. The house hadn't been painted since shortly after World War II and very likely never would be painted again; it was the property of the World-Wide Church of the Thirteenth Apostle, a missionary church that legislated against almost everything in life that could be dispensed with, as long as it didn't cause physical hardship. Robin had found it necessary to run away three or four times before he was reluctantly granted permission by the Apostolate Council to play ball with the Baptists. Also his father had threatened to remove him from the Tidrow household and place him in military school, a certain loss of one soul to the devil.

Robin's Aunt Fay was in the kitchen frying chicken when he walked in.

Fried chicken, corn on the cob with crock butter, pickled squash and first-crop tomatoes, biscuits as big as a man's fist—at least the Thirteenth Apostolates believed in eating well, to keep up their strength for prayer meetings, knocking on doors and bracing natives in the bush, and Aunt Fay was the best cook in the Lambeth Sanctuary.

In general their strict religion was kinder to the women, who labored like pioneers but saw the beauty of life reflected in their children; the men, who as wage-earners were more exposed to the wickedness and deceit of the world, often were guarded and humorless, even around each other.

"Did you win?" Fay asked him.

"Uh-huh." He glanced at the oilcloth-covered kitchen table, which was set for dinner. That was his job, but the game had started late. "I'm sorry it took so long."

"That's all right, Robin. Ellis called from Washington, he won't be home before eight. So you have a half hour to get cleaned up and read Scripture."

"Yes, ma'am." Robin looked at the right-hand top of the refrigerator where the mail would be, if there was any, specifically one of the tissue-weight light blue airmail envelopes from overseas. It had been nearly two months this time.

"No, nothing today," Fay Tidrow said with a sympathetic smile.

"That could mean he's coming home," Robin said, feeling suddenly jittery with anticipation; this time it was more than just a hunch, or wishful thinking. He had become expert at divining the meaning of noncommunication on the part of his father.

Sometimes The Commander was so busy he couldn't write, or if he had time to write then he was in a part of the world where it took weeks just to get a letter out. Robin's father had been a Naval officer; now he worked as a hydrologist for a government agency, which sent him to places Robin had trouble locating even on the detailed maps of his Rand McNally International Atlas. Water was life, and apparently there was plenty of fresh water to be had in the world. A seven-thousand-year supply less than a mile below the surface of the United States; a prehistoric lake the size of England and Wales combined trapped underneath the Sahara Desert.

Putting all this water to use was his father's job, and it was important and interesting work. Unfortunately he was able to spend only four or five weeks a year at home. Robin and his father had learned how to make the time count, so that looking forward to The Commander's return relieved the austere months of church meetings and Bible study and no movies or television.

And his father always needed the closeness and the fun as badly as Robin did; sometimes when he returned he was gaunt from poor food or illness.

Last year Robin had suffered through the longest stretch yet, five months without a word. When at last The Commander arrived Robin was shocked to see him. He was only thirty-seven, but his hair was turning silver. There'd been an accident on the job, followed by weeks in a primitive hospital. He bore, across one set of ribs and down to the small of his back, a rippled bad scar, as if from a stuttering blade.

So they didn't do anything really strenuous during the Caribbean vacation that followed. In Tortola they chartered a 41-foot sloop. The weather held blue and perfect. They explored St. John's, Virgin Gorda and the Horse Shoe Reefs. Two divers, tank-saddled, awkward as horseless knights before the plunge, performing steeply in the moody blues beneath the maelstrom in the airless eye of heaven. Briny cogitations of brain-coral. Regiments of little checkered flicker-fish. Wrack-ribbed schooner and crusted iron. Dropsical octopus like a leathery leaf blowing across the bottom sand. The Commander made superb conch chowder and cheeseburgers. Robin was active, courteous, good-humored and eager to please. He worked hard to make fatherhood effortless. Even so it was more than a week before all of his father's strength and his low-key sense of humor returned; gradually the night sweats and tormenting dreams ceased. . . .

"Robin," Fay said gently for the third time, finally getting through.

Robin gave his head a shake and looked up at her.

"Don't you want to get started on your bath?"

"I was just thinking about——"

"I know. Wouldn't it be wonderful if he decided to stop traveling, take a less demanding job. But we all have our mission in life, Robin. Think of the lives that have been saved. Hunger. Famine. Pestilence. Drought. Those are your father's enemies. We can be proud."

Robin dawdled in the bathroom, soaping and scrubbing only when he heard the door of Ellis Tidrow's junker car slam, and he was late getting to the table; a couple of beads of water slid along the angle of his jaw as he unfolded his napkin and bowed his head. Ellis Tidrow looked at him with glum forbearance, recited Scripture at length and added his own prayers.

Tidrow was a long shy nervous man who talked with downcast eyes, often rubbing his high forehead in distraction if the conversation went on too long. He regarded even the ordinary occurrences of daily life as a series of curses. "We're cursed with a rainy day," he would remark upon arising and looking out. Or, "We're cursed with that dog again," when the neighbors' Collie came around to see what Robin was up to. He handled finances for Thirteenth Apostolate missions, working out of the church's international headquarters, which were located on the edge of a Washington slum. But he yearned to be in the field, preaching to the heathen.

Dinner wasn't over when Fran Marshall appeared at the back screen, fluttering there like a giant moth. Fay invited her in.

Fran was tense and pale; her eyes went to Robin and stayed on him.

"I hate to bother y'all like this, but we're havin' just a awful time with Brian, and maybe if Robin could talk to him like he did those other times——"

"We have Vigil tonight," Ellis Tidrow said firmly.

"It isn't *strictly* necessary for the children to attend," Fay reminded him. "And if Robin can be of any help to that poor little child——"

"Sure," Robin said eagerly.

"Prayer is the only answer for a child like that," Tidrow explained, reasonably he thought, while Fran stood on one foot and then the other, embarrassed.

She was a tall Blue Ridge Mountain girl with blonde hair so lank it looked runny. Just eighteen, already she had two children, the oldest of whom was the autistic Brian, and she was at least five months pregnant again, showing up big in the homely summer dress she wore. She might at least have taken the trouble to put on some underwear before rushing into his house, Tidrow thought.

He looked at Robin, again trying to evaluate the mysterious quality that attracted people to him. Jehovah had denied Ellis Tidrow children of his own, then further frustrated him by placing in his care a boy who was reckless, troublesome and headstrong. Tidrow had good reason to believe that, if Robin was not totally godless yet, he was a budding heretic. Perhaps it was a blessing that Robin seemed to have some influence over Brian Marshall, but Tidrow was prey to doubts. He was terrified of any kind of mental illness. There were Dark Legions at work in the afflicted; our state hospitals were piled high with the victims of Satan's whims. *You who would heal, read your Bible and know the truth!* If Robin so easily communicated with the otherwise unreachable Brian, it could be devil's work. And Robin *did* have red hair, a most mournful sign.

Tidrow sometimes dreamed uneasy dreams about his redhaired charge; once he had awakened with a taut erection and an outpouring, even though he'd never been able to sustain an erection long enough to impregnate his wife. Devil's guile . . . and devil's laughter in the bare orderly rooms of his mind. Prayer was his salvation. Intense, scouring prayer.

He yielded to the silent pleading of the women and gave a quick nod in Robin's direction. Robin, grateful to escape the grinding repetition of Wednesday night Vigil, hopped up and was out the door just behind Franny.

For a woman with her center of gravity distended, Fran was light-footed; Robin caught up to her only after they crossed the road. They walked the rest of the way side by side, Fran breathing hard and trying not to get off on a crying binge.

Robin didn't know what to say, so he took her hand. She held him very tightly.

The Marshalls owned six acres of woodlot and boggy

meadow. They lived on a grassless plot under shade trees, the crowns of which looked high as clouds in the night sky. The house, from the outside, was a twin of the house in which the Tidrows lived, but without the Italianate lean. Inside there were treasures. Both Fran and her husband Whit were descendants of mountain people who had sold their heritage for fifty cents an acre to coal and timber interests, but they had passed on a love of craft to their offspring.

Robin heard Brian long before they got to the house; tonight it was the peculiar chanting cry which usually accompanied his "rounds." He would walk a very nearly perfect circle, exactly six and a half feet in diameter (Whit had measured), speeding up the walk at intervals with a kind of jog-step-skip. He was capable of maintaining the ritual for hours, until he fell over gray and soggy from exhaustion, as exhausted as his bewildered parents.

He was on the long back porch which Whit had shored up and glassed in to take advantage of sunny winter days. Whit and Fran kept their workbenches on the porch, along with an assortment of broken-down antiques, odds and ends of junk and barrels of discarded clothing, all of which they turned into dazzling artifacts. Whit made tables and chairs and hourglass dulcimers and open-back banjos. Fran made sweaters from Collie dog hair spun on her ancient flax wheel, Star-of-Bethlehem quilts that brought three hundred dollars apiece in the cities, and such traditional mountain items as artificial flowers from wood shavings and maple-split baskets colored with dyes boiled from walnut or pulcoon root.

Robin was always happy to hang around the porch, and he'd learned to make a few things himself, such as gourd birdhouses and corncob pigs; Whit had promised to show him how to construct a whimmydiddle. But that was a complicated toy, and what with teaching at a college across the border in Maryland and trying to find medical help for Brian, Whit had very little free time any more.

The baby, Bernice, was crying in her cradle in another room. Fran looked despairingly at Brian and went to pick up Bernice. Whit tugged at his vast beard and rocked and stared at Robin with drowned blue eyes. Whit was having a few beers to help him manage his distress.

"Brian was making good progress," Whit muttered. "He really was."

Robin didn't say anything. He sat cross-legged on the floor near Brian. Obviously Brian had done it in his pants again. For a while there he hadn't been doing it in his pants, and responding to simple verbal commands. Now he was back to a familiar pattern and crying out helplessly.

Robin felt sad because Brian was sane and bright and beautiful, and because he knew what Brian himself knew, that Brian was doomed. And that was the reason for the frantic making of rounds, the slamming of the same door over and over again, or the repetitious clenching and unclenching of hands while he sat with his back to a wall, ignoring all attempts to distract him. These were Brian's methods of trying to solve the enormous riddle of the inside self and the outside self, his attempts to push the right buttons as Whit pushed buttons on his typewriter and produced something coherent from the mental and physical collaboration. But Brian would never never be able to do it.

During his Visits Robin could perform simple tasks for him. When Robin took control Brian dressed and undressed skillfully, bathed or fed himself. But after the Visit ended and Robin withdrew, Brian was as perplexed as ever. He could imitate the Robin-self for a while, but always something went wrong: as the cells of the body eventually lose their ability to duplicate themselves perfectly, Brian's brain soon produced only the most bizarre examples of rote. He could not easily feed himself, or remember to take down his pants at toilet time, but he could go around and around in monotonously exact circles.

Robin could not have told anyone how he managed a Visit. Of course separation was easier in his own bed at the end of a tiring day, just as he felt himself drifting off to sleep. In that state he could Visit almost anywhere. Fully awake he'd never been able to do it so completely with anyone but Brian, who lacked defenses of any kind, and absorbed much more stimuli than he could cope with. Robin's technique for projection was to mold thought into thought-force and then mentally pitch it; when he really wanted to he could make an impression on even the most rigid mind, just as if he were lobbing a rubber ball dipped in paint against a concrete wall. With more receptive people it was like throwing his thought-ball at a picket fence, occasionally having it sail between the pickets. When that happened Robin often got startled looks that made him grin.

For a few minutes Brian didn't acknowledge him at all as he

made his rounds, but Robin patiently kept bouncing the ball his way, and after several returns he cleanly entered Brian's mind.

As usual he was nearly swamped by the violent wave energy, the drowning boy attempting to smother his rescuer, but he'd become adept at holding Brian off until he had the chance to harmonize all that dissonance and disengage Brian from the rounding impulse. That took time and effort, and meanwhile the body continued to skip and jog and the voice chanted hoarsely.

A couple of times Robin glanced at himself, sitting outside the circle Indian-fashion with his head down and his eyes closed, lips a white line, perspiration rolling down his brindle cheeks, but he was too busy to pay much attention to the physical body, and it was no longer a novelty to gaze upon himself from a distance. He began to tune and regulate the intensely disorganized brain-wave patterns, imposing his own quieter and slower rhythms on the overburdened thalamus.

Before long Brian slowed to a trudge. The chanting stopped and was replaced by a low cry.

"Daz!" Brian said over and over, meaning: Dad. Robin aimed Brian at his father, where he clung to Whit's knee perhaps too tenaciously, almost paralyzed. But it was better than making rounds.

Robin regretfully withdrew as Franny came back with the baby on her hip.

She glanced at Brian and bent to kiss Robin's wet forehead. He looked up at her, dazed.

"I just don't know how you do it," she said.

Whit took the newly docile Brian off to bathe and change him for bed, although he was at the point in his drinking where he needed a little help himself.

Fran yawned and turned off lights, making the porch dark; she smiled sweetly and distantly at Robin. Robin excused himself and left.

But he lingered in the woodlot for several minutes, staying to hear Fran sing softly to Bernice as she rocked the baby in her arms. He perceived her, as if reflected in the eyelight of his torrid devotion, moving slowly within the glass, hair twisting down her back and pale as the pith of a tree struck by lightning.

Robin was astonished to find that the Tidrows had been to Vigil and returned, which meant he had spent nearly two hours with Brian. No wonder he could barely keep his eyes open. His aunt was scrubbing the kitchen floor, cheerful despite the fumes. She had saved two biscuits from dinner, and Robin devoured them with generous helpings of plum preserves. He explained that Brian was doing better now. Fay nodded and beamed at him. Her hands were redder than his sunburned nose. Robin wished she wasn't down on her knees doing a floor that didn't need doing very badly anyway, and he felt a pang of remorse.

Fay caught a flash of this emotion and looked up again.

"I'll finish it for you in the morning," he offered, but Fay said no, it was her work, thank you, Robin.

He wondered how she could go on living with and drudging for a man who offered so little in return. Robin, who knew a lot of things without having to be told, understood why they didn't have children. What always happened to him when he played with his prick in the tub or in bed almost never happened to Ellis Tidrow. He didn't know what the problem was, but there was deep shame in it for a man. But Fay generously accepted this failing, and did without her brood, and tried not to overwhelm Robin with all the love she was meant to lavish on a houseful of kids. Her religion truly meant something to her, and she was ennobled by it. Her husband, on the other hand, dug into his Bible like a cave, burrowing away from life, which he hated. He wanted only one thing from life, and that was his Heavenly reward for having endured it.

Robin had once tried to have a sensible conversation with Tidrow on a subject that Robin found complex and fascinating. He framed a metaphor that wasn't bad for someone his age. I put on my uniform, he said, and I go down to the Little League park and I play a game, and for seven innings I don't think about anything much except the game and how it comes out. It's my whole life, I'm really *serious* about it. Then we win or lose, and I make a couple of dumb mistakes I hate myself for and need time to think about, but the game is over, and all I can do is take off the uniform and wait. There'll be another game any time I want to play, and next time I know I'll do better.

So what if, Robin said, I'm sitting here and talking to you, and this is what we think is life, but it isn't, really, it's just that we're wearing these bodies because it's part of the equipment we need to play a certain kind of game, one you have to make up as you go along. But some day this game will be over, and when it is we'll take off our bodies and rest a while, maybe talk it over with some friends who have been there too. Then after we've had, like, a good night's sleep, only it could last a hundred years, we'll leave wherever we are and find another body so we can play again. We won't remember anything about the last game we were in or the one before it, and we won't think about all the games we have left to——

He came very close to being thrashed by a usually nonviolent man. Instead he got a fundamentalist lecture on the nature of man's relationship to a wrathful God and the everlasting torments of the hell that awaited atheists, and for better than two weeks Ellis Tidrow thought seriously of putting Robin out of his house. But this would have meant surrendering a soul that might be saved, and it also meant the loss of four hundred dollars a month which Robin's father paid for his keeping, a sum which allowed Ellis to tithe generously and enjoy increased stature in Lambeth Sanctuary. So he reconsidered and Robin stayed; but thereafter he kept a closer eye on Robin's studies, and Robin was forced to smuggle into the house the books which Franny checked out of the adult section of the public library for him.

Robin's bedroom, on the third floor of the old house, was furnished with a sagging bed, a chifferobe with doors that wouldn't stay closed unless they were tied with string, a study desk and a wooden chair, but he was permitted to decorate according to his enthusiasms. A Cincinnati Reds pennant was tacked over the bed. Next to a framed photo of one of his heroes, personally inscribed by Johnny himself, were several photos of his father: graduation day at Annapolis, in action as a member of an elite UD team. There was a recent Polaroid shot of Robin, standing on tip-toe, holding up a big barracuda he'd hauled in almost single-handledly off the Montezuma Shoals. His father had written across the top of the photo *Skipper's big 'un—Bequia, Christmas, 1971.* Robin also owned a single small photo of his father and mother together, taken before he was born. His mother had died when he was two, and Robin retained only vague impressions of her. The Commander seldom said anything about her. She'd been a fashion model. She'd died, of complications from an infected tooth, while The Commander was on sea duty. It seemed a strange way to die.

The occult books Robin kept well hidden, because he knew that Ellis Tidrow made a habit of searching his room for conclusive evidence that Robin was a communicant of Satan.

There was a loose soap dish mounted on the tile wall above the claw-foot tub in the bathroom; the tile cement had cracked in a big square, and by being careful Robin could pull out both the dish and the tiles to which it was attached. The tile wall was cemented to wood joists, and between joists there was storage space for three or four books. Robin did a lot of reading in the tub, certain that he would never be interrupted behind his bathroom door.

In the books he had first encountered the theory of reincarnation, which confirmed his own hunches about the immortality of the soul and led to his rash decision to try out the idea on Tidrow. He learned that what he called Visiting was a form of astral projection, also known as an out-of-the-body experience, or OOBE. There were few reported cases, but Robin already knew that all souls traveled, or Visited, from time to time, mostly at night while the body rested. It wasn't usual to remember Visits as clearly as Robin always remembered them: for the well-being of the entity (as it was often called), Visits were distorted and recast as dreams.

It was rarer still to Visit as he Visited with Brian Marshall. And Robin discovered that almost nothing had been written about some of the other talents he exhibited intermittently and sometimes involuntarily. Once while waiting at the Little League park for his battery-mate Harkaday to show up, he had idly run two fingers along the chain-link backstop, leaving a three-foot gap which people had puzzled over for days. Robin was tempted to try it again, but he didn't want to cause any more talk.

As far as he knew, nobody else could do his tennis ball trick. He would take a ball in his two hands and clasp it hard against the solar plexus, bending over as he did so. This turned the ball inside out, but he could just as easily restore the fuzzy side without losing any of the bounce. He showed the trick to Bob Brownell, who was in the seventh grade and did magic at little kids' birthday parties. Bob pestered him for weeks to tell him how the illusion worked. Eventually Robin got bored and made up a lie, explaining to Bob that he had had two balls all the time.

Bob still thought it was a hell of a good trick, and he was probably practicing right this minute.

What else? On those days Robin felt the obligation to get cracking and really polish up his skills he could make his alarm clock ring by staring at it, and on the Fourth of July he'd caused the clock in the Lambeth courthouse to toll twenty-six times at ten minutes after two in the afternoon, a feat which required so much energy it nearly knocked him out, and left him feeling sort of nauseated for a couple of days. Again in one of the books he'd found a word to describe this phenomenon: *psychotronics*. His mind had an affinity for machines.

Fran was good about not asking questions, and she and Whit didn't go around talking about how *weird* he was just because he could influence Brian. But Fran was more than just a close friend. He really loved her, and she had to have deep feelings for him too. On an afternoon in late winter she'd been nursing Bernice in the rocker on the sunporch; when he got tired of whittling he climbed into her lap to be rocked too, and after a drowsy warm time with all three of them drifting off to sleep he'd raised his head and asked if he could taste her milk. Fran was quick to expose the other breast to him.

Mother's milk was hot, sticky and sweet, and he'd had plenty of it long before he tired of the excitement of suckling her, feeling her own aimless rocking excitement as she stroked the back of his head. In a couple of years, then, he'd be grown up enough and taking care of Fran . . . once the thing that was going to happen at the bridge happened to Whit because of his drinking.

Robin's favorite toy of the moment was a limberjack, or dancin' doll, which Whit had made for him. The featureless doll, about ten inches high, was jointed at shoulders, hips and knees, the pieces held together with small nails. A turn of the wooden rod attached to the middle of the doll's back made him jiggle and dance, the clumsy oversized wooden feet rapping on the surface of Robin's desk. Tonight, though, he was depressed rather than amused: the limberjack reminded him too much of Brian.

He put it away and went to bed, yearning, for the first time in months, to Visit with his own kind, to be able to talk of chain links neatly separated without cutting or melting, of the Fourth of July bell-tolling and of the new talent that was slowly developing, the ability to see, merely by touching another, bits and pieces of his past and earthly future.

Robin knew that there were hundreds and maybe thousands like himself, not through actual contact but through wavefronts, a non-Visiting mental seismograph. But he couldn't just pick up and go Visiting without knowing who he intended to see, knowing exactly where to find him. There was a hard and fast rule: once out of the body you didn't go wandering aimlessly around. That was much more dangerous than hitchhiking on a lonely road in the middle of the night, and it could lead to terrible trouble. Ellis Tidrow thought he could imagine the horrors of all the demons of hell, but one look at the creatures who swarmed in the ether (which was both space and the source of life itself), just beyond the reach of the normal range of the senses, would have sent Tidrow into a state of permanent screaming insanity.

They scared Robin, and he was used to them. During his first, tentative short-range Visits he had learned to ignore the creatures. It was fatal to be intimidated by their cries and swoopings, or their seductive protestations of friendship. Instinctively he had realized they could not physically harm or sever the cord of scintillating blue light that connected him to his physical self, but if they could weaken him with fear or seduce him with flattery then they might invite themselves back to the sleeping body. Once in residence they never left voluntarily. And they made appalling houseguests.

Although he'd been disappointed in many previous Visits, he knew where he wanted to go tonight. And so he rose, marvellously, as something drowned; trapped; dangling upward in the swift-drawing flue of the moon, poised—hands floating—weighted only at the heels by the thought of flesh, not flesh itself, clubfooted with desire to be loose above the stressful earth. He kicked once and rose again beyond the sleepers of this house, one quiet and slow-breathing, another shaking in his night of Pentecostal fevers; he rose through roof and branch and hovering leaf and traveled eastward, past night-clinging crow and covert owl, airborne like a blaze of static over the half-stoned torrent of a river, the last blue fall of the mountain. He passed through levels of ghost-dancing and places of screams, where wolf-like creatures leapt at the moon's off-eye and fell back in a blood bath of frustration.

The hag-dogs studied him with fang and lolling tongue. Black magicians with bloodstream wings and languid claws solicited in whispers rarified as adders' tongues. He saw incuba and succuba. He saw a goblin ugly as a fried kidney.

Robin found peace in endless fathoms of light, felt the throbbing sense of his twin, like a heavy vein pulsing on the outside of the unborn corpus of summer. When he was close he went straight down to her, asleep in her bed in the house by the bridge.

She was lying on her back and breathing with a whisper through her lips, one straight-out hand clutching her shabby panda. Her pajama tops were half unbuttoned and twisted. No boldness in the ten-year-old body, only the mild cruciality of youth, nipples flat and trivial as vaccination marks. He rejoiced in the ear-pretty and protectionless look of her. But she didn't know he was there, although the cat on the window seat had raised its head, eyes like glassy gold in the light from the hall. Robin formed demanding thoughts to test her forgetfulness.

Gillian!

She stirred and clutched her panda tighter and murmured peevishly, but she wouldn't open her eyes or acknowledge him. Robin looked around the familiar room, where he'd played often a few years ago—before they inexplicably grew apart. She had a lot of things he admired, particularly the solid brass mailbox salvaged from the demolition of the old Pennsylvania Railroad Station. He liked the marionette theatre and the comfortable bentwood rocker. The rare dolls in display cases didn't interest him, of course. By contrast his own room had always been so barren. When Gillian Visited they preferred to play out of doors, in the flowery dells and hollows around Lambeth, Virginia.

Gillian, stop pretending! You know it's Robin. I just want to talk, that's all. There's a lot I need to tell you.

He was getting through, in a limited way. But she flopped over on her stomach, sleep unbroken, hugging the panda. Robin was angry enough to wish he was there in the flesh; he would smack her butt so hard she'd jump straight up out of the bed.

Why don't you Visit any more, or let me Visit? Come on, Gillian, this is dumb. What I can do you can do. You're my sister. . . .

But she wasn't, quite, and maybe that was the trouble. He had married and fathered and otherwise loved her through many past lives and the plan this time was to be brother and sister, only heartbeats apart at the time of their birth, a mirror oneness. But something had gone wrong with the fetus in the crowded womb. The umbilical wrapped chokingly tight around the neck and Robin was forced, just an hour before birth, to locate another body so that he and Gillian could be born while the conjunctions and the solar eclipse were in full force.

Therefore they were psychic rather than blood twins, but it seemed to make little difference during the first three years of their lives. Through constant Visiting they were nearly inseperable. Then Gillian had begun to deny the powers she was born with, and deny him as well.

It isn't right for you to act like this, he thought petulantly. *I need you. There's nobody else I can tell . . . things.* He gave in to a final burst of anger. *Damn you anyway, Gillian! I won't hang around all night. I'm going!*

If she knew or cared she showed no sign. Robin thought in parting: *You're going to need me some day, wait and see,* and then he was grimly gone, returning in two slow blinks of an eye to his cold and lumpy mountain bed.

Gillian sighed and stirred and changed sides in her own bed, flinging the eyeless panda to the floor, pawing at the rumpled sheet with a slim tanned foot, all skindeep dreaming now, too young to be aware that she could break anyone's heart.

Six

At ten minutes past four on a sullen Christmas Eve the last of the workmen got into a station wagon and drove away from the town of Bradbury, Maryland. Whitecaps were visible a couple of miles distant on Chesapeake Bay, and the wind from the southeast was spitting particles of snow, although the weatherman had not predicted a white Christmas for Bradbury. The overly green artificial Christmas tree in the square shuddered with each of the wind gusts. One of the metal ornaments blew away and went bouncing through the square, ending up in front of the railroad station, where three new cars of a commuter train awaited a 4:37 departure.

The grapefruit-sized iridescent ornament attracted the eye of a great bald eagle floating high above the station. They were rare in these haunts; this one was old and forgetful. Faulty reckoning had brought him again to what had been acres of piney roost and good hunting ground. The eagle circled lower, alighting on the cupola of the station. Closer inspection satisfied him that here was nothing good to eat. The streets looked remarkably free of the usual edible debris that attracted the small birds and rodents which the eagle fed on when black duck was scarce on the northern estuary.

He took wing again and flew over a blue taxicab, marking it in passing with a chalky dropping. He flew low past department store, pharmacy, bank and cinema, seeing nothing but his own stylish reflection in the window glass. But it was getting almost too dark to see much of anything, and still there was not a light showing anywhere in town. The eagle soared, over the silent municipal generating plant, the firehouse and the consolidated school, where the school bus was waiting with opened doors. Then he was out of Bradbury, out beyond the railroad tracks and the ten-foot-high fence topped with barbed wire.

The eagle sensed, before he saw, the fleet of helicopters flying in low from the west, and he gained altitude immediately, heading back to the uninhabited inlets where he made his home. Men lived for years along the Chesapeake without having a glimpse of him or his kind. Few of the bald eagles were born here any more; the tons of pesticides and other inorganic phosphates washed into the west bay by Agnes in '72 had made their nesting situation all the more cirtical. Too many flawed eggs were laid. Young were born deformed, unable to survive more than a few days.

The lead helicopter flew in over the barbed wire at an altitude of one hundred feet. The helicopter had plush accommodations for a dozen passengers, but only five men besides the crew were aboard. Two of the men were responsible for the design and construction of Bradbury, Maryland, a job which had been accomplished in almost exactly a year's time.

Two other men were bodyguards for the fifth passenger, a one-armed man named Childermass, who stared out the window by his leather chair as four helicopters, big and booming, made a slow circuit above the town. There were roller-coaster lines on his forehead. One gray eye was larger than the other, and his mouth was the size of a buttonhole. His backswept blondish hair looked as stiff as the crest of a furious kingfisher. Altogether it . was a strange, disordered face, round and desolate as the moon.

He was watched closely by the designer and the builder. When the helicopter had gone around once Childermass sat back in the seat and groped the stump of his left arm. After eight months it refused to heal properly, and minor surgery was again required. The arm had been blown off on a rainy night in Washington after a carefully conceived plan had gone awry. Its absence caused him frequent pain, but not as much pain as the memory of the humiliation he'd suffered.

"Well," he said, holding out his hand, "let's see how clever you boys are."

A machine like a desk-top digital calculator was passed to Childermass; he placed it in his lap, picked out a code with two fingers and looked out the window again. It was almost fully dark now. For ten seconds nothing happened, but in a concrete bunker below Bradbury an idling computer came to life and began to issue commands. Wheels turned slowly at the generating station, then accelerated to a blur.

All over Bradbury the lights came on. The Christmas tree in the square was suddenly gorgeous; it could be seen for miles across the flatlands of the Aberdeen Proving Grounds. Four traffic lights turned red to green and back to red again. Television sets in the window of the appliance store flickered with cabled images. In the cinema a 16-millimeter projector began to show Marlon Brando in *The Godfather*. The 4:37 commuter train left the station on time and began its mile and a half circuit inside the barbed wire, with two other scheduled stops before it arrived back at the station on the square. The school bus closed its doors and proceeded east until it reached a grade crossing, pausing there while the train went by at twenty miles an hour. The blue taxi drove to the bank, the laundromat and then to the firehouse, passing the town police car and a delivery truck, which were also making driverless programmed circuits of Bradbury, Maryland. Christmas music filled the air, but anyone standing in the streets below would have had a difficult time hearing it because of the reverberating racket from the four helicopters circling overhead.

In the lead helicopter the two men who had worn themselves to a frazzle during the past year broke out the champagne and whooped it up. Childermass smiled a tight, elliptical smile.

"It's the biggest electric train set a boy ever had," he said.

Not being movie buffs, they were polite but puzzled. Childermass didn't bother to explain.

For a couple of days while she cooled out from the high fevers and slept almost constantly, Gillian was aware in her wakeful moments that everyone who came near her wore hospital gowns, caps and masks, and those who touched her did so with gloved hands. Even her mother and father appeared in masks— although she couldn't be certain she'd actually seen them; her eyes wouldn't focus part of the time and she seemed to be gazing at all the faces through an annoying thickness of polyethylene. *Oxygen tent.* It was also difficult to hear; voices were obscured by the soft aspiration of oxygen into the bulky tent and by a persistent vibrato ringing in her ears, like the sound of gut string on a mountain fiddle when it's bowed a certain way; it was loud but not unmusical.

Probably the trappings and the obvious seriousness of the whole business should have upset her; she was in a hospital, and there were indignities to be endured, swabbings and needles and rectal thermometers and the rest, but she was apathetic. Trying to figure out what had happened to her was tiring. Better to sleep.

Without any transition she was aware of, Gillian found herself weak but fully conscious in another room, in semidarkness relieved by a fan of lamplight on the ceiling in one corner. Her vision was perfectly clear and the oxygen tent had been replaced by a nasal cannula. She felt throbbing pain in her right hand and turned her head on the banked pillows. Her arm was taped to a board, and the back of the hand was swollen where the intravenous needle had been inserted into a vein. There were pretty heaps of flowers on a window ledge. Beneath the windows a small Christmas tree stood on a table, surrounded by ribbony presents.

Gillian cleared her throat.

"Mer Christmas," she whispered, to no one in particular.

A nurse with all-pro shoulders and severe-looking eyeglasses approached the bed. Little blue and white name bar on one starchy breast: *Mrs. D. Ombres.* Just behind her was Gillian's grandmother Min, who spent most of her time in Palm Springs. She was sun-darkened, gnarled and well oiled, like an ambulatory piece of fine furniture.

Gillian was pleased and astonished to see Min.

"Hi," she said, and made a face. Could that rusty croaking thing be her *voice?* Talking was an exotic skill she would have to master all over again.

The nurse began to take her pulse. Grandmother Min came around to the right side of the bed.

"Well, hello. How do you *feel?*"

"Sort of . . . dull, and . . . dreamy, I guess." Gillian licked dry lips. Min held the pitcher of water so Gillian could drink through a bent glass straw. When she had had her fill she asked what time it was.

Min looked at the tiny face of a watch sunk in a grotto of diamonds.

"Twenty past nine."

"No. I mean——" Gillian looked at the little perky Christmas tree, and at a wall of holiday cards beyond.

"Oh. Well, it's the twenty-seventh of December, Gillian. The year's almost gone."

"It *is?* When did I——how long've——"

"They carted you off to the hospital on the twenty-first. So it's been a week."

Mrs. Ombres smiled and let go of Gillian's wrist.

"Right back," she said.

"Carted me off——?"

"How much do you remember?" Min asked, putting down her Dashiell Hammett omnibus and sitting on the edge of the bed. Gillian winced.

"Sorry. Hand sore?"

"Uh-huh. Well . . . I think . . . Larue was over for the night. I remember we went shopping, and saw a movie. I don't know what movie. Then I remember . . . doctors. Nurses. Everybody wearing masks like . . . they were afraid to breathe on me. My head . . . burning up. How sick am I?"

"You were *very* sick, luv, from some sort of scary tropical bug they thought, so as a precaution you were put in isolation for four days. Then they decided it was flu. One of the new monster strains. Not much of it in the U.S. so far, thank God. But only one case in a thousand hits as hard as you were hit."

"How long have you been here, grandmother?"

"When Katharine called I flew in right away. We've all taken turns sitting up with you since you got out of isolation. And of course you've had your nurses twenty-four hours a day. That big husky one is Mrs. Ombres. I suppose she went after the plug-in thermometer, it's about that time, but your temperature's been close to normal for the past twenty-four hours."

"It's . . . a real shame about her car."

"How's that? I'm just getting deafer and deafer in this ear."

"Her car . . . all smashed up. Not an accident. What kind of kid . . . would use a hammer on a brand-new car? Why does he hate her so much?"

"I guess you must have heard us talking about it. The young man is someone she's been trying to help, out of the goodness of her heart. What a stunt he pulled! She's just all broken up about it."

Gillian already knew that, although she wasn't quite sure how she knew all about Mrs. Ombres's new car, or the confused, resentful boy she'd taken into her home. But while silently counting Gillian's pulse the nurse had communicated her unhappiness, the betrayal of a trust that hurt worse than damage to the car . . . Gillian abruptly found herself thinking of something else.

"Who died?" she asked.

"Could you speak a little louder, Gillian?"

"You . . . went to a funeral. Just before you left the desert."

Min nodded. "An old and dear friend. But how did you know about Lucille?"

"I heard . . . the music just now. Smelled the flowers. And . . . I can see her. Wearing silk. Isn't it? Peach-colored silk."

Min withdrew her hand from Gillian's cheek, smiling so big her gums showed.

"Yes. She . . . I don't remember talking to anyone about the——"

"You don't have to *tell* me," Gillian said, a bit irritably. "I could see. Cancer?"

"Yes. Who would have thought Big C would ever catch up to Lucille? God, she was tough! And so vigorous. Tennis in her seventies. We used to joke about it all the time, while friends dropped like flies around us. 'Not me,' Lucille said. 'Cancer wouldn't *dare.*' "

Gillian smiled slightly and closed her eyes. Mrs. Ombres came back with the IVAC. Min got up from the side of the bed.

"I'll just call Avery and Katharine and tell them you're doing so well."

Mrs. Ombres pulled the privacy curtains around Gillian. Min looked at the telephone, but that whole corner of the room was suddenly misty. Instead of phoning right away she went into the bathroom to freshen up. Looking at herself in the mirror was a shock. Her left eye was filling up with blood; it was as red as a tomato. She'd had laser surgery twice to correct this weakness of the minute blood vessels of the sclera, the last time four months ago.

Couldn't anybody do anything right any more? Min didn't recall ever hemorrhaging this badly. It wasn't immediately dangerous, but the eye was unsightly and she hated wearing shades indoors. She lowered her head, not wanting to look any more. Her hands trembled as she washed them.

East of the Long Island village of Beach Meadows, Hester Moore took the cove road. It was four o'clock in the morning; in the headlights of the rented Maverick wet snow fell like parachutes. There hadn't been a car behind her since she left 27A more than ten minutes ago; nevertheless when she reached the cedar-screened entrance to the Nally place she dutifully made a sharp left off the cove road, dimmed her lights, eased up to the shuttered summer house and turned around, then killed the parking lights and the engine and settled down to wait out the third of the designated ten-minute surveillance breaks.

This close to Peter the wait was supremely frustrating; Hester had a high-tension headache from all the driving, and her fear, not of being followed but of what she must do when she got to Peter's hideaway, had her close to tears. She knew she was going to make a stupid hysterical fool of herself. Why couldn't she just drive on and get it over with?

The Nally house was elevated above the road. From where she waited Hester could make out the few scattered lights of Beach Meadows, and a good portion of the cove road. If anyone should be coming after her, she'd see the headlights almost as soon as the car left the village. But she was absolutely certain she had not been followed, at least not from the airport eastward. She'd lost hours carrying out Peter's precise, perhaps fanatical instructions. Getting off the plane at the last possible instant while her skis went on to Denver surely would have been enough to confuse even her most diligent pursuers.

Hester passed the slow minutes by briskly hitting the underside of her chin with the backs of her fingers, an exercise designed to massage away the little frog's belly there. Her only physical shortcoming, practically, except for a few tiny acne scars which were easily concealed. Hester's hair was pitch-dark and she could wear it in a dozen flattering ways; she had kind of buttony trusting dark eyes and expressive red red lips that could be sneaky-funny or poutingly salacious depending on her mood.

For now her lips were cold and compressed. It was *very* cold in the little car with the engine shut off, but Peter said they had gear sensitive enough to pick up the sound of an idling automobile engine from a mile away; even if the car was concealed they could detect the heat from its engine at a range of several hundred yards with something called a thermal-imaging device. He should know about such things; but sometimes he deliberately tried to scare her just so she'd be more careful.

Hester punched up the display on her pulsar watch: nine minutes gone, and she decided that was enough. She started the Maverick, which had been reserved and was ready for her only a few minutes after she left the Denver plane. There'd been no time for the rental car to pick up a hitchhiking bug, and she'd driven on and off the Long Island Expressway several times to foul up hypothetical tag-teams. That part had been exciting; she loved fast tricky driving, although she would have preferred her own little MG for the abrupt screeching exits from the outermost lanes of traffic. There'd been some close ones on the L.I.E. tonight, but the fun of it had long faded, it all seemed so futile and hopeless and paranoid now, and what was she going to *say* to Peter?

Three miles down the cove road the Maverick's headlights lit up the weaving dune fence and she cut the lights before heading up the rutted road to the house. Snow came at her thick and wild from the north when she got out of the car; clutching her shoulder bag against her ribs, Hester put her head down and ran to the porch.

The house which she had borrowed from Connie Sepoy was a stout old-timer with little personality on the outside; inside Connie's architect husband had gutted and simplified until it was basically one large raftered room, lofty as a church, with dramatic clerestory windows, sleeping balconies and play-pens and conversation pits and a big dining deck around an island kitchen. Only a few massive pieces of furniture. The house was well insulated against the storm outside, the porch entrance acting as an airlock. Hester was very quiet going in. A gas-log fire on the main floor burned at the minimum. She stood getting accustomed to the textures of the dark. She made out Peter sprawled asleep on his stomach on one of the balconies, went gingerly up a flight of free-standing stairs. She was half-undressed before she reached the bed. By then her eyes had fully adjusted to the night shapes of the house. Peter's head looked surprisingly dark against the pillow; the Grecian Formula for Men she'd bought him was working already. Hester slipped out of her pants and in a panicky excitement clutched at her breasts, bringing up the nipples. Her eyes were brimming with tears. She moved closer and bent to touch his sleeping head.

To her horror she felt the scalp shift uneasily to one side beneath her fingers, felt the dead coldness of skull underneath, realizing at the same instant that she had not seen him breathe at all beneath the blanket.

With a cry more chilling than a scream she backed away from the bed, and stepped on a bony bare foot behind her.

"Hester!"

She turned with her arms raised protectively, saw the steep ridges and angles of his face brought out by the distant blue light of the gas fire; she looked back at the bed, at the artifact of wig and round beach stone and rag-doll limbs. For one blind moment as he groped to reassure her, Hester almost swung at him. But then she snorted and choked and exploded in tears, and was dead weight in his hands.

"Hester, I'm sorry—I can't take chances, ever."

"You can trust me! Don't you know that by now? I just wanted . . . get in with you, make love to you, make it all right somehow! Oh God——"

"I was checking behind you," Peter whispered. "Everything looks okay."

Peter got rid of the things in the bed and eased her down, and went down with her, but Hester had lost all sense of her physical self.

"I know how tough this has been for you, Hester——"

"You don't know . . . anything! Listen——" But all Hester could do was sob, brokenheartedly, for a while. Then, slowly, she became accustomed to and was gratified by the tender long tracing of his fingertips from the small of her warming back deeply down between her legs where eventually she melted, just melted, like a pat of butter on a hot day. . . .

There was light outside. Maybe she'd dozed. Hester rolled over and looked at Peter lying on his back. His eyes were closed and he was breathing deeply. She stared at him, entranced. Only a little more than two months ago they'd met in a crowded restaurant on the East Side. Peter had asked to share her table. Hester was half way through her own meal. She looked him over warily, but he was presentable; just a little shabby, like an unemployed intellectual. She liked his eyes. She had a night school class in accounting to get to, and she really was in no mood for conversation. But that was a funny thing about Peter. Once you started talking to him, even if you had a brush-off in mind, you couldn't stop talking. His eyes invited confidences, he seemed more accessible and sympathetic than any psychiatrist. He could turn a statue into a monologuist. Even before she finished eating Hester had decided to cut her class. And before the evening was over she'd talked herself into a crush on him. A crush that was the real thing now, deadly real . Hester didn't know she was crying until she saw her tears fall on his sleeping face.

"What's wrong?" Peter said, not opening his eyes.

"Peter, I tried . . . to tell you about the computer. I got hold of the access code . . . and . . ."

He looked up at her for a solemn long time, his expression not changing.

"Peter. The computer says . . . that Robin is dead."

She couldn't bear watching him; nor could she look away. The only immediate change was a slow hardening, a quiet shift of his eyes away from her face, as if suddenly he couldn't stand the sight of her. *In the old days,* she thought with a distinct chill, *bearers of bad news were killed.* There was a change in the rhythm of his breathing, a rasp in the throat. He threw his legs over the side and left the bed. He put on old warm clothes with a rigid intensity, walked downstairs, walked out of the house. Hester followed part way, going as far as the porch with the rust-red blanket around her. There she stood shivering and watching as Peter, desperately willed, thrust himself across the decayed dunes against a gray snow-flecked sky. She watched until he disappeared, wondering, now that so necessary a part of him had died, if he would ever come back.

Seven

After young Dr. Newbold Jr. changed the dressings on her leg during his 8 A.M. rounds, Irene Cameron McCurdy prepared to go visiting.

Her hairdresser had made the trip up to Washington Heights yesterday to get Irene in shape for New Year's; Irene had slept sitting up in her hospital bed to preserve the hair set. In the no-nonsense morning light that flooded her eighth-floor hospital room, Irene studied the mirrored tint job and found the color garish but acceptable; Hedy had been forced to work with limited facilities. Irene used a lot of base to overcome that blotchy postoperative look, considered the splendor of the lapis lazuli lounging pajamas which she wore and did her eyes to match.

A nurse's aide helped her out of bed and into the wheelchair. The leg was agonizing but Irene managed to smile. She'd been through a similar vein-stripping operation on the left leg two years ago, so she knew how to handle a wheelchair, even with the propped up leg straight out in front of her.

Irene chose from a suitcase so many of her enameled, shield-like bracelets and rings that she looked, from the elbows down, intimidating and gladiatorial. From another suitcase she took several items and packed them away in a tote. The big scrapbook she wedged between her good leg and the chair frame. Then she was on her way down the hall, with a cheerful word for each of her friends on the floor.

She stopped in front of the room which she had discreetly reconnoitered the night before. The door was open a few inches. Irene leaned out of the chair and knocked. No reply. Unlikely the child was sleeping, because no one slept around here much after eight, what with medical rounds and breakfast and the Puerto Rican scut workers who talked very loudly always—but then, Irene supposed, if you grew up in such *large* families, apparently it was necessary to *clamor* for attention . . . she pushed the door open and smiled broadly at Gillian, who was sitting up in bed wearing white headphones, listening to music and making notes on a score.

"May I come in?" Irene asked, doing a busy burlesque pantomime. She didn't wait for a signal from Gillian but went rolling right up to bedside. What a beauty this girl was! Irene thought, with a touch of proprietary envy. Her illness had left her with a dusky ring around each eye and obviously fever had burned away pounds and pounds, but they could recover so quickly at that age.

"HELLO! IT'S GILLIAN, ISN'T IT? I'M IRENE CAMERON MCCURDY FROM JUST DOWN——"

Gillian smiled gamely at the intrusion and took off her headphones, dialing out the music.

"—down the hall. All by yourself this morning? I had such a nice chat with your grandmother yesterday evening, I was hoping I'd see her again."

"Min had to get back to Palm Springs, there's some sort of huge charity thing she's been working on for a year."

"She told me so much about you, I just had to meet you at the first opportunity. I think we have quite a lot in common."

"Oh."

"Not that I can lay claim to being *gifted,* although I've always been sure that I have just a little more ESP than the average person——"

Irene was watching Gillian closely. This was one very well-brought-up young lady who had been taught early never to reveal her feelings to strangers, but Gillian's reaction was that of someone who expected to be handed a rattlesnake fangs first. Irene shifted course and nodded wisely.

"I know, I *know*, dear. Right now you'd rather not talk about it because you feel you've talked too much, but I promise I haven't breathed a word to anyone."

"Mrs. McCurdy, I don't think I——"

"Irene, and I want you to know that you can trust me! At a time like this—when you've virtually been *born again*—you need someone who really believes, and cares. That's why I'm here. I'm an authority on. . . ." Irene looked hard at someone passing in the hall outside and wheeled herself tight against the bed, where she was eye-to-eye with Gillian. "Psychic phenomena," she said. She opened her tote and pulled out a well-thumbed paperback book, which she handed to Gillian. "Here's my biography of Peter Hurkos."

Gillian looked at the photograph of a much younger Irene Cameron McCurdy on the back of the book.

"Who's Peter Hurkos?"

"A man who had a very serious accident years ago. He fell off a ladder while painting a house and nearly killed himself. But when he woke up in the hospital, he discovered to his amazement that he'd become clairvoyant. He could literally see incidents from the past, and the future, of perfect strangers!"

Irene smiled encouragingly at the frowning Gillian. "It was almost as if Hurkos—now get this—could tune into some huge cosmic television set. He saw his own child in danger in a burning room, he saw . . . but it's all there in my book. I urge you to read it. His clairvoyance was a direct result of the concussion he suffered; in your case it must have been the abnormally high fever."

"What did my grandmother *say* to you, Mrs. McCurdy?"

"Gillian, Gillian, now you mustn't upset yourself. She told me how you described the funeral of her friend, and in such exquisite detail, and then there was the nurse whose car was vandalized, and the other nurse, that lovely Jamaican girl who was on days with you. She didn't know she was pregnant until you told her. Oh, so many little incidents only a true clairvoyant could reveal—and I'll bet there's lots more you haven't mentioned!" Gillian looked steadfastly out the window. "I think you must be one of the very special New People. More and more are coming through all the time."

"Mrs. McCurdy——"

"Eye-rene."

"Yes, ma'am. I . . . it was probably just dreaming, that's what it seemed like, and I don't . . . want to say any more about it."

Irene said sympathetically, "Doesn't it help, though, to be assured that you're not alone in the world? Of course it's all new and baffling, poor Peter Hurkos was convinced he was losing his mind. . . ."

Bad choice of words, and Irene knew it. She opened her scrapbook.

"I think you're right not to say any more until you have it all straight in your own mind that something truly wonderful has happened. Oh, I mean it! And you have so much company, children just your own age. This charming little South African girl who sees underground water as a shimmering cloud, and all the tots who are bending silverware and moving pendulums at a glance, doing really phenomenal things pk-wise; now look at this, would you just skim through this story, Gillian?"

Irene referred her to a lengthy newspaper article about Japanese children, ages five to fifteen, who were performing spectacular feats of telekinesis under scientifically controlled conditions.

"There must be literally hundreds of them, all second generation post-Bomb, and doesn't *that* give us something to think about. Well, pk is interesting, but the most significant talent is psychometry. If you'd like, we could work on just a couple of . . . experiments."

"No," Gillian said. "No." And she looked to be at the point of tears. "Whatever it is . . . it'll probably just go away. *I don't even want to think about it.* And right now I have to learn this music." She closed the scrapbook, put it and the paperback about the psychic within reach of Irene, and picked up her headphones. Irene, unfazed, left the books where they were.

"Why don't you keep these for a while? And that scrapbook is just the recent tip of the iceberg, I have tons of research material. Now I'll be in 819, Gillian, whenever you have a question or two."

Gillian settled back without comment, turning the volume up.

Irene smiled and wheeled herself away from the bed. She left Gillian's door partly closed as she had found it and continued up the hall to her own room, fizzing with energy and excitement, forgetting about her aching leg. It hadn't gone quite as well as she'd expected; obviously Gillian was going to resist the fact that she was part of a miracle . . . an unprecedented transitional stage in the growth of mankind! Irene liked that phrasing so much she jotted it down as quickly as she could. Then she sat gazing out her windows at the towers of the George Washington Bridge a few blocks away.

More like a naturalist than an occultist, Irene had waited and watched nearly twenty years for the first puzzling and tantalizing signs of the New People to become manifest, and now at last they were popping up like wildflowers after a spring rain. But what a lot of luck to come of a dismal trip to the hospital! There were so many fascinating questions to be answered, but Irene knew very well she had to be careful with Gillian, who would not remain in the hospital many more days. She had to win the girl's confidence, establish herself as a worthy guide for the emerging psychic. In retrospect Gillian seemed frightened—perhaps a bad experience already? Gillian was not just another entertaining mover and shaker, a parlor poltergeist and a threat to cutlery everywhere, she was a cosmic visionary with access to the time-less flow of life itself, the secrets of being and becoming. Prop-erly nourished and motivated, she would speak for the universe.

Irene made another note, and when she looked up she was aware of her own face in the window glass. But she was not dismayed, as she often was, by the evidence of years, nor was she reminded of Cocteau's glum metaphor: "Look at yourself all your life in a mirror, and you'll see death at work like bees in a glass hive." Today Irene Cameron McCurdy had heard—how-ever faintly—the music of the spheres, and she was enthralled.

Gillian always had had a substantial gift for aural and visual mimicry: at the age of six she could do her mother's hand ges-tures to perfection, and nowadays even though she might go for a while without seeing or hearing Streisand, she could re-create Streisand with puckish accuracy almost on demand. *Doncha think I'm pretty? Ya don't have to give me ya ansa right away, why doncha think about it f' three uh four munts?* As she listened through headphones to flute, piano and cello, the mild pressure of words forming in her mind was not too much of a distraction at first; it was a little like listening to the radio late at night, hearing a fitful voice suppressed by a stronger signal. Automatically she went to work on the voice, although it was so far away in time she couldn't remember whose voice it was.

I'm not near enough, Gillian. Need help to

No.

More like: *Gil-yan.*

She felt a tingle of satisfaction at getting the boyish inflection right; still she couldn't visualize him. He'd sort of popped in out of nowhere. But somehow in achieving the voice she had allowed his faint words—her tingle changed perceptibly to a chill —to come much more powerfully, accompanied by the reality of a—*mind*—that could just push aside the music and make difficult any mental effort other than awareness of him.

Yes, he was real, and now he moved in like a storm front; Gillian tried to blank him by increasing the volume of *Vox Balaenae* and concentrating on the score in front of her.

A painful, thrusting urgency: *No, don't, Gillian! I want to Visit. Keep working. Try to see—*

She felt especially uncomfortable as she silently mimicked the voice, her throat muscles working hard because of abrupt downshiftings to a sturdy baritone. How sweet—his voice was changing! Gillian sensed that she had it perfectly, but she was afraid of further accommodation. She would not visualize as he wanted because it could mean an apocalypse of the mind, the dreadful shadow-shows of childhood screaming forth from the subconscious. Gillian tried to switch to someone else. The chesty contralto of Irene Cameron McCurdy was still very much with her, a little practice and she could do a pretty fair McCurdy— but this *boy* just wouldn't let her go.

Need help to come all the way through to you. New games, Gil-yan. Want to teach you   all the new games.

Gillian snatched off the headphones and got out of bed too quickly, which resulted in dizziness and a loss of balance. She clung to the foot of the bed, bit her lower lip with a sharp canine tooth until the pain brought tears but stilled her panic.

The dreamy glimpses of life and death and secrets she could tolerate because they happened so effortlessly and involved her not at all; but this was different. Gillian felt thin-skinned to the point of invisibility and in danger of dispossession. It gave her the shakes. They came rattling up from her cold knees, they hurt her bones and set the blood to throbbing in her throat and temples. If she could just get *out* of this goddamned hospital . . . the phone was ringing.

"Gillian? Are you crying?"

"Oh, Larue! No, I'm just . . . I'm so bored, I want to go home. I'm glad you called."

It was blissful then to curl up in the chair by the phone and talk about school and music and friends, and make plans for a ballet and a concert; laughter, the one imperative in Gillian's life, came easily when she had Larue's ear. She had never been more passionate about the familiar and ordinary things of the day, but even as they chatted Gillian felt a pang or two, a puzzling sense of incompleteness or loss, like the slowly fading aftermath of some of the hopeless crushes she'd had in her life.

Eight

The four Cabinet-level visitors to the underground complex at Bradbury, Maryland, gathered in a leather-paneled Regency drawing room following their tour of the operations facility. When they had been provided with cigars and cognac, a skinny bearded former ad man named Braintree took over the indoctrination.

He showed them a clip from a National Geographic Society television documentary on the human body, first shown over the Public Broadcasting System on October 28, 1975. In a laboratory experiment in biofeedback training a young man with electrodes attached to his forehead controlled the movement of a toy electric train with his alpha waves—the speed of the train depended on the size of the waves which the subject emitted.

"A commonplace experiment," Braintree said. "With a little practice any of us could learn to do it. No unusual mental powers are required." The screen went blank. An assistant wheeled a cloth-draped cart toward Braintree. He removed the cloth, revealing an assortment of sculptures made from metal alloys. The largest was a cube eight inches on a side, with a deep groove in one surface; another looked like a mottled doughnut and the third could have been a badly tooled cogwheel.

"These simple psychotronic machines are derived from models created by Robert Pavlita, a Czechoslovakian textile designer who claims that his inspiration was the journals of a fifteenth-century alchemist."

The visitors were getting restless. A gentle-looking academician named Byron Todfield grinned wryly and blew smoke rings at the ceiling; a JCS Old Warrior and a Statesman, a vicarish figure charged with consequence, look disgusted. The fourth visitor, Boyd Huckle, who was more valuable to the Chief Executive than his frontal lobes, appeared to be half asleep as cigar ash drifted down to dull the shine on one of his three-hundred-dollars-a-pair cowboy boots.

"We may suspect," Braintree continued, "that Mr. Pavlita is having his little joke, but there is no denying the efficiency of his machines. Each has the property of accumulating energy from human beings, at which point they act as generators, releasing that energy to perform various tasks. This one——" and he indicated the cube, "—will drive a small electric motor for several minutes. The cogwheel dramatically increases plant growth. The doughnut kills insects placed within its circle."

"Electrostatic energy?" said the Old Warrior.

"No, sir, because static electricity won't work under water—but this generator will. Water even enhances the effect. Nor is it magnetic energy or temperature changes, or anything we understand at the moment. The shape of each machine seems to dictate the work it can do. For instance—film, please."

The room darkened slightly and they viewed a 35mm movie strip shot by a professional, in color, under excellent lighting conditions.

"This was made a year and a half ago in the physics department at Kazakh State University in the USSR," Braintree explained. "The subject is Petr K. Woronov, a well-known theoretical physicist who does not pretend to have psychic ability."

The film showed a small windowless room empty except for a table made of clear acrylic. There was a cordless electric fan at one end of the table. Woronov, a round-shouldered elderly man wearing a pin-stripe suit and a shirt open at the throat, approached the table carrying a psychotronic machine much like the cube which Braintree had exhibited to the group from Washington. Woronov placed the machine at the opposite end of the transparent table and stepped back about four feet, where he stared at his machine. Within a few seconds the fan blades began to turn; they became a pink blur as the fan oscillated smoothly. White numerals appeared on the screen: 1.2×10^{-3} dynes. The force required to make the fan blades turn. The camera zoomed in. The film ended.

"That was Woronov, all right," said Todfield, whose profession was Intelligence. "And the camera always lies."

"Granted the demonstration could be rigged," Braintree replied. "But we've duplicated it many times at Psi Faculty, with various subjects. And we've greatly expanded the applications of our psychotronic machines, which of course is why we thought it necessary to interrupt your holidays. May I have the other film, please?"

Again the room darkened as the projector whirred softly.

"This film," Braintree said, "was made at Psi Faculty ten weeks ago. The walls of the room are concrete, four feet thick. The camera ports are two and a half inches of heat-resistant glass. The manganese oxide and aluminum thermite device is a common cartridge-type which generates a temperature of between three and four thousand degrees Fahrenheit for up to eight seconds. The table is three-quarter-inch stainless steel plate. The generator in this test, as you can see, resembles a crude pre-Colombian figure in bronze. Notice the wave pattern of grooves on the 'head' of the generator. This is the so-called 'staring pattern'; the subject holds the figure in his hands and moves his eyes along the grooves, thus charging the generator with the vital energy which mystics and investigators have known by various names. The ancient Hindus called it *prana;* for Paracelsus it was *munis* and Mesmer in his work referred to 'animal magnetism.' Currently we think of this energy as bioplasmic or psychotronic energy. Incidentally, when the subject has charged his generator it can be dangerous for anyone else to pick it up: temporary paralysis may result. It's a very potent force indeed. Oh. Gentlemen, our subject—code named 'Skipper.'"

Even Boyd Huckle, from his slouched-down position in the cozy armchair, was paying attention now, squinting in fascination past the smouldering tip of his long cigar. Boyd needed glasses but he wouldn't wear them.

"Why's his breath fogged like that? Where's he at?"

"In what we call, for obvious reasons, the Cold Lab. Skipper doesn't mind the cold. It's beneficial for telepathic and pk transmission, for reasons only our theoreticians could explain."

The Old Warrior cleared his throat and said harshly, "How far is he from the bunker?"

"Four hundred and fifty yards, sir."

The film returned them to the concrete room. The camera panned from the psychotronic generator to the explosive cartridge lying on the steel table. It was apparent that there was no physical link between the two.

The Statesman said hesitantly, "So what he will try to do, then, from a distance of about one quarter of a mile, is discharge energy from the generator, which in turn will set off——"

Even as he was speaking the movie screen glowed with actinic light, a total whiting-out of the picture. Only the Old Warrior, who was wearing tinted glasses that darkened protectively as the light blazed into the room, was able to go on watching until, eight and a fraction seconds later, the terrible burning ceased. More than half the table had been consumed, leaving a jagged smoking remnant, spidery runs of molten steel on the concrete floor. Freeze frame. The Statesman made a wisping mournful sound like a leaky radiator. The lights of the room came up to full.

"Sound waves," the Old Warrior muttered. "Ultrasound could do that." No one else said anything until Boyd Huckle called for more cognac.

"It's gonna be cold upstairs," he said. "Best fortify ourselves."

He was still drinking from a crystal goblet when they took the elevator to the lobby of the Bradbury post office and walked outside beneath uncrowded stars in a sky of purest indigo. The driverless Bradbury taxi came down the street, waited politely for a red light, then pulled up in front of the station across the square from the post office. The empty commuter train arrived and stopped with a squall of steel on steel, a gasp of air brakes. Television cameras monitored the group from Washington, but they weren't conscious of this surveillance.

The Statesman looked around as if something was preying on his mind.

"I *know* this town," he said. "I mean I've seen it before, I mailed a letter in this same post office. Damn it, it's just a *little* place, not too far from Camp David as I remember——"

Braintree smiled. "That's right, Mr. Secretary. Lambeth, Virginia. Our scenic designers, the best Hollywood has to offer, duplicated a good part of Lambeth brick for brick. We borrowed some of its . . . artifacts as well. The school bus, for instance, it's the same one Skipper used to ride every day to the consolidated school."

"What's the point of spending twenty-two million bucks on a replica?" Boyd Huckle asked.

"Verisimilitude; a study aid, you might say. It's been very helpful to Skipper as he developed the sort of eidetic imagery essential to working with more complex machines that have psychotronic potential—the computers that run Bradbury, for example."

"You lost me, Mr. Braintree. Just what the hell is eye-detic imagery?"

"Imagination. The ability to look at a picture or object and retain a faithful impression for minutes, hours, or even weeks afterward. Many children have it to an astonishing degree, but unfortunately contemporary modes of education hinder the free development of the imagination, so a valuable tool for the expansion of consciousness is blunted . . . oh, here we are, gentlemen."

A heavy-duty tow truck, this one with a driver, turned into the square with a late-model stock car attached behind it.

The Dodge Charger was red and blue with big white numerals painted on the sides and top. There were several decals advertising sparkplugs and oil additives. The car looked as if it had been around and around the track a few thousand times, as well as up against the walls.

But the strange thing about the car was the copper mesh that completely covered it except for the tires.

"What's that?" the Statesman said, with a trace of apprehension. They had been promised a surprise.

"A rolling Faraday cage," Braintree replied. "Are you gentlemen familiar with the concept—no? Well, in short, the copper mesh eliminates the possibility that the car can be operated by remote control, like the taxi over there, or the train. The cage blocks all electrical transmission. The car has been modified for operation solely by a psychotronic machine. To conclude our demonstrations today, we thought you might be more convinced of the reality of the work that's being done at Psi Faculty if you took a little spin around town."

"Hold *on,*" said Boyd Huckle.

"Now wait," the Statesman protested. "I don't think——"

The Old Warrior said, "You mean you intend for us to climb into that vehicle, *without a driver,* and——"

Todfield grinned tiredly and unwrapped a roll of stomach mints; then he stood with his feet wide apart, hands behind his back, hating every minute he was forced to spend in the clutches of a rival service. The stock car was part of something fiendish, no doubt, dreamed up by Childermass, and Todfield felt certain he was going to look like a bloody fool no matter what choice he made at this point.

Braintree was trying valiantly to reassure everyone. Workmen had uncoupled the car from the tow truck and were checking for possible magnetic or electrical fields with meters. Despite his uneasiness Todfield was intrigued. He walked over and examined the Charger more closely.

"How do we get in?" he asked a mechanic.

"No problem, sir. We just peel back the mesh to open the door, then reweave it. Easy stuff to work with."

"And how does it run?"

"Damned if I could tell you that. We bolted in a couple of sealed metal boxes where the alternator and ignition systems should be. There's two more boxes either side of the steering gear case, which has been modified. I couldn't tell you exactly *how* he steers, but four notes of the musical scale are involved, which activate a gadget about the size of my two fists. It's a computerized squeezebox—you know, an accordion."

"I hope he'll be playing my song."

The mechanic chuckled politely.

"Up to me, I'd a pulled the competition engine, that's some kind of *bomb* there under the hood. But the scientists said no, they wanted as few modifications as possible. Skipper gets some kind of a kick out of it, all that power."

"Is he old enough to drive?" Todfield asked sardonically. "He sure doesn't look it."

"Oh, yes, sir, he's a good driver. That is, if you consider he never gets within three hundred miles of the vehicle." Todfield and the mechanic stared at each other, and the mechanic smiled edgily. "I guess I shouldn't talk so much, I don't even know what kind of clearance you got."

"Don't you recognize me?"

"No, sir."

"I'm with that Other Firm. As a matter of fact, I run it."

"Oh. Well, I guess there's no question then about security. Would you like to get in?"

Todfield nodded, put two fingers between his teeth and whistled piercingly. The others stopped talking and looked at him.

"Come on, you chickenshits," Todfield said.

Todfield and the Old Warrior were given walkie-talkies; a bunkered voice checked each one to make sure it was in working order. The Statesman carried a portable FM radio which clearly received nine stations in the Washington/Baltimore area.

They all squeezed inside the Dodge and were locked into seat belts: three of them crowded together on a bench back seat that had been installed in the stripped interior just for this occasion, Todfield in a front bucket riding shotgun. There was no seat behind the small steering wheel. Both walkie-talkies were receiving a time check at ten-second intervals on the same frequency. The Statesman's radio played Bach.

"Gentlemen, I hope you're not too uncomfortable," Braintree said, looking in on them.

"I'd sooner might prefer to be sittin' in an electric chair," Boyd Huckle said.

"Enjoy your ride." Braintree closed the only working door; the other had been welded shut. The copper mesh basket surrounding them was quickly rewoven, ending radio communication. Both Todfield and the Old Warrior checked and rechecked their sets. Not a peep. The FM radio was as dead as a tomb. The Statesman, who was seated in the middle of the back seat, swallowed hard.

"I wonder if all this is necessary," he said.

Todfield looked back; it was swiftly getting dark and the copper mesh made it difficult to see out. Another car had pulled into the square, a bronze Olds or a Buick, and Braintree got in. The commuter train had left the station and was picking up speed. The courthouse clock tolled five. The Dodge Charger just sat there, shocked-up behind, low in front, in a cold silence that proved exacerbating. The interior of the stocker smelled of grease and oil and much stale sweat. But it was still equipped with a roll cage, and they might be grateful for that, Todfield thought. Particularly since the brake pedal had been removed, along with the floor shift lever.

"Assuming they already tuned this heap for him and warmed the engine, then all he has to do by using his eye-detic energy and his *psy*chotronic imagery, I hope I'm sayin' that correctly, what he has to do is kick that fat engine over, and move on up through the gears, and make all the turns in the right places, and hit the brakes short of punchin' us through a brick wall or a chain-link fence. . . ."

"Probably he has only one gear to play with," Todfield murmured. "Just too complicated otherwise."

"Gentlemen, with the horsepower that's under that hood, even low gear is good for sixty-plus."

"It just isn't possible," the Statesman said, "for him to steer this car through town at *any* speed without——"

"He must have some sort of visual aid," Todfield concluded. "Probably minicam TV. Even so, from where he's sitting, it's a feat for a computer."

They'd all been waiting for it, but still they were startled to hear the low-pitched rumble of the engine, feel the shimmer of power through the seat of their pants.

"He'p me, Jesus," Boyd Huckle said with a humble smile.

The headlights flashed on and the brakes were released without finesse; the Charger went screeching through the square past the out-of-date Christmas tree, painting the bricks with foot-wide stripes of rubber. The men inside were pressed back into their seats by the force of the acceleration. Todfield felt the blood draining from his head to his groin. The car fish-tailed at the first intersection, as if it wasn't sure where it wanted to go. It slowed momentarily, then leapt toward a pharmacy diagonally across the intersection. Todfield threw up his crossed arms but the car swerved at the curb, hit it solidly with one of the big back tires, bumped back into the street and careened toward the driverless police car, which was heading on down to the square in faithful duplication of its daily rounds.

"He can't control it!" Boyd Huckle screamed. "The sonofabitching maniac, don't he know he can get us killed?"

The stock car rammed right again, leaving the path of the oncoming cruiser, and continued up the street to a red light. It stopped for the light and sat there burbling and chuckling, outrageously full of power.

Eating power as well, and Todfield wondered how long the generators could last. Surely no more than four or five minutes, then the car would sit dead in the street until it was towed away, prepared for the next trial. In the meantime——

Todfield could almost feel the mind that controlled them all, idling, pondering something really spectacular to impress them before time ran out.

He saw, half mile away, the commuter train curving slowly along its track. Top speed for the circular track, about thirty miles an hour. In the back the Old Warrior had had enough, he was clawing at his seat belt. But it couldn't be released without the locking tool, they were all quite helpless.

The Dodge Charger surged forward as the light changed, and went speeding toward the train.

No, Todfield thought, *no, don't, for Christ's sake, you're not good enough yet!*

They left the business section behind and crossed an iron bridge over a lagoon fringed with wintering cattails, and at this point it became devastatingly obvious to the others that they were in a race with the train for the crossing.

Four hundred yards—three hundred, and approaching at an angle. For the moment they had the train beat. Todfield watched the small adjustments of the steering wheel that kept the car centered on the road. *And what happens now if one or more of the generators quits?* No way to suddenly repeal the law of mass and momentum; the Charger was going to make a deep and ugly dent in the side of the first coach . . . and then be turned to twisted scrap beneath those grinding wheels.

Todfield grabbed for the steering wheel, but he could just touch it with his fingertips—he understood perfectly why he had been given the choice seat; of the four of them he was the smallest, and had the least reach. He sat back, feeling sluggishly horrified as the Charger ate up the last fifty yards to the crossing. And now it seemed that the car was slowing up a bit, losing its slight edge over the train.

"We're going to hit it," the Statesman said, not very loudly.

As if in reply the sound of the engine changed brutishly, there was a new increment of power seconds before something vital in the transmission snapped and froze, but by then they had bounced across the tracks a few feet ahead of the looming train.

By the time the smoking stocker had rolled to a safe stop, the other car was alongside.

Workmen quickly scissored through the soft mesh and unlocked the seat belts. Aerial bombs, called maroons, were going off overhead, followed by fancy multiple-break shells that filled the sky with clusters of chrysanthemums. Someone was celebrating, or lording it over them. The FM radio was playing again. The Statesman took two wobbly steps and hurled it against a rock. Then he collapsed on his knees in the dirt road. The Old Warrior was choking on bile. Boyd Huckle, his face shaded from amber to pink by the pretty explosions in the sky, reached with a trembling hand for his cigarettes. He looked thoughtfully at the rear lights of the train receding toward town.

Todfield moved very carefully getting up and out of the car, but he wasn't careful enough for his chronically bad stomach. He threw up on his trousers and his shoes. Then he wiped his mouth with the back of a numbed hand and looked up to see Childermass a few feet away, agitated with glee.

The expression in those mismatched eyes confirmed Todfield's closely held suspicion that the man was a dangerous psychopath, and he cursed the unknown shotmaker who had managed to take off only one of Childermass' arms. Todfield had assassins galore to finish the job, and it was long past time to let a contract. But of course that was wishful thinking. There was too much of MORG now, they were everywhere in the foundations of government like deathwatch beetles. And it was too much to hope that Childermass would ever succeed in hanging himself, with just such folly as they had survived moments ago.

"Toddie, ain't he a whiz?" Childermass exulted, waving at the gaudy display, his voice almost too high-pitched for human ears.

Todfield, shivering, looked around as Boyd Huckle came up beside him. Boyd wasn't about to challenge Childermass either. They'd been treated like bare-assed pledges at a frat initiation, but they would have to be good sports about it.

"Did you practice it much before you put us on for the ride?" Boyd said. Sky rockets continued to whistle and thud overhead, the burning magnesium turning them all into chalk-faced clowns.

"Of course, Boyd. We worked it out to the split second."

"Mighty reassuring."

"But we had to be convincing. What good's a demonstration, if it's not absolutely convincing?"

There was a pyrotechnic message for them off in a field, outlined in blazing pinwheels.

HAPPY
NEW YEAR

Boyd pulled at an earlobe and handed Todfield his cigarette to drag on.

"Oh, I'm convinced," Boyd said quietly. "I'm convinced you better kill that little shitface before he causes some real grief."

Nine

It was a little after three in the afternoon on New Year's Eve
when Hester Moore finished altering the black coat and the
black trousers with the shiny seat, and plugged in a steam iron
to warm up. There was music in the house by the cove: New
Orleans funeral music, with struttin' ragtime sallies and break-
aways. Hester tried the iron with a wetted fingertip, but her spit
didn't crackle. She picked up a dilapidated black umbrella and
strutted into the bathroom where Peter was standing naked in
front of the mirror, shaving.

"It's bad luck to open an umbrella in the house," he said.

"I'm not superstitious." But she collapsed the umbrella anyway, and sat low on the edge of the Roman tub to watch him
shave. His hair had turned out well, a shade of brown that
looked right with his normally ruddy complexion; just a few
streaks of white remained around the ears. Hester had trimmed
away most of the shag. With heavy glasses and pipe and a cal-
culated slouch he was transformed. Whipsnade Professor of
Economics at NYU. Or one of the bright young Jesuits in the
Cardinal's office.

"Have you always had thievery in your bones?" she said ad-
miringly.

"No. I was carefully taught."

"Suppose the housekeeper had walked in while you were upstairs burgling the rectory of good old Immaculate Conception?"

"It's a very old house, and it'll fall down one these days. I would have started talking about support walls and beams and bracing. I would have drawn diagrams until she got bored and remembered something else she needed to do. People want to believe what you tell them, it simplifies their lives."

"I believed you when you told me about Robin. But it was hard to believe, I mean suddenly the place where I worked sounded so sinister. How long did you watch me before you decided to take a chance?"

"Six weeks."

"And how long before you started to trust me?"

"I set out my mousetraps. I was a big piece of smelly cheese. Nobody tried to take a bite."

"I don't know how you had the nerve to do that, after what you'd already been through."

The iron would be hot by now and she had work to do, but Hester liked sitting there looking at him. In a couple of hours he'd be gone and then it might be a very long time before she saw him again . . . if he made it back to her at all. Just three days ago she'd been certain that the computer's terse obituary meant the end of it.

    PARAGON EST 2115 HRS
    ID: DEJA VU
    FOR VISUAL DISPLAY
    REF: SANDZA FILE

    . . . .

    ?CURRENT STATUS?

    . . . .

    DECEASED/DETAILS FOLLOW:

    ON 18 JUNE 1975 AT APPROXIMATELY 0200
    ROBIN SANDZA FELL OR JUMPED INTO THE
    EAST RIVER FROM THE PROMENADE OF CARL

SCHURZ PARK VICINITY EAST 86TH ST/ FOUR
WITNESSES INTERROGATED BY POLICE
PROVIDED SIMILAR ACCOUNTS OF THE
INCIDENT/THE BODY WAS NOT RECOVERED/
ON 19 JUNE THE OFFICE OF THE CORONER

Peter had stayed away for hours while she tried to read, tried
to sew, napped fitfully. When at last he walked in, half-frozen,
cold rain on his face, she could see at a glance that no proof of
his son's death would ever be good enough: having survived this
long on luck and nerve and will, he probably would not have
believed if they had shown him a disinterred corpse in a coffin.

Four witnesses had seen Robin take the long plunge into the
tidal river; why wasn't that enough? Hester had decided it was
enough for her, but she couldn't say so. Peter mattered too
damned much . . . more than she mattered to him, another truth
that was unwelcome. But he needed her close, not to talk to, not
right away, just to touch if he wanted. He needed, on a dreary
afternoon, the reassurance that he was not totally alone.

Hot vegetable soup made with beef and bone marrow; dark
imported beer at room temperature. A real fire, not the tame
gas-log affair but hefty logs graying on the hearth, fountains of
sparks, the sting of hardwood smoke, the always-changing, entrancing flames. Her head was in his lap, his fingertips light on
the nape of her neck.

"Did you always know that Robin was a psychic?"

"No. He kept it from me for a long time. That wasn't difficult
to do, I saw very little of him while he was growing up. I think
he *wanted* to tell me, long before he got around to it. But he was
worried sick he'd do it badly, and destroy the relationship. He
knew I'd be pretty damned disturbed."

"Were you?"

Peter smiled. "We were in St. Thomas—April of '74. He was
growing up fast—every time I saw him he was six months, a year
older, and I was beginning to think it was a terrible waste of both
our lives. By then I knew I wanted out of MORG. It wasn't a
matter of age, or nerves, or reflexes. I still checked out pretty
good: simple reaction time of .14 seconds, or .26 seconds in a
six-choice situation. I have the perceptual speed and dynamic
visual acuity I had when I was a kid. I can still make the long

shots, up to fifteen hundred yards when you've got, at most, twelve inches to work with. But it had all . . . gone flat, somehow. I'd lost my sense of outrage. I felt like I had overstayed my adolescence by about fifteen years.

"Anyway, we both had a lot on our minds during the flight down, there was a kind of awkwardness between us. By then Robin had read me, he had a good idea of who and what I was, he knew the names of men I'd killed. Even so he loved me. It was my love he was afraid of losing, because he felt like a god-damn monster."

"Poor Robin."

"We chartered a boat, fished for jack and pompano, did some diving. Our usual routine. When he finally got all the emotional knots untangled and confessed——"

"You couldn't believe a tenth of what he told you."

"No. So he flipped a Kennedy half dollar fifty times. Forty-seven times it came down heads. Robin said he could keep it up all afternoon, but it was boring. Then he unsheathed his diver's knife and asked me to stand behind him. He wasn't wearing anything but swim trunks and burn cream on his shoulders and nose. He stood in the sun on the stern deck with his right arm outstretched, palm up. He put the knife in his palm and concentrated on it for a couple of minutes. His hand was steady. The knife suddenly flew and stuck with tremendous force in the mast twelve feet away. Robin retrieved the knife and held it up, and I remember how the sun flashed on the blade. He passed his other hand over the blade and it wilted like an unwatered flower. Then he straightened the blade, not quite as good as new: it was about an eighth of an inch out of plumb."

"Good Lord. What did you do?"

"I smiled; asked him how he did it. He said, By wanting to, that's all I know. Robin looked tired. I went below to get him some lemonade and fix myself a drink. I poured a hell of a lot of gin over ice and drank it before it was cold. The sight of a tempered steel knife blade curling over at the tip wasn't easily dismissed from the mind."

"No indeed."

"When I tried to apply reason to what I'd seen, my mind just —balked. Nothing looked quite right to me, but I didn't blame that on the gin. I couldn't tell if I was looking at water or artfully contrived, blue concrete. I had the eerie notion I could walk on it, all the way to Buenos Aires. I wondered if the multiplication tables still worked. I wondered if the sun was going to set as usual, or if it would hang in that particular spot in the sky forever——"

"In other words, you freaked."

"I finally realized what was affecting me: simple terror. I'd dealt with terror before. You have to get yourself moving. Do something, anything, but don't just stand there paralyzed. So I took Robin his lemonade. He was anxious and uncomfortable. I don't know how I looked to him. I imagine my smile was badly hung. But when I gave him the glass and touched his hand I found that I could breathe again. After that I was okay. Different, but okay."

"When did you decide to quit MORG?"

"On the spot. It was obvious that Robin was going to need me, badly. I had an obligation, a moral obligation to complete an assignment I'd been working on for a year. Then I could come home to stay. Ellis Tidrow had been wanting to return to missionary work for some time. Borneo, New Guinea, one of those Godforsaken places. I told Robin I was ready to be a full-time father. At first he was afraid I'd made the decision because I thought he needed a keeper. When I convinced him otherwise, he was—overjoyed. God, we had a beautiful time the rest of that week, making up for some long-gone years."

"Smoke getting in your eyes?" Hester asked.

"No, I'm crying."

"Oh," she said.

"Don't worry, I won't go apeshit on you."

"It isn't apeshit to cry when you love someone."

Peter moved her, but tenderly, got up to walk off his emotion. He added another log to the fire. He came back to her. He was angry now, though not at himself. Hester closed her eyes and touched him blindly, erotic because of the tears she had seen.

"I think Childermass planned to take Robin from me the night I introduced them," Peter said. "Robin had prepared a couple of reasonably difficult demonstrations. Ball bearings on a formica table top. He kept several of them in constant motion without rolling any off the table, a feat which I couldn't duplicate using both hands. Childermass wrote down a long series of numbers, sealed the original in a metal box, kept a check list. Robin held the box in his hands. From eight feet away Robin ran the numbers off on a digital calculator, almost faster than the eye could follow. It was obvious, even then, that Robin's talents . . . had no practical limitations.''

"I don't understand why you had to tell Childermass that Robin was a psychic."

"Do you remember what MORG stands for?"

"Multiphasic, Operations, and umm, Research something-or-other."

"Research Group."

"MORG. That's . . . really grotesque, when you think about it."

"Just a bastard little agency that never made it at DOD. Except for Childermass it would have been dismantled along about the beginning of the Korean War. But Childermass is one of the great bureaucrats and demagogues, the equal of Hoover himself. He took an agency nobody knew much about and created a sphere of influence in the Cold War climate of the fifties. All he needed to become really powerful was a few hundred million dollars. He got the swag by scaring people. He tricked and lied and blackmailed. He conned large numbers of otherwise sensible men into believing that the CIA and the FBI weren't enough. We needed MORG. And did we ever get it."

"I don't think you answered my question about Robin and——''

"I was so tired of the gangster work, the neighborhood protection rackets. Which is all it ever amounted to despite the rhetoric and the chauvinism. We were protecting our no-doubt vital interests in neighborhoods like Cambodia, Peru, and the Trucial Oman States. And the old ways always worked best: a payoff here, a killing there. I was damned tired and just a little careless long before I recognized the symptoms. I ought to have quit cold, but Childermass argued me out of it. I accepted double salary and a title in an area where my training and judgment might be valuable. A sensitive post. Too sensitive, because Robin had access to everything inside my head. Sooner or later that would have caused trouble. So I told Childermass. Hell, I all but invited him to steal my son."

"You didn't know Childermass was interested in psychic phenomena."

"No. The Russians and the Czechs had been diddling with it for years, reason enough for Childermass to sink a few million into Paragon Institute. Nothing much had come of his investments. But it was all there, just waiting, for Robin."

Peter got up to open a bottle of Irish beer and poke up the fire. Hester curled deep in the tub chair, looking out at him like a dreamy animal in a winter den.

"That's one reason why I don't believe my son is dead," Peter said quietly. "Dr. Irving Roth is a liar. His computer also tells lies, and four 'witnesses' will lie to their graves because they've been handsomely bought. Childermass leaves nothing to chance. Robin was too valuable to be let out of Paragon by himself, particularly at two in the morning."

"What if he . . . broke out for some reason?"

"And jumped in the river with four people watching? It's a little too neat, Hester."

"I guess so."

"Childermass found himself in possession of a unique natural resource. The Russians don't have one. The Chinese don't have one. He wanted Robin locked up—the euphemism is 'involuntary sequestration'—where his researchers could devote full time to him. He didn't want any questions asked about the boy, ever. Robin's 'death' was easy to fake, but there was a bigger problem."

"You?"

Peter nodded. "Childermass knew that as long as I was alive there was no chance he could get away with any of it. Robin was scheduled for five days of tests at Paragon Institute. In the meantime Childermass had an urgent request. One of our Russians had died in Vladimir prison after eight long years. As soon as he was in the ground the Ukrainian NTS got his wife out; she had refused to leave Russia as long as Sergei was alive. There was a chance she had some information, one of many pieces of a puzzle we'd been working on for a long time, and because I'd known them both it seemed likely Katya would be willing to cooperate with me. She was old and sick and we were working against time, so I flew to Finland immediately. But I was a few hours late; Katya had lapsed into a coma and was failing so rapidly there was no chance she would recover. I saw her briefly. Maybe it *was* Katya. Or maybe it was some other old woman they'd drugged for the occasion."

"Who do you mean, they?"

"Our Baltic group. The Principal is, or was, a man named McGourty. I think I killed him, but to this day I don't know for sure. Good old McGourty. He sprung for dinner at Kalastasaturppa and got me to the Helsinki airport in plenty of time to catch the 7:30 P.M. Finnair flight to Copenhagen. From there I was connecting direct to New York on SAS. I said goodbye to McGourty at the gate. The plane was a DC-9, I think, and the flight was lightly booked, maybe twenty-five passengers in all.

"We were boarding in a light rain, walking across a stretch of wet tarmac, when the bomb went off prematurely, almost blowing the tail section off the plane. The explosion dismembered a couple of cargo busters and a ramp rat. Most of the boarding passengers were injured; fortunately there was a big catering truck between us and the blast. I don't know what caused the bomb to go off at the airport instead of over the Gulf of Finland. Maybe one of the cargo busters pried open the wrong suitcase. I came to in the back of an ambulance parked on the ramp. I remembered vaguely having dinner with McGourty, and there he was again, bending over me on the litter, talking to me, looking very concerned. I couldn't hear a word he said. He had rolled up my sleeve. I saw the needle in his hand. I couldn't tell you why I reacted like I did. I might have seen something, just for an instant, in his eyes. I think now that McGourty heard the explosion as he was driving away from the airport, turned around and came back in case it was necessary to finnish off a bad job. And that's a bad pun, but I got both hands around his throat before he could jab me, and if he wasn't dead when I left him on the litter and drove off in the ambulance, it's only because I wasn't at full strength at the time."

"All those people dead because——"

"Childermass wanted to be sure I didn't come back from Finland. He could have put me up for bids, I can think of half a dozen professionals who would've considered the money worth the risks. Childermass has always been a free spender when it comes to his pie-in-the-sky projects, but my life wasn't worth two hundred and fifty thousand bucks when five thousand would do the trick, and to hell with the rest of the people on that plane. By the time he assigned a reliable assassin, I had my wits about me. It took me six weeks to get home. I had it figured— why he'd done it; what he wanted. I got in touch. He said he knew he'd made a hell of a big mistake, and he wanted to talk. Just the two of us."

"Did you trust him?"

"We worked it out so there was no possibility I was walking into something. But he was so eager to get rid of me he was willing to do the job himself. Childermass isn't a coward, but he's never carried a weapon and as far as I know he's never killed a man. It can be hard to do that first time. He was counting on me to be a little lax. Hardware fixed him up with a High Standard Model 10 riot gun, which is an automatic shotgun a little more than two feet long, with a pistol grip, loaded with Sabot cartridges that generate twenty-two-hundred foot-pounds of energy at the muzzle. It's one of the most evil weapons ever devised. He had the gun under his rain slicker. We met after midnight, in the middle of a parking lot at RFK stadium. His car, a VW, and the stolen car I was driving. I circled until I was satisfied he was alone in the bug. I parked eight feet away, and parallel. He got out. It was raining. He had his right hand through the side slot in the coat. I still didn't expect anything. But the engine was running: I had one foot heavy on the brake, the other on the accelerator.

"He should have brought that shotgun up firing through the glass of the off-side window—hell, he could have blown the side right out of the car. But he couldn't see well because of the rain, and maybe he didn't trust his fire-power. If he'd done it right, there wouldn't have been anything left of me above the belt buckle. But he wasn't a pro, he wanted the door open. I'd rigged a little something, just to set him back on his heels, make him nervous. A three-thousand-candlepower torch that went on as soon as the door was opened, hitting him full in the face, blinding him. He lost his cool and tried to drag that shotgun out from under the slicker. He was back on his heels, still holding onto the door with the other hand. I hit the gas and took off. Childermass lost his balance and fell down hard on his butt with his left arm still extended, and the shotgun was hung up at a bad angle. The jolt triggered it and that big, heavy Sabot slug blew his arm away at the elbow."

"Oh, God, that's terrible! What did you do?"

"Drove fifty feet; stopped. Looked back. Put it in reverse. I figured by the time I ran over him, back and forth three or four times, he wouldn't miss the arm at all."

Hester's face was totally drained of color. "I don't believe . . . you would have done that."

Peter reacted with a fierceness that startled Hester: he took her face in his hands. The pressure of his fingertips made heavy indentations along her cheekbones. She sucked air painfully through clenched teeth. Hester tried to look away, and couldn't.

"Hester," he said softly, "what are we talking about here? I never owned a white horse. I was never in a fair fight in my life. I never gave the other guy a chance to draw first. It is a very ugly thing to die by shotgun. It's probably worse than being blown up by a bomb ten thousand feet over deep blue water. I would have run over him, Hester. I would have mangled him. But they were monitoring or observing visually from somewhere, and they filled the area with cars in a hell of a hurry. I got out alive because I had clouted some kid's Roadrunner with a big mag mill in it, and because I had less to lose than the man driving the chase car; speed and desperation gave me the necessary edge."

Hester's stomach was churning. Her right cheek stung where one of his fingernails had gouged her.

"Please . . ."

Peter released her. He turned his head away as if he felt contempt for her, for unpardonable weakness. His contempt hurt worse than a beating.

She had said: "It could be—the one reason why he won't give up, why he's still after you."

And Peter had said: "Revenge isn't that dear to Childermass. No, he's hunting me out of fear. He's afraid I'll take Robin away from him. And Robin has become more important to him than MORG itself."

Hester watched Peter scrape the underside of his jaw with the old-fashioned straight razor which he'd stropped to a delicate edge. He had good steady hands today. He'd slept soundly two nights in a row, so he wasn't sick to his stomach half the time from sheer nervous fatigue. He could hold on to his meals and he'd put on four or five pounds since she'd been cooking for him, he didn't look quite so gaunt any more. In another week

. . . Hester's eyes stung with sudden tears. She wished now she had lied about the girl poor Raymond Dunwoodie had mentioned, the psychic. *"I checked all the hospitals, Peter. I couldn't find a trace of the girl. Maybe she wasn't treated—you know, she might have been feeling okay and they just sent her home."* But it wasn't so easy to lie to him. Not when he sat very close and still, his eyes motionless like a chilly kind of waking death, with those metal-hazy glints that made you mindful of the savage potential of the smaller jungle cats, the ones even the best of the cat keepers and trainers don't try to work into the act.

So she'd told him all she had learned about Gillian Bellaver. *Those* Bellavers. He praised her detective work. There was a tremor of excitement in him, a renewed sense of purpose. Hester couldn't shake the feeling that she had made a disastrous mistake.

Peter finished his shave and rinsed. Hester got up and went back to the ironing board and pressed the priestly suit of clothes he had stolen the day before, along with a clerical collar and a plain black homburg and a black satchel like the satchel doctors carried in that remote era when doctors made house calls. No one looked too closely at a priest in a hospital, no matter what time of the day or night he was seen there. No one asked for credentials.

When Peter had it all together Hester studied him critically from across the room.

"If I'd walked in the door just now I wouldn't have known you," she admitted.

"I feel about as authentic as a two-dollar hairpiece," he grumbled. "I was never big on disguises."

"You'll be great, Father, um——"

"Van Bergen."

"But the timing?"

"Couldn't be better. New Year's Eve, the hospital's half empty. Reduced staff, and by ten o'clock tonight there'll be at least one discreet but swinging party for those nurses stuck with floor duty. I'll have plenty of time to talk to the Bellaver girl. And if she's all Raymond claimed she was——"

"Then somebody else could be interested," Hester said. "The ones Raymond talked to before you met him in the park. He *had* to be talking to MORG, Peter. There was no call from Raymond

Dunwoodie logged at the Institute on that day. I checked."

Peter studied her. "Maybe you're taking too many chances lately."

"Oh, Peter, anybody can get a look at the telephone log!"

"That place is heavily miked, Hester! And I tried to explain to you how the Psychological Stress Evaluator works: they'll have random print-outs on every employee. It's a long-distance device that evaluates physiological tremors under stress, you don't have to be hooked up to it to give yourself——"

"Okay, okay."

"So you spent a few minutes bashing with their computer and got away with it, but maybe you've done something else that strikes Paragon security as a little odd, and they don't need much to make them suspicious. One slip and you'll be another in a fairly long line of people who have passed through Paragon Institute on their way to a cloudy corner of limbo."

"You have to get scary, don't you? I'm fine! Nobody's after *me*. You're the one who keeps disappearing and, and, God, I don't *see* you, days at a time, weeks, all I can do is call and call that fucking subway number, and maybe once in a while some *wino* answers——"

It astonished Hester that she would so easily go off on a tear, perversely showing him even more weakness; she'd planned to be as stoic about Peter's leave-taking as he was. But once she got started, the flicker of concern in Peter's eyes might have prompted genuine hysteria if he hadn't held her so soothingly close.

"Just don't get hurt," she begged him. "And don't stay gone so long this time."

"Hester, I couldn't keep going without you," Peter assured her, and although Hester was basically too sensible to entirely believe him, there was nothing she wanted to hear more.

Ten

With his wife in Minneapolis for the birth of a grandchild, Dr. Irving Roth, Director of Paragon Institute, found himself with nothing better to do on New Year's Eve than attend a party of the Hudson Valley Medical Association for some globe-trotting Russians. It was a big, formal, and dull affair in Riverdale, the kind of thing where you had to wear a name tag on your tuxedo. The buffet wasn't bad. Roth overate, as he'd done throughout the holiday season. Pounds and pounds he didn't need. He was already wide, like a wrestler, but he had short arms and no air of aggression—his smile was too smooth and appealing. All in all, a bit of a charmer. His hair was fading from the top of his head like grass on a drought-stricken lawn.

Roth spoke to men he hadn't seen much of since med school, and he spoke to a disconcerting number of colleagues who thought he'd retired and moved to a more leisurely part of the world.

"I'm doing basic research," he said, when the question inevitably came up. No one pressed for details, but several with research projects of their own were interested in the numbers.

"Well funded, I hope," said a physiologist with a goatee who was looking for a sponsor. Roth smiled the comfortable smile of a man up to his elbows in the public trough. He told the physiologist he needed to make a phone call, helped himself to a third martini, vowing to drink only half of it, and went wandering. It was a depressing house: drafty, with slate floors and dark wainscoting high as a man's head.

"Irv? Irving Roth?"

Roth turned, smiling automatically.

"Oh, hello, doctor, uh——"

"Tofany," the man said. He had a kind of cheerful, old-fashioned, turn-of-the-century look: Teddy Roosevelt glasses and strawberry-pink coloring, topped by a confection of pure-white, billowy hair. "Hubert Tofany."

"Let's see, tropical medicine, isn't it? And you're at Columbia."

Tofany nodded. "I saw you come in. I was hoping I'd have the chance to talk to you tonight—I've meant to look you up. Do you have a minute, Irv?"

"I was looking for a telephone, but it's nothing urgent. Grandchild due out in Minnesota."

"I have six grandchildren myself. The oldest will be ready for medical school in a couple of years."

Roth chuckled and shook his head as if to say *Time sure gets away from you,* and then he decided to finish the third martini after all. Every damn drop.

"What piqued my interest, Irv, I recalled hearing you were heavily into psychic phenomena these days."

"As an adjunct to noetics and transpersonal psychology, yes, I suppose you might say I'm interested in Psi."

"I mention it because of a patient, unusual case. I was brought in as consultant when it seemed there was a good possibility she was infected with one of the really hot viruses that slip into the country from time to time. We had her in isolation at Columbia until we were certain it was nothing more than a particularly vicious flu mutation, similar to the one that was so devastating in Recife last summer."

"Uh-huh."

"The patient is a young lady of fourteen. She was stricken suddenly, and ran a high temperature. It peaked at one hundred six and two tenths."

"Wow."

"Apparently without doing any real damage; they can stand a lot at that age. She convulsed at least once before we saw her, but an EEG two days ago showed normal wave patterns. Now she's almost completely recovered, in fact we may let her go home tomorrow. It can't be too soon for Gillian. She's had some interesting paranormal experiences these past few days."

"Paranormal?"

"I'm not sure what you'd call them. Visions, perhaps."

"She saw herself standing before the gates of Heaven, that sort of thing?"

"Nothing so comfortably rooted in mysticism. She was able to describe to me, in great detail, a malpractice suit I was familiar with, because it involved my son-in-law. The case was settled two years ago."

"She remembered reading about it in the papers."

"The case was tried in Texas, and even then it rated only a couple of paragraphs."

"Hospital gossip, then."

"Gossip about a two-year-old case at Houston Medical Center? I don't think so. And Gillian knew too much to have casually pieced it together from idle chatter. For instance, she could describe accurately General Robert E. Lee's aide-de-camp for whom my son-in-law Josiah was named. There's a portrait of Captain Brakestone hanging in the den down there in Houston, but Gillian couldn't possibly have seen it. I think the whole thing is rather remarkable."

"What else has she done?"

"Before it began to trouble her and she stopped talking altogether, she kept the floor nurses entertained . . . and, I think, a little apprehensive. She was like a, a mental magnet, picking up items of personal information. By that I mean the sort of thing you might not even discuss with your closest friend. Everyone was talking about Gillian on the floor, and I suppose all the attention, plus a certain amount of notoriety, made her cautious."

"But it could have been a short-lived phenomenon. That isn't unusual. We're a long way from understanding how the human mind works. The high fever, well, that could have resulted, in view of the essentially passive condition of the recuperating patient, in some sort of biocommunication, perhaps a veridical hallucination or two. . . ."

"Oh, yes, I see."

"It would be more significant if the girl had been aware of definite Psi experiences before she became ill."

"Well, one of the reasons she fainted at the skating rink——"

Roth said alertly, "Skating rink? Are you talking about Woll-man Rink in Central Park?"

"Yes."

"She fainted there, and was taken to the hospital?"

"Roosevelt. Then that evening I had her moved uptown to Washington Heights."

"Do you remember what day it was?"

"Before Christmas. Tuesday, I think, the twenty-first, because we were due at the Amerdeens at eight, and I——"

"Doctor, I'm sorry, you *were* saying, weren't you, that the girl had some sort of paranormal experience at the rink——"

"That's what Gillian told me, two days after her fever broke and she was able to piece together what had happened to her just before she collapsed. Gillian and her girl friend had been aware of a, some sort of bum, derelict, the park is full of them as you know, he may have been making a nuisance of himself. Asking for handouts. For some reason Gillian felt as if she knew him. At least she knew his name, and his background; he was from some little place in New Jersey. It all, she said, just popped into her mind."

"His name was——?"

"Raymond. Dun something. Dunkirk, perhaps."

"Please go on."

"Gillian remembers feeling a little woozy, out on the rink. She already had a touch of fever, and she was looking forward to a long nap when she got home. It was when she made a turn on the ice that she was severely jolted by the sight of the bum, Raymond, lying on his back, a gunshot wound in his head."

"Gunshot wound!"

"It was dreadful and gory, and that's what precipitated her faint."

"But he wasn't there, it was just a, call it a hallucination."

"Of course."

"Gunshot wound, she's definite about that."

"Oh, yes," Dr. Tofany said.

Roth had finished his third martini without tasting it, and he was feeling rather nastily on edge, a little worm of a blood vessel prowling in his left temple, usually an unfailing commandment: thou shalt lay off the hard stuff, take deep breaths in a well-ventilated room, and think benign thoughts about the human condition.

He said, "With your permission, doctor, I think I'd like to talk to the girl. Gillian?"

"Bellaver."

"Oh. Those Bellavers?"

"Her father is Avery Bellaver."

"The family oddball?"

"I found him cultivated and sensitive, although not very . . . accessible, which may account for his reputation. His wife is a raving beauty."

Roth consulted his watch.

"Let's see, nine forty-six, the hospital's just a few minutes from here——"

"You wanted to see her *tonight?*"

"Clairvoyance, or precognition, is neither rare nor a sign of abnormality, but Gillian has no way of knowing that. She could be one very badly confused girl. Frightened. I think she'll confide in me, however. And it would be far easier now, tonight, than after she's discharged, at home with the family."

"Yes, I understand that."

"New Year's Eve, my wife's in Minneapolis——" Roth spread his hands and grinned wryly. "And I'm here, surrounded by two hundred doctors talking shop. I might as well be working. At least I won't wake up tomorrow with a hangover."

Dr. Tofany also smiled.

"She's in 809 Herlands North, and I do appreciate your taking an interest. Why don't you give me a ring in a day or two?"

The only phone line in the house not tied up by other doctors was a pay phone that had been installed for the convenience of the household staff. It was located in an alcove between the busy kitchen and the butler's pantry. Roth made a credit-card call to Minneapolis, and was so brusque with his wife she had to ask him if he was feeling well. The baby hadn't come yet. Roth told Grace-Ann that he would be at home in Pelham in about an hour and a half, she could reach him there after the blessed event. He managed to sound cheerful saying goodbye to her, but she was out of his mind even before he hung up.

Roth was thinking about the dazzling day before Christmas when Raymond Dunwoodie called him from Central Park, and he had a serious attack of the guilts again; he would feel everlastingly guilty about Raymond. They should never have let him try to send from inside the high-frequency electrical field, an experiment that for unknown reasons always had a terrible effect on the organism. A promising young psychic had been reduced to fumbling in trashcans because of a directive Roth should have been sufficiently cautious to ignore. That's why he always tried to be patient when Raymond was desperate, and shamming, and inventing stories in hopes of cadging a few bucks. (They could have taken care of him, for God's sake, put him on some kind of pension. The ethical poverty of his employer, the essential lack of respect for human life, shamed Roth). The story about the girl at the ice rink was too good to be true, of course, but Raymond's voice sounded different that afternoon. He wasn't whining. He was excited but not overwrought. There was a suggestion of forcefulness that surprisd Roth, so he took time off on a busy day to taxi to the park, expecting almost anything but the sight of Raymond so pathetically dead on a high rock overlooking the rink.

He'd reported it the same day, and later the startling explanation came back to him. Raymond had been seen with Peter Sandza. The decision was made by the MORG team to take out Sandza, because opportunities had been scarce and Childermass was having fits. Unfortunately the attempted assassination went wrong, a grotesque climax to the downhill life of Raymond Dunwoodie.

Roth had his opportunity then to explain about the psychic girl of Raymond's, but the more he thought about it the more it seemed a terminal fantasy. If she did exist, with Raymond dead how could she be located? So Roth kept the story to himself.

Now, purely by chance, he knew that Raymond had been telling the truth, and Roth quickly had to do something about the girl. It was time to make another phone call—suspiciously past time, depending on how they cared to look at it. He could be in trouble.

The vein in his temple was acting up again. He was standing, and his right leg was going numb from the pressure of the garters he wore only with his formal threads. He ignored the black maid who was prowling around hoping to get possession of the telephone, wiped oily palms on a paper napkin, turned his back, hunched over the receiver and placed a second call.

As usual, once he reached the primary number, there was waiting involved. He was uneasy, thinking of the girl in the hospital, wondering if somehow she might get away from them again; but this time he had her name. Gillian. Just fourteen. Robin Sandza's age. . . .

The phone rang and Roth picked up the receiver.

"Hello, Doctor," Childermass said pleasantly. "How's tricks?"

In her last night in Washington Heights Hospital, Gillian, for sheer lack of anything else to do, considered throwing a tantrum.

She was in a ludicrous state of frustration; hollow, but not hungry; despairing, but not quite enough to support a good soul-cleansing cry. She had taken her sleeping pill, but she remained starey-eyed awake. Television was contemptible, all music bored or annoyed her, and there was nothing to see through her windows except another part of the sprawling hospital. She had a mysterious rash on her bottom that made it difficult to sit still for any length of time. She had bitten her nails to the bleeding quick. She didn't feel attractive enough to go to bed and try to get some pleasure from her body; she couldn't be horny even when she concentrated on an image of Robert Redford at the tennis club, the heart-stopping way his eyes gleamed in his sweaty overheated face when he smashed back a powerful serve. It was hard to have erotic fantasies when your hair needed washing. She knew if Bob could see her now he wouldn't smile, that great cheeky morale-building smile that was specially *hers;* he would probably throw up instead.

The old year dragged minute by minute into oblivion. The hospital floor was dismally quiet at five minutes past ten. Most

of the rooms around Gillian's were unoccupied; no one liked to
be in the hospital at this time of the year if they could possibly
put it off.

Even a visit from İrene Cameron McCurdy would have been
preferable to going nuts by herself, but Mrs. McCurdy had entertained right up until eight o'clock, a parade of gimpy garden-
club ladies, and she was undoubtedly fast asleep by now. Gillian
considered another slow stroll up and down the hall, but there
was nobody much to talk to, only a couple of unfamiliar nurses
at the brightly lit eighth-floor station. Nor could she while away
an hour on the telephone; her friends were out for the evening
or having fun in a warmer climate, her mother was God knows
where, and her father had left for Boston, where he was to read
a scholarly paper at some kind of meeting.

There were some books piled on the window ledge, and Gillian went through them unhopefully, stopping when she came
to the paperback biography of Peter Hurkos which Mrs.
McCurdy had written. Gillian frowned; she thought she had
returned it, along with the scrapbook which had sat untouched
in her room all afternoon. Maybe she had taken another book
back by mistake. She decided to go down the hall and leave the
Hurkos book. It was something to do. There might not be time
in the morning, and tomorrow she would have nothing else on
her mind but going home.

Gillian changed slippers and chose one of her newer wraps
from the closet. The single nurse visible at the station opposite
the elevators had her back turned when Gillian left her room.
Gillian went the other way, past a room half lit by the light of
a silent TV set: the man in the bed had fallen asleep. There was
no activity on the floor. It was so quiet she felt a little spooked.

She was never going to be stuck in another hospital, Gillian
thought grimly. If she had babies, she would have them at home.

Irene Cameron McCurdy's door stood part way open and
Gillian looked in. There was a night light near the floor in the
corner opposite her bed. Irene was sound asleep on her back,
both legs elevated slightly to ease continuing circulation problems. She made snoring sounds that were a little louder than the
rasp in the throat of a contented cat. A vaporizer breathed
foggily. Irene before retiring had sprayed some flower scent in
the air. Gillian found the moist sharply sweet air all but un-

breathable as she put the book on top of the dresser.

"Who's that?" Irene said calmly from the bed. Gillian turned. "Oh, it's you, dear."

"I thought you were asleep, Mrs. McCurdy. I was just returning a book I forgot."

"That's very thoughtful," Irene murmured. Gillian walked toward the door. "But you don't have to go yet."

"Well——"

"I'll be asleep soon. I had a little something extra for the pain tonight, it's very . . . relaxing. Would you mind sitting with me for a few moments? Since I was a little girl I've dreaded going to sleep alone. That's silly, isn't it?"

Gillian approached her. "I feel the same way sometimes," she said.

Irene smiled and patted the bed.

"Sit right here. Such an exhausting day. So you'll . . . be going home tomorrow. We won't lose touch, though. Oh, no. There's so much we need to talk about."

Irene held Gillian's free hand. Irene's hand was on the plump side and felt papery but it wasn't unpleasant to touch, and Gillian was sure that the woman would soon fall asleep.

"We must think of . . . how to care for all the New People," Irene murmured. "I know that there are many in High Places who are already using their considerable psychic powers to check the Forces of Darkness; but their power, compared to the power of the New People, is a drop of rain compared to an ocean. And so we cross the threshhold of a new age of consciousness. But not everyone is to be trusted. Remember that. History teaches that evil at its most exalted is merely a wretched excess of good. Good becomes righteous; righteousness becomes evil. Are we in the dawn of a Great Awakening, or in the last moment of twilight, just before the plunge into an abyss of ignorance and terror? I don't know the answer to that question. There are those who will prefer another Dark Ages to the Triumph of the New People, the blinding purity of the psi Enlightenment. I do ramble on, don't I? Are you there, dear?"

Hearing no response, Irene softly increased the pressure of her hand on Gillian's. Irene felt snoozily adrift, in and out of clouds that were faintly lit as if by shafts of light from a celestial source. It was almost too much effort for her to turn her head on the pillow and look up at the profiled face of the tall girl sitting next to her.

When she did look Irene saw enchantment, an expression of traumatized concentration.

"Papa, don't, don't do it!" Gillian squeaked in a girlish voice that Irene somehow recognized although it had been years, so many years.

"Get off her, Papa!" Gillian now demanded, growing rigid, and Irene was astonished to feel the shock-wave heat of anger coming off Gillian's skin. Irene instinctively tried to withdraw her hand, but now Gillian wouldn't let go. This effort was too much for Irene's failing resources; she felt herself powerlessly drifting again, near to nodding off. She might have peacefully lost consciousness but for a bolt of alarm, the organism warning of sudden massive exsanguination, of oncoming fatal shock.

That peaceful feeling was not due to the pills she had swallowed half an hour ago. Irene knew instinctively that she lay there dying while her life flashed before Gillian's eyes.

"I will kill the both of you!" Gillian growled. She had commenced to shudder and jerk about on the bed, but her grip on Irene was unbroken. Gillian had one slippered foot on the floor. Her foot tapped imperiously as she roundly cursed the father of Irene Cameron McCurdy. She also cursed her father's plump groaning mistress, who had spread herself belly-down on the mossy trunk of a fallen tree, blonde hair locky and all adangle in her eyes, the fat of her cheeks quivering while he shoved and grunted from behind, still impeccably attired except for the opened fly.

Tap, tap!

"Ah, God—!" Gillian cried, crazed with the pain of the spied-on infidelity. "How *could* you, Papa?"

But, mercifully, the image that held her tranced was beginning to fade; Gillian's foot now made soft wet sounds on the slickening tiles of the hospital floor. The limp hand she held had become as cold as a toad in a snowbank.

Gillian's first conscious thought following her psychometric vision was that she had embarrassingly wet herself while she sat there woolgathering, letting an old lady talk herself to sleep.

Then, despite the still-cloying odor of flowers in the hot damp room, she smelled what it was.

Roth left his car on the second level of the hospital parking garage on West 168th and entered the hospital via an overpass walkway that connected the garage with Herlands North. There were few cars in the garage, and he passed no one on his way in.

The clock on the wall beside the guardhouse in the hospital entryway, just inside the steel-and-glass doors, gave the time: 10:27. Roth hadn't visited the hospital since the new Y-shaped, buff-brick building had gone up. He found it depressingly like entering prison. The ceiling was a plane of white fluorescence that created a shadowless environment. The guard sat elevated behind thick glass and his voice rattled through a speaker. Roth stated his business and was issued an after-hours pass which he wore clipped to a lapel of his tuxedo.

A couple of nurses wearing hooded cloaks and boots went by on their way out. One of them smiled at him and said, "Oh, where's the *party?*"

Roth grinned and turned thumbs down. He walked to the elevators. After a considerable wait one came down to him, doors parting to reveal an intern leaning fogbound against one wall. He was missing a shoe and he'd put his girl friend's flow-ered underwear briefs on over his trousers.

"Fella, is this your stop?" Roth asked, holding the doors for him. The intern licked his lips and looked around without seeing anything.

"Botanical Gardens?"

"Try the Lenox Avenue line," Roth suggested. The intern stumbled off the elevator and stood looking around with an expression of tuned-out melancholy. Roth hoped he would find a conference room to crawl into and sleep it off. He pushed the right button and the elevator took him to the eighth floor.

Overhead lights had been dimmed here, to the restful yellow of a harvest moon. Several bright narrow spots were focused on the nurses' station, but no one was on duty.

In fact there was no one to be seen anywhere on the floor.

They came by car from different parts of the city, all of them arriving by ten thirty-five. Thirty MORG agents had been put on alert. Some of them were a little red-eyed. A siren went by on Fort Washington Avenue; the wind whistled drearily on the unprotected roof of the parking garage while they waited for the minibus with the communications gear, which arrived from midtown at ten thirty-eight.

The Principal pulled up a minute behind the bus. He was a part Paiute Indian named Don Darkfeather, a very tall man with the sinister thinness and crude energy of a whip. He had eyes like two black thumbtacks in a piece of tobacco-colored corkboard. His was an attitude of ruthless command. He had been directing MORG's P and C operation in the New York metropolitan area since the day after the shooting of Raymond Dunwoodie in Central Park. His predecessor had been reassigned to a newly formed antiterrorist unit based in Prudhoe Bay, Alaska.

Darkfeather's agents were equipped with belt transceivers, wrist microphones and earpieces as well as more powerful walkie-talkies. The team was composed of penetration specialists, crack drivers and shotmakers. The shotmakers carried high-velocity weapons: riot guns and revolvers loaded with the pancaking Superbell slugs, which made terrible man-stopping wounds wherever they hit. Beneath his regulation dark gray trench coat each man wore a multi-layered Kevlar vest that could stop a .45 slug fired at close range. None of them had to be reminded that the man they were going after was one of the three or four best shotmakers ever turned out by MORG.

Darkfeather's instructions were brief.

"Don't overlook anybody," he said. "Sandza could've made himself a part of the scene by now."

"Sir, what if he has a fuck with him?" It was the MORG word for civilian.

"If you have to hole a fuck to get to Sandza, okay. We'll sweeten it later."

"Doctors, nurses?"

"Nobody's sacred," Darkfeather said.

"What about NYPD?"

The Indian tugged at one long sideburn and reconsidered.

"Don't hole a cop," he said. "That does take a lot of sweet-enin'."

Roth walked down the hall to 809, Gillian's room. The door stood half open. There was a light on by the bed. He knocked softly at the door.

"Miss Bellaver?"

When she didn't reply the doctor walked in. He could see at a glance that the room was empty.

He was standing with his back to the bathroom. When he heard a door hinge creak he turned, a smile forming.

"I didn't mean to——"

Roth bit his tongue in astonishment. A priest was standing in the bathroom doorway, pointing a gun at his head. Obviously he was accustomed to handling firearms. There was authority in his stance.

"What have you done with her, doctor?"

The voice was familiar, and Roth felt an onrush of shock that threatened to topple him.

"Arrghhhh," he said, fright stifling his power of speech. His body stiffened defensively as he remembered the beating, months ago, that had crippled him for more than a week. There had been few marks anywhere, although the pain even with opiates was nearly unbearable. He knew he couldn't survive another beating like that, but this time he saw in those hellish eyes that Peter Sandza did not intend to go to any further trouble, he would simply pull the trigger when he was ready.

Dr. Roth couldn't speak, but he could vividly picture gunshot trauma, and there was a heavy rising mass just beneath his diaphragm.

"I don't have *time,*" Peter said in a toneless low voice. "Get yourself sorted out fast and take me to Gillian Bellaver. Or I'll start putting your lights out."

"I——" Roth said, and found that his tongue was manage-able, his throat not entirely paralyzed, "don't know, where, she is. I just, g-got here my-m-my——"

"What I'll do, Doctor, I'll go for the back of the neck. Kiss one off the third cervical vertebra. Now you know what that does, it turns you into a living head for a few years; maybe they'll be able to fix you up with one of those wheelchairs you operate by pushing a button with your tongue."

"*Wait!* I know you don't have any reason to believe me, but for God's sake, man, will you l-listen! She is a patient here, but I just learned that tonight. Maybe they moved her to another room, I don't know, but I can, if you'll give me a moment to check, one of the floor nurses——"

A smile flickered. "They're tied up belly to belly in a spare room down the hall. I counted on a long session with the girl, didn't want interruptions. All right, strange as it may seem I think I believe you. I might even believe you if you told me you came alone."

"I did!"

They had become aware of an intense, maddened moaning out in the hall; the sound turned the hairs on the back of Roth's neck spikey as pine needles. And, at the same time, someone was using a mop. Peter's eyes widened a fraction, and he seemed momentarily unable to cope with this intimation of Bedlam, one poor soul placidly mopping the floor while another went audibly insane. Then with his free hand he motioned Roth out the door.

Roth hurried outside looking the wrong way, but he caught a glimpse of something terrifying to his right just as Peter came up behind him and shoved him hard. Roth took two off-balance steps to the opposite wall and froze there. He looked starkly over his shoulder at some kind of apparition, wearing slippers steeped in blood, that glided toward him with little Oriental shuffle-steps.

Gillian's skin was as deathly white as watered milk. Her eyes rolled like the eyes of a frightened horse, and she was chomping her tongue. There was no crazy mop-lady; it was just the sound of an incredibly bloody robe, caught up on one ankle, that slopped along behind her. Gillian had stripped herself half na-ked; her nightgown was in tatters, most of it pasted to her shapely legs. Roth saw that her body was smeared with blood as well, and she kept making those unbearable sounds. But he saw no slashes, no deep pumping wounds, and he guessed that she wasn't, couldn't be, as severely injured as she looked.

He made a fumbling move to intercept Gillian, but Peter got

to her first. Peter slapped her hard across the face, causing blood to spray from her bitten tongue. Gillian came to a cringing stop, hands motionless, eyes still and looking huge and halo-shiny in her drained face. The moans continued until he popped her a second time; now there were finger-welts on both cheekbones. From the small amount of blood on her mouth and chin Peter assumed she hadn't done severe damage to her tongue. He saw it all coming back to her, whatever horror she had so pathetically fled; he moved deftly, ripped off the rest of the sodden gown, threw it against the far wall.

What a godawful load of blood, none of it hers. Whose, then? Had she murdered someone? A fantastic notion crossed his mind. He yanked the stinking slippery girl from the trailing robe and held her tightly against him. She was rigid and unbreathing in his arms.

"Find out where she's been!" Peter said harshly to Roth. The doctor took off at a half run down the hall, following the trail of blood swabbed on the floor.

Peter upended Gillian, carried her into the room, kicked the door shut and stood her against the wall by the bathroom door. He soaked a towel and began to clean her. She was cold to the touch and still cringing, her eyes shut. He rubbed brutally; she shit on the towel. Peter sighed and threw it away and got another and rubbed harder. It hurt and Gillian groaned, but that was a healthier sound, one of protest, and Peter was encouraged. He helped himself to a fistful of her long hair and banged her head lightly against the wall.

"Look at me," he demanded. "Whatever it was, it's over now. You're safe and you can face it. Don't let it get the best of you. I said open your eyes and look at me, girl!"

Gillian trembled, but she looked at him. One inward eye, he noted, and great bones: probably a beauty when she didn't look like something he'd fished out of a sewer. He used a corner of the towel more gently to sponge her flecked lips.

"All the blood is gone," Peter insisted. "I wiped it off you . . . no, don't."

The impulse to hysteria was running wild under her skin. He lashed a flank with the twisted wet towel and she yelped.

"Don't go off again. Talk to me. What's your name? Tell me your *name*, goddammit!"

"G-Gillyun."

"Louder. Gillian what?"

"BELLAVER! Don't hit me any more."

It was more of a warning than a plea. She still couldn't control her miserable trembling, but there were signs of warmth, there was a healthy flush in the triangle of her throat, and great areas the length of her body were mottled where he'd scrubbed so hard.

"I'm cold," Gillian said, her voice blurred by her defective tongue. "You're tearing my hair out! And I d-don't think you're a very n-nice——"

When the tears came, copiously, Peter stepped back, breathing a little heavily but satisfied with his rescue operation. He wondered just how close she'd come to spending the rest of her life in a very expensive sanitarium wearing a fixed placid expression like a heavy coat of wax.

He left Gillian long enough to get a terry robe from the closet. He helped her into the robe and sat her in a chair. She sobbed and coughed herself blue in the face and then tried to bundle up in a tight ball, to retreat as far back into childhood as she could get. Another familiar symptom: she wanted to sleep and sleep, like naptime on mother's bed on a rainy afternoon.

Peter knew his time was critically short. Nevertheless he pulled Gillian, wailing and complaining, from the chair, and began to trot her around the room.

"Walk! Stop the baby stuff. At least *act* like you're grown up."

"You prick! You *ass*hole!"

Gillian struck at him, then flinched when he brought his hand back. He kissed her instead, tenderly and with as much lust as he thought she might be familiar with at her age. Gillian found this new approach confusing, shocking and indefensible, and as she grew slack in his arms gradually the kiss became a comfort to her. With his own eyes closed Peter readily lost awareness of her youth; the snug pressure of her uncovered cunt against his body was mature enough, even insinuating.

Then her lips parted and Peter tasted bitter blood. He took Gillian by the arm, this time hearing no complaints, and led her to the wash basin to rinse her mouth.

The cold water stung her lacerated tongue and she made mewing sounds of pain. She swallowed some of the water and almost heaved, but it stayed on her stomach.

Peter put a hand calmingly on the back of her neck.

He felt grotesquely ambivalent toward this unusual girl, as if he'd just given birth to her, as if they were already lovers. He was in the worst possible danger, or he would've taken her with him . . . and Peter knew Gillian would accompany him without question. He had saved her from the fury and the terror, and in a sense he owned her now.

Gillian looked up wide-eyed at the strange priest who had beaten and then half seduced her. Then the truth occurred to her, which Peter read in her eyes.

"No, I'm not a priest, it's just a lousy disguise. Look, I have to go now, Gillian. If I stayed any longer I could get killed. I know you can't make much sense of what I'm saying, so just remember the words and think about it later. I have a son like you, Gillian—very much like you, I think. He was taken from me. I have to find him. I believe you're the only one who can help me, so I'll be back to see you. In the meantime there's a man named Roth; watch out for him. He'll be sympathetic and helpful and charming. You can't believe anything he tells you. Don't, under any circumstances, admit to him that you have the powers of a clairvoyant. And stay away from a place called Paragon Institute. Once you're inside I may not be able to get you out."

The hall outside Gillian's door was getting noisy, and Peter frowned. He picked up the black bag which he'd brought with him to the hospital.

"I want you to go to the telephone before all hell breaks loose up here. Call your father or someone else you can trust, a lawyer would be ideal, and tell him to come get you tonight. Say that you'll be waiting in room 909, which is the room directly above this one. I've already checked it out, and it's unoccupied. The stairs are just across the hall. Get dressed, walk up to 909, shut the door and wait until the one you called has come for you. Do you have all that, Gillian?"

Gillian spat pink water into the bowl and nodded wearily.

"What's . . . your name?" she asked him.

"Peter."

"Peter." Gillian nodded again and tried to smile. *Peter.* She liked that name. For no good reason tears began to run down her cheeks. She reached for a towel to dry her face. "Peter," she mumbled, "Mrs. McCurdy's dead." She found it increasingly painful to talk because of her tongue. "Ah . . ." Gillian caught her breath and made another attempt. She urgently had to tell him, while she could still get the words out. "Just bled and *bled*. All over. Soaked . . . me. God. I think *I* did it, Peter. I made it happen."

She lowered the towel and looked around, desperate for his understanding.

Peter was gone.

Gillian experienced a sharp cramp of fear. No, she needed him! But she wasn't going to cry any more. And he'd made a very sensible suggestion. She knew she must leave the hospital right away, and go home. There she would be safe until Peter came back—

Soon. It *had* to be soon.

Gulping air, hiccuping, Gillian went straight to the telephone and sat hunched over it, her mind momentarily a blank. Voices outside brought her around; she was afraid someone would come in. There was no man to call, as Peter had hoped; but all her life when she'd most needed help she'd been able to depend on Mrs. Busk, the Bellaver's housekeeper. It was New Year's Eve, but Mrs. Busk would be at home with her hair in rollers, waiting for Guy Lombardo on TV. Once alerted and aroused she had the moxie to drive straight to the hospital, strong-arm her way inside, and take her Gilly home.

Over everyone's dead body, if it came to that.

Eleven

In the hallway near Gillian's door Peter encountered a handful of middle-aged and elderly patients standing in groups clucking about the blood on the floor or complaining of interrupted rest. Farther down the hall, at the end of the wing where the trouble seemed to be, two women had their arms around another, immensely broad woman who was pulsating with terror and trying to faint.

"Father, where have the floor nurses gone?"

"Father, there's a woman in that room down there . . . just awful. . . ."

"I know, I know," Peter said. "You can all be most helpful now by going back to your rooms and staying there. It appears we have a maniac on the loose."

His warning emptied the halls even faster than he'd anticipated. Except for a man with a surgical neck brace who kept moving, doggedly, with the aid of a walker, toward the nurses' station. He had that old soldier look.

Peter said, "Colonel?"

"Brigadier."

"Where are you going, sir?"

"Been trying to raise someone on the bloody howler in my room. No luck, New Year's Eve, entire infirmary has gone to pot tonight. I'll just try the telephones at the service desk."

"Those phone lines have been cut, sir."

"Have they? What do you know about it?"

"Brigadier, I could use your help. We may still be able to do something for the woman. Would you follow me, please?"

Peter didn't wait for him; a couple of doors were quickly closed along the hall as he ran toward room 819. He glanced at the nameplate on the door. MCCURDY, IRENE C.

She was a flaccid thing on the bed, minus the considerable weight of approximately five quarts of blood. There was a bright, bouffant, artificial-looking arrangement of hair that didn't go with the stone-gray and shrunken face. Her teeth were bared in an expression of utter distaste. The room was like a greenhouse. The reek of blood, still dripping stringily from bed to floor, had Peter holding his breath. As far as he could tell it had all drained out of Irene McCurdy somewhere below the waist, probably under more pressure than the normal pumping action of the heart would provide. Area of recent surgery? Peter couldn't make himself go and look.

As he'd expected, there was no sign of Dr. Irving Roth. The doctor had left a partial footprint at the edge of the slowly spreading, viscous pool where he'd walked on his way to the bed. Gillian had made long sliding tracks. She'd slipped and sprawled and finally made it out of the room on her hands and knees.

Peter heard the creaking of the walker, the old soldier's rasping breath behind him.

"Extraordinary. It was like this in the trenches, you see. Very bad in the trenches. All those marvellous lads."

"Yes, sir. I'm going for help. Don't let anyone disturb this room."

"Haven't you a ritual to perform, Chaplain?"

"It'll keep."

Peter made some vital calculations as he went down the hall. Time of Roth's arrival on the eighth floor, approximately ten thirty. By the wall clock at the nurses' station it was now ten forty-seven. Peter felt a little stunned. The stairwell door closed behind him; he went up three steps at a time, carrying his black bag.

So he'd spent nearly a quarter of an hour with Gillian Bel-laver. During that time Roth had investigated Irene McCurdy's condition. It would have taken him all of thirty seconds to estab-lish that there was nothing to be done. Then, if he was any kind of medical man, he would spend a minute or two longer puzzling over probable cause, before the animal alarm reminded him he'd better set about saving his own skin. He needed the kind of muscle that could handle Peter Sandza, armed and known to be exceedingly dangerous. He'd looked at the telephone, hesi-tated, and run like hell.

To the elevators? No. There were only two elevators for Her-lands North; one had been on the blink for a while. Tough to get it repaired during the holidays. Hester, who had gone over the hospital with care while plotting Peter's Outs, had timed the service provided by the remaining elevator. Average off-peak waiting time was three minutes twenty seconds. If Roth had hung around punching buttons for any length of time on his arrival at the hospital, he'd remember and shun the elevator as a means of escape.

Which left the stairs. Up or down? Considering that fat Rothie had a weight problem, he'd find it a lot easier going down. Seventh floor? No, the good doctor would be anxious to put as much distance between himself and Peter as he could.

So jog down to six or even five, and run to the nurses' station. Arrive more than a little out of breath, and identify yourself, and tell them there's trouble up on eight, get some help quick. Dial main-floor security. One man on duty in the guardhouse by the doors, and he can't leave. Activate the pocket-pager and locate old Fred. Retired cop, of course. Maybe, just maybe, Fred would call in right away. Get in touch with a Dr. Roth at the station on six, Fred. Bzzz, bzzz. "Security. You called?"

Elapsed minimum time, say five minutes. Eight at the outside. Clock time, ten thirty-eight.

But it had been at least ten forty-five when he'd left Gillian's room. By that time Fred should have been on hand, supported by a contingent of security men from other sections of the hospi-tal, maybe even NYPD if a unit was near enough. All of them leveling guns at the door waiting for him to emerge. Peter could picture Irving Roth lurking somewhere in the background, a sickly expectant grin on his face.

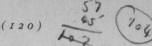

Roth hadn't notified hospital security after all.

Possibly he'd been so frightened he'd kept right on running to the nearest exit, claimed his car and was half way home by now, the sweat running down his spine like ice water.

Peter rejected the idea; it didn't jibe with his on-the-run, paranoid sense of the fitness of things.

Suppose there was someone else Roth could call on in an emergency. Not plodding ex-cops or nervous young security-trainee machos stuck with the undesirable New Year's Eve duty, but an elite force, men who could sift buildings and whole neighborhoods through a fine-mesh screen, allowing nothing to escape.

Oh, yes, Peter thought. He liked that.

If it was true, as Roth had claimed (and there had to be a grain of truth in the man somewhere), that he hadn't known of Gillian's whereabouts until tonight, then it made sense to assume Childermass had encouraged the doctor to drop by and see her. And Childermass would easily have made an important connection. Gillian at the ice rink in Central Park, Peter there on the same afternoon. Therefore it was not unreasonable to believe that Peter knew all about Gillian, and would be combing hospitals looking for her. Worthwhile assigning men to the Washington Heights hospital, just in case.

Roth had located the MORG Principal, and he had confirmed Peter's presence.

They had to be at work even now, quietly and meticulously, closing all the Outs, but not in such a way as to communicate the faintest tremor of activity to Peter. They would stay low and wait, then do it with a big bang if necessary, sweetening at leisure.

Peter had momentary misgivings about Gillian's future. But if she'd paid attention and did just as he said, probably she was in no immediate danger from Roth or MORG itself. The Bellaver name and the power of their wealth would make even Childermass cautious about how he approached her.

It might help Gillian to ease on out of the hospital if he made an uncustomarily noisy exit himself, at the same time drawing off much of the strength of the MORG teams on hand.

Easy to draw them off; very likely impossible to get rid of them once he had.

Take a little time to think about that problem on the long way down.

He had reached the tenth and top floor of Herlands Pavilion. There was a sign on the door. Red letters. NO ACCESS. CONSTRUCTION STILL IN PROGRESS ON THIS FLOOR. Metalclad door painted gray, impressive-looking lock. It wasn't as good as it looked, if you knew just which tools to bring. He opened his black bag. Penlight, lock picks. Twenty seconds, silently jiggling tumblers, and he was on the other side of the stairwell door. He closed it carefully behind him.

Colder here. The surgery floor was ninety percent completed, even the exit lamps were all in place. The red glow provided enough light for Peter to ease his way around the piles of builder's remnants. He had the Baretta automatic in his hand. They hadn't started to move in the complicated machinery yet, and only half the tiles were laid along the floor in front of him.

He was beginning to feel sick to his stomach again. Not from fear, exactly, but from a suffocating sense of *déjà vu.* Once again the nightmare scramble to avoid the Pit, each time coming closer to sliding in, falling headlong in the dark Forever.

So if you're afraid of the Pit, the thing to do is climb right in to show your contempt. Of the Pit, and the locking-tight terror it inspires.

Anyway, the roof was no longer a possibility. The simplest Out of all to cover, once they were on the alert.

Peter had a small pry bar with him, but someone had left a larger one on a partly dismantled packing crate near the elevators. He used both tools to open the doors of elevator one. He made some unavoidable noise getting them apart, but the sound of elevator two falling in its shaft was enough to obscure the clanking of the pry bars and the rolling-back of the doors on ten.

With the aid of the pencil flashlight he took a sighting on the cables in the center of the shaft. Because of the oversized hospital elevators they were a little farther away than he'd counted on, but the cables looked relatively unused, not dangerously slicked from grease and wear. He didn't look down at all. Yesterday the elevator had been in the basement, bunches of wires dangling from its control panel. It had better still be there.

Peter tucked the flashlight away and took a pair of black

leather driving gloves from his bag. He'd spent more than an hour on the gloves after Hester had purchased them, gluing and sanding with care. Climbing straight down a hundred and ten feet of rope was no great accomplishment if you knew the technique and had the stamina; climbing the same number of feet on braided steel elevator cable verged on the suicidal. On the taut cable he wouldn't get much help from his feet in braking the descent. Almost all of his weight would be pulling at his gloved hands. And he couldn't predict how long the sandpaper grip would last. If the gloves wore slick midway on the cable, then he would ride it smoking to the roof of the elevator below, hitting the roof with enough impact to drive pelvic bone fragments through a lot of irreplaceable soft tissue.

He had made a clip-on strap for the bag, which fitted snugly enough under his left arm. He waited until his eyes had adjusted to the available light. The faint gleam of the cables was just visible in the shaft. He couldn't rely on depth perception. Elevator two was now rising in the adjoining shaft, its machinery humming high C.

Peter stepped to the lip of the shaft opening. The black bowling shoes he wore gave him a soft sense of contact with the steel plate, but he would have preferred to do this in his bare feet. He hooked the fingers of his left hand in the horizontal door slot and leaned out, reaching with his right hand. He touched one of the cables and held on and then, grunting, let go with his left hand and pushed off like a circus flyer on his way to a triple somersault. He brought his feet up until he was nearly parallel to the drop; simultaneously his left hand crossed his body to the wire. He enjoyed a half second's weightlessness while he set his grip, but brute anxiety caused him to cling too tightly, and the sandpaper surface of the driving gloves worked very well.

As Peter swung around the cable with enough momentum to wrench his arms from their sockets, he had the wits to keep his feet together, maintaining a precarious airy balance. He loosened his grip just enough to compensate for the arc of his body and the tug of gravity and slipped a rocketing eight feet down the cable. Then he got the thin soles of the shoes on the wire for extra traction and came to a swaying stop, leaning back for balance. He breathed through his clenched teeth. Circus act. No applause please, save for the end.

Elevator two had stopped on the eighth floor. The doors opened, but Peter couldn't hear voices. Strict discipline. MORG had come to sweep up. Distantly he heard the old brigadier calling for help.

Where are you, Gillian? Peter thought. It was drafty as a chimney where he was hanging, and the sweat of his armpits felt like chilled mercury, sliding in lazy droplets down his sides.

He started to lower himself. Hand over hand, a foot at a time.

In 612 Herlands West Father Karl Krás⸗o sat nodding over his prayers, forgetting, in his weariness, some of the native tongue. He had hoped, by reciting Psalms in Czech, that he might get through to the man on the bed, but more likely it had been at least forty-eight hours since Jonas Krásno had paid attention to the sound of his brother's voice, or to anyone's voice. The hero-brother was just too far gone, yet the big chest, undiminished by the spreading rot inside, continued to heave as if under a ton of weight; he made each breath last an incredible minute or longer while he gathered strength to fight for another. Father Karl found it difficult to keep his mind on prayers while the struggle continued; even the private duty nurse in attendance at Jonas' bedside was staring at him, gripping the arms of her chair as if the intensity of his desire to survive was consuming her as well.

Father Karl took off his glasses and poured a little cold water on a cloth, held it against his aching head. He smiled. *Ah, but you should have seen him at his greatest,* he thought. Thirty-eight, no almost thirty-nine years ago. He could still shudder at the memory of the Carpathian winter and their suffering as Jonas prodded them through waist-high drifts of snow. Nazi ski patrols everywhere. Jonas was sixteen but seasoned, fully a man. They were the children of Max Krásno, and so marked for death like the rest. The world remembers Lidice, but not Drbal. It was almost a hundred miles from their doomed Moravian village to the ruins of the Slovakian castle near Strečno in the Malá Fatra where they hoped to find a partisan group willing to take them in. A hundred miles of frostbite and starvation, no nourishment except stonecrop tea and a few bats Jonas had trapped in a cave and roasted like squab.

Yolande had died in Jonas' arms only a few miles from the castle, a pathetic blue lump in the torn fleece which he stripped from his own back in a last futile attempt to keep her warm. Despite the medicinal tea she coughed her lungs out, bits of bloody tissue at a time. Had Jonas accidentally smothered her, a hand over her face to muffle the sounds in the sifting-down night while spotlights raked the trees? For almost a full day after they reached shelter he refused to let them take Yolande from him. Karl slept and slept, exhausted. On waking he attacked his big brother in a frenzy partly caused by fever. *Yoan-ash! Yoan-ash! Why didn't you save her?*

He would never forget the look of bewilderment and anguish on Jonas' face, the tears that didn't quite flow. *Bad luck, Karl.* It was all Jonas said. The next day he went back to join the Resistance in Brno. He killed a lot of Nazis in the war, perhaps some S.S. who had been responsible for the horror of Drbal.

Let me now make amends, Karl thought. He put down the cool cloth and reached for his glasses and the rosary of heavy hand-crafted silver, a luxury that sometimes embarrassed him. His ordination gift from Jonas. *Glory be to the Father, and to the Son, and to the Holy Spirit. . . .*

But it had been longer than a minute since the last breath, almost two minutes. The nurse was standing beside the bed, a hand on Jonas' wrist. Karl rose wearily himself, unable to believe that it could be over. The nurse picked up the receiver of the telephone. Karl hesitated a few moments longer, his eyes on the motionless chest. Then he sighed and kneeled.

Lord, accept the soul of Thy repentant servant Jonas. . . .

Jonas had performed his Act of Perfect Contrition several days ago, and he had received Extreme Unction, the Last Rites of the Church. Now there would be a wake for the few who cared to come, and a Mass for the Dead. In two days, three at the most, Father Karl could return to his parish duties in England.

The young resident doctor, a woman, was at bedside in under three minutes. She pronounced Jonas dead. Karl packed the reliquary and the eighteenth-century statue of St. Florian, patron saint of a once-formidable family now all but extinct, and went out into the hall.

Cosima was there, wiping tears from her cheeks. She had been waiting since two o'clock in the visitors' lounge opposite the nurses' station. She looked admirably fresh and resiliant despite the tears, sustained, no doubt, by her dancer's vitality.

"I know he didn't want anyone to see him, but . . ."

Karl nodded. "He was your father. Go in."

He waited for Cosima in the lounge. One of the floor nurses gave him a cup of coffee. When Cosima rejoined him she was more pale than before, but dry-eyed. She bummed a cigarette from Karl. They walked to the elevators.

"You must be starved," she said.

"I'm all right." His voice was hoarse from the hours of reading aloud. "A little sleepy."

"A drink, then."

"That would be welcome."

"Would you like to spend the night? Jessica's gone home for a brief visit. There's plenty of room."

"No, thank you, Cosima. I'm comfortable at the rectory. Tomorrow is a Holy Day of Obligation; I'm celebrating the six-thirty mass for Father Pannell."

She toyed with the big square horn buttons on her lambskin greatcoat.

"I should call Charles and John. No, it can wait until tomorrow. So now the fighting starts in earnest. All the hate comes out."

"But you won't be a part of it."

"I do not care about *one cent* of my father's money! I have a good life. Pardon me for even mentioning our . . . sibling inadequacies. I know this has been a terrible experience for you, Uncle Karl. Now there's no one left."

He smiled tiredly. Jonas had been a stranger to him for more than twenty years. He thought of the Jonas Krásno who had died, a rich suspicious alienated man, despised by his associates and all but one of his children. And how had Jonas come to that? How had he changed so? Of course he had been embittered by the war; gradually his hatred of the Germans was transmuted into a scathing intolerance for all the failings humanity is prey to. He had lived this long, perhaps, by becoming a driven man, interested only in the accumulation of riches and power. A tragically familiar story. Father Karl preferred to remember the boy who had fearlessly hurled lye in the face of the Gestapo chief, survived a bullet in the back, lugged two helpless children across a wilderness of snow. . . .

When he and Cosima left the elevator on the first floor of Herlands East he was thinking of the occupation of Drbal, of the men in black leather trench coats who came first in their powerful cars and killed his father. Cosima was preoccupied with her own memories. Neither of them were immediately aware of the two men who walked through the sliding glass doors at the entrance.

"Hold it right there!"

Father Karl looked up in surprise and saw guns aimed at them. The dark gray trench coats these men wore caused a single thought to flash through his mind: *Gestapo.*

Classical conditioning theory argues that all behavior is a response to, and dominated by, stimuli occurring in the external environment. If he had not been so profoundly tired, if his long vigil had not prompted total recall of the sacking of Drbal that began with machine-gunnings in the square and ended, hours later, in a ghastly firestorm, Father Karl might have stood flat-footed and unresisting. But the impressive stimulus of the thought-form *Gestapo* had the double effect of disassociating him from the here and now; at the same time it shut down the reticular activating system of the brain with almost surgical precision, thus making imperative the primitive and most natural response to the danger that threatened him. The Gestapo had found them at last, and the hero-brother lay dead.

Father Karl bolted, pulling the startled Cosima along by the hand.

"Run! Run! Run!"

So bright everywhere; he had to go up to his room now and quickly pull the shades over the glaring noon windows so that they, so *nothing* could look in. He would be safe on the floor in the airless hot corner by the shelves where he kept his sailing-ship models. Yolande would not make a sound, they would hold each other tightly while the stalking boots went back and forth and then faded away down the crickety stairs. The boots could not come in—ever—because the Archangel Michael had once paid him a sickbed visit and smiled his blessing. Therefore his room was a consecrated place and protected from evil by the powers of a guardian angel, if he could—

—only

Father Karl had the stairwell door half open when two more of them came around a corner at him. One of the MORG agents kicked the door out of the priest's hand and when he reached inside his coat for his rosary another agent shot him twice in the stomach from six feet away with a revolver loaded with wadcutters. The flattened slugs dealt him heavy mortal blows; Karl sat down stunned by their force, robbed of breath.

Cosima fell screaming across him but he wasn't aware of her weight, suddenly he had almost no sensation from the chest down. They pulled Cosima off him almost immediately, but her sheepskin coat was stained like a slaughterhouse pelt. Karl felt very sorry for her: she was always so clean and tidy and delightful in her movements and now she was forced to struggle like a wild thing, haywire and screaming, to get back to him. *Oh my child, don't worry about me.* He had lost aural perspective; voices had a way-out, end-of-the-tunnel ring. Men, more men everywhere. Men going through Cosima's tote, men with walkie-talkies. *Got him!* Me? Karl thought. Preposterous. I am simply not worth all this fuss. Men in white smocks broke through the ranks and kneeled beside him; they opened his coat and the rosary fell out. Others were bearing Cosima away; her eyes rolled toward him a final time and cords stood out in her neck.

Karl opened his mouth to speak to her, but he couldn't speak and his jaw sagged. He regretted that he would not, after all, be able to see her dance in London in the spring. One of the interns put the precious rosary in his fist and held it up so he could see and Father Karl was grateful, he died with his gratitude frozen eternally in his eyes.

In the grounded elevator in the basement of Herlands North, Peter took off the priest's collar and the black suit, bundled the clothing and put the bundle on the roof. He slid the elevator hatch cover closed and got down from the sawhorse. He was now wearing a white short-sleeved cotton shirt and wrinkled white trousers and white shoes. From his valuable black bag he took a different pair of glasses, mod half lenses that perched half way down his nose. He rumpled his hair and filled his shirt pocket with ballpoint pens and a pocket flashlight. He hung a stethoscope around his neck. It looked a little wrong, carrying the bag around, but it was Peter's security blanket. It held his .38 Baretta automatic and two additional full magazines.

He by-passed the elevator core common to the three wings of Herlands Pavilion and proceded to the basement of Herlands South, which contained the giant laundry for the complex. As he'd expected, the laundry was deserted. He found a selection of hand-pressed smocks that were segregated, for the power elite of the hospital, on one rack. He chose a smock ticketed for a Dr. Chen.

It had been a while since he'd heard voices but he heard several now, following the dungeon-like slam of a metal door. MORG or Hospital Security, he didn't know which. Peter picked up his bag and walked unhurriedly into the locker room provided for the laundresses and then into the adjacent shower room where four nozzles dripped slowly. By using the shower knobs for footholds he climbed to the oblong clamshell windows near the ceiling and opened one, propping it open with a steel rod. He wriggled through and dropped, damp and grimy, into a short humid passageway with locked black doors at either end and another door midway which was marked DANGER/HIGH TEMPERATURES. He noted the door with the green chalk mark in the upper right hand corner, went to his bag for tools and picked the lock.

On the other side of the door he found himself in the old hospital, specifically an area that included the morgue, the crematorium and an autopsy room. The paint job here was Barbizon green, dusky as a landscape by Corot. The brass gates of the dim elevator devoted to transport of the dead were standing open: there was an occupied gurney inside. Peter rolled the shrouded corpse out into the hall and took the elevator to the third floor. There he got off and crossed the hall to a lab.

Inside a round young black man with a bottle of beer in one hand was tapping out a query on a computer terminal. A centrifuge was on. The pathologist glanced at Peter but didn't speak.

Peter nodded and smiled and walked up beside him. He put

the bag on a counter top, took out the Baretta automatic and placed the muzzle against the black man's head. The pathologist put down his beer and tried to come to attention, but his belly was wedged tight against the computer console. He grew more and more tense but he didn't say a word.

"Don't you talk?" Peter asked him.

"Talk about what, dude? You here to steal, just help yourself."

"Turn the centrifuge off."

"Spoils the batch, you know? I can hear okay."

"I might miss something that's happening out in the hall."

The pathologist gave him a sideways speculative look, then reached out and turned the machine off.

"How does it go from here on?"

"We walk out of here and down the stairs to the Emergency Ward and walk through to the ambulance bay. You talk. Talk about anything you please. Tell me all about your fascinating life. But if you stop talking for even one second you'll lose my interest, and if I lose interest in you, Dr.—"

"Paradies. Sydney Paradies."

"I will fucking do you the honors, my man. There are no alternatives. Don't try to find one."

"What you want is out, right?"

"You said it, Dr. Paradise. So let's go see what Emergency looks like tonight."

Chief of Security at Washington Heights Hospital was a former 5th Division precinct captain named Adam Hazell, who lived with his wife and two of his four children in a five-room apartment in the Inwood section of Manhattan. The Hazells were having a rollicking evening with a few old friends, everybody getting slowly lit but not too rowdy, when the call came through at four minutes past eleven. It was his senior man on the four to midnight shift, Tony Megna. Tony spoke to him over the phone as if somebody was standing right beside him telling him every word to say. There was a lot of trouble, lobby floor of Herlands West, but Megna wouldn't spell it out, he just kept repeating in a strained voice that Hazell should get down there right away.

Adam Hazell drove down Broadway from Dyckman Street, his head throbbing in the cold polluted air. He found the Fort Washington entrance to Herlands West blockaded by three of the type of sedan known as SGI, for Standard Government Issue, and a lot of men in identical dark gray trench coats. They had parked their sedans on the plaza directly in front of the low steps.

All the city cops were out in the slushy street. Three blue-and-white radio cars and a 34 Sergeant's car, all flashers off. The cops were just standing around breathing clouds and looking at the stalwart men in gray.

On the inside the hospital lobby was teeming; Hazell saw at least six more of the gray coats and a couple of his own uniformed men. Hazell approached the sergeant, the only superior on the scene, who was leaning against the side of his car with his arms folded.

"Adam."

"Cass. What the hell?"

"I don't know, Adam. A shooting. They won't let us in."

"*Who* won't let you in?"

"Those guys. Feds of some kind."

"Are they narks?"

"Hell, I don't know, but there's dozens of them, it's like they've took over the goddamn hospital."

"If there's been a shooting, it's city property and you have—"

"Adam, I tried. They read me some kind of directive, for Christ's sake."

"What?"

Sgt. Casden looked at the patrolman next to him, who flipped open his notebook and recited in a gritty voice, "National Security Decision Memorandum number M18, gives them precedence over all local, state *and* federal authorities in matters judged to be vital to the security of the United States."

"Matters? Judged? By who?"

One of the men in gray approached them. "Mr. Hazell?"

"Yeh."

"Would you come with me, please?"

"Just a minute," Hazell said rudely, and he turned to Sgt.

Casden. "It was me, Joe, I'd start rousting brass. Buck this thing up through Division, and right now."

"On New Year's Eve?"

Hazell said grimly, "It's called covering your ass, Sergeant." He went along with the man in gray, who was not talkative.

It was obvious where someone had had his guts shot out, hard by the stairwell door. Across the hall in an improvised trauma room they'd brought in a shock cart and a team of doctors and nurses were working in a controlled frenzy over the gunshot victim. They had stripped him to his underwear. His black suit had been ripped or cut from his body, there were pieces of it all over the floor. Hazell, as he went past the room, took in the discarded clerical collar and the rosary dangling from a clenched fist.

Mother of God, he thought, horrified. They've shot a priest!

The Feds had set up their command center in a first-floor conference room. Two of them were looking through the priest's wallet and his passport. The head man, some breed of scalp-lifter, was using a radio/telephone contained in an attaché case. Another agent yelled into a walkie-talkie, getting nothing back but a weak burst of static. The entire hospital was a dead area for most police frequencies, but Hazell didn't say a word, he wasn't doing these people any favors.

"Okay," the Indian said calmly. "It appears we made a mistake." He hung up. "You Hazell?"

"Yeah."

"I'm Darkfeather."

He offered an ID folder with his picture on an embossed plastic card. All five prints from the right hand, not just a thumbprint. Some kind of magnetic code below the latents and the signature tape. On the reverse side was a curt directive from the Chief Executive, his seal and signature.

"What is all this, Darkfeather? The cops outside——"

"Will stay outside. Can't have NYPD complicatin' our procedures."

As an ex-cop Hazell was familiar with most of the clandestine intelligence organizations in the U.S., such as USAINTC and the DCDPO, which were aggressively accumulating dossiers on citizens who remained blissfully unaware that such agencies existed. But MORG was a new one; MORG had Hazell puzzled as well as a little frightened.

"What're you, some cowshit branch of the Treasury? I never heard of this agency!"

"We don't put a whole lot of coin into public relations, Hazell."

Hazell handed the weighty folder back and said in exasperation, "Okay, Chief, so do I get told what you're doing here?"

"We're lookin' for a very dangerous man. He slipped into the hospital tonight, dressed as a priest. He looked a hell of a lot like that bona fide priest, Father Krásno, out there. A very natural, human mistake was made. But our man is still kickin' around in here. He can't get out. Nobody gets out unless I say. We'll track over every inch of the hospital and flush him. I want you standin' by in case we need instant verification of personnel or a fix on layout. That's it."

"That's it? You shot the wrong man? You shot a priest dead in the lobby of this hospital, and that's all you have to say? Don't you know how this looks?"

Darkfeather just stared at him. Maybe he wowed the women with his hawklike eye and tooth enamel, but Hazell wasn't impressed.

"We have a whole bunch of people who are *only* concerned with how things look. Now they go to work. I expect those cops on the street will be hearin' from their borough commander just anytime now."

An agent, who sounded as if he'd run several blocks, came into the conference room.

"Sir. I think we. Spotted. Sandza. Emergency, Old Heights. Broadway and. Hundred sixty-fifth. Lousy radio, so I——"

"Positive ID this time?" Darkfeather asked, not turning a hair.

"Lou deMasio. Says it's been four years, but. Sandza's not somebody you. Forget, once you've known the. Fucker."

"He is *so* right," Darkfeather said. "Let's show a little hustle, now."

Adam Hazell suddenly found himself standing in an empty room. He blinked and trailed the MORG agents out into the hall. The lack of activity around the priest caught his eye. A solemn straight line divided the oscilloscope; a black nurse moodily crossed herself and turned away from the table.

Car doors popped outside, and the first of three chase cars, all of which were equipped with 307 four-barrels, fired off the plaza, hit the street with a crunching thud—it was packed with men—then swerved, bit down with screechings of fast rubber, went flat-out and dirty for all the money.

Poor bastard, Hazell thought. *Whoever you are, you don't deserve this.*

Sydney Paradies was saying, "So I gave some thought to OB-GYN. The hours, they're not so bad with a group. Sharing the labor, so to speak. The methods are a disgrace, like they did it better in the Dark Ages, you know, but the babies never stop coming. I always thought it was for the bread. Med school, the *fan*-tastic drudgery, my wife comes home from her day at Gimbels, can't stop crying, feet so sore she can't stand up. I knew I wasn't going to be one of your great surgeons, the heart guy all the rich bastards had to have first, but hell. *Path?* You know what Path is? It's four rooms in Park West Village, and a couple of weeks in the Adirondacks every year. The only trouble is, I love it too much. I love secrets. I dig looking deep at the neat little cells and the ones that aren't so neat any more, the strange exploding ones the body doesn't know about yet. Is it the cops, man? Don't see any cops on the floor. They waiting for you outside?"

"Maybe," Peter said, nodding as if he were hearing an impressive diagnosis.

He was walking alongside the black man, one hand on the Baretta in the pocket of his smock. They moved without haste down the long wide hall of the Emergency Department.

It was like any night in Emergency when the people out there are generally at loose ends, spoiling for a good time and not careful enough with their valuable bodies. Broken bones, smashed heads, heart muscle with the big wasted patch the size of a silver dollar, delirious drunks, the leftovers from a husband-and-wife home massacre. A blanket-shrouded propane burn case was rushed in through the portals, bottle of fluid swinging above her blackened head. A feverish child sat weeping on the side of a gurney. In Treatment 2 the team had a convulsing patient on their hands; his projected vomit had splattered the ceiling and was dripping down all over them. Fogies, crummies and weirdos with vague complaints peopled the hall.

Peter looked at every face. He hadn't seen anyone yet who excited his curiosity. The only law visible was a tall cop who stood chatting with a nurse at the admitting desk, which was located opposite the entrance doors.

"Dr. Paradise?"

"They always called us that, instead of Par-a-dees, makes my mama so mad."

"We'll go outside and have a smoke. Keep talking to me."

"There's a cop," Dr. Paradies said, dragging his feet.

"Don't worry about him."

"See anybody else?"

The doctor was quickly developing a fugitive mentality. Peter didn't respond; he had now noticed a couple of things that dampened his expectations of a clean escape.

Someone had carelessly left a dark gray trench coat across a chair in a treatment room. So that meant at least one MORG operative was sitting around or prowling the hall in his shirt-sleeves. He could have been the man with the gauze eyepatch and the sorrowful expression, or the man with the bandaged arm stretched out on three folding chairs.

Peter looked at a door marked *private*. It stood open an inch or two. The room beyond was dark. From inside one man could monitor half the emergency ward. Behind the Admitting desk there were two doors with cloudy glass panels in them: one-way glass, for general security purposes?

If so, at this moment he and Dr. Paradies might be under observation by a roomful of MORG.

Peter doubted that anyone could make him all that quickly, but he kept his head down, chuckling at something the doctor said. He wasn't feeling funny. The itch in his blood told him he had to choose a quick and unexpected Out, and he needed to act immediately.

The tall cop left the Admitting desk and sauntered in front of Peter and Paradies on his way outside. Peter glanced at the radio car, which was backed into an ambulance bay, rightside door open. The patrolman behind the wheel was drinking coffee. Apparently they'd dropped someone off for treatment.

Peter followed the doctor outside. Not enough open space;

hospital on two sides, a concrete wall across the drive. Steps to a parking lot, chain-link fence all around, high sodium vapor lamps. Twelve or fifteen cars were parked behind the fence overlooking the emergency entrance. So the only fast and sure way was down the drive. Paradies dropped his cigarette pack and had to go down on one knee to gather up loose filtertips. Peter leaned against the brick hospital wall and checked behind him through the double glass doors. The man with the eyepatch was walking slowly toward him. He walked like a man trying to decide if he should cut loose and be the hero of the piece. Peter winced.

"What do we do now?" Paradies said, shivering and cupping his hands around a match. The cigarette twitched between his lips.

"Enjoy your smoke," Peter told him; "I've decided to give myself up."

Paradies looked up in shock as Peter walked across the short stretch of tarmac to the police car. He got there just as the tall patrolman was getting in beside his partner. Peter slid in next to the cop, drawing his gun as he did so, closing the door behind him. He pushed the muzzle of the Baretta deep into the armpit of the cop he was crowding and said,

"You're under arrest."

"Whaaat?" the tall cop said. He had started to resist, but then he got a crick in his neck trying to look at the gun.

"You're under arrest—for impersonating police officers. I'm taking you in. *Move* this thing."

The cop behind the wheel said, "Hey, look, buddy, just what the hell do you think you're——"

"Marty, Marty, he's got a piece! It's sticking in my armpit, Marty!"

Marty raised his hands a few inches off the wheel in a gesture of exasperation. He looked sidelong at Peter, who regarded him calmly over the straight edge of the glasses.

"Okay, okay, what do you want me to do?"

"Take Broadway. Uptown."

"What for?"

Peter dug the Baretta viciously into the armpit of the cop next to him; the cop sucked air through his teeth and said, "Just *roll it*, we'll talk while we're driving."

Marty put the car in gear and went bumping down the drive to Broadway. There was a blinking yellow caution light on the side of the hospital building, but not much traffic; Marty made a swooping turn into Mitchell Square. Peter saw, with a quick motion of his head, two MORG sedans whipping around in the parking lot, just as a couple of chase cars came down Ft. Washington and made smoking sliding turns into One Hundred Sixty-Fifth Street. Peter also had a glimpse of MORG agents equipped with walkie-talkies running from the Emergency Department, and one of them was Eyepatch. They'd made him, all right. But something, probably faulty communications, had prevented them from closing the ring in time.

"Any particular place you want to go?" Marty said in a surly tone of voice.

"The GW," Peter said.

"The GW? You want to go to fucking *Jersey?*"

"That's right."

"A little out of our sector," said the cop whom Peter was holding hostage.

"Just take me for a nice long ride. Right now you're the only two people in the world I feel safe with. I want to enjoy your company."

The two cops exchanged looks. Marty did the humoring.

"Sure. Sure, why not? We'll like cruise around, and maybe after a while you want to talk. That's okay with us. So what's your name?"

"Peter."

"I'm Marty, Marty Coranallis, and that's Patrolman Dominick."

"Hi, Peter. Why don't you call me Dom?"

"Hi, Dom."

"Should I move over a little? The front seat's all busted down; too many lardasses in the Three-Four."

"I have enough room, Dom. How about this gun in your armpit, I'm not hurting you, am I?"

"Tell the truth, I'm just a little uncomfortable—you keep looking back. Something bothering you, Peter?"

"Yes, there is."

Marty said, "But you don't want to talk about it yet, that it, Peter?"

"Just keep making the lights, Marty," Peter told him.

The four MORG sedans stayed a block behind as the NYPD radio car drove up Broadway to One Hundred Seventy-Eighth Street. More cars were proceeding parallel and northbound on Riverside Drive, on Ft. Washington, Wadsworth and Amsterdam Avenues.

In Chase Two, Darkfeather's assistant, a man named Beau Cliff, said, "Why don't we take him off their hands?"

"Two reasons, Beau. There'll be a lot of gunplay if we chivvy in now. Those two cops are bound to get holed. The New York Police Commissioner is one of Childermass's pets. After the business on the Staten Island ferry two years ago, Childermass made the Commissioner a solemn promise. So we can't be held accountable for any more Inspector's Funerals. Peter probably knows that; that's why he grabbed those cops. No chance he'll get away from us. Let's ride easy for now, until we find out what it is Peter wants to do next."

"What do you suppose he's telling those cops?"

"Whatever it is," the Indian said, "they won't believe him."

Gillian, wearing the belted white Misty Harbor trench coat which had been one of her Christmas presents, sat in a chair by the windows in room 909 Herlands North, and chewed her fingernails to splintery ruin.

When she heard the tapping at the door she got up quickly, grabbed her overnight case and was half way across the room when the door opened and two men dressed in dark gray appeared in the slab of light from the hall.

One of them switched on his flashlight. Gillian gasped and turned her face aside.

"So this is where you've been hiding."

The other one, a hand pressed to the button in his right ear, said, "Recall signal. Full scramble. They've got him."

"What about——?"

"Full scramble!"

"Okay." The flashlight was switched off. Gillian didn't look up. She felt a hand on her shoulder and shied nervously.

"Little girl, you stay right here in this room. Understand? You'll be sent for."

When the door closed Gillian opened her eyes. She saw a roomful of sparklers. Her heartbeat was running away, yet her extremities felt bloodless and prickly-cold. After all those days in bed, just a few minutes on her feet made her feel sick and faint. Gillian yearned to fall across the bed and close her eyes. But she'd been discovered; naturally they blamed her for what had happened to Mrs. McCurdy. Something awful would happen to her if she didn't get out of the hospital. She couldn't afford to wait any longer for Mrs. Busk. So she picked up the case she had dropped, sighed deeply and walked a gently swaying tightrope to the door.

"**M**arty and me have been partners a long time," Dominick said. "Six years." They were driving across the Hudson River on the lower level of the George Washington Bridge, heading for the apartment towers on the heights of Ft. Lee, New Jersey.

"That is a long time," Peter said, seeming rigidly preoccupied.

"You're not a regular doctor of some kind, are you, Pete?"

"No, I stole this smock."

"In other words, you're in disguise?"

"Yes."

Dominick chuckled. "That's a pretty clever disguise."

"Thanks, Dom. It didn't work, though. They were waiting for me."

"Somebody's after you?" Dominick said sympathetically.

"I once worked for a government agency you never heard of. It's big, though, and very powerful. I turned my son over to them. I'd tell you why, but that's a pretty long story. Anyway, my son disappeared. They told me he died, but that's a lie. They needed him, so they just took him. It's a frightening power these people have. They can make a man disappear any time they want. Did you know it's a statutory offense for a MORG employee, past or present, to reveal information about the agency?

He may not even confirm that MORG exists. Laws like that are passed because a man named Childermass understands the workings of government better than any man alive. Government must grow or wither away, so it loots the public treasury in order to grow. When there's money available—and power for the taking—there'll always be a Childermass to encourage good men to look the other way, and exploit their worst fears. Maybe it's possible to stop Childermass. Somebody's got to do it. But I'm only one man, Dom."

Officer Dominick looked cautiously at Peter. Were those tears in his eyes? God help us, Dominick thought, he's liable to go berserk right here in the car. Start blasting away at all his imaginary enemies.

"Yeh, well, that's *right,* and if you don't mind my making a suggestion—maybe we can help, Peter."

Marty Coranallis picked up his cue.

"You see, Peter, me and Dom have had a lot of experience dealing with—you know—the kind of people who get their kicks from bothering other people, harassing them——"

Dominick said, "My brother-in-law lives over here. In Teaneck. There's this place he took me to once, all-night diner on Route 93 in Leonia. What'ya say we stop and have a cup of coffee and——"

"Don't stop!" Peter yelled, scaring them. "Keep this car moving."

Dominick swallowed a little taste of vomit. "Okay, Peter— look, man, we're on your side, we're just trying to help."

"Marty?" Peter said.

"Yeh?"

"You know the riverfront below Ft. Lee?"

"Not too familiar with it, Peter."

"What I want you to do, Marty, is get off in Ft. Lee, and follow 505 along the water until you come to the old One Hundred Twenty-fifth Street-Inglenook ferry slip. There's a lot of construction going on where the rail yard used to be, quite a few sudden detours. What we have to do when we get to the torn-up area is lose the cars that have been following us."

"Following——?" Dominick said.

"Hold your head still, Dom, and keep your hands in you lap! Marty, there are four, maybe five—hell, I don't know the exact number any more—but they're all back there, and the two in the lead are the chase cars. A red Camaro and a silver-and-black Granada. They've got the works. Those two cars will easily hit one-forty on the flats."

Marty checked his side mirror and said in a low voice to his partner, "He's right about the Camaro and the—. I noticed them before, back at the toll."

"You'll have to lose those two cars if we're going to have a chance."

"They look like Feds to you?" Dominick muttered.

"Who knows?" Marty said. "Maybe something's going on here."

"Have you done any high-speed evasive driving?" Peter asked him.

"A little. My brother, on the state cops, they sent him out to the Coast to the Bondurant school. That's some course they teach out there. He showed me a few wrinkles. Cornering on all kinds of surfaces, skid turns, high-speed reverses——"

"When I give you the word I want you to drive for your life, Marty. Because if the people who are in those cars can make my son disappear—and me disappear—they can make *you* disappear too."

They were approaching the Ft. Lee off-ramp. The chase cars a hundred yards behind them tightened up a little.

"Peter," Dominick said, "I'm worried that gun's going to go off—you know, by accident, when we hit a few bumps."

"You do have something to worry about there," Peter agreed.

Gillian opened the door of room 909 and went out into the hall. A squat florid nurse with a wart like a second nose was standing by the water cooler near Gillian's door; obviously she was on guard duty.

"Hello, dear," the RN said. "Where are you off to?"

Gillian looked at her and didn't say anything for a few moments. She licked her flaky lips.

"Home," she whispered.

"Oh, but."

"I'm going home," Gillian repeated, not looking the nurse in the eye.

"You can't leave the hospital without being discharged by your physician, so I guess it *will* have to wait until morning. I understand you've been very sick. You don't feel at all well now, do you? Poor lamb. What a terrible upset evening we've had around here. Things are getting back to normal, though. My name is Evelyn. Why don't you go on back into the room now, it's all clean and made up and everything, and I'll bring you a pill to help you sleep, soon as your file comes up from eight."

"Please get out of my way," Gillian pleaded.

"Oh, come on, don't be cross with Evelyn. Things will look so much brighter in the——"

She started to take Gillian by the arm. There was a sudden disturbance, of cyclonic intensity, farther down the hall by the nurses' station.

A woman was shouting in a terrible hoarse voice, "Don't tell me! Don't think *I* don't know! There's a madman loose in this hospital, and I'm not staying one more minute!"

"Oh-oh," Evelyn said, and she scampered back to the station. Gillian followed.

One of the largest women she'd ever seen was having an argument with the other nurse on duty. The woman was about six feet four inches tall, and the etchings of her face put her age in the middle sixties. But she was wielding a four-footed aluminum cane with considerable force, slashing the air. She wore a ratty long coat trimmed in blue fur, and a campaign hat with plastic flowers pinned to it.

"Don't trifle with me, de Graff," she warned the nurse who was trying to placate her. "Or you'll be wearing a plate in your head tomorrow! I refuse to be murdered in this hospital."

Evelyn made it to the sanctuary of the station before she spoke up.

"Mrs. Toone, doctor put you in here for your BP. What do you think is happening to your BP right now? You should see yourself, Mrs. Toone, you're the color of raspberry sherbet."

Mrs. Toone pointed her cane at de Graff.

"Out of my way!"

"What's the point, Mrs. Toone? Honestly, there is *no* danger.

The FBI is here. I think it's the FBI. You'll just do yourself in if you keep acting like this."

Mrs. Toone pushed her aside, grounded the rubber-tipped cane and stalked off to the elevators.

"Could I come with you?" Gillian asked timidly. Her voice was slurred, difficult to understand.

Mrs. Toone stopped and peered down at her.

"What's that, girl?"

"I'm afraid . . . to stay here."

"Sure you are! Anybody with any sense would be. You just come right along with me." She stabbed the elevator call button with her stick.

"Mrs. Toone! That is a very sick girl! She may not leave——"

"Oh, shut up, Evelyn! Either of you tries to lay a hand on us——"

"I'm calling Security right now. Security will deal with this, Mrs. Toone."

The nurses' call board was lighting up. Evelyn couldn't get through to Security. The working elevator, which had been on the lobby floor, came promptly up to nine.

"I'm warning you, Mrs. Toone! You're making a very serious mistake, taking that girl with you."

"Goodbye, goodbye!" Mrs. Toone cried delightedly as the elevator doors closed.

Then she turned and looked more closely at her companion.

Gillian stood there unresponsively, a hand on the railing, her eyes wide open. She was in some sort of fugue state, Mrs. Toone decided. All the brutal excitement, the tales of violence and the fear . . . she felt rather fizzy and darkling herself. The old BP. Just be calm now. Mrs. Toone put her arms around Gillian. The child whimpered softly. Oh, so dear, Mrs. Toone thought, what a purrrrecious! The arteries in her neck felt like overblown balloons, and her head felt strange, an unpleasant burning sensation that was not a fever and not an ache. A burning she could taste and smell; it was like old truck tires. She tightened her arms around Gillian, oh, oh, getting so dark now.

Mrs. Toone was just a tiny bit afraid that she'd overdone it this time.

Benny Alonzo, the night watchman at Medina Brothers' site number four, Marina Vista, heard the throaty roar of the big mills coming down the slope of the palisades toward the fenced equipment yard. He heard them dodging through the wilderness of forms that had been constructed and now awaited the continuous pour that would complete the foundations for the condominium complex. Two, three, four different engine sounds—winking red lights were reflected against the dirty windows of the trailer.

Benny gulped the last of his roast beef sandwich and made it to the door as the lead car hit the temporary bridge outside, whumping and rattling across steel plates that spanned a newly dug channel.

It was a New York City patrol car. A red Camaro appeared behind it, maybe fifty yards away. After the Camaro came a whole weaving procession of cars. Foglights. Sirens. Red flashers hidden behind grills.

Two of the cars, arriving by different routes, got tangled up at the unmarked bridge approach. One of them wheeled sideways into a pile of canvas-covered reinforcing rods, many of which pierced the car and its occupants. The other car bounced high over the wooden curbing of the temporary bridge and dived down into the murky channel. A reinforcing rod, hurled a hundred feet through the air, whanged the side of the trailer a foot from where Benny stood gawking in the doorway.

And still the cars kept coming, pouring it on, tip-tilting, yawing and bouncing, slewing into cars already disabled. Benny had never seen a spectacle to equal it.

Then, as suddenly as they'd appeared, most of the cars were gone, trailing off in the dark downriver, leaving a few wrecks behind to litter his dooryard. Back in the kennels the construction company's attack dogs were going nuts. A blown engine was vividly on fire. Injured men crawled along the rutted ground and collapsed; victims cried out from the depths of the steel-sided channel.

Benny grabbed a big fire extinguisher and went out to give some assistance.

South along the river, in the direction the cop car and the

Camaro had gone, there was a deadly crash, accompanied by an explosion and a fireball. Benny turned and stared at it. The chase had ended.

"**N**o way I can shake them," Marty announced, calmly enough considering what was howling along behind them. "This old crock is about to come apart. The wheel, no goddam response any more!"

They were on a short stretch of pavement puzzle-cut by a length of rusted railroad track. Each ponderous jolt sent death rattles through the frame of the car. The brake linings were almost worn out, and the drums had begun to smoke.

"Marty, see that beacon ahead?"

"Up the hill, you mean?"

"It's not on the hill, it's on the roof of a soap factory that's coming down. A railroad spur line runs straight through the middle of the factory. Okay, we'll follow the rails inside. Stay as far to the left as you can once we're in the factory. Watch out for the support pillars, any one of them is big enough to pulverize us."

The red Camaro had gained on them. Half of the back window of the police car blew out in a twinkling frost, showering them with glass and a few spent shotgun pellets.

"Shit!" Dominick yelled.

"Ignore that," Peter said. "They won't shoot to kill. We should be picking up the spur line along about here—okay, there it is. Follow it, Marty."

There was a junkety knocking under the hood.

"Pistons!" Marty groaned. "We won't get another mile out of this——"

"All we need now is a couple hundred yards. Floor it, Marty! Here comes the factory."

Directly in front of them a few yellow warning lights blinked in front of the factory shell. Marty steered frantically for the high black oblong into which the rails disappeared.

"Left, left!" Peter screamed.

One of their headlights was out due to the violent uses to

which the car had been put; they had only a glimpse of the huge piece of demolition machinery that had been parked inside the ruined factory, the fat ton of rusted teardrop that seemed suspended in dusty space directly in front of them.

Marty hauled the wheel over. They were close enough flashing by the wrecker's ball to see patches of mortar and brick dust clinging to its pitted surface. Then Marty had his hands full avoiding the pillars and loading dock remnants that cluttered the factory floor.

The wheelman of the Camaro that entered the shed at sixty miles an hour instinctively steered to follow their taillights, but his reaction time was half a second too slow. The impact drove the enormous wrecker's ball back about eight feet; it quivered on its cable and swung forward once again, just as the second chase car ran inside the shed and vaulted over the top of the squashed-down Camaro, meeting the doomsday ball head on. Simultaneously the gas tank of the Camaro blew up like a land mine and scattered the wreckage of the silver-and-black Grenada throughout the factory. Cables parted at the second impact and the iron teardrop thumped down on what was left of the Camaro and the clumps of burning men inside.

"Jesus God Almighty!" Dominick said as the police car emerged on the far side of the structure. "You set it up! You really had the whole thing worked out, didn't you?"

"I had it worked out," Peter said. "Don't slow down, Marty. We've got a couple of jumps on them now, but they never stop coming at you. Understand that. They *never* stop. So keep driving."

Gillian had forgotten what it was like to be so cold.

After leaving the hospital she trudged down Broadway against the wind, shuddering deeply, her head bent. Despite the coat and a wool dress she felt unfleshed; her unprotected bones were knocking together. It seemed to Gillian that she had walked a very long way, but when she stopped to get her breath and turned there was the hospital looming up behind her. So she had to be walking in place, it was like one of those dreams. Big slow stepping-stone steps while the sidewalk changed, by dream-magic, into a corridor; soon she would be back inside, but tiny as a bug this time in those hostile, brightly shining spaces.

Two Puerto Rican boys walked slowly by, stopped a few feet away, stared at her. Gillian paid no attention. She was trying to breathe, trying not to be a bug-thing no matter how much she deserved to be. The boys argued about her but the older one shook his head finally; they walked on.

Gillian thought she might make better progress getting out of her dream-entrapment if she took her boots off. Barefoot she'd always been the fastest girl at camp.

She sat on the curb and managed to wrench one boot off, but she hadn't the strength to tackle the other.

The gutter was rancid. She sat there panting. Someone yelled obscenely at her from a passing car; a thrown bottle splattered glass not far away.

Gillian didn't look up. She was trying to remember what she was doing out there, alone, late at night, on the street. Running away, yes. But *why* was she running away? Did it have something to do with the tall stricken woman who had fallen down in the elevator? It had taken Gillian a very long time to pry herself loose from the woman's steely embrace.

Her eyes funny, bulging out of her head like that. Bloody nose. What was wrong with her anyway?

What's wrong with me? Gillian thought. Get up from here. Coat all filthy. But——

A car stopped. Headlights as startling as flashguns. Gillian looked up warily.

Someone familiar.

"Oh my God, my God—Gillian?"

"Mrs.—Busk?"

"Yes, yes, oh God how you're shaking!"

"I am?" Of course she was. It had gone on for so long now it seemed a natural sort of thing. To tremble and not be aware of trembling. "I got out. Couldn't wait in the hospital. Stinks there."

"Let me help you up, darling. The car's right here. I drove by once, saw you, couldn't believe my—something made me come back and—what's this?"

"W-what's what, Mrs. Busk?"

"All down the back of your nice coat. Like blood—"

"*Take it off!*" Gillian screamed. She was already plucking at the toggles, hands frantic but ineffective. "Off, offf, offffff!"

Mrs. Busk helped her. Gillian snatched the coat from her and pitched it in the gutter.

Then she collapsed in the leather hollow of the right-hand seat in her mother's costly Porsche, her ears ringing from stress. Mrs. Busk made a sweeping U-turn and made most of the lights going down Broadway.

After a couple of miles Gillian stopped gasping. Mrs. Busk looked tearfully at her.

"Oh, Gillian, what's happened to you?"

"Music," Gillian demanded.

Mrs. Busk dialed around the FM band. She found Brahms: Third movement, Second Symphony in D Major.

The speakers in the car were exceptionally fine. Little by little the gentleness of the *Allegretto grazioso* had an effect on Gillian. She sat up straighter, immersed, distracted.

Mrs. Busk drove like an angel, floating the blue car through the city streets. The city going by was like a waxworks to Gillian. It was a remembered city, and not too well remembered at that. Where had she been, and why could she not get back? Never mind, the music was like food for her, nothing need exist for now beyond the sphere of the delicate, entrancing melody.

The police car stopped on the old railroad pier that jutted 90 feet into the Hudson. The remaining headlight was too weak to illuminate the end of the pier. The river going by out there had a high spoiled sheen. Across the river Manhattan dwelled fabulously, but its lights and spires had melted together in a cold haze, as if the city had been conjured by a sorcerer with a faulty technique. The right front tire of the car was slowly hissing down as the engine idled.

The three men sat silently looking at the river, too whipped after the chase to speak. The car reeked of excretions, of the bitter salts and oils of their bodies.

Peter banged open the sticking door and got out, still holding his gun on them. Tears ran freely down his cheeks. There was a biting west wind, an almost invisible presence of snow in the air.

"What are you going to do now, Peter?" Dom asked.

"Both of you come out here. This door. Keep your hands where I can see them."

The police officers slid across the seat and climbed wearily from the car. They stood side by side. Marty rubbed his trembling hands together. He looked like he might fall down any second. The river slapped and sucked at the big pilings.

"Get rid of your revolvers," Peter told them. "In the water."

They unholstered their service revolvers and threw them away. Two splashes.

"That's one eighty-seven fifty twice," Dominick said sullenly. "And you know we have to pay for those .38's ourselves, Peter."

"Try not to make me feel like a prick, Dom. Both of you back off now."

"Peter, look, man, how long can you keep it up? There's gotta be someone who can help you."

"BACK OFF!"

For a nasty moment Dom was certain Peter meant to shoot them. He tugged at Marty's sleeve and the two policemen began to walk, moving sideways, watching for missing or badly rotted planks.

"Peter, you may think there's no milk of human kindness left, right now I bet it seems to you like the whole world has dried up at the tit. But take it from someone who's been through a hell of a lot with you, who's come to know you as a friend: we're all human, we've got our limits, and it looks to me like you've reached yours. I honestly don't think you understand what you're doing any more."

Peter waited until they had moved twenty feet from the car. Then he went around to the driver's side and got in, put the car in gear.

Dominick ran toward the car, heedless of the rough footing.

"Hey, Peter, now wait!"

The window was rolled down half way. Peter looked back, mania in his eyes, a fatuous smile of satisfaction on his face.

"They'll have to follow me to the bottom of the river this time!"

With the damaged engine revving to the limit Peter took his foot off the brake. The police car leapt, fishtailed clankingly, released a monster burst of oily smoke and plunged off the end of the pier. Dominick ran, stumbled, went down on his hands and knees, rolled over with his palms full of splinters, trudged the rest of the way. He barely had a glimpse of the streaky dim headlight in the murky water before the electrical system of the car shorted out. The river belched a couple of times, and the last breathy bubble smelled indescribably of the deep-down bed, of the waste and corruption to which Peter had consigned himself.

Dominick walked back to his partner, shuddering, thinking of how cold the river could be in mid-winter. Even the men in the sealed wet suits who specialized in retrieving bodies couldn't take it for longer than a half hour at a time.

Marty was standing on the pier, head on his folded arms.

"He did it," Dom said. "He drove right in the fucking river! First I thought he was crazy. Then I decided he wasn't so crazy after all when those Feds started chasing us. Now I don't know what to think."

"Just leave me the hell alone," Marty murmured.

"I'll see if I can find a phone," Dom said.

Katharine Bellaver was driven home by a friend at one in the morning.

"Good to have our girl home again," said Patrick, the guard on the gate at Sutton Mews. "And a happy New Year to you, Mrs. Bellaver."

There was yellow fog along the river. Somewhere a bugle was blown flatly in a parody of celebration. Mrs. Busk met her at the door. Katharine requested strong coffee. She drank it while Mrs. Busk told her all she knew.

Katharine asked only one question. "Do you know for sure there was blood on her coat?"

Mrs. Busk could not be certain.

"Find out where Wally is," Katharine said grimly, referring to Wallace Mockreed, the family lawyer. "Tell him I want him here, I don't care if it's four in the morning."

Katharine was wearing a heavy floor-length Halston gown she couldn't walk in very well; she'd already ripped the hem walking up the front steps. She had Mrs. Busk unzip the gown for her and she went upstairs to Gillian's room wearing a pair of sheer briefs and nothing else.

Gillian's room was dark and almost cold and Katharine's teeth began to chatter. She had a nervous headache. Music was playing almost inaudibly. Chopin? Katharine saw Gillian motionless on the bed and thought she was asleep. She looked through one of Gillian's closets for a robe to put on. Then she started to examine the clothing Gillian had worn home from the hospital to see if there were stains on the underpants.

Gillian sat up stiffly on the bed, leaning on one elbow.

"Hello, Mother."

"Hello, Gil. How do you feel?"

"I don't know—just glad to be home." Her voice was indistinct; she could barely pronounce words. Her head lolled. If Katharine hadn't been well versed on her daughter's attitude toward drugs, she would have guessed that Gillian was spaced out. Katharine sat down with her. Probably her imagination, but Gillian seemed to draw cautiously away.

Katharine put a hand to Gillian's forehead, but Gillian wouldn't be touched.

"Don't."

"Okay."

"Are you mad at me because I came home?"

"Of course not. We just want to be very careful you don't get sick all over again. This is the sunniest room in the house, but it's the coldest at night. I think you ought to have a blanket over you."

Gillian, who was wearing pajamas, allowed herself to be covered. Obviously she was dead tired, but jumpy and restless.

"Tell me about the party," she said. Katharine had a few anecdotes on the tip of her tongue. Gillian snuggled down and closed her eyes for a few moments, but then she looked up an' around apprehensively. Katharine tried to hold her hand. (lian ripped the hand away with surprising force. ·

"I said don't!" She was throbbing with *angst*.

"Gillian, why not?"

"You might——"

She couldn't force herself to complete the thought. Her eyes roved.

"Is he still here?"

"Who? There's no one in the room but us, don't be silly."

"Who's being silly?" Gillian cried, indignant and hurt. "What do you *mean?* I hear his voice."

Gillian's eyes filled with tears. Her head went round and round. Katharine swallowed hard, feeling helpless and afraid, but she couldn't be specific about her fears.

"Are you sure you're not mad at me?" Gillian said at last, in a distinctly childish voice.

"Gillian, stop! You're not six years old any more. We have a, I hope we have, a more mature relationship than that."

"Yes. We do. I really love you, mother, but you're always putting me down. Why do you do that, it's so hateful, I don't want to hurt *you.*"

Katharine grimaced. "It's that other way consenting adults pass the time. I never stop to think—. I'm sorry. Gillian, I want you to tell me something. Did someone come into your room at the hospital? A man who—shouldn't have been there? And did he——"

"No. No."

"You don't want to remember."

"I don't remember! Nothing happened at the hospital. I was —tired of being by myself, I wanted to come home. That's all, do we have to make such a big thing of it?"

Gillian got out of bed and went into her bathroom. Katharine heard her pissing. When she came out she ignored her mother. She went instead to the marionette theatre, a nineteenth-century French antique that was wider than a door and stood about six feet high. Puppets lay in a leggy clutter on the stage. Gillian picked up Mr. Noodle, humming a little tune to herself.

"It was so sweet," she said. "They played and danced and sang for me when I came home. Skipper sang all the songs we made up a long time ago."

"Who?" Katharine said, getting up.

"Skipper."

Gillian reached for another figure at the back of the stage. She turned around holding him fondly in her hands. Skipper was about a foot and a half long, human in his proportions, cleverly articulated. His head was walnut, his body pine. Unlike the other puppets, some of which were turn-of-the-century antiques, Skipper had a freshly carved look. He wasn't wearing one of the traditional costumes. He had a freckled boyish face, and a thatch of red hair. The room wasn't well lighted, but Skipper's hair looked almost real to Katharine. She was stunned to see that the puppet had been provided with realistically carved balls and a man's cock that hung down between his shapely wooden thighs.

"Where did you—get that?"

"What do you mean? I've always had Skipper." Gillian pulled the string that caused his lower jaw to move up and down in a mime of speech. Then she pensively touched his long cock with a fingertip. "He never had one like this, though. It was tinier, you know, cute and crooked, and sometimes it stuck up, sort of like the end of my little finger."

She turned Skipper around and around. His eyes winked alternately shut. Gillian winked back. She kissed the brick-top crown of his head and put him back on stage with the others, drew the curtains closed.

Katharine made herself smile.

"Gillian, would you like to spend the rest of the night in my room?"

"Yes. Oh, I would like that, mother."

"Some warm milk might help you sleep."

"I'd love some warm milk."

Gillian also wanted the housecats for company, but sometimes they made themselves scarce for no good reason. So Gillian went to bed upstairs without them. Katharine sat up with her daughter. They played a game of stink-pink, just like old times. Katharine then entertained with gossip about some of the less obscene pecadilloes of those members of the cat-pack with whom they were both acquainted; occasionally she paused to wipe tears of fatigue from her eyes. At last Gillian fell into a heavy unmoving sleep.

Katharine helped herself to more milk, laced it with brandy, debated calling Avery at his hotel in Boston, decided it should wait until morning. She stood for a long time looking at the unconscious Gillian, who slept with one hand curled lightly between her breasts. Something was stuck in Katharine's craw, and the memory of it slowly twisted her mouth out of shape. She turned abruptly and almost ran downstairs and entered Gillian's room, her heart pounding. She went straight to the marionette theatre and pulled the curtains apart.

The Skipper puppet wasn't there. In its place was a badly mangled marmalade cat which had gone by the name of Sulky Sue.

Katharine felt the essence of her sanity shifting about in her head like heavy smoke, looking for a way to escape into the open air. She clamped a hand over her mouth. The threatened scream was bottled up in her throat.

Sulky Sue didn't look run-over, nor did the corpse smell of death. There wasn't any gore to be seen. Sulky Sue looked as if she had been taken apart by a devilishly inquisitive mind, then put back together, but badly, as if the mind couldn't quite remember what a cat was supposed to look like. Oh, yes, of course, it was similar to some of Gillian's youthful crayon drawings. Vivid coloring, but the tail depended from the body in an unlikely place. One ear was much larger than the other. The feet were crudely clubbed, not defined by toes. And the eyes. . . .

Katharine didn't look any closer. She went to the closet and stripped a cleaner's storage bag from one of Gillian's dresses and, using a big ruler instead of her hand, she bagged the strange, orange-and-persimmon cat-thing.

Now what? Gillian mustn't under any circumstances see it.

Mrs. Busk had retired for the night. Katharine carried her burden downstairs and rang for Patrick. When he came to the door she made up a story about having found the poor animal dead on the kitchen doorstep, obviously struck by a car, could he get rid of it *please*?

Patrick glanced inside at the tumbled mass of fur, shook his head sympathetically and was about to carry it away when Katharine said with a little laugh,

"Patrick, when you—when you've done that, I'd like the entire house searched."

Patrick may have connected the dead cat with her anxiety, but he asked no questions. When he returned he had another member of the private patrol force with him.

Katharine dreaded going into Gillian's room again; she couldn't have done it without knowing there were armed men just down the hall. She turned on all the lights and searched the bedroom herself. The Skipper puppet just wasn't there.

Either it had been taken, and the cat substituted, or——

But absolutely she had *not* imagined Skipper, she'd seen him lying limp and smug in Gillian's hands, and gross as a dildo. Of course that was the purpose it was intended for, but what was Gilly doing with it? Was Skipper some girlish-kinky thing the kids at Bordendale were passing around? Katharine had too high an opinion of Gillian's good taste and sensitivity to believe it. Nevertheless she'd cuddled the loathsome thing.

Well, *where was it?* She was on the verge of waking up Mrs. Busk, but wouldn't that be something: she'd look like a real idiot accusing the doughty old housekeeper of making off with a doll that had a penis-replica capable of——

Patrick and his partner came to the door and knocked. Patrick had an armful of squirming alley cat, a black and white neutered male with a regal Egyptian head. Mr. Rudolph.

"Found this little fellow hiding in the powder room downstairs."

Mr. Rudolph leaped down and ran. He wanted no part of Gillian's room tonight.

"Mrs. Bellaver, the house is secure. If you'd like I'll have Donny here stay a while."

"Oh, I don't think that's necessary, thank you, Patrick."

When they were gone, Katharine sat down on the bed and made an urgent reappraisal. One, the room had been almost dark. Two, her common sense had been overruled by the crushing fear that Gillian had been raped earlier that evening, and this fear resulted in a grotesque but appropriate hallucination. So blame it all on a temporarily dislocated psyche. Gillian had fawned over some other doll, one that reminded her of childhood's Skipper.

As for the cat—it had been injured, all right, perhaps much earlier in the day, and had gradually made its way upstairs to die in Gillian's room, in that snarly nest of puppets behind the curtains of the marionette theatre.

Katharine could devise no other explanations; and she badly needed something to get her through the remainder of the night.

The helicopter from Washington flew low up the Hudson River, slowly angling toward the Jersey shore where floodlights on the old railroad pier were concentrated on a salvage operation.

The pilot circled an area delineated by pink flares. The chopper, gravid with sitting men, eased into the blown-down winter grass and coughed itself dead. Childermass got out behind his bodyguard, who openly carried a machine gun. He was greeted by two of his executives on MORG's domestic side, usually referred to as "Homefolks."

"I was watching Dietrich in *Dishonored* tonight," Childermass said as they walked toward the pier. "I wonder if either of you have seen it?"

"No, sir."

"No, sir."

"It's a gem. Dietrich never showed to better advantage than she did under Von Sternberg's direction. She is sexual, enticing, drolly wanton. There is more passionate energy in one of her studied glances than in four hours of *Hamlet*."

"I'd like to see it sometime."

"So would I."

"I own one of the two complete prints in existence. I understand Dietrich herself has the other one."

They walked between parked cars, hearing the grinding groan of the winch on the back of a big wrecker brought in to haul the police car from the bottom of the river.

"What's the box score?" Childermass asked.

"So far, we have seven deads."

"Two men missing. They may have drowned."

"Nine injureds, three serious."

"Three vehicles totally destroyed. Five others damaged."

Childermass shook his head ruefully. "Peter fixed us up tonight, didn't he?"

"Yes, sir."

"Yes, sir."

"What happened to Darkfeather?"

"He was thrown clear of one of the chase cars that crashed and burned."

"But he was burned himself. Just a mass of charcoal."

"Still alive when they got to him. At least his eyes looked alive, that was the one part of him that wasn't burned."

"But when they tried to move him he just broke into pieces."

"Oh, too bad," Childermass said with a frown.

They walked almost to the end of the pier and stood watching as the winch chain slowly wound around the drum. There were frogmen in the flashy water. The car wasn't visible yet at the end of the taut slanted chain.

"Any animal must react to threat if he is to survive," Childermass mused, "but he must not over-react."

"Yes, sir."

"That's right."

"Tonight Peter over-reacted. But after all. How long has it been, a year and a half? We may have succeeded, at one hell of a cost, in driving him nearly insane."

"Crazy bastard."

"Crazy."

Childermass fixed them rebukingly with his larger eye.

"There'll never be another like him. He had savvy and a fanatical sense of balance. His skin had eyes. I honestly believe there were pits in his skull with a thermo-sensitive capacity, like those of a rattlesnake."

Childermass paused, as if searching his memory for a quotation that might serve as epitaph.

"Some guys didn't like his style, but I liked it a lot," he concluded.

The rear end of the police car had broken the surface of the river. Soon water was streaming out of the drowned vehicle from a dozen openings. Frogmen pried open one of the doors and aimed torch beams inside.

"He's not in there!" one of them called to the watchers on the pier.

Childermass' head jerked up. He smiled apprehensively. He stared at his executives as if accusing them of abetting a Houdini-like bit of showmanship. His bodyguard snicked the safety off the machine gun. Childermass walked briskly away from the end of the pier, stopped, walked back, leaned so far over that one of the execs frantically grabbed the back of his coat.

"Drag the river!"

"We'll drag the goddamn river!"

"We'll find him, sir."

"No you won't," Childermass said. "Because Peter has done it again."

He then flew into a tantrum that lasted more than five minutes. He repeatedly kicked the side of a car. He snatched the machine gun from his bodyguard and shot out two searchlights. Grown men got in each other's ways trying to make themselves scarce. Childermass dropped the machine gun and hit himself in the face with his fist until they were able to subdue him and sit him down and pour whiskey into him.

The whiskey calmed Childermass, but it also gave him the giggles. A punched eye swelled. His executives squatted around him looking like blanched owls. Finally Childermass staggered to his feet and lurched toward the salvaged police car. It had been raised to the level of the pier, and dangled there.

"Sir."

"Sir."

"Don't bother me! So it's another laugher, right? But the laugh's not on *me*, boys. This time it's on Peter Sandza. You want to know why?"

He picked up a piece of driftwood and brandished it for emphasis. Then he turned and howled his punch line at the river.

"BECAUSE ROBIN DOESN'T CARE ANY MORE! HE DOESN'T *CARE* IF HIS FATHER IS ALIVE OR DEAD!"

He teetered on the edge of the pier for a few moments, but even his bodyguard didn't want to go near him during this emotional crisis. Eventually Childermass collected his wits, dropped the piece of wood and came walking fast back to the little knot of men. He seemed anxious to get away from the lights and off the exposed pier.

"What the hell," he muttered, wiping tears from his puffy eye. "It's New Year's. Let's all fly over to Fun City and get laid. My treat."

Twelve

Robin awoke still tasting the oily river, and his stomach was badly unsettled. He got down off the high double bed with its posts of oak almost as big around as telephone poles; he was wobbly on his feet. He had on his old yellow cotton pajamas, washed so many times you could read a newspaper through the material. The pajama shirt hung unbuttoned. Someone had mended the tear under one arm.

He swallowed several times, finding his throat a little raw, and then a cramp propelled him into the bathroom. He retched until he was worried he'd rupture his navel. Nothing much came up but bright yellow bile. His head ached from his exertions. He looked around the bathroom with teary eyes. Everything was on a vast scale, even for him, and he was getting closer to six feet all the time. Half an acre of tiled floor, probably a billion of those little six-sided tiles, a square basin big enough to bathe in, a curious tub like a big sea shell that stood four feet off the floor. Wherever he was, it was a dumpy old place, older than the house in Lambeth.

Thinking of Lambeth and his Aunt Fay caused the tears to run and run until he washed his face in cold water. When he finished his fingers still tingled but the stomach cramps had stopped. His pajamas were spotted and wet, so Robin took them off before returning to the bedroom.

He'd had a noiseless visitor. The drapes were open; sheer curtains billowed in a lavish morning breeze. The air, scented by a forest, felt and tasted good, it melted on his tongue like a wafer. Also it gave him a raging appetite. That had been anticipated. On a round table in the center of the bedroom he found a tray with an icily sweating carafe of fresh orange juice. And there was a typed note for him.

> GOOD MORNING ROBIN!
> WOULD YOU TAKE THE YELLOW AND
> GREEN CAPSULE AND THE WHITE
> TABLET WITH YOUR JUICE THEY'LL
> GET RID OF THE NAUSEA AND HELP
> YOUR HEAD KINDEST REGARDS
> GWYNETH

Gwyneth?

Robin poured a generous glassful of the juice, sipped eagerly, remembered the pills and studied them with suspicion. He compromised and swallowed the tablet, which was so small he had trouble picking it up with two fingers. Anything that small probably wouldn't kill him. He hadn't seen anyone in this place yet, but he didn't trust them no matter what.

Because the juice tasted okay he finished what was in the glass. Then he looked around for clothes to put on.

With a little effort Robin found most of his old stuff, including a lot of things he hadn't taken to that other place in New York, because they'd told him he was only going to be there for a few days. Also there were new Levi's, the style he liked, and body shirts and walk shorts and a couple of dress-up outfits, including a double-breasted knit blazer from Saks Fifth Avenue. In other drawers he found neatly packed away games and books and pictures and other precious memorabilia. One closet was filled with his sports gear.

"Robin?"

The sweet clear voice startled him just as he was about to give in to the push and shove of memory and start weeping again. Someone outside, calling him. Who was she, and what did she want? He grabbed a pair of stringy cut-off Levi's and a faded red tank top and put them on. Then he walked barefoot onto the balcony which was outside the tall windows that opened like doors, and there he had his first look at his new surroundings.

Blue-green mountains and a far sparkling lake and, nearer, fieldstone buildings with steep slate roofs in a naturally wooded setting. A school? Nearer still he saw a garden with squared-off hemlock hedges, beds of marigold and gracefully curving footpaths walled with roses. Beside the house there was a private swimming lake studded with rock outcrops, ringed by perfect specimens of spruce. A wooden bridge arched above a spillway. A multilevel, flagged terrace in the wide angle formed by the wings of the house went down to the water's edge.

The girl swimming in the green water raised an arm when she saw him.

"Hi! Come on down and finish your breakfast!" She dived beneath the surface and he saw her stroking underwater, fluid as an otter, toward the terrace.

A tall man wearing a white mess jacket and pinstripe gray-and-black trousers was waiting for Robin in the bedroom doorway. He smiled, revealing crinkled lines around the eyes.

"This way, sir," he said.

Robin followed him. The hallway was an interior gallery rich in wood, with a carpet like an abstract painting in tones of burnt orange, rust and brown. The gallery was lit by high opposing windows, three of them, each the size of a badminton court; the streaming hot light of the morning sun was regulated by stained glass louvres which appeared to have a religious motif.

"We'll take the elevator to the terrace," the man said. "It's faster than walking down all those steps. By the way, I'm Ken."

"What is this place?"

"It was the home of the Chancellor of Woodlawn College for Women, before the school went broke. When Psi Faculty took over the campus it became the Director's office and residence."

"Psi Faculty?"

"Dr. Charles will explain all that to you," Ken said, smiling again. He showed Robin the cabinet-sized elevator, which descended to the first floor. They walked through a chapel which had been turned into a luncheon/meeting room and out onto the terrace, past a grotto with a trickling waterfall. Here religious statuary had been removed, replaced by a huge piece of stone that looked like a cross to Robin, except for the top part, which was in the form of a loop.

"What's that?"

"It's called an *ankh*," Ken explained. "It's the ancient Egyptian symbol of—immortality, I think. Dr. Charles knows more about it than I do, you could ask——"

Another man in a mess jacket was setting out breakfast on an oval-shaped, wrought-iron table painted a subdued shade of yellow. The table had a pebbly glass top and was shaded by a large fringed umbrella.

"Bart," Ken said, "this is Robin."

"Hello, Robin," Bart said. He had a lot of brassy curly hair and keen blue eyes and a smile the equal of Ken's. "Why don't you sit here, facing the water? Dr. Charles will be along in a minute. Would you care for more juice?"

"No . . . thank you."

"Okay, well, there's iced Persian melon to start, or sliced fresh papaya if you prefer that, it's really good with a big spoonful of Devonshire clotted cream. We have toast made from the terrific wholegrain bread they sell down at the co-op, or frosted bran muffins, those are especially good with raspberry jam. I'll take your egg order now . . . no eggs? Could I tempt you with a small filet of poached speckled trout? Fresh-caught at five o'clock this morning, just a half mile down the road from here."

When Bart left him Robin picked up a spoon and dipped into the pale soft melon, but his throat tightened before he could take a bite.

He got up and walked to the edge of the lake, thinking about the girl he'd seen swimming. He hadn't been able to tell much about her from the third-floor balcony. The half submerged rocks at the water's edge were fringed with green-gold streamers, some sort of aquatic plant life. But the water had a decided flow even this close to shore and it looked clean, so clean and clear he could see the round brown stones on the pebbled bottom out to a depth of seven or eight feet.

Robin wondered what had happened to him after he'd lost his balance on the wall that separated the promenade of Karl Schurz Park from the East River fifty feet below. It was all he could remember, black night and a half-circle of encroaching, ultimately blinding lights and the fine mist coming down, making the footing treacherous on the incurved iron railing that was supposed to keep people from jumping in and drowning. Everybody said the tidal river was bad there, washing swiftly seaward; so if he'd fallen in why hadn't *he* drowned?

He wished he was dead, because if he wasn't ever going to see his Dad again. . . .

Robin's face got miserably flushed before he started crying, and the tears were hotter still, as if his insides were one huge blister he'd cruelly pricked, allowing the corrosive and scalding fluid to drain out. In trying to stop the tears he smeared them all over his face like a child, which made him mad and caused him to bawl in frustration as well as pain.

"Hey now, good gosh, what we're going to have here is a big old saltwater pond if this keeps up."

The voice was feminine, exaggeratedly gruff; the hand that touched him was meant to be friendly. But Robin jerked away, doubly humiliated now that he knew he was observed.

She stood back toweling her hair while Robin got himself in order, blinking and wondering what he could blow his nose on, it was getting messy. She handed him the towel. "You want, I'm through with it." Robin dried his face and sneaked looks at her. She stood a dozen feet away, hands on hips, appraising him with a tight compressed smile of concern.

The first thing he noticed was how good her hair looked even when it was fluffed half-dry; it didn't stand out ratsey all over her head and show unappetizing expanses of scalp. She plucked a brush from the waistband of her lowslung, mint-green Lee Riders and gave her mane a few licks until it settled down thick and lion-toned, shading to smoke, curling like woodshavings on her bare shoulders. She had a firm small body with just enough hip-swell and pear seat to distinguish her from boys.

From the navel up she was heartily woman: she wore a bouclé halter top fully loaded with good brown jugs, each a perfect seemly roundness . . . and nipples that, by contrast, made aggressive high-rise peaks in the material. The quantity of down on her arms and legs glinted like hazy golden wire. A drop of water ran down one ankle and into the space next to her big toe. Her feet were quite small, and so were her hands. She had vegetable-green elliptical eyes and heavy lashes to shade them and subdue the explicit gaze. Her nose was small and cunningly snubbed, like a child's nose that had not changed over the years. The rest of her tanned; her nose peeled, but prettily. She had a set of dimples and minor beauty marks in unexpected, catchy places and, when Robin finally put the towel down and looked directly at her, she exhibited a dead-center dazzling smile that seemed to show all of her white teeth, a smile that worked on him like gravity.

"I'm Gwyneth," she said, "but I like Gwyn. Do I call you Robbie?"

"Robin."

"Okay. I'm starved. Why don't we sit and if you don't want to eat, we'll talk while *I* eat."

Bart was right there with her breakfast when they reached the table. Herb tea, two scrambled eggs and trout, a serving of which was also placed in front of Robin.

"Even if you're not hungry you don't have to chew or go to any trouble, the trout fairly melts in you mouth. Who are you looking for?"

"They told me I was going to meet someone named Dr. Charles when I——"

Gwyneth shook her head, trying to suppress her amusement; her dimples whitened in her cheeks.

"Okay, you've got me. I'm the good doctor. What's the matter, don't I look old enough? Go on, flatter me—tell me how old you think I am."

". . . Nineteen . . . ?"

"Twenty-eight. Well, ho-ho, I'm cheating. I'll be twenty-nine on the fifteenth of July. So you're just in time for my birthday. Let's see, you were thirteen in February, right? Boy, you're really sprouting for someone who's just thirteen. How tall are you?"

"Five ten and three-quarters."

"You'll easily grow another four inches—maybe five, you've

got long bones. Don't you want to ask what kind of doctor I am?"

"What——"

"M.D.; speciality's neurobiology. Nerves, the brain; you know. I also have an advanced degree in theoretical physics. What am I doing with that? *I* don't know, seemed like a good idea at the time. Listen, I'm just stuffed full of smarts! Graduated college at sixteen, graduated Columbia Med three and a half years later. They didn't want to accept me in the first place, I was so young. Took a lot of hassling to change their minds. Special favor to me, Robin, just try a forkful of the trout."

Robin humored her, but he could barely get the bite of fish down. He looked unhappily at her. Gwyneth's own appetite flagged.

"I *know.* Oh, I know the feeling; you're hungry but you just can't—my uncle said you took it so goddamn hard. What else? I want you to know I ate him out good for the way he handled you. What a tactless man he can be. God, you might have died!"

On the promenade, headlights blinding; he runs and runs, but there is no place left to go.

Childermass, stepping out of one of the cars.

"I'm your father's friend! He would have wanted me to look after you!"

"Your uncle?" Robin said, dismayed.

"Childermass." Gwyneth shrugged, disclaiming responsibility for one's relations. "He's . . . sometimes I think he's like a displaced tyrant from a fairy tale. A king of the legendary present. Honestly, he does have his good points. I'm told your father would have trusted him with his life."

"*I* don't trust him," Robin said, not looking at her. "And I don't believe my dad is dead."

"That's understandable. But you know he lived, chose to live, dangerously. Robin, the information I have is still sketchy, but . . . do you want to go into this now?"

"Yes."

"He was on assignment in Lamy, one of those West African plague lands squatting along the Equator, miles and miles of swamp and jackal bush and no civilization to speak of. The country is one big clap-trap, medically it's back in the stone age, but there's a volatile mix of tribes and territorial disputes have been going on for thirty centuries. Now it seems there's a prize worth dying for, a potentially big oil field under the delta, exploitable at today's prices. So the tribes are getting tons of arms from the usual sources and having at each other in mercenary style."

"My dad——"

"I can't speculate on what he was doing there. I know he was riding in a Land Rover with two other men, in daylight, in a supposedly secure area. The Rover was raked with automatic weapons fire, and all three were killed. By the way, my uncle's organization has been trying to raise your Aunt Fay on Inanwantan radio for the past couple of days, but the weather's been very bad in that part of New Guinea. If they can't get a message through on the missionary frequency, they'll send a helicopter up in the mountains as soon as the weather clears."

"If . . . he's dead, they'll be bringing him back, won't they?"

"Robin, the area in which your father was killed is completely cut off now. In that part of the world they have to bury the dead quickly. Eventually I hope his personal effects will be returned. All the legal matters on this side are being taken care of by my uncle, who has power of attorney. Your father's estate, including insurance, comes to a little over two hundred thousand dollars. After taxes the remainder will be placed in a trust account for you. I think most of your things, other than what you had in storage, are already here. We're really trying to make the transition as painless as——"

"What kind of place is this? What am I doing here?"

"I think the best way to explain Psi Faculty is to show you around," Gwyneth said with a pleased smile.

Gwyn usually rode to work on her ten-speed bicycle, but when she had a guest she drove an electric cart. A carillon was pealing as they cruised soundlessly over a watercourse and through bowers; they were splashed in passing by hot droplets of sun.

"Those mountains are the Adirondacks; that big lake out there is Lake Celeste. We own four hundred and eighty acres, and there's a mile-wide greenbelt surrounding the campus. It's a government reservation, chief, so once in a while you'll see

some old poots patroling with a dog or two. Don't be intimidated, that's just to keep the campers and hunters out of the
woods, they can be a nuisance sometimes. My grandmother
went to school here; Woodlawn had a terrific reputation in the
old days. But the endowment was just too thin, they couldn't pay
their bills any more. My uncle picked up the whole thing for a
song. Half of the buildings are in mothballs, so to speak, but
we've put all the lab space to good use and built more to suit
our needs. How long were you at Paragon Institute, Robin?"

"Six days."

"Did anyone explain to you what "paragon" means?"

"No."

"It means the best there is; something that can't be equaled
—the incredible power of the human mind. Paragon Institute is
basically a testing facility. Here we have the money and the time
to study the fundamental stratum of existence, which is consciousness, along with the scientific, philosophical and social
implications of psychic research. We call ourselves Psi Faculty,
Psi being the twenty-first letter of the Greek alphabet——"

"Isn't it the twenty-third letter?"

"Ho-ho, I just wanted to see if you were napping! Twenty
-*third* letter of the Greek alphabet, and the ideogram stands
collectively for all paranormal experiences. Here's something
that might give you a chuckle."

They swooped down on the quadrangle, enclosed by four-
story stone buildings jacketed in ivy and by the newer carillon
tower, which rose to a gothic peak of one hundred feet, well
above the loftiest tree in the vicinity. Where the walks converged
in the placid quad there was a statuary grouping that looked, on
approach, like the *Burghers of Calais,* their bronzes weathered to
a shadow-darkness in the brilliant sunlight.

"A corny Annunciation stood here," Gwyneth said. "I had it
hammered to bits my second day on the job and commissioned
this piece. Do you recognize them?"

Robin shook his head. There were two skinny figures; the
other was portly. Two were on their feet but the fat one had
fallen; he looked to be in a panic. They were all in headlong
flight, which was complicated by a burden of chains which
dragged them down, even distorted them physically. One of the
figures had flung an arm across his eyes as he pulled in despair
with his other hand at the crude links fastened to his chest.

Gwyneth hopped out of the car and strolled companionably around the seven-foot statues, tapping an elbow, rubbing haunches, naming each in turn, reading from plaques at their feet.

"Herman von Helmholtz, German physicist, 1821–1894: 'Neither the testimony of all the Fellows of the Royal Society nor even the evidence of my own senses would lead me to believe in thought-transmission. It is clearly impossible.' Lord Kelvin, English physicist, 1825–1907: 'Nearly everything in hypnotism and clairvoyance is imposture, and the rest bad observation.' Thomas H. Huxley, English biologist and noted progenitor: Quote. 'Supposing the phenomena to be genuine, they do not interest me.' Unquote. Three of the finest minds of their century. The century immediately preceding this one, I might add."

Robin, looking up at Gwyn, shaded his eyes and said nothing.

"Maybe we ought to erect a monument to the cow as well," she said, coming back to the cart.

"What cow?"

"In Europe it was once commonly believed that beasts could be possessed by demons and controlled by the evil of Satan. So animals, even birds and insects, were tried by ecclesiastical courts, just like witches and heretics. They were excommunicated, tortured and condemned to death."

"That was in the middle ages."

"There was a trial in the year 1740 in France, the cow I mentioned. The cow was judged, declared guilty of satanic influence and executed. Not so far back in time, in what historians consider to be a reasonably complex and sophisticated age. So we've come a long way in our thinking, haven't we? Responsible investigators are allowed to quietly pursue the notion that the psychic system has a prehistory of millions of years; that a tele-magic sympathy exists between all living things; that there are planes of existence and hierarchies of consciousness barely conceivable at our present level of knowledge. Yet ninety-nine percent of the population of the world struggles along on a primitive level of consciousness, very much like twilight sleep. They think trance-thoughts; their actions are merely reflex movements. There are otherwise sensible people living in this area who believe that the moon landings were a clever illusion staged by a government desperate for prestige. Twenty years ago we could have shown them a visitor from the planetary system of 61 Cygni, on television, live from the Oval Office of the White House. Fact. But they weren't ready for it then, and they won't be ready twenty years from now. If such people become sufficiently agitated by wonders beyond their ken they will listen instead to a new crop of ecclesiastics, inquisitors and exorcists who are prepared to purge all monsters, whether they be space man, cow or clairvoyant."

There was a heavy mist of perspiration on Gwyneth's upper lip. She glanced at Robin, whose head was lowered in gloom. She put a hand on him and sighed.

"What it is, I get so wound up sometimes I go off like one of those clown-cannons loaded with flour, dusting everybody in sight. We're not exactly heroes up here; for the most part psychic researchers, those who are considered the least bit far-out in their thinking, are the fools of the scientific community. I've got good staff but I could use a dozen more top people. If I could find them, motivate them. . . ."

"What you said is the truth. I know I'm a monster."

"Hey, that wasn't meant personally."

"And there has to be a special place to keep the monsters. A zoo. No matter what name you call this place, it's still a zoo."

"Come on, Robin!"

"Only I'm not ready for this or any other kind of zoo," he said, his eyes slits, his face tense as a fist. He got out of the cart and started walking back in the direction from which they had come.

He had trudged half way to the house when out of the corner of his eye he saw the cart flashing past him through thickets of birch and black cherry. A white-throated sparrow piped shrilly in the woods like a boatswain welcoming the admiral aboard. Gwyneth was parked on the path below him and waiting, leaning against her cart, when he appeared.

"So where are you going?"

"I want to get my things. I don't want to stay here."

"Could I take a shot at an apology?"

Robin didn't say yes or no, but he stopped a few feet away. Gwyn pushed her hair back with both hands, revealing all of her graceful neck.

"Okay. You're a guy I like a lot on short acquaintance. All I really know about Robin Sandza is what I read in a highly confidential report from Paragon. Transcripts of the tapes you made, and so forth. I admit I was—goddamn well stunned by your ability. I understand there are films. I'd like to see them too. What I said about monsters—we're all in the same born-again hotbed, shuffling and scuffling toward a state of grace, most often doing the lousy thing and making the unforgiveable gesture, but sometimes muddling through. But you've made a couple of quantum-jumps toward the perfect state, you're a twenty-first century kid who arrived a little early. Robin, we're all going where you've been already. You make me feel—humble, believe it or not, and just a little too anxious to please and impress. After they fished you out of the river and pumped your lungs out and sedated you, you were brought here because my uncle didn't have any better ideas. It's big and peaceful here, there are a lot of ways to have a great time in this country if you want to.

"Now, technically, your Aunt Fay is your legal guardian, but we can't even *find* your Aunt Fay. The law in New York says until you're sixteen you need an adult to look after you. Who's it going to be? Your second cousin doing time for embezzlement in Joliet? Your great-aunt Harriet living off her dividends at Leisure World? I don't think you're psychologically equipped, after the tragedy you've experienced, to go knocking around the world on your own. So—give us a chance, please. Stay awhile. Do your own thing. Swim; go hiking; learn to ride a trail bike. I can guarantee, because I run the place, that there'll be no pressure on you to participate in any of our work. You'll be left strictly alone if that's what you want, and, owww, oh, goddamn it!"

Gwyn leaped high and wide and turned around once in the air while grabbing at the seat of her pants. She want hopping and skipping past Robin and he saw the horsefly soar away. She rubbed the bitten place, tears standing out in her eyes.

"Oh, the damn *flies* we've got around here! Robin, would you see if he welted me?"

The fly had bitten her very low on the back, a finger's width from the ivory rim of one soft cheek. A goodly lump was raising. Gwyn bent over, shoving the low pants even lower. Quite obviously she wore no underpants.

"Rub some spit on it for me? That usually helps when I don't have anything else handy."

Robin wet his fingertips plentifully and coated the bite. Gwyn straightened and hitched up and wiped her tearing eyes on the back of a wrist.

"Ohhh, thanks. It feels like he took a big chunk out. I guess he got a whiff of asshole."

She looked quickly at Robin and tossed off a shrug. "Excuse that last remark. I do get a little vulgar from time to time."

They were standing close together in an open place where the sun was powerful; Gwyn continued to look up at Robin, but neither moved to get out of the other's way. A breeze stirred strands of hair on the crown of her head. He was totally interested in the wavering of her hair, in the mild steady eyes. He found other things that fascinated. Her lips seldom closed all the way. The upper lip had a pronounced arch. She had a serrated front tooth, a visible, strong pulse in her throat and a natural scent that would, in time, prove electrifyingly erotic.

Gwyneth, rising on tiptoes to more nearly approximate his height, balanced herself with one hand on his shoulder; she reached out to touch his pinked sensitive nose with the ball of her thumb.

"We have the same trouble, huh?"

Robin swallowed and thoughtfully bit his lower lip.

She stroked his nose kiddingly and dropped the hand, but she did it with a languid, wistful slowness, keeping light fingertip contact all the way to his beltline. Then she put both hands in her own front pockets, thumbs showing.

"Give me a shot at being a friend?" she said.

In response to the blue uncertainty of Robin's smile Gwyneth lowered her eyes submissively, willing to wait him out.

At the two o'clock staff meeting Gwyneth said, "I think, despite Robin's problems, we've already developed a relationship that can only improve with time." She looked around the table and added, "He's taking me to dinner tonight."

The four men and two women in the conference room smiled at her.

The dinner wasn't a success. Robin was docile, not giving. Gwyn knocked herself out to jolly him and sometimes he smiled, but she'd find him looking at her as if he couldn't convince himself that she really existed. She'd never encountered this much reserve in any male, regardless of age; Robin's attitude perplexed and ultimately defeated her. He withdrew completely then, and threw up high walls.

For a week and a half afterward Robin deliberately avoided contact with her. He slept much of every day and prowled nights. He had the run of the campus, and Staff stayed tactfully out of his way. Gwyn spotted him early one morning, just before daybreak, huddled high and dry on a rock in the middle of the swimming lake. She wondered how he got there without getting wet. He spent long nocturnal hours in the Faculty library, turning the pages of rare books that made up a part of the six-thousand-volume occult collection. Most often he studied maps. He caught a cold and was plagued with a low-grade fever and his appetite didn't improve. One side of his face swelled up from poison oak. He looked and felt miserable.

Analysis of the films made of Robin while he slept showed he was leaving the body for four and five hours at a time.

"Apparently trying to arrange a meeting with his father in the astral," said Newvine, the Faculty psychiatrist and den-mother, a transvestite whose nickname was "Granny Sigmund."

"And not having any luck," a co-worker commented.

"He's been studying all those detailed maps of Equatorial Africa," Gwyneth said. "He could be looking for the body. He needs to be convinced it happened."

"I doubt there is a body," said an Englishman named Salt-marsh, who was on loan from the University of London's Council for Psychical Investigation. "Bloody mercenaries would have chucked the lot of them into a roadside ditch. Wouldn't be much left by now, would there? Rags and a rather cloudy odor."

Gwyn made a face. "For God's sake, they *must* have buried the poor man! But Robin is going to go bats pursuing his father's ghost, or his earthly remains. I've got to divert him somehow, it's getting critical. I'm afraid Robin will induce a psychopathological condition we can't handle without resorting to the phenothiazines. And drugs may very well close valuable pathemic channels."

"May I make a suggestion?" Granny Sig said. The transvestite was a vast figure with Kerry Blue hair and little round glasses perched on apple cheeks. She laughed a lot, shaking and reddening without ever uttering more than a wheeze of sound.

"I wish you would, Granny Sig. I had him in the palm of my hand, practically, but——"

"I've studied your excellent resumé of your first attempts to befriend Robin. You possess a rare flaw, my dear. That flaw is flawlessness. You are brilliant in several fields of study, physically vital and competent at all types of games. You have this maddening ability to pick up expertise in areas that actually don't interest you very much. You can tune your '57 DeSoto like a fine watch, explain role-reversal among coyotes, discuss ballistics with a sharp-shooter and list six plausible ways Johnny Bench can break out of his current batting slump. You have social graces and a funnybone. You also possess an intimidating sexual confidence. Gwyneth Charles is a creature of so many parts that trying to explain her to the uninitiated leaves one in the despairing position of the blind man in the parable who tried to describe the elephant."

"Gee whiz, I've loved hearing all this; however——"

The transvestite shook and trembled with internal laughter, turning the color of a thrombosed vein.

"I have seen you, operating at perhaps half power, demoralize a roomful of excellent men of our acquaintance. Just think of the impact you must have had on that thirteen-year-old boy."

Gwyneth chewed her underlip. "He's no ordinary——"

"We are speaking of emotional capacity. For the moment think of him solely as a sexual being. Genitally he is in a splendid state of development. We have filmed him masturbating to a climax. We may assume that from the wealth of pornographic material available to all growing boys he has adequate technical information. By his own admission he has not experienced sexual intercourse. More importantly, he's had little contact with pubescent females. His most profound sexual experience to date involved the lactating breast of a mother-surrogate with whom he strongly empathized."

"I bet I know where you're going with that."

"Yes. Your long-range plan for Robin is not without the possibility of considerable danger——"

"Not *again*, doctor!"

"But since you are committed to this course of action, I urge you to re-think your strategy."

"What you're trying to say is, I hustled him to the brink too fast. But I wasn't really working at it——"

"Oh, my dear, two overt contacts within an hour! And you revealed no corresponding areas of vulnerability to which he could respond. Consider his adolescent daydreams: who is he mooning over as he pounds his peenie? Last month's centerfold girl? The saucy sprite selling deodorant on TV? That mountain wench on whom he was severely fixated? It doesn't matter, they are safely removed from the reality of the act as he commits it. I'm certain that he doesn't think of *you;* perhaps he makes a conscious effort not to. Because you are much too immediate and larger than life, and more woman than he can possibly cope with. Showing him even a portion of your superb derriere was a terribly intimidating, not a provocative act. A blow to his burgeoning sexuality. He may want you, it would be inhuman of him not to want you, but he feels unequal to the task, which could have repercussions."

"You mean I might have driven him into the clutches of Ken or Bart?" Gwyneth said sarcastically, but she had flushed to the roots of her hair. Several of those in the room were having a hard time containing snickers.

Granny Sig smiled peaceably.

"Oh, I'm sure there's sufficient time to restore his confidence. But another bit of advice? Don't fuss over him. Let him make a fuss over you, for a change."

"Ah-hum," Gwyn said, enlightened.

Robin was unaware that the campus of Psi Faculty was as tightly guarded as any facility at Langley or Ft. Meade. He saw no helmeted police with packs of vicious dogs; there were no checkpoints protected by machine guns. Visible security measures included warning signs, a few floodlights at night, some not very formidable gates across access roads. These were tended by dyspeptic middle-aged men with pot bellies who were armed with nothing more lethal than a clipboard.

He occasionally ran into the only active daytime security patrol, two men in faded Forest Service green who chewed toothpicks and prowled the back woods in a pickup with a big German shepherd who rode in the truck bed. The shepherd whoofed and ranted and bared his teeth when anyone approached, just as he'd been taught. But nobody had figured out a way to keep him from wagging his tail at the same time; obviously it killed him not to be liked. Robin also saw pipe-smoking government employees ruminating over soil samples and seedlings; he saw logging crews and maintenance men and meteorologists from the weather station on a bald bluff overlooking Lake Celeste. They liked to strip to the waist and throw a frisbee around during their lunch break. At intervals he saw a helicopter in an otherwise empty sky. Nobody followed him or showed unusual interest in his presence. If he wanted to get on Gwyn's trail bike and ramble for miles he could do so.

He had absolute freedom, and he was totally a captive. Even before Robin's advent part of the MORG reservation had been used to experiment with new types of protective sensors and hardware. The security system that monitored several square miles of campus and woodland was based at the meteorological station, which was a blind. It contained surveillance and tracking devices adapted from all the latest cameras and telescopes which NASA crammed into its spy satellites. The woods were gridded with sensors and honeycombed with sector control bunkers. Each team of operators had at their disposal arsenals which could handle any sort of intrusion. By pushing buttons they could soak the night sky with burning magnesium, destroy bridges or create lethal pitfalls in the winding roads. They could gas every living thing on a two-acre plot in a matter of seconds. Fields were sown with pop-up land mines that contained enough metal fragments to shred an elephant. Heat-seeking missiles awaited low-flying jets.

More canines, monstrous cousins of the tail-wagger in the pickup truck, were available at a nearby farm. Nice old men who scratched their bellies and yawned a lot could kill you in ten different ways if you aroused their suspicions. Ken and Bart, who looked after the house so well, were a particularly murderous team. Ken liked the long silent stalk and the sudden knife; Bart, who had an almost mystical grasp of anatomy, killed inventively with whatever came to hand.

The 250 cc. engine of the trail bike could be blown by remote control if Robin exceeded certain limits of exploration. His every moment in the house was photographed at eight frames per second, with conventional lenses and infrared film.

After three weeks the men assigned to plotting and anticipating his every move began to see a pattern of dependability emerging; he was getting used to his new home, settling into a routine. He made no real overtures to Gwyn, but he became more talkative around Ken and Bart.

Near the time of her twenty-ninth birthday Gwyn planned to spend several days with an old beau, a novelist, who was in residence at Yaddo, the artists' colony down the road in Saratoga Springs. Prior to departure she said nothing about her trip to Robin, but she left him a brief cheery note.

It was immediately evident that he was shocked by her absence. A couple of times he went into Gwyneth's apartment, which was on the third floor near his own bedroom, just to look around. He read and re-read the handwritten note. He borrowed a Swiss Army knife from Ken, who had quite a collection, and walked the woods searching for pieces of basswood to whittle into figures. He began to eat all of the sandwiches that Bart packed for his day-long odysseys instead of throwing them away after a bite or two. Hour after hour he worked feverishly at his woodcarvings, broke many of them in dissatisfaction, started anew. He cut his fingers several times, covering the damage with Band-Aids.

Granny Sig had Ken and Bart down to her shop on the quad for a consultation.

"His level of prescience has been very low due to emotional trauma. Now that he's showing signs of recovery, we must be very careful around him. If Robin knew the extent of our protective arrangements, he would be upset and frightened. Later the security precautions will make no difference to him; if anything he'll be flattered knowing it's all for his sake. Right now we wouldn't want to alert him to any of the bloody truth about your misspent lives, my dears."

"He actually reads minds?" Ken said uneasily.

Granny Sig laughed and laughed, sounding like a broken bellows.

"That's a serious misapprehension. One of his remarkable talents is the phenomenon of psychometry. And all *that* is—well, someday we may actually know how the mind transcends time and space; "reality" as we know it. For now let me say that there is a bioplasmic universe, and in that universe is a record of every human impulse, word and deed—from lives past and lives to come. Robin, by touching you, or something that belongs to you, makes a connection between the timeless world and the physical world, what clairvoyants call a "vision." He culls from your past or future—which is all one, anyway, part of the huge collective consciousness."

Ken said, "Do you suppose he'll read anything off that knife I gave him? It was practically new, I never used it."

"Not to worry, then."

"Won't he get a lot of wrong vibes from Gwyn?" Bart asked.

"We pondered that problem at length. All I can say is, Gwyneth is not in possession of any single piece of information that could betray her. She will never have to lie to him. Shortly we will stage a set-piece for the ultimate benefit of their relationship, but Gwyn won't know about it in advance; she'll have to improvise, responding to opportunities as they happen. And, as the boy falls deeply in love with her, he will soon be no more perceptive about Gwyn than he is about himself. Clairvoyants are notoriously unable to divine their own fortunes."

It was raining lightly and getting dark when Robin made his way home that afternoon on the bike, skirting a cove of Lake Celeste. He wasn't looking for it, but through the tamarack and the spruce he couldn't miss Gwyn's car parked on a flat promontory; it was one of her "thinking places," where she would gaze uninterruptedly for hours at the perfect reflection of the trees on the face of the water. The car was a red and white DeSoto, twenty years old but beautifully maintained; she had referred to it proudly as "one of the really great, tacky, tail-fin, park-n'-grope Dee-troit honeywagons."

She was home a day early from Saratoga Springs. He wondered why. He skidded to a stop and looked down at the car. Headlights winked on and off twice in the settling gloom.

Robin took a slippery needled trail down to the lake shore, pulling up next to the DeSoto. Gwyneth was slumped behind the wheel. She didn't look at him but raised a hand in wan salute.

He killed the bike engine and put the kick-stand down, but he didn't get off.

"Thought I heard my old banger," Gwyn said. "How've you been?"

"Okay."

She sat up and eased the door open and got out. She took a tender deep breath, looked at him and through him.

"You said you wouldn't be back before——"

"Tomorrow, but alas the reunion ended today. Once again I couldn't stay the route with good old Vic."

Gwyn smiled somberly, wiped the mist of rain from her forehead and walked down to the edge of the lake. She was barefoot. She walked stiffly, as if her left side hurt. She stood for a few minutes with her feet in the cold water. Robin wandered around and scuffed at rocks. Gwyn came back.

"We're getting wet," she said.

"What happened to your side?"

"What? Oh, I . . . bruised it. Hurts. Kind of."

"Your mouth is cut."

"Where? Here, you mean. So it's cut, okay."

"How come?"

"Oh, shut up, Robin," Gwyn said mildly. Then she lifted her hands, palms up, a gesture of apology. She winced. "Sorry. I got hit a couple of whacks, that's all. The ribs are the worst this time. I've learned not to stick around for the full cycle. Tears and recriminations were on tomorrow's schedule, if I stayed out of the hospital. Vic is stalwart and charming for a day, he drinks for a day, he becomes incomparably . . . compulsively . . . destructive."

"Why would he hit you?"

"I can't explain that very well. It's not because he doesn't like me."

"Oh."

"Throw the bike in the car and I'll drive us home."

He would have liked to ask more questions; it made him edgy and angry to think that she had been hurt. But Gwyn wasn't angry, she just looked very sad; her lips moved soundlessly a couple of times as she drove, as if she were now phrasing all the things she wished she could have said to Vic.

Then, catching Robin looking at her, she smiled and leaned over and pounded a chummy fist on one knee.

"I'll be okay."

"Not if you hang around what's-his-name," Robin said a bit fiercely.

"But it's over. All over. Finally."

"How long did you——"

They had reached a wide place where three unpaved roads intersected. Two muddy sedans were parked there. A man in a hat and a pale trench coat was getting out of one car and into the other. He looked up, briefly, just as the DeSoto's headlights flared on his face.

Robin was staring through the rainy window. He bucked as if touched by a live wire.

"MY DAD."

"What?" Gwyneth said, startled from her despondent reverie. She looked back but didn't stop. Robin had rolled down the window, saw only taillights vivid in the slash rain as the sedans went divergent ways.

"Gwyn! Stop! Go back! I saw DAD."

"Oh, no, Robin——"

"*Please!*" he shrieked at her, lunging dementedly to grab the steering wheel. Gwyn rode the brake on the slick clayed surface; the DeSoto spun like a top and slid a hundred feet.

"Robin!"

She fought him off with one hand and tried to control the skid; the car crashed into a springy alder thicket overgrowing the road and stopped.

Robin threw open the door on his side, fell out, bounded up and ran back down the road.

The cars had disappeared. Robin fell headlong again as Gwyn restarted the engine, delicately gained traction and followed. She caught up to Robin standing dejectedly near the place where he'd seen the man.

Raining harder now, rain thudding on the car top.

His chest heaved and his Rubenesque hair was matted to his forehead.

"Robin, please get back in the car."

He shook his head violently.

"It may have looked—you could not have seen——"

"BUT I DID."

"Robin, no Robin, your father is *dead;* I can prove that to you if you'll only——"

He turned; in place of eyes she beheld a shocking luminosity in the headlights.

"They never sent him back; so there's no proof!"

She had to go after him.

"Robin, come home with me."

"We could be following them!"

"Where? Which road? I didn't see the way those cars went. Be sensible. If it could have been—by some miracle—he'll get in touch, won't he? *Well, don't you think so?"*

Robin lowered his head. There was a little blood where he'd bitten his underlip; it washed away quickly. Gwyn took him by the arm. She had to pull him, one sticky, sluggish step at a time, back to the DeSoto. They rode shuddering and in silence the short distance to the house.

He was just out of a hot tub when she called his room an hour later.

"Robin, could you come down to the study for a few minutes?"

Gwyneth had changed into a long tropical skirt and put her hair up. She was drinking Scotch. Her eyes looked a little muzzy. He sat on the seat of a wall-sized bow window that overlooked the swimming lake. At the perimeter of the terrace Japanese lanterns were lit. The rain had all but stopped. Clouds like chimney smoke rolled away toward the Hudson Valley. In the last full flash of day, trees dripped diamonds.

She brought him a nine-by-twelve envelope from the safe.

"I've had these for a week. I never intended showing them to you. I know I may be making a mistake, but—" Gwyn tried to undo the string-tied flap but her fingers blundered. Robin took the envelope from her hands, opened it, slid out several glossy black-and-white photos. For three or four minutes he stared at the top one. Flat road in a hot country. A baobab tree. Sunflare off the icy shards left in the windscreen of the Land Rover, which had gone off the road and was inclined at an angle of about twenty degrees from the horizontal. Thirty or forty brightly peened bullet holes in the metal. Man in bush jacket sprawled head down out of one side of the vehicle. In the background, two black men dressed in guerrilla fatigues. Paratrooper boots, heavy weapons, bandoliers, berets. Toothy grins. The photography, in all respects, was excellent.

Robin reluctantly abandoned the first photograph. The next one was a full shot of another native soldier, fully equipped but barefoot. He pointed exuberantly at the body in the road. Black blood; swarm of flies about the shattered head.

Robin looked up open mouthed at Gwyn, who was squeezing her glass in both hands.

"Go on," she said stonily. *"Keep looking."*

He flipped the two photos face down on the seat and sat with the third in his lap. Closeup of another body inside the vehicle. Sweating soldier with tribal scars holding the head back by the hair, a look of frantic excitement in his eyes. Five, possibly six round dark bullet holes in the victim's face alone. Although the features were distorted by various fluidic pressures, he was easily recognizable.

"Is that your father?" Gwyn demanded.

Robin didn't speak. He turned this photo face down with the others.

"Where did you get those?"

"Childermass."

"Why—would anyone—take them?"

"Gloating privileges."

"What?" Robin said, trembling with rage. He blinked rapidly. His lips were like suet. She was certain he was going to faint

"I'm so *sorry;* it's an evil, dirty business, and I honestly did want to—but if you go on thinking, the rest of your life, that y. might run into him on the s-street; or, or, every time the phone rings you——"

Robin got up and left the room. Gwyn heard him pounding up the stairs with a growling wail that wrenched the heart out of her. She sat down, prickly with nausea, and pressed the cold glass against her head. She wept a little, fitfully, while she nursed one more drink.

About ten o'clock Gwyneth went upstairs to her apartment. She found three wood carvings, the figures hand-polished to a high luster. Tranquil sylvan setting. Mother and two cunning children, a boy and a girl, seated, a large picnic hamper between them. Detail was rendered beautifully: the palm of the mother's hand, the folds of her skirt, the curve of a child's mysterious smile. The figures engrossed her; she was thrilled by this display of youthful talent. Now she understood the reason for all the Band-Aids she'd noticed on his fingers.

A birthday card accompanied the carvings.

I WISH YOU
was all it said, all the words he had needed.

She thought she heard Robin in his room. Thrashing in his sleep, crying out. Gwyneth finally overflowed, crying enough tears to sop one bell sleeve of her white crewel-work blouse.

There was a big shower in her bathroom, a modern instrument of torture like an iron maiden, needle spray coming at her from half a dozen different directions. The ribs which Vic had belabored in his love-rage ached horribly, but she stuck it out. She used a loofah to get the blood going even more fiercely.

Gwyn came out red as a radish, breathing hard and pleasantly exhausted, wrapped herself nearly head to toe in a big orchid towel and lay down tingling on her bed to orchestrate emotions. Before she was completely dried she discarded the towel and reached for the little bottle of concentrated hash oil she kept close to hand. She measured a small drop of the valuable stuff directly onto one fingertip. Sitting in the lotus position, she held the firm viscous drop aloft and stared at it. Then she looked down at her gently rounded crinkle-free belly and the soft fume of droplet maidenhair. Without uncrossing her legs she lay back, inserted the finger quickly deep into her anus, withdrew it immediately, placed it inside her vulva, withdrew again and let her fingertip loll deliciously on the fat and uppity joy-button.

Within seconds she was jumping up and down at the brink of what could be a night-long orgasm, to be maintained as long as she wished with a further judicious application of hash oil. Her skin flushed again and her head was a heavy ball of vipers, entwining sensuously, hissing like flame as the incredibly potent oil was absorbed by soft erogenous tissue.

Gwyneth place another drop on the heart-beat nipple where it could not be absorbed too quickly, at least by her. She was avid then to put her hands on herself, to claw out and cling to the steamy pulsating heart, to rub against walls and furniture, fall panting and grinding on the rough carpet, wearing the skin off her hips and behind while she wore out her need. She forced herself to obtain a small measure of self-control, and went keenly along to Robin's room. She was a stifled madhouse, a sweltering storm.

He was sleeping, but poorly; he sat shock upright when she came in.

"Who's that!" ·

"Gwyn, darling. Are you all right?"

"I was dreaming. I've got a—terrific headache."

Gwyneth kneeled on the bed beside Robin. She put a hand on his forehead. He was still groggy and had night sweats.

"I was in the bath. I thought I heard you, so I came right away."

"I'll be——"

"I can stay with you," she said urgently.

"I——"

"I *want* to stay with you. Robin . . . I have something good for your headache."

She hitched closer to him, sat knee to knee, her other knee raised, making him fully aware of skin tone and stressed muscle, the blood's enormous pulse, the bawdy thoroughbred heaving of her breast.

"What is it?" he said in all innocence.

"Oh God Robin, put your arms around me, please please please before I lose my fucking *mind!*"

But she couldn't wait for him to make even the first sampling move; she gathered him in, flocked his face with butterfly kisses. She treated him to alluring flights of fancy with her tongue. Her hands were loving and roving, then lewd and to the point. Not a moment too soon she was astride him, a nesting pungent lapful, and the loaded nipple was between his teeth.

"Tastes funny," Robin murmured, very nearly his last cogent thought for the remainder of the night.

Five thirty in the morning. The stones of the house were sweating. Conifers in the gunmetal greenery of the garden stood limp with beads of moisture. Fathoms of curling fog, white as bone, wisped hotly from the surface of the black reflecting lake. Two whistling swans glided rosepetal smooth in malicious self-admiration to a far bank where the tall spruce, dim sentinels dark as midnight, began to perish in illusion. Birdsong was chilled, isolated. Gwyneth, in bluesy linen and charming sou'wester, drifted along paths far from the hardpan of the soul, cherished by the spirit that unknots the troubling flesh, all her sins exemplary.

She heard the whisper of giant wings an instant before the bird appeared, directly in front of her and only a few feet off the ground. Gwyn recoiled with an oath, thinking the raven would crash into her, but with a rushed tilt of his iridescent black wings he flew off without a sound above the shrubbery, and was swallowed in cotton mists.

Dirty birds, she thought, hating them because of what they symbolized. Several of the ravens haunted the campus, and some of them were large enough to trigger magnetic-wave detection alarms. The one that had almost bumped her had a wing span of more than five feet. Security men occasionally took pot-shots but without much luck; the ravens had learned to be devious and seldom seen in order to survive.

"Is that you, Gwyneth?" said Granny Sig Newvine, and presently she became visible down the path Gwyn was taking. Mild light had struck the grove and, stirring in bare shadow, Granny Sig came forth, vocal, extravagant, stinking of candor, lovely in cloche maroon and supplemental swag. She carried a ferocious-looking walking stick.

"Oh, yes. There you are. Was it that bird? I saw it too. Well, you look—vital, as always. Not badly used, as I might have expected after so many hours with your tot-cocky soulmate."

"You know already?"

"Guesswork," said Granny Sig, with a hint of a simper.

"The time was right for—laying ghosts. I would say we're rid of his father once and for all. Robin is totally mine now."

"With the aid of a dollop of hash oil, to break down lingering inhibitions?"

Gwyn said dreamily, "They say that making love in the astral is nirvana; for pure sensation it eclipses anything we can manage in the flesh. But we managed pretty good last night."

"Robin is somewhat adept in the astral, you are not. Be careful, dear."

"What are you afraid of, Granny Sig?"

"For one thing, your proclivities toward the left-handed uses of sex."

"You're being an old Puritan. Using drug and sex rites to implement paranormal experiences is standard occult practice. The release of sex energy through ritual copulation can be *very* creative. It's white magic. I'm not fool enough to dabble in black magic——"

"You are focusing the libidinal forces of this mind-boggling youngster on yourself. He may prove to be quite extraordinary sexually——"

Gwyn said with a flippant shrug, "Study the films if you want to. It's going to be a class act."

"No joking matter. I think Robin will become far too much for you to handle——"

"Ho-ho-ho!"

"Sheer youthful braggadocio. I have a very healthy respect for the kinetically destructive powers of the sexually aroused. You can satisfy, even exhaust, the physical body, that's purely a matter of mechanics, but what about the "double," the bioplasmic body we know so little about? What happens when it is subjected to conditions of prolonged spasmic orgasm without emission? Can you satisfy Robin in the ethereal? What happens if you don't? You may find yourself in possession of a *tulpa,* a living nightmare beyond your control."

Mention of the unruly and often terrifying *tulpas,* part of the lore of Tibetan mysticism, caused Gwyneth's skin to prickle momentarily, but then she scoffed.

"*Tulpas* are thought-forms, and I'm a hard-headed realist. And Robin is—he's—all boy. I'm really awfully fond of him, Granny Sig. I'm going to take good care of him."

"Very well," Granny Sig murmured. "I only want you to be aware of the possible dangers. Where do we go from here?"

"I think Robin and I will take a brief *wanderjahr:* he ought to enjoy canoeing on the Ampersand for a week. Hard physical work, and those deep downy sleeping bags at night—lovely! When the relationship is really firmed up I want to introduce him to the kabbalists."

"The Fifty Gardens of Knowledge?"

"Even now, on sheer raw ability, he must be somewhere around the Thirtieth Gate, farther than any of our earthly geniuses can go."

Granny Sig said reverently, "Solomon passed through the Forty-Eighth Gate; by the grace of God only Moses has sojourned in the Forty-Ninth Garden."

"Robin will pass through the last gate."

"To the Final Garden, the Ultimate Mystery?"

"The creation of life itself. And why not?" Gwyn said exultantly, feeling very much up on her luck.

They reached higher ground where the fog was parting. Ahead of them the sun had risen; the blue and speckling day exploded.

Thirteen

Paragon Institute took up part of the block between East 86th and 87th Streets in Manhattan, facing Carl Schurz Park and the river. The main entrance was at the corner of 86th and East End, a handsome Federal house of aging red brick. Paragon also owned the row house next door and the two houses immediately behind them, each with a private entrance on a narrow mews which lay in the permanent shadow of a twenty-story apartment building.

On the evening of the fourth of January it snowed for hours. The fifth dawned clear and very cold, a morning of blue shadows, red faces, vapor breath and crunching footsteps.

Roth, asleep on the couch in his office, flinched and burrowed under one arm when the drapes in his third-floor office were opened part way. He muttered bearishly.

"Dr. Roth?"

When he didn't respond Hester Moore came over and put a firm hand on his shoulder.

"Doctor, you had an eight o'clock breakfast date on your calendar."

For a few moments she thought he was going to ignore her.

She looked around the office, strewn with papers and files. There were two horoscopes visible in view boxes on one wall. At a glance the charts appeared to be identical.

Roth sat up. His shirt was unbuttoned almost to his shaggy stomach, and he needed a shave.

"Time's it now?"

"Seven forty-two."

He smiled and yawned.

"Good to see you back, Hester. How was your vacation?"

"Oh—fabulous."

"Where'd you go?"

"Skiing. In Colorado."

"You don't have much color. You ought to be the color of new pennies by now."

"It was overcast most of the time, but I loved it anyway." Hester drifted toward the view boxes. "I didn't know you were an astrologer, doctor."

For having just come out of a sound sleep, Roth was fast and agile on his feet. He blocked Hester away from the view boxes without making an excuse for his rudeness and took the transparencies down.

"I can draw up a chart, that's about it. The fine art of interpretation I leave to others." Roth rubbed the crown of his balding head, smiling edgily. "Tell my, uh, tell him I'll be a little late. Worked all night."

His hand slid down over the wiry paunch of his chin and he began pulling open desk drawers, looking for his electric razor. "Oh, bring a pot of coffee for me?"

"Yes, doctor," Hester said. She walked down one floor and through a doorway, emerging into a sunlit foyer where a bodyguard stood with folded arms on a carpet designed by Léger. Hester had just a glimpse of the man who sat inside the private dining room behind a *Wall Street Journal,* which he held with one hand. All she saw of him, really, was his stubby hand and a flighty swept-back hairdo; he might have been a man-sized cockatoo sitting there.

Hester's blood didn't run cold, as she'd expected, but she felt distinctly uneasy.

"Miss?"

"Oh! Ah, Dr. Roth will be just a few minutes late."

"Thank you." The bodyguard looked toward the dining room. "I'll tell him."

Hester swallowed and nodded and was about to turn away, but at that moment Childermass put down his newspaper and smiled, catching her eye. Hester froze outside the door, and quickly progressed from an initial stage of awkwardness to feeling downright foolish as she tried to raise a pleasant smile that would get her gracefully away from there.

He beckoned; she had to go in.

"Hello," Childermass said, "and how are you this morning?" He seemed to know he couldn't do much with his little mouth, it was—she couldn't think of a kinder analogy—asshole-tight and just about as attractive, but there was a pert twinkle in his eyes. Hester was fascinated to see that he was wearing makeup to conceal a bad shiner.

"I haven't seen you before, do you work for Roth?"

"Yes. Well, there's two of us, Kristen and myself. I'm Hester."

"I know Kristen. She's a very pretty girl. You're a very pretty girl yourself, Hester. Have you worked here long?"

"Almost a year."

"Well, well. Is the Big Man going to keep me waiting today?"

"Oh, only a few minutes, sir."

Childermass beamed at her for a few moments longer, then his eyes became inexplicably cold as, without saying another word, he resumed with his newspaper. Hester beat it out of the dining room, hurried past the guard and went down another flight of stairs to the kitchen.

"Coffee for Dr. Roth," she said to the cook. She continued on to an adjacent washroom, bolted the door. She sat down on the john with her knees together and rode out a trembling fit.

There'd been nothing about his appraisal of her, nothing in the routine compliment he'd offered like a leftover Danish pastry to trouble her so, but Hester had the super-creepy feeling Childermass was acquainted with her life from the first baby tooth—he knew everything there was to know about her liaison with Peter.

She felt better after patting a little cold water on her cheeks and in the hollows of her throat. With time to analyze her irrational upset Hester realized that she'd simply heard too many horror stories about the man from Peter. She had a bad case of

—what was Peter's term?—"fugitive mentality." If Childermass had any cause to be suspicious of her he wouldn't sit there making boring small talk. No, they'd have whisked her away to some grim little room and . . .

Fugitive mentality again. Hester smiled at herself in the tarnished mirror, hated the smile more than the dopey one she'd flashed at Childermass. She grimaced instead, finally stuck her tongue out at herself. Now that she was back at Paragon she had important things to do; if she hoped to be of any use to Peter then she needed to be nervy and on the attack and not the least afraid of possible consequences . . . and right now Dr. Roth was waiting for his coffee.

At six minutes past eight Roth slid into a chair opposite Childermass, facing a diffused glare from the snowy park across the street. Hanging baskets in front of the wide windows were dripping scarlet poinsettia leaves. The poinsettia was not one of Roth's favorite plants: he thought of them as the whores of horticulture. He preferred desert plants, with their austere and delicate flowers.

"Good news this morning?" Roth said to the Wall Street Journal.

"A sampan loaded with junketing congressmen has gone down in the Styx. Sabotage is suspected, but not condoned."

Roth laughed and drank his grapefruit juice. Childermass put the paper aside.

"So how are things at the hospital?" Roth asked.

"Sweetened," Childermass said indifferently.

"I can't imagine that all the law suits have been filed yet."

"I'd say we're one jump ahead of everyone who has a possible claim."

"Any fuss from the Bellavers?"

"People of quality don't 'fuss.' They make inquiries. They spend money if necessary, quite a lot of money, to get all the facts. Then, if they have a case, they hit like a *tsunami*. So far the family firm is still looking into it. They seem puzzled by the whole business."

"The girl hasn't talked, then."

"It isn't likely she'll say a word. She left two bodies behind her."

"Gillian may have no idea she was responsible for the death of McCurdy and Toone. She may not remember a thing that happened to her that night."

Childermass scowled.

"Retrograde amnesia? That tired old bit?"

"The organism will produce some bizarre effects in its efforts to prevent total mental and emotional collapse. Amnesia is the most common reaction to sudden intense shock. If you'd seen Gillian, blood head to foot, you'd wonder how she could possibly survive the experience with her mind intact."

"That's a good point. She may not be totally sane. The family is certainly keeping her under wraps."

Roth buttered a half slice of toast. "But they haven't consulted a psychiatrist, or packed her off to a good sanitarium. According to the agents who found her hiding in 909 and the floor nurse who spoke to her, Gillian appeared a little upset, but she didn't behave irrationally. I think she'd already done a good job of blacking out Mrs. McCurdy. The Toone woman was bad luck, my God, she was *asking* for trouble with her blood pressure." Roth ate his toast in two bites and said grimly, "I'm inclined to accept a prognosis of, say, selective repression, which may last a few hours or a few days. It could all be coming back to Gillian by now. If so, God help the unfortunate kid."

"I'd say the sooner we get Gillian in here, the better."

"Agreed. I've been working on it. A matter of reaching the people who will recommend me to the Bellavers. Complicated. Like finding your way through a maze . . . meanwhile, the girl is a danger to everyone around her. Her ability to psychometrize is entirely spontaneous. She must create an enormously powerful electromagnetic field. Of course not everyone exposed to it bleeds. But the list of those who *will* bleed, and fatally, is a long one. Someone with a peptic ulcer could go in a matter of minutes. The smallest vascular weakness in heart, brain, kidneys———"

"Is she as dangerous as Robin Sandza?"

"As far as I know she hasn't caused as much havoc as Robin, but it's only a matter of time. Look at this."

From a folder Roth took the two horoscopes he hadn't wanted Hester to see. They were identified by number.

"Robin Sandza and Gillian Bellaver. If you'll lay one over the other you can see that, allowing a few seconds' adjustment for local mean time, they were born virtually at the same moment: on February 4, 1962, at nine minutes and fifty seconds past midnight Universal Time. Gillian at Doctors' Hospital just up the street, Robin at the Naval Hospital in Bethesda, Maryland. Allowing for minor hereditary differences, mostly coloring, they resemble each other physically according to their common ascendant. It was the moment of the new moon in the sign of Aquarius. Tho moon, the sun and five planets were all in the same sign. A rare and significant astrological event. It also coincided with an increase in solar activity.

"These children are Aquarius with Scorpio rising, a powerful combination for good or evil. Psychics were predicting that a child born at the time of the Great Conjunction might be the new Messiah. But what about—a thousand children? So far we know of two who are extraordinary—"

"Statistically speaking, how many could there be?"

"I'll put the computer to work on it. Some of them wouldn't have survived, of course."

"But we do have a phenomenon on our hands," Childermass said, with so much excitement he couldn't hold his fork. "Robin Sandza's psychic twin."

"When they were babies," Roth mused, "they may have been in touch telephatically. Each other's imaginary playmate."

"Even the most backward tribes, the most primitive cultures on earth must have welcomed the birth of *their* Robin Sandza. By now those children are well on their way to becoming the magicians, the prophets, the great healers of their tribes. But there's no place for kids like them in our great culture, because they're so superior to what we hold sacred. Now ain't that a kick in the head?"

"And history teaches that what a culture can't assimilate it destroys," Roth said moodily.

The rest of their breakfast came from the kitchen, but neither man even picked at the food.

"Once you have Gillian here," Childermass said, "we'll make arrangements to move her to Psi Faculty."

"But how do we—? Another 'suicide' without a body would be an unacceptable coincidence. By the time the Bellavers get through with us—"

"We'll stage an 'accident' this time. There'll be a body—decapitated, so no one will have the stomach to look too closely."

Roth sat back and took a deep breath. He looked unwell.

"That's heavy. Very heavy."

"I don't think you realize how serious my responsibilities are. Gillian Bellaver and Robin Sandza must be protected—we have to be protected from them. I report to a committee of five men, doctor. Five of the most powerful politicians on earth. Yet two of them want Robin Sandza destroyed, and the others are wavering. The Chief Executive is said to be "very concerned." They didn't know what real power was until they saw Robin at work. Ultimately we're all in the protection business—self-interest is the only constant in life, and murder is always preferred to impotence. I expect an attempt on Robin's life before long, probably from the Langley gang. Deep snow at Psi Faculty places a burden on our security. Darkness comes much too early these days."

"How can you hope to find a—a substitute for Gillian on short notice?"

"We have the body already. It's being flown in from Copenhagen. The girl died two days ago of a cleanly broken neck. An amazing physical resemblence to Gillian. Fortunately they grow those willowy ones by the acre in Scandinavia. The victim was quick-frozen within minutes of her death. We paid twenty-five thousand dollars for her in a natural state. This one was easy; it took us over a week to locate a ringer for Peter Sandza."

"Oh. What did you need him for?"

"I'm sure that's something you'd rather not know."

"Of course! I meant—I'm just curious about Sandza. Wondered if you picked up his trail again."

Childermass smiled meanly.

"Doctor, you're scared shitless."

Roth flushed with shame.

"He's a—a vicious and unprincipled man. He came within a whisker of killing me."

"We're grateful you're in one piece. But seriously, I don't

think he would have killed you. Out of desperation he may resort to you again."

"W-why?"

"He assaulted you once, looking for the truth, but even though the beating was severe it was a hasty job by Peter's standards. At leisure Peter is much more effective. He's a skilled torturer."

Roth didn't say anything. He rubbed his sweating palms on his trousers.

"I thought you told me—you were beefing up the security force around here."

"Oh, we are. But short of placing you in solitary confinement there's no way to guarantee your safety."

Childermass let that soak in, like a solution of chilled acid. Then he hunched his shoulders apologetically.

"These days, Doc, we're spread kind of thin. We need to maintain a twenty-four hour watch on Sutton Mews in case Peter decides on another move in the girl's direction. And we're making every effort to uncover his confederate at Paragon."

Roth was astounded. "Confederate? Someone who works *here?*"

"Oh, he must have penetrated Paragon months ago. I would say, knowing Peter, that it has to be a woman. He may have doubled one of our own dollies. That would be like him. But we're painstakingly checking and rechecking everyone. I've had to call agents out of retirement to do this job. Your *bauernfrühstück* is getting cold, doctor. Dig in."

"I'm trying to drop a little weight," Roth muttered. He poured coffee instead, despite a queasy stomach. "When I get through to the Bellavers, what—how much do you think I should tell them about Gillian?"

"That depends on what they're ready to believe," Childermass said. "By now they should be eager for the advent of a miracle worker named Irving Roth."

Fourteen

"Mrs. Bellaver? This's Jake, up here in Bedford?"

"Oh, yes, Jake, how are you?"

"Fine, Mrs. Bellaver, and we all want to thank you and the mister for that wonderful Christmas bonus. Although that isn't the real reason why I called. Your secretary said maybe I shouldn't bother you, but I just got to thinking, and the more I thought about it the less sense——"

"Something wrong there, Jake? The horses——"

"The horses are all in excellent condition, ma'am. Ambrosia and Fan-Fan are both in foal, and that yearling we picked up at auction last July is proving out to be——"

"You said something didn't make much sense to you, Jake."

"Well, yes, that's right, Mrs. Bellaver. I know Gillian's been bad sick and all, in fact she just got out of the hospital."

"Yes, she did."

"Knowing how sick she was I couldn't believe it when Jody Pete—that's my middle boy, had all that back trouble when he fell out of the loft—Jody said he seen her down by the stables, it must have been a few minutes before seven o'clock this morning."

"Jody saw—? Well, that . . . Jake, he must be mistaken. Gillian's right here at home. She's feeling much better but she's still weak, she hardly leaves her room."

"I know you think this is—crazy, and a terrible waste of your time, but Jody, he's about Gillian's age, had this crush on her long as any of us can remember, he swears to me, Daddy, I know it was her, it was Gillian. Gillian talked to him, he says. Kept asking where Pony was. She was just real tearful about not seeing Pony there at the stables."

"Pony—? You mean that cute little Shetland we bought her for her fourth birthday?"

"Yes, ma'am. Came down with a blood infection if you'll remember, I don't expect Gillian had him more than eight, nine months altogether. That's what struck me as bein' so strange; if it was some other girl, looked like Gillian, tried to fool Jody, how would she've known about Pony?"

"You've got me, Jake, but Gillian is upstairs in her room right this moment. It's a hundred miles round-trip to Bedford. What time is it now, nine-thirty? Even if she could have left the house without any of us being aware of it——"

"Yes, you're right, obviously this has got to be some kind of uncanny coincidence. What I thought, if there was a chance she was up here, just getting over being so sick and all, then you'd want to know about it."

"Just a moment please, Jake, did Jody mention what she— what this girl was wearing?"

"Hold the line and let me check." Katharine put the receiver down momentarily and tuned her mind to the distant, eerie flutings from Gillian's room. Miss Chowenhill looked inquiringly across the ground-floor office at Katharine, who smiled noncommittally and put the receiver to her ear as Jake came back on.

"Mrs. Bellaver, he says blue jeans with patches and tape on 'em, those rough-out Frye boots like they all wear, a regular Navy-style pea jacket, and a blue-and-white knit cap."

"I see. Well, I can only repeat that it's a mistake, a case of mistaken identity, but thank you for letting me know. And—if you should see this girl, try to find out a little more about her."

"I sure will."

"Jake—there's no chance Jody Pete dreamed this whole thing up?"

"Why, he couldn't even think of such a thing! I'd bet my life on that."

Miss Chowenhill was on another line. She looked at Katharine again as Katharine hung up.

"The Zaire Delegation, his Excellency would like to postpone the interview until five o'clock, and make it his apartment at the Carlyle instead of the UN."

"Okay," Katharine said absently.

Katharine followed the sound of the flute to the second-floor bedroom, passing Rosalind, one of the day-workers, on the stairs.

"Sure would like to change those sheets in there," Ros grumbled.

"In just a few minutes."

Gillian's breakfast tray was on the floor outside the door. Katharine tried the doorknob; locked. She rapped a couple of times. Gillian continued to play her flute, the melody lost and sad and fundamentally haunting, a melancholy exercise which caused Katharine actual physical pain as she bent to examine the breakfast tray; she felt as if sharp splinters were lodged between each rib.

The fluting stopped. The door opened almost immediately and Gillian looked out at her mother, who was down on one knee.

"Oh, hi. What are you doing?"

"I wanted to see if you had anything to eat."

"While you're snooping around like that why don't you have a look in the toilet?"

Katharine stood, clenching both fists.

"I can't believe you said that!"

"I . . . I guess I shouldn't have, I'm sorry."

"And why is this door always locked? You've been very sick, you might need help in the middle of——"

"I don't lock the door!"

"It was locked just now and it's *always* locked, what do you have to hide in there, Gillian?"

Gillian flung the door wide open, crashing it against the wall.

"Ye, gods, come in, come in, if it's so important to you!"

She was wearing tattered shorts and a limp sweater out at one elbow. Her hair needed combing and had an odor. And she was much too thin. Gillian went back to the messy bed, clutching her flute. She lay face down with her feet in the air. There were some sordid-looking yellowish bruises high on the inside of her thighs.

"Gillian——"

"I'm not eating because my tongue is still sore. I did drink some milk, and that filled me up."

"Ros wanted to know if she could change the sheets and freshen up in here."

"Oh, okay." Gillian rose and started pulling everything off the bed. Katharine opened a louvered closet door. Gillian stopped what she was doing and stared at her.

"You used to have a blue-and-white knit cap."

"Still do, it's there on the shelf, I think."

"Do you wear your Navy pea jacket?"

"Of course, all the time, you've seen me wear it a hundred times."

"And your Frye boots?"

"When I go riding in cold weather, otherwise I ride barefoot. Mother, what the hell's—I mean, really, I don't understand—"

"I imagine Jody Pete has seen you wearing all those things."

"Jody Pete? Up at the farm? Sure. I suppose so. Why'd you bring *him* up?"

"He . . . he was certain he saw you at the farm this morning. About seven o'clock."

Gillian laughed; she was startlingly loud.

"Bananas," she said, shaking her head. "Real-ly bananas."

"He's not what you'd call an imaginative kid. I've always found him very sober-sided and——"

"I *know* Jody Pete, you don't have to tell me about him. Why would he make up a crazy story like that?"

Katharine smiled. "I really don't know. He daydreams about you, I guess."

"Oh, sure."

"You're feeling better, aren't you, Gillian?"

"I am. But I get tired easy. I sleep a lot."

Gillian stood very still and tall, hands at her sides, staring at a point a little to the side of Katharine's left shoulder. Her air of secrecy and self-enforced wretched solitude was oppressive.

"Try not to lock me out? Can't tell you how that worries me."

"Mother, there has to be something *wrong* with the goddamn lock!"

"Then just don't close the door, Gil."

"I like a little privacy. A *little.* This much," Gillian said, holding thumb and forefinger half an inch apart. She was sullen and twitchy. Katharine held out a hand to her. Gillian backed off.

"Don't. I asked you not to."

". . . Why can't I touch you any more, Gil? Why are you being so hostile, have I——"

"*Pri*-vacy, mother. Just allow me a little privacy please! I am not your cuddly little babykins any more, I don't want to be— fondled, and if you find anything hostile in that I am sorry, very truly sorry."

Gillian plugged a cartridge into her eight-track deck and turned the volume loud, loud, loud. She stood with arms folded, her back to her mother, braced against the impact of the sound. Katharine sensed that she was crying. She gathered up the bedsheets and went out. There was nothing of Gillian in those sheets; they smelled of dried night sweats and dribbled urine and raunch, as if a family of weasels had denned in them. But the sheets had been on the bed for only two days. Katharine shuddered and threw the soiled bedding down where Rosalind would find it when she came back upstairs.

As she did so she saw Gillian's door close; she imagined, despite the Jaggerish rock-fury pounding at the stout walls, that she also heard the lock click into place.

Wednesday, January 5
10:56 A.M.

"Hello, Mrs. Bellaver, hold the line for Dr. Hansel, please."

"Hello, Katharine!"

"Well, Park, I guess you wouldn't be this cheerful if it was cancer."

"Kath, everything came back from the lab totally negative. I will double check it, as I usually do, but for the moment I can say that you have nothing to worry about."

"Except, possibly, getting pregnant. At a rather advanced age for childbearing."

"It's not unheard of for women to go on conceiving into their early fifties."

"But is *is* unusual to go through menopause and then, two years later, to start menstruating again. Heavier than when I was a kid, and I flowed like Niagara until after I had Gillian."

"Yes, I know. Cramps bothering you?"

"No, I just feel sort of draggy and really depressed at times. I went through change of life, I made up my mind, well, that part of life is over, but I'm no less a woman: better than ever, goddammit. And now here I am, puberty all over again."

"Kath, I can't tell you *why* it happened, at this point I only know there's no abnormality involved, thank the good Lord. You have a healthy uterus and two functioning ovaries after, uh . . . uh . . . this little hiatus. You did stop rather early, you know, forty-three and a half, these days the norm is closer to fifty years."

"Is that a clue? I've heard of false pregnancy, but false menopause?"

"Yes. The subjective symptoms of menopause can be totally misleading. I'll want to see you again next week. Meanwhile take your iron tablets and have that prescription for a new diaphragm filled, unless of course——"

"OH, NO; no sir, no way!"

11:15 A.M.

"Hello, Larue? Katharine Bellaver."

"Mrs. Bellaver! Great to hear from you!"

"How did everything go in Boston?"

"Oh, those lousy rotten critics! Mrs. Bellaver, it's a beautiful show, but it hasn't happened yet, it just needs more time to *happen.* There was so much love in the company, and now there's so much bitterness. Neil Simon's coming to see it! I'll bet he'll have a lot of good ideas. If the producers would just get off my father's back and stop acting so morbid——"

"I know how brutal it can be out-of-town. Once when I was ready to throw in the crying towel George Abbott told me, 'You take your baby steps in Boston; you find your legs in Philly, and you come home wearing seven-league boots.' "

"I'm praying *so hard* . . . Gillian's all right, isn't she?"

"Much . . . better, and she misses you."

"Maybe I could come over?"

"Well, let's give her another day to rest. What I was thinking, Friday night for supper, around six? Then Seamus will drive the two of you to Lincoln Center for the Philharmonic——"

"Sounds fabulous . . . Mrs. Bellaver, Gil must be about to go, you know, really batshit by now, all that time in the hospital and then cooped up at home, do you think it would be okay if she spent the night at my place after the concert? I'd really love the company. There's nobody here now but Bjorn and Aase, and, you know, they say like two words a week in English."

"I'm sure it would be a welcome change of pace for her; yes, it's a lovely idea, thank you, Larue."

I I :35 A.M.

For once the door wasn't locked, or even closed all the way. Inside the bedroom Gillian sat with her feet up on a window seat, playing the flute.

"Hey, Gil."

Gillian looked around at Katharine without taking the flute from her lips.

"I talked to Larue a little while ago."

"Oh, she's back?"

"I invited her for dinner Friday night."

"I'd love to see her," Gillian said after a pause, and picked up the flute again, turning her face to the sunny window.

"Also she thought you might like to spend the night with her after, say, the concert at Fisher Hall."

Gillian thought about this arrangement and nodded. She blew a few wrong notes, frowned, put the flute down and stood up.

"I think I'll take a nap."

"A nap? You slept til——"

"I explained to you that I get tired easily, mother. Can I help that?"

"No. I wonder if you shouldn't see the doctor. I could make an appointment for later this——"

"No, mother. I'm okay. I'm eating better, aren't I? I'm not feverish."

"I still don't think you're in shape to go back to school on Monday."

"Well, then, I'll stay home for a few more days, I have things to do anyway."

"Tootle your flute? Twiddle your toes?"

"Ugly, mother. Very ugly."

"I do . . . get . . . exasperated."

"*You* came up *here*," Gillian said reasonably, and pointed to the door. "Could you close that on your way out?"

"It might get mysteriously locked again."

"It might. Better if it's locked when I'm sleeping."

"Why?"

Gillian clapped her hands together in a mock-prayerful attitude and cast her eyes heavenward, but she answered the question.

"Things could happen, otherwise."

"I'm not sure what to make of that."

"I just don't like the idea of—being looked in on while I'm lying here. You might get the wrong idea. You might try to wake me up. Maybe I wouldn't wake up right away, and you'd—panic. Try to move me, or something. To a hospital. That would be very bad for me, mother."

Katharine listened to her heartbeats becoming loud and violent as slammed doors.

"That sounds ominous."

"Oh, don't make a big thing of it," Gillian said softly. She smiled, a rare smile these days, not wanting Katharine to be offended. "I'm getting to be very grown up. I can take care of myself if you give me half the chance."

"What are we talking about here?"

Gillian's eyes were half closed. "Things . . . well beyond your understanding."

"I will always make an effort . . . to try to understand . . . anything you may want to tell me."

For just a moment Gillian looked at Katharine almost longingly, as if she wanted to embrace her.

"That's fair enough, mother. Now—if you don't mind?"

Katharine was on her way upstairs when the rock music began. She knew it was no use going back to hammer on the door and protest. The door would be locked, and Gillian oblivious. She felt a cramp coming on, hurried to her own bathroom and took the prescribed medicine. She batted back the tears stinging her eyes. Then, for the third time that day, she changed the large pad she was forced to wear to accommodate a heavy menstrual flow.

When she finally reached the atelier, Katharine called Miss Chowenhill and canceled everything on her calendar for the remainder of the week.

3:24 P.M.

Today the music was endless, deliberately and provokingly endless. Even behind a fat cushion of Valium Katharine felt ravaged.

"Avery, we need to get into Gillian's room."

He replaced the musty book he'd been consulting and looked down at her in some surprise from the third step of the library ladder.

"Katharine? I didn't hear you come in."

"She must have made her own tapes, two-hour tapes. Otherwise it couldn't just keep playing and playing without a pause."

"Don't you feel well? You look———"

"I'm doped, loaded to the gills, isn't that obvious? But it does no good. I can still feel, a little bit, and *hear*, and, oh my God, if I could just turn off my mind for a little while what a blessing. How can you stand it? Don't you realize something's going on, she———"

"The music, yes. It is too loud. Mrs. Busk says they've complained from across the street."

"Damn, Avery, pay attention to what I'm trying to tell you! Gillian's in danger of———"

"Danger?"

"Of, I don't know what, but something is seriously wrong with her! Something is wrong in that *room*, she as much as told me so, we've got to get in."

"The door's locked?"

"Of course!"

"But Mrs. Busk has———"

"Mrs. Busk had a spare key; it's missing from her ring."

"You knocked?"

"Five times in the last hour. *Pounded.* She isn't—it's as if she —nobody sleeps that heavily." Katharine gently massaged the sore skin of her constricted temples.

"I'll call a locksmith," Avery said, searching for the phone book.

"No! I don't think there's time. Avery, you're clever with

watch repairs and things like that, it's a fairly simple privacy lock with a keyhole on this side——"

He needed ten minutes to find his case of jeweler's tools, three minutes to jimmy a good lock.

Gillian's door swung open a few inches. The room was dark for mid-afternoon of a brilliant day. The rock music, close up, jarred Katharine to the roots of her teeth. She went in first and glanced at Gillian lying heavily across her bed, a sheet half covering her. She was unfamiliar with Gillian's stereo equipment and it took her a few seconds to turn off the tape. Even then the silent room seethed with halucinatory sound.

Avery was standing near Gillian, looking down at her.

"Katharine, just a little light, please, from the windows?"

Katharine parted the drapes a hand's breadth and hurried to the bed.

What she saw of Gillian stunned her: whitish moons of sclerota visible beneath the taut eyelids, lips waxen, limbs stiffened, her skin very pale. And no breath, no breath at all . . .

"Gillian!"

Avery caught her hand an inch from Gillian's motionless breast.

"No, don't touch her," he said, calmly enough, but the pressure of his fingers caused Katharine to rise on her toes in pain.

"She's——"

"Don't!" he said, more sharply, taking hold of Katharine's other hand as well. "Gillian isn't dead. Nor is she . . . there, right now."

"What the hell are you talking about, old man? Look, look at her!"

"The body is all right. Her respiration and pulse rate have slowed way down and the body temperature has dropped, probably to about twenty-four degrees centigrade. She's in a state of, I believe it's called tonic immobility." Avery looked over his shoulder at the stereo equipment, seeming unaware of Katharine's efforts to wrest herself free. "Oh, yes. Might have expected it. She required the enormous energy of the music. These ceremonies vary little in form, whether among the Ashanti, the Bavenda, the Hopi. The ritualist first utilizes the energy of sound; then he intones a name of power. Finally he performs a circumambulation, a ritual movement, until the exercise results in a deep trance. Much easier then for the novice to separate from the physical body. Of course those who are adepts, or specially skilled at astral projection, need no extraordinary preparations in order to separate."

He blinked and looked at Katharine again, surprised to see that he was holding her tightly enough to break both wrists, and that she was having hysterics, a drug-muffled, hum-drum and giggly version accompanied by bleatings and sudden violent snaps and twists of the body.

Fortunately Avery was a big man and well conditioned from his sojourns among primitive peoples. Still holding fast to his wife, he trotted her out of Gillian's room, up the stairs to his own bedroom and into the bath, where he thrust her under a frigid needle shower. He held her there until she regained her senses. For good measure he popped a capsule of smelling salts under her nose.

"That's enough!"

"The water is bloodied, Katharine, are you hurt?"

"I'm just h-having my p-period."

"After two years of menopause?"

"Let me go, I have to get back to Gillian!"

"But I can't let you disturb . . . the body. That's always taboo. Katharine, listen to me? Every living thing in this sphere has its shade, or doppelganger, or whatever you want to call it. I believe the popular term is "astral body." It's connected, probably by way of the pineal gland, to the material body, but it has the freedom to travel in other planes, other spheres. That's what Gillian is doing now. A great many people, when they think they've had an especially vivid dream, actually were experiencing——"

"Astral projection is occult bullshit dreamed up by so-called intellectuals who need something to sell the crazies, the gullible old ladies who can't get it on with their ouija boards any more."

"I don't think so, and I've been around a bit more than you have. The aborigines of central Australia, who have no written language and live in conditions of grueling hardship, have an astonishingly complete metapsychical system that rivals the insight of the most advanced mystic. Notions of time, ritual and protocosmic archetypes are molded into an elaborate mythos which they call *alcheringa,* which means past-presentness, or "dream-time." Life doesn't begin and end with the material body. Life is thought, and therefore timeless. By *thinking* it we've created this world, a great grinding machine in which we are all caught up; but as Rimbaud said, 'real life is elsewhere.' "

"He must have b-been crocked on poppies at the time," Katharine sneered, and she hunched down inside the big towel Avery had wrapped her in. "I don't know or care about your theories. I want my Gilly—I want my daughter back."

"She'll be back."

Avery's insistence that Gillian was not with them in the house brought on a fresh spasm like dry heaves.

"Yesterday—Jake called. Some nonsense about Jody Pete seeing Gillian at the stables up there when I know good and well she was *here*. That scared me, though, and then Gillian—acting so weird all of a sudden. We never had a locked door between us, never."

"It's quite possible that he saw, not Gillian, but her——"

"Ghost?"

"No, ghosts are seen only after the body dies. It would have been a wraith—but as real, as substantial to Jody Pete's eyes as you and I are to each other."

"But she spoke to him!"

"That *is* unusual. But not unprecedented."

"I don't believe any of this! She's sick, some sort of relapse, we have to get her back to the hospital!"

"Katharine, I don't know what brought on Gillian's spell of wandering, where she goes, what she's looking for. I do know it would be disastrous if we move her body. It would be unimaginable hell for her to return and not be able to find it."

"My God. I truly believe—you've spent too much time with your headhunters and blood-drinking savages. You're obsessed with their addlepated superstitions!" She struggled up from her seat but Avery calmly stepped between her and the door. Katharine shook with outrage.

"My daughter is dying and you——"

"No, Katharine."

"Dying!"

"No."

She hit him viciously in the face. It hurt, but he didn't budge. "Don't, Katharine."

Avery had made fists. Katharine was shocked. She realized then he would knock her down, restrain her forcibly if she tried to shove her way past him. *Insanity.* He was the least rebellious of men, always graceful when conceding. Katharine tried to think of the razor words that would humble him, remove his liver and dim his lights, reestablish her preeminence in the relationship. But the pecking order she'd always taken for granted had been impressively annulled not by Avery's willingness to do violence but by his conviction that he *must* do it for her, for Gillian: for the two women in the world he loved.

"Please, please, Avery, let me go." Her teeth chattered; she wept dispiritedly.

He began to peel away the sodden towel.

"Get you out of these wet things. Then I want you to lie down in my bed. Rest. I'll look after Gillian. Nothing will happen. It was a shock coming across her like that. But she needs to be alone, for a while. Try to understand, Katharine."

Katharine protested fitfully, but she was a rubbery lump in her husband's hands. Thirty seconds after he put her in his bed her eyes closed. Thirty seconds after that she was asleep on her side, arms wrapped around a pillow.

Avery went downstairs to Gillian's room. He remembered having partly closed the door on his way out with Katharine. Now it was completely closed.

And locked.

For the first time he felt deeply concerned: the skin of his forearms and the back of his neck reacted, it was like the hairs-on-end, sizzling warning that comes just before lightning strikes. He put his ear to the door to try to hear Gillian. The room inside was breathlessly still. He doubted that Gillian had returned, reentered the body, gotten up to lock her door.

Someone, then, or something, was ensuring her privacy. For good or for evil, he couldn't say which.

9:52 P.M.

Avery was nodding before the fire in his library, books at his feet, more in his lap, when a slight shift of attitude allowed one of the volumes he was holding to fall to the floor. He woke up with a leaden lifting of his head, yawned until his jaws popped, stared at the flames.

He felt watched. He looked back over one shoulder.

Gillian was standing in the doorway, shirttail hanging frayed, legs bare. She was drinking from a quart container of milk.

"Hello, Gillian."

"Daddy." She ambled toward him and flopped on the carpet with her back to the fire, crossed her legs, finished drinking. "Um. Nothing tastes good to me any more but cold milk. My second quart today."

"Highly nourishing."

"But constipating. What are you reading?" Gillian picked up the book that had dropped, losing some of its pages. "Demonic possession? The pages are like dried blades of grass. Must be two hundred years old."

Avery studied her.

"The facts, such as they are, never seem to change."

Gillian wrinkled her nose to indicate disinterest and put *Demonic Magick and Pacts* aside.

"Gillian, I think it's only fair to tell you that I was in your room late this afternoon."

She leaned forward, arms crossed on her knees.

"You found a key?"

"I picked the lock."

"Mother with you?"

"Yes."

Gillian laughed, but she wasn't in a particularly rosy humor.

"Her idea, then. Was she very, very sorry?"

"I expect she'll recover. Katharine has a remarkable resiliency."

"What did you tell her?"

"The truth of your situation, as I saw it."

Gillian glanced at the work on demonology.

"The truth isn't in there, Daddy. It's a—different sort of thing altogether."

"Will you explain?"

She was silent for so long Avery thought she intended to ignore him. Then she stretched out at his feet, gazed unwinkingly at the fire.

"Something went wrong with me in the hospital," she said. "The high fever might have caused it. Skipper says some of us Come Through the hard way, after an accident, or a severe shock of some kind, But he didn't have to Come Through, he could always Visit, he didn't fall out for a while, like I did. When I was three and a half, four years old, I began to lose my . . . Visiting privileges, and I lost track of Skipper. Now I have to learn to Visit all over again. It's like learning to swim in heavy surf. Scary sometimes. There are things—not in this world but just outside it, like shadows on a window, oh God!—but Visiting gets a little easier every time I try it."

"Who is Skipper?"

"I had a puppet by that name which sort of looked like him; for a while after he was born he hated *Robin*, he thought it was a dumb girl's name."

"Robin, or perhaps—Robbie?"

"Sometimes I called him Robbie." Gillian was delighted. "Do you remember?"

"It wasn't so long ago. There was always a place at your tea parties for Robbie. We had to be very careful where we walked so we wouldn't accidentally step on him. Now Robbie has—come back, has he?"

"I know what you think. I am not nuts! I was one of *twins*, Dad. The other one died in the womb before delivery, so Robin and I couldn't be together like we planned. But he is alive, and real, I swear it! And he's the only one who can help me." Gillian sat up shaking her head. "I'll do what he wants," she said quietly and desperately. "Whatever he wants, if he'll only tell me how to—control myself. He can do incredible things, turn it on and off at will. . . ."

"Gilly, where's Robin now?"

"In the flesh? I don't know. He just Visits when he has the time and feels like it. And sometimes he talks to me, from a long way off. Tells me to meet him in one of the places where we used to play."

"Like the stables at the Bedford farm?"

"That was one of our favorite places. I waited and waited, but no Robin. It isn't funny, we're not playing hide-and-seek any more. He can be mean sometimes! I love him, but he's really changed. Maybe he can't help himself. I think something really bad is happening to him. No, he wouldn't hurt me, but he could do something really stupid, like have me wait for him in a place where I can't defend myself; I could get in such horrible trouble I might not ever make it back all the way."

Gillian got up, one hand casually worked into her long hair, and took a meditative turn around the library.

"Why do you need his help?" Avery asked. "What is it you're so afraid of, Gillian?" A few moments later he said again, softly: "Gillian?"

"Oh, I'm sorry! I thought I heard——"

"Is Robin here?"

Her jaw muscles were knotted. "No."

Gillian came over and sat on a padded arm of her father's big chair. She was careful not to touch any part of his body with her own. She made a couple of torturous false starts before she was able to continue in a low, tired voice.

"Have you heard about a woman named McCurdy?"

"I don't think so."

"They hushed it up, then. She was on my floor of the hospital. A little hard on the nerves, but she—meant well, actually. She'd had surgery. Something to do with her legs. The night before I was supposed to come home I was desperately bored, almost berserk. Because I didn't have anything else to do I went down the hall to Mrs. McCurdy's room. That I remember pretty well; it was stuffy hot in there, she had a vaporizer going. I wanted to turn and walk right out, but she was awake and heard me. She asked me to sit on the bed and keep her company. I must have held her hand; yes, I'm sure I did, it happened while I was holding on to her. Maybe it's called a "vision." For me it's like looking at part of a movie. Now I don't remember what it was all about, but I still feel how badly *hurt* she was after so many years. She never forgave her father, never. I hated him too. It poured out of me and into Mrs. McCurdy. The hating. That's when she began to bleed. To death, to death, to *death*. God damn me. I killed her."

Gillian's hands fumbled helplessly for the solace she couldn't seek from him; her head was low. Avery wanted to touch the tender exposed nape of her neck, but a powerful instinct weighted his hand.

"Gillian, she could accidentally have torn loose her sutures.

I know there has to be a sound medical explanation for what happened to Mrs. McCurdy; and I'll find out——"

"No. No other explanation. Robin says—it's us. But he doesn't think it's so tragic. He didn't seem to care when I told him about Mrs. McCurdy."

"Do you remember what happened to you after you left her room?"

"Yes. No. Part of it, I think. Faces. A priest. He seemed to know what I'd done. Blood all over me. He was kind. He helped me. Told me I should get away from there. I wanted to go with *him*, but he was in some kind of trouble. Said he'd come to see me. I'd like to talk to him, get it all straight."

"Gillian, a priest was shot and killed at the hospital, not long before Mrs. Busk found you sitting in the street."

She looked up, nerves pulled so tight she couldn't shed a tear.

"That's it, then, why he hasn't come."

"But I want so very much to help you. And I don't know how."

The water is bloodied, Katharine, are you hurt?

I'm just h-having my p-period.

After two years of menopause?

"Daddy?"

"Yes, Gillian?"

"I'd like to kiss you. A—a kiss couldn't do any harm."

Avery smiled gallantly. "I can't imagine that it would."

Eyes big with apprehension, she touched her lips precariously to his forehead.

"It's obvious how worried you are. Now I almost wish I hadn't told you. But I knew you'd make the effort to understand, you've seen some amazing things. That holy man in India who duplicates the miracles of Christ. Of course Robin can do the same. More. He doesn't really have a Messiah complex, though."

"Gillian, if you don't trust Robin, how can you believe what he tells you? Are you convinced he won't hurt you?"

"I never *said* I don't trust him. Sometimes I'm just a little afraid. He's always been reckless. He plays hard. He thinks he'll become more and more powerful, and that nothing can ever go wrong." She picked glumly at her underlip. "I do trust him," she said after a few moments. "But then what other choice do I have?"

"Another guide. If we could find one for you. Someone with

the wisdom and experience that Robin seems to lack."

"Okay. Maybe." Gillian was apprehensive again. "But I wouldn't want Robin to find out and be mad at me. Oh, that wouldn't be so good."

"I'll have to look up some people who may be difficult to find. We'll talk more about it in a day or two."

10:40 P.M.

Gillian shampooed her hair in the wash bowl while warm water filled the tub. The FM radio speaker in the bathroom was playing softly: Judy Collins, then a medley of Kristofferson hits, performed by the nonsinging Kris himself. She fluffed her hair with a towel, and avoided looking directly at herself in the mirror. She knew she had a bad color. There were too many bruises, and too many gawky ribs showing. She yearned for the terrace of the family getaway pad high above Acapulco bay, a terrace built to catch the sun all day long, and she had a taste for all those crisp and fattening Mexican specialties that came from Magdalena's kitchen. She was tired, just hurting tired from trying to please Robin on one plane or another. He had the stamina of a hunted fox and an endless fancy for rough initiation jokes.

When she dropped the towel from around her waist and turned to step into the tub she discovered, at the last possible moment, that the water was now scalding hot.

Gillian wanted to cry, scream, smash something, preferably Robin's freckled nose. He didn't show himself; maybe it was just too much trouble. But he was there. She choked down most, but not all of her resentment.

"I don't like what you did to my cat, either," she said, then held her head high and waited, gently rubbing a breast that had taken too much abuse lately.

Thursday, January 6
12:16 A.M.

Katharine was sighing and weeping in the dark; Avery heard her before he opened the door to his room. The room was quite cold, she had dropped the thermostat very low. The lamp he turned on shone directly in her face and she flinched as if shot, eyes closing in pain. Katharine was sitting in a padded rocking chair. She'd put on one of his robes; only the tips of her toes showed beneath the hem, and they were lined up in a tight little row.

"What is it?" Avery said, crossing the room to light another lamp. He glanced at the bed and saw where she'd been sleeping. He stared mindlessly.

"Oh, my dear," Avery said. "Oh, oh, my dear——"

"It stopped, finally. Used a big towel. Stopped it."

"Oh, my——"

"Don't, Avery. God knows couldn't b-b-b—bad as it looks. Big heartbeat. Slowing down now. I'm weak, that's all."

He came back to her.

"Could you dress yourself? Walk?"

"But I won't. No hospital. Staying here. Gillian—needs me. Don't call anybody. *I won't go.*"

"Gillian's all right, I talked to her only a couple of hours ago. I was thinking . . . just as far as Min's house tonight. Would you spend the night there?"

"Why?"

"At Min's I don't think you'll be in danger of—sudden hemorrhages like this one."

"And how do you know that?"

"Gillian claims that she can cause such bleeding by proximity. But if you remove yourself, even fifty yards from——"

"What sick nightmare have you dreamed up this time? Do you have my daughter believing she's a vampire?"

"You're not thinking clearly, Katharine; you've lost a great deal of—move to Min's, please, for the remainder of the night."

"No!"

"If you don't go, and right away, I'll call Parker Hansel. You know the course of action he will surely take."

"Where is Gillian now?" Katharine demanded.

"In her room."

"*All* of Gilly?" she said, with a dreadful smile.

"I can't be absolutely certain. The door has been locked again. A little while ago I was certain I heard—voices behind the door. I did talk to her this evening, in the library. There's so little I can tell you now. Gillian's problems seem to involve a rather unique case of possession. But the tragedy that is threatening each of us is beyond the scope of any nightmare. We will need all of our wits to survive; our strength. Bear this in mind: Gillian loves us. She means us no harm. May I pack some things for you, Katharine?"

She had begun to rock herself, self-absorbed as a child; her mouth shaped words which she kept to herself. There was a humming sound in her throat, and her eyes were busy, as if they were following the bouncing ball in an old one-reel sing-along, following tenaciously in the dark theatre of her mind, following even to oblivion.

Then, suddenly, her head snapped up: her long throat was taut with terror.

"*It's started again,*" Katharine said, and she broke into tears.

2:10 A.M.

In his deep seat in the library Avery faced the ashes of his fire. He was almost too weary to keep his eyes open.

There were several phone numbers scratched on the pad which he held in his lap; he'd been phoning for more than an hour, trying to track down two colleagues he thought might have the information he required. One, on a field trip, was completely out of reach. The other, Richardson, he'd located after awakening a considerable segment of academic London. But Richardson had provided a name, and a number to try in New York.

For several minutes now Avery had been holding the receiver

of the phone on his right shoulder, checking occasionally to be sure that the line was still open. He heard nothing but the sounds of his own cabinet clock. Time seemed to pass more quickly late at night when time alone claimed his attention: when he was feeling his years the seconds had a cruel velocity. But Katharine was safe, tucked away in his mother's bed next door on Sutton Mews. Min's elderly Scots houseman probably thought they'd had a violent quarrel. It didn't matter what he thought. As Avery had anticipated, the dangerous bleeding stopped almost as soon as Katharine left her own house. He hoped she was asleep now. Avery had instructed the houseman to look in often, but he was not to bother Katharine unless something seemed wrong. . . .

"Hello?" A sleepy, possibly irate man, whose help Avery desperately needed.

Avery stirred and took a deep breath and resumed with the telephone.

"I realize it's a very late hour," he said. "Thank you for taking my call."

Then he listened for a long time, making no comment, lines deepening in his forehead, until the man at the other end of the line ran out of breath.

Finally Avery had his chance to speak.

"Yes," he said, "that *is* quite a remarkable coincidence, Dr. Roth."

Fifteen

Friday, January 6

Hester's new friends, the Bundys, had decided on Vanilla
Creme for the bedroom and a lustier color for the living room,
called Fiesta Red, which went well with the heavy Mexican furniture and earthy artifacts they'd collected while living in semire-
tirement in Cuernevaca. Also, Meg swore, it was the exact shade
of the dress she'd worn for the climactic *zocalo* number in *Holiday
in Guadalajara,* their last film for MGM in 1952. Miles disagreed,
provoking a spirited dust-up, which Miles attempted to settle
Friday afternoon by borrowing a 16-millimeter print from a
collector and screening it on a dirty wall of their new living
room.

Hester enjoyed the gaudy and corny movie, which was slightly
older than she was. Jane Powell was adorable and Red Skelton
had some delicious business, like the taco eating contest with the
little Mex boy who turned out to be triplets. The dancing, by
petite Vera-Ellen and the Bundys, was spectacular, although the

back-lot sets didn't look much like the Guadalajara Hester had toured three summers ago.

Meg's disputed dress was almost, but not quite, the shade she recalled. Meg blamed deterioration of the negative and a bad print. Miles, aglow with gin-fired nostalgia, conceded peaceably, and they all got back to the decorating.

Hester had volunteered to paint the bathroom, not much of a chore for her: she was speedy and efficient. Meg tackled the living room in more leisurely fashion. Miles, for his part, moved furniture, stirred paint, drank more gin and ambled around in jeans and shoddy sneakers while he reminisced in hilarious fashion. Hester dropped her brush more than once in the throes of a giggling fit. The Bundys certainly had had a lot of fun during those last golden years of the old Hollywood, before TV and the bitterness and paranoia generated by the witch hunts all but destroyed the place.

At six o'clock Miles went out for Chinese food. Hester and Meg cleaned up, opened more windows to dilute the paint fumes and sprawled on cushions in the living room.

Meg was, had to be, in her middle fifties, the farmer's daughter gone silver-gray but still in robust good health and with a damn fine figure; there was just the nicest hint of earth mother about Meg. Miles was as dapper and California *recherché* as he looked in all the bygone flicks. They'd danced every day together, for the fun of it, they thought, while operating their modest dance-and-drama school in 'Vaca. Neither expected to appear professionally again, in movies or elsewhere. But a recent successful pastiche of glorious moments from the classic MGM musicals had featured them; suddenly they were in demand, sought by those promoters and packagers waxing fat off candyland camp. So the project they'd settled on was a funny-sentimental salute to the postwar film capital, scheduled to go into rehearsals in February. And here they were back in New York after a quarter of a century, loving every minute of their new adventure. Already they'd been to Roseland twice, just kicking up their heels.

"All the regulars, the old-timers, applauded," Meg said dreamily. "But it wasn't a rowdy scene, everyone crowding in, talking at once, trying to cop a feel or two. They stood back at the edge of the floor, politely and expectantly, as if we were royalty. Billy the bandleader announced that we would dance for them. Then—it was eerie—almost in one voice they requested a waltz. Imagine, a waltz! So we did that bit of introductory dialogue from *The Perfect Gentleman*, Miles and I meeting late at night in Waterloo Station. We'll have to run that one for you sometime, kiddo. We set the scene, you could almost *see* the billowing clouds of train smoke, and then we danced, and it was like falling in love all over again. Everyone at Roseland seemed to be caught up in this magical spell. I saw tears as we drifted past them; we heard them whispering, 'Welcome back,' and, 'We've missed you'—sentiments like that. Gee, did we have a swell time."

"What was Judy Garland *really* like?"

"You too? Truth is I didn't really know her, even though we were on the lot together for years. We made that one picture together, I think I had four or five scenes with Judy. What I remember most vividly about Judy is running across her absolutely naked in a dim corner of the stage behind some scenery. Oh, I don't mean *bare assed*, she had on this ponderous hoopskirt costume. I'm talking about the naked emotion she displayed, over a chocolate éclair someone had smuggled to her. You know she had a terrible problem with her weight, they just didn't allow her any goodies when she was working, which was practically nonstop. So here was Judes clutching—*fondling*—this enormous chocolate eclair, it must have been a foot long, but I couldn't tell for sure because one end of it was in her mouth: she was licking, sucking, all but ravishing it, I felt like some kind of voyeur just watching her.

"Judy almost choked on her sweet-treat when she saw me out of the corner of her eye. She stood there with that naughty thing melting and oozing in her two hands—even away from the lights it was plenty hot on the stage—and there was goo ear to ear. To add to her misery she began to cry. She didn't know me, and she was afraid I was one of the company spies who reported every move she made to the director or to Louis B. himself. Poor miserable kid! I told her I loved chocolate éclairs myself (although I never wanted to blow one), and then I helped her get her face in order because they were hollering for First Team. There was no place to hide the rest of the éclair, but she wasn't about to give it up. She wrapped it in a big hurry and shoved it at me and said in that inimitable voice, 'Here, I'll love you forever, just don't let anything happen to it.' "

"What did you do?"

"Well, I was wearing this working-girl's apron and had some storage space, I was able to stuff the éclair out of sight. I figured I wouldn't have to keep it more than a few minutes. I forgot I was in the background of the scene they'd been resetting the lights for. A second A.D. grabbed and hustled me into place, and there I stood, babes, for an hour and a half while Judy flubbed twenty-three takes in a row beneath those big arcs they used to simulate desert sunshine. Calamity. I could smell the éclair going bad right under my nose. As soon as the shot went in the can I got out of there, but Miss Garland was right behind me, drooling. Her dressing room was full of spies, so she dragged me to another hidey-hole and demanded her éclair. I wish you could have seen the look on her face when I reamed it out of the apron. She was *furious!* She stamped her foot and said over and over, 'Jesus Jumping Christ, look at it! What did you do to my éclair?' She wanted to lick the wrapping but I wouldn't let her. By then it was virulent enough to wipe out half of Culver City."

Miles came back staggering under a load of succulent Cantonese vittles, but after laying out the cartons he discovered he'd forgotten eggrolls. He was willing to trudge another ten blocks in the biting cold to redeem himself, but Hester had commercially packaged eggrolls in her freezer, and she ran down two flights to get them.

Hester had been having such a good time with Meg she hadn't watched the clock, and she was startled to see when she entered her kitchen that it was now close to seven. She grabbed the eggrolls, charged back upstairs, ran into the Bundys' flat, dropped the package where Meg would find it and ran out the door again.

"Phone call!" she blared. "Ten minutes! Start without me!"

Meg trailed her to the door. "Use *our* phone, you can eat and talk at the same——"

"Long distance!" Hester shouted back, and the apartment door slammed behind her. Meg shook her head and went back to the kitchen.

"I'll put the eggrolls in, would you close the other window in there, Miles? It's getting drafty."

"The place is shaping up," Miles observed, crossing the half painted living room. "Hester's been a lot of help, hasn't she?"

"Hester is a goddamn jewel," Meg said from the kitchen.

Miles put the window down but he didn't lower the blinds. He stood with his hands behind his back looking out until, below, he saw Hester hurrying down the front steps of the brownstone, getting into her parka. He looked at his watch.

"Hester's gone out to make her phone call," he observed.

"Uh-huh."

"That makes every night this week, at seven o'clock on the dot."

"Do you want a little moo goo gai pan, or a lot?"

"A lot."

"Tummy, tummy," Meg admonished.

"I'll work it off in bed," Miles advised her. In the kitchen doorway Meg clutched at her heart, miming terror. With a smile every bit as endearing as Fred Astaire's, Miles gave her the finger, then lowered the blind and closed the slats. After turning on another lamp he visited the bathroom. He returned to the table rubbing his hands together in anticipation of a feast.

"The loo looks terrific; how do you suppose she does it without leaving any brush marks?"

"Deft," Meg said. "Hester is deft."

"We'll have to do something for Hester," he said, sitting down.

"I know."

"What?"

"I'm giving it some thought," Meg said, pouring strong tea.

Peter had warned her to use only the public telephones on the street, but there was a scarcity of those in her immediate neighborhood; she had to run all the way to Thirty-Sixth and Lex. Hester arrived almost completely out of breath, her face scalded by cold. Her watch, which kept excellent time, told her it was already twenty-one seconds past the hour. She tore off a glove and pressed her dime into the slot and began poking the stainless steel buttons. When she had punched out the number she huddled up against the phone box, trying to keep her face out of the abrasive wind.

Hester let the phone ring nineteen times before she gave it up for the night.

By then she was sobbing. She had not seen Peter since shortly after 2 P.M. on New Year's Eve, when he left her alone on Long Island. All she knew about his subsequent problems she had inferred from a few paragraphs in the *Daily News:* a priest, obviously mistaken for Peter, shot and killed. It was a brief story, not followed up. A full week had passed, without a word or a sign from Peter himself. She wanted to scream at the unresponsive phone.

Alive? Dead? Where are you, Peter?

Tonight she didn't even get her dime back.

No longer in the mood for company but feeling the pressure of a social obligation, Hester walked back to her building between Second and First. When she rejoined the Bundys she was still falsely radiant from the cold, but even so they could tell Hester was more than a little heartsick. She was thankful that Meg and Miles had the class to respect her privacy and make no mention of her sadly altered mood.

While there was snow in the streets of New York City, the state of Virginia south of Charlottesville was enjoying an unusually balmy week.

From the Puma helicopter flying at four thousand feet, a soupy red sun could be seen as it set behind the Blue Ridge. Near the sun in the faded sky, but perhaps a thousand light years from our solar system, was an object bright as an evening star, an exploding nova.

Nick O'Hanna, one of the supergrades aboard the chopper, pointed it out to his chief. Byron Todfield looked up from the fresh file of intelligence grist he was studying, but he wasn't all that interested in something which was happening outside his sphere of operations. Another supergrade, the druidical Bose Venokur, was reading Mishima on the trip down to the Plantation; he quoted from *Spring Snow:* "History is a record of destruction. One must always make room for the next ephemeral crystal." Nobody paid any attention to him. One of the body-guards from Watchbird Section swore under his breath; he was losing at blackjack. The mighty helicopter flew on at a cruising speed of 165 miles per hour.

They reached the Plantation a little before six and the helicopter landed in the compound on the south bank of the James. The night sky was clear but already there was a haze over the fallow land, thickening to mist in the low-lying bends of the river. Around them as they hurried into waiting vehicles, lights burned like droplets of napalm. O'Hanna shivered momentarily, crisis-conscious. He didn't know much about what went on at the Plantation because it hadn't been his business to know. Still, he'd heard a few lurid stories.

The drive to the manse took a couple of minutes. It was a brick Colonial house with a veranda that overlooked the river valley. There were smaller outbuildings in the style of the main house, boxwood hedges that had been planted before the Revolution. A houseboy in knickers was at the door to take their coats.

Their host, a small man wearing mirror sunglasses, came down the wide curving staircase to greet them. His name was Marcus Woolwine. He was pleasant, even effusive, and though he shook hands well he bothered O'Hanna: but then Nick had never liked looking at a man and seeing little more than his own badly posed and eavesdropping reflection. Woolwine's assist-ant, by contrast, was a milk-fed slab of young farmer, cornshock hair and red cheeks, but O'Hanna didn't care for the set of his mouth, a lip that met his underlip sharp and slanted as the blade of a guillotine. O'Hanna felt uneasy again; no, he didn't like these men, and the implications of their power disturbed him.

"How's Peter?" O'Hanna asked.

Woolwine smiled. "Your friend is working out in the .gym."

"What?" O'Hanna said, amazed. "He was pretty sick when he——"

"Dangerously ill, I would say: dwelling far out on the ragged edge of nervous exhaustion. A temperature of a hundred and three. Spot of pneumonia in the left lung, no doubt from the ingested filth of the river. We also discovered a good-sized duodenal ulcer. But he's fit again——"

"After five days?"

"I've been called on to perform much more difficult feats of

rehabilitation in seventy-two hours or less," Woolwine replied
tartly. "The mind heals the body far more effectively than any
drug. Come see for yourself. Mr. Todfield, will you be speaking
to him at this time?"

"By all means," Todfield said.

They reached the outlying gym via an enclosed and heated
walkway. Peter, wearing a red sweat suit, was lifting weights. He
was assisted by a lovely blonde with intriguing ginger ale-and-
verdigris eyes. She was the sort of girl who could be sunny and
indomitable without triggering insulin shock. Peter lay on his
back on a bench doing leg lifts, twenty pounds on each leg. He
had worked up a healthy sweat. He had a good sunlamp tan
going, and seemed in a bonny frame of mind.

O'Hanna, Todfield and Venokur crossed the maple floor. The
blonde girl glanced at them, then touched Peter's shoulder. He
got up and flashed a smile at Nick O'Hanna, studied the other
men.

"Peter? Goddamn, if you don't look great!"

Peter shook the offered hand. "I've never felt better, Nick."

"I want you to meet my boss, Byron Todfield. And this is our
chief of Hothouse Section, Bose Venokur."

Peter shook hands all around. "Just get in?"

"A few minutes ago," Todfield said.

"I suppose Nick told you what's happened to me—and to my
son."

"The full story. Of course we've always known a great deal
about you, Peter. You're a resourceful and valuable man. I wish
we'd had you on *our* team. It's absolutely amazing how you've
survived Childermass's treachery, not to mention a full-scale
manhunt."

Peter looked at his friend O'Hanna.

"I might not have pulled through this time. But for Nick."

O'Hanna said, "We've wondered why you didn't come to me
sooner, Pete. I mean, opposite sides of the fence and all, but you
know I would've believed you."

"My old Navy buddy," Peter said with nostalgia. "But there's
an axiom they drill into us at MORG, from the very beginning.
You can't trust the FBI, or NSA. Above all you can't trust the
Langley gang. I was afraid you'd hear me out politely, then turn
me over to Childermass."

O'Hanna scowled. "Jesus! That madman. Not a chance."

"The important thing now is—" Peter turned to Todfield. "Do you think you can help me, sir?"

"You *bet*," Todfield replied vigorously. "But I have to say to you, Peter, that as of this moment we still don't know where Robin is. We'll keep trying to locate him. In the meantime— you'll have all the moral support and material help you could ask for."

Peter nodded soberly.

"Thank you. Thank you." He couldn't stop nodding then; his face became pinched-looking and his eyes were blurry. "Thank you. Because the important thing is, the thing is, I have to find my son. My son. I've got to. Find him. Find Robin. Find Robin." He turned to the wall and began hammering it with a fist. "Find Robin."

The girl stepped in protectively and put her hands on Peter's shoulders.

"Peter, don't," she said. She looked at the incredulous men. "He's a little tired," she explained.

Peter sobbed once, a wild gulping sound, and then he was motionless as the winsome girl slipped an arm around him. She cupped his raised fist with her free hand.

"Your friends will be having dinner now," she said softly. She addressed O'Hanna: "Is there anything else you'd like to say to Peter?"

O'Hanna swallowed bitterly.

"The boss is sticking around for a couple of days, Pete. We'll —we'll be talking to you."

As they walked away Peter turned: he seemed to have recovered totally from his frenzied agitation over his son. He was grinning.

"Hey, Nick."

Nick turned distractedly. "Ole buddy."

"How are they biting for you?"

"Oh—just fair, I guess."

"Keep at it," Peter advised him.

"Sure. You keep well, Pete."

"I've never felt better, Nick. Listen, we'll be out on the flats first thing in the morning."

"How about a dip now?" the girl said to Peter: her voice had acquired a seductive furriness. "The ocean's warm as spit this time of night; great for a long lazy swim."

They heard Peter laugh, deep in his throat, as they left the gym.

Outside Woolwine and his young assistant joined them. Woolwine was itching with self-satisfaction.

"Gentlemen?"

"Jesus," O'Hanna muttered, shaking his head. "To see him like this—you should have known him—that was always one hell of a *man*. Where does Peter think he is?"

"Fishing with you, in the Florida keys. The two of you left Falls Church on Sunday afternoon, flying down in your Cherokee to your lodge on Lower Matecumbe. You've been there ever since. It was useful to provide Peter with a continuous memory beginning moments before he collapsed on your living room carpet on New Year's night. So bear in mind when you talk to him that you're catching bonefish and boozing a little and soaking up sun, getting decently but not gaudily tanned—we don't want Peter calling attention to himself in the dead of winter when he's turned loose in New York again."

Venokur said thoughtfully, "For a robot he seems altogether too emotional."

"What a curious idea," Woolwine said, looking at him in mild surprise and then (as if he hadn't seriously observed Venokur before) with contempt. "I don't create robots. That's hackwork. Mr. Sandza is engaged in a life and death pursuit, a quest of epic proportions. He must find his son. Our primary aim is to strengthen his resolve, to make him even more single-minded and resourceful. We don't want to do anything to blunt the cutting edge of his high purpose; he mustn't lose a jot of animal cunning. His outburst seemed somewhat theatrical, I grant you, but you should remember that he is in a stage forty trance, and will remain at that deep level until we finish our implant counseling. Let us say, Wednesday of next week. By Wednesday I assure you he will be without flaw."

"You can do some amazing things here," Todfield said respectfully.

Woolwine chuckled, mollified.

"I think we can at that, sir."

The limousine carrying Dr. Irving Roth and his Paragon associate Dr. Maylun Chan We paused at the gates of Sutton Mews and was waved through as soon as the guard verified that it had the correct number of passengers.

"So this is Sutton Mews," Maylun said. She had the not-uncommon physical perfection of Oriental peoples: clean, spare, eyes like matched black pearls, she seemed too exactly made to have come from any womb. A small tooth-white scar on her forehead was a valuable flaw, a hint of fallibility. "I've seen these houses from the deck of the Circle Line. I always wanted to know who lived here, the lucky devils."

"Nothing but goddam Bellavers," Roth said. "The whole block."

"Not what you'd call a pretentious house. But oh, so charming."

"He's not a pretentious man."

To prove Roth's assertion Avery Bellaver met them at the door. He took their coats and hung them up, then escorted his guests to the library where Katharine was waiting.

Roth saw immediately that Katharine Bellaver was under a bone-breaking strain; she looked glazed by opiates. Nevertheless she was still a dazzler, and he smiled warmly at her.

Then Roth looked expectantly at his host.

"Will Gillian be joining us?"

"Gillian isn't here—she went to the Philharmonic, and she'll be staying overnight with a friend." When Roth didn't speak Avery said, "From my conversation with you I was under the impression that Gillian wasn't dangerous unless she came into contact with a—a potential bleeder."

Roth touched the bald spot on his head. It looked as vulnerable as a bit of underbelly. "But exposing her to a large crowd —I really wish you hadn't let her go."

Katharine spoke up. "I thought she needed—a touch of normalcy in her life. Good music, someone her own age to talk to." Her voice threatened to break, but she controlled it with a frowning self-hatred which he found clinically interesting. "I wanted to get her out of this house, and away from—him."

Roth had no idea who Katharine was referring to. "We can hope that it was a wise decision."

Katharine defended it. "You don't know what's been happening. *You* don't know what's going on."

"I know very little," Roth replied humbly. But he had guessed a hell of a lot. Maylun was setting up her Nagra tape recorder. "Do you have a recent picture of Gillian?" Avery produced a framed photograph from his desk. She looked very different from the girl Roth had seen for only a few seconds in the hospital corridor. She looked modest, intelligent, self-sustained. A heroic width of forehead, ravishing eyes, spacious smile. Roth was extravagant about her beauty and asked those questions that could only solicit answers flattering to parent and child alike. In this manner he began skillfully to pick at the lacings of the pitiably straitened Bellavers, setting them up for the difficult investigation that lay ahead.

It was past midnight when he finished with his questions. For three or four minutes longer no one spoke at all. Katharine sat absent-mindedly rearranging her abundant hair, pausing to cough dryly into a handkerchief. Avery's eyes were inflamed; he scraped at the bowl of his pipe with a sharpened kitchen match, a sound that got on everyone's nerves. Maylun rewound the tape she had made. Roth, who was stiff and sore from sitting so long, got up and stretched and then helped himself to the pitcher of Ind Coope bitter; he'd already put away three pints of one of the world's great ales, which Avery Bellaver had flown in by the barrel direct from the brewery in England. Roth envied him that touch of gracious living.

He faced the Bellavers as they sat side by side on a sofa.

"All you know of Skipper, or Robin, is what Gillian has told you. Neither of you has seen a manifestation."

Avery shook his head. Katharine shuddered.

"Seen—? No."

Roth smiled indulgently. "What is it, Mrs. Bellaver?"

She lowered her eyes.

"The night Gillian came home from the hospital she showed me a—puppet. Her Skipper puppet. It had red hair. It was a lascivious, grinning thing with a—a man-sized cock. Gillian claimed she'd always had Skipper. But I never saw it before."

"Where is the puppet now?"

"Wouldn't I like to know? It disappeared. An hour, two hours later, I went back to the marionette theatre. Not there. In its place was a mangled cat."

"A mangled cat," Roth echoed.

"Yes. No, not exactly what the word implies. But dead. Distorted. A cat *shape*. It had Sulky Sue's coloring, although it was difficult to tell—I had Patrick get rid of it."

She stared at Roth with pinpoint eyes.

"I'm not making this up," she said huskily. "Patrick saw it too."

"The cat," Roth said with a fixed marveling smile.

"Yes, the cat!"

"Then there most certainly was a cat," Roth conceded. "A hit-and-run victim, perhaps?"

"That's—just what I told myself. But—the puppet—"

"I think Gillian made you believe in Skipper for a little while. *She* believes, most passionately."

Avery said, "There is no Skipper? No Robin?"

Roth shook his head. "No, sir. As a child Gillian invented him to fill a need; obviously he took the place of the twin who died shortly before birth. Now, faced with a crisis, she's reinvented him, or perhaps a more adult version equipped with telemagical powers, to help her out. Nevertheless Robin S—Robin is a fantasy."

"Dr. Roth, I can't believe my daughter is mad."

"Of course she isn't! But the psychometric power she possesses is frighteningly real, and dangerous. Are you familiar with the short story about the man who went on a time-travel expedition, and changed the fate of the world by inadvertently stepping on a butterfly in some prehistoric epoch? When he returned to his own time he found that, because of his carelessness, it was now a grotesque, savagely distorted world with nothing beautiful in it any more. Gillian, as she flashes back and forth in time, is like our man who crushed the butterfly. Her very thoughts can significantly affect reality as we know it. She urgently needs professional help to cope with her power."

"*Can* you help her?" Katharine demanded.

"Yes. Try not to worry, Mrs. Bellaver."

Roth polished off the mug of Ind Coope. He felt persuasive and confident; things were going much better than he'd hoped. He had not missed the relief in their faces when he abruptly dismissed Robin as delusional. Words could be magic too, and his magic was potent tonight.

"I think it would be a very good idea," he said, "if we sent for Gillian now."

At mid-concert, between Brahms's *Tragic Overture* and the excerpts from Elgar's *Dream of Gerontius,* Gillian had felt unwell and needed to go to the lounge in a hurry. Larue, worried that she might faint, accompanied her, but Gillian took a tablet and her spell of nausea soon passed. Crowds, a little too much excitement. They strolled the lobby through *Gerontius* and except for a minor headache Gillian felt okay.

Larue suggested they skip the *Marosszek Dances* and go back to her place.

Gillian wanted to walk, and she argued that the cold air would pick her right up. It was about a half mile from Lincoln Center to Larue's building on Central Park South; Larue tried to discourage her. Gillian worked out a compromise: she would ask Seamus, the chauffeur they'd borrowed for the evening from her cousin Wade, to follow them in the copper-colored Rolls. But she was determined to start exercising, she hated having to stop midway on a longish flight of stairs to catch her breath.

"Do you think the show will make it?" Gillian asked during the course of their walk. She was referring to the musical Larue's father was trying to whip into shape in Boston.

"Just might."

"Either way he's out of a job, once it opens in New York."

"I know."

"Then where will you go?"

Larue sighed. "London, I think. A movie. My mother might be in it. We'd all be together for a while, that wouldn't be so bad."

"I'll miss you if you go."

"I'll miss you too. You could come visit. Do we have to talk about sad things?"

The bedroom Larue occupied in the duplex apartment overlooked Central Park from the twentieth floor. The moon was bright, and, as Gillian took off her clothes, she could see the white rectangle of skating-rink ice glistening through leafless trees.

Larue was downstairs making hot chocolate and warming cinnamon doughnuts. Gillian brushed her teeth and put on her
nightgown and gave her hair a few licks. Then she took a turn
around the room, which was grandly furnished in Louis XIV, a
style Larue hated. Everything in the apartment was rented, including the bath towels and the cutlery. Larue had brought only
clothes and a few personal things with her.

On one wall there was a blown-up photo of her late half
brother Michael. He was wearing a USC athletic jersey. He had
the long bones and grayhound look of a basketball player. His
hands were on his hips and his head was thrown back as he
laughed about something.

Larue came up and saw Gillian looking at the photo. She put
down the tray she was carrying, went silently into her dressing
room and came back fastening her own gown between her
breasts.

"From the time I was old enough to follow him around I
wanted to marry him," Larue said.

Gillian looked compassionately at her.

Larue's face squeezed up; she tensed all over. The spasm
passed in a few seconds.

"Sometimes I think my heart's going to stop beating," Larue
said matter-of-factly. "One of these days I'll think about how
beautiful he was and how much I loved him, and my heart will
stop and I'll die too." She sat down and poured chocolate for
them, taking great care not to spill any.

Gillian sat near her on a chaise and nibbled a doughnut.

"Anything good on TV?"

"Junk," Gillian said.

The French telephone rang and Larue answered. Her mother,
calling from Yugoslavia. The connection was poor. The conversation went on for a long time. Larue didn't say much, but when
she spoke she was obliged to use a great deal of volume. For the
most part she sat slumped with her eyes closed, the receiver of
the phone on one shoulder. Her fingers stealthily pressed and
smoothed her forearms, as if she were afraid her skin might be
crawling.

When she hung up Larue said, "They're six weeks over, with
another two weeks to go, and she has to report for another flick
in Spain in ten days. My mother goes from one picture to an-

other. She's tired and lonely and probably balling somebody she doesn't like very much. Basically my mother is a very good person, and she has an old-fashioned sense of sin. Nothing is discardable when it comes to human integrity, that sort of thing. I heard an actor say that in show business emotions are used as hard currency. Well, my mother spends too much. Most of us are like her, don't you think? On the other hand, my father is —too costly. He doesn't make friends, he creates dependents. Gets the job done, I suppose. Once in a great while someone like Mike happens. Totally giving. No predjudice, no fear." Larue looked at her brother's laughing face. "He paid for all the giving, though, all the demands. Do you read Frost? Frost said, 'Home is the place where, when you have to go there, they have to take you in.' Mike took everybody in. That was part of his karma."

"What was the other part?"

"For the grace to go on living he had to accomplish beautiful, difficult, dangerous things." She held her hands out, brought the spread swooping left hand slowly against the clenched right fist.

"Oh, Larue," Gillian said softly, sorry that the mother had called to further upset her.

Larue's hand flew gracefully once more; she watched it with a brooding eye.

"Isabella knew he was going to die. She tried to prepare me."

"Who's Isabella?"

"A witchy friend in Malibu. Just darling. Her entire family is witchy, going back to the seventeenth century."

"God, I never heard of such a thing!"

"Where've you been, Gil? Well, I suppose New York isn't a very big witching ground."

"You believe in witchcraft?"

"You don't understand. Along with dope it's the number one fact of life out there. If you're a girl and good-looking they come up to you on the street or the beaches, for God's sake, warlocks looking for recruits. The covens will fuck you over fast if you don't know how to protect yourself. Oh, it's creepy in southern Cal. Last year I met this guy at the Renaissance Faire. He had a thing going for me right away, but I was with friends, I wouldn't split with him. For a week after that I had big trouble.

Nightmares every night. I felt drawn to a certain occult shop I passed on the way to school. When I refused to go in I suffered terrible headaches. Isabella said I was under psychic attack. But she broke the spell."

"How?"

"I don't know; it's white magic, folk magic. She's under oath not to talk about it."

Gillian brushed doughnut crumbs from her lap into a napkin. She got up and went slowly to the windows and stared out for so long Larue became restless.

"Are you sick again?"

"No. Thinking."

"I guess you find it a little hard to believe. About the psychic attack. Those things go on all the time. Gil, I thought we had the sort of relationship where we could tell everything that was on our minds. Everything, no matter what."

Gillian turned and looked intently at her friend.

"We do."

"Because I've always been straight with you."

Gillian smiled and nodded. She looked again at the photo of Larue's beloved Michael. Then still smiling, she stretched out on the canopied bed.

"Larue?"

Larue came and lay down near her, chin in hands, eyes inquisitive.

"I'd like to tell you about Robin," Gillian said.

The telling took considerable time. Larue was fascinated, as Gillian had thought she might be. Larue asked sensible questions about all the aspects of the relationship that puzzled or intrigued her. At one point she sat up and, closing her eyes, stretched out her hand, trying to imagine the astral world just beyond her fingertips.

"What's happening there?" she said.

"Everything that's happening here, and more. It's a busy place."

"What do you look like? When you're there."

"Just the same. But I could look different if I wanted to; or if I were condemned to."

"How do you mean, condemned?"

"Evil doesn't stop with this world; it goes on. But where it exists in the astral, it exists visibly. You just can't hide your thoughts or emotions in the astral."

"And that's the first place we go? When we die?"

"Always."

Larue said excitedly, "Would Mike be there?"

"Well—he might be. But he was so young when he died. If he has a cycle to finish, part of the eighty-four–year cycle, then he'll be coming back soon."

"At times I've felt like he was still really close to me. Keeping an eye on me."

Larue suddenly put her arms around Gillian and hugged her tightly. Gillian went rigid with distress; then she struggled.

"Larue, don't."

"Don't be afraid—if anybody's going to be afraid it should be me. I had terrible nosebleeds when I was a little kid. I used to get so nauseated and dizzy I'd faint. I can't *stand* the sight of blood! But nothing's going to happen. You've got to get over this, Gil, being scared to touch or be touched."

They wrestled strenuously for a few moments, but Gillian had little stamina and Larue won easily. She lay her head on Gillian's damp breast and listened to the alarmed heartbeat.

"I'm all right," she said soothingly. "I'm all right. Nothing's going to happen. Don't be upset, Gil."

After a while Gillian relaxed and tenderly touched the back of Larue's head. They breathed together, ruddy and warm.

"You're crazy," Gil said. "I really love you. I've never had a friend like you. Now get up, you're breaking my ribs."

Both girls sat up smiling without pretense, secure in their poignant admiration for each other. Gillian leaned forward and with her tongue licked away a few crumbs of cinnamon and sugar from the side of Larue's mouth.

"Do you suppose you could get in touch with him?" Larue asked.

"You mean Mike? Oh, no, I don't think so. It would be like trying to find you down there in the subway. If I didn't know just where to look I could ride the trains forever and not see you."

"But what if he's close to me right now, just on the other side, like a few feet away?"

"I don't know," Gillian said doubtfully.

"If you could only talk to Mike for a little while. Find out how he is."

"Don't cry, Larue."

"I would never ask another f-favor of you as long as I live."

"I guess it isn't such a big thing to ask. I just don't know how lucky we'll be."

Gillian walked around and around and stopped in front of Michael's photograph.

There was a flare on the glass, and she couldn't see him well. She lifted the frame down from the wall. The flare persisted, but she was infected by his sense of fun, by the horseplay that had him laughing. Gillian laughed too until the reflected light, or, more accurately, the light that seemed to shine from the center of his body, hurt her eyes.

Blinking, tearing, she shook her head sharply.

"Gillian?"

"Awfully *bright* in here," Gillian complained, holding the frame with one hand, rubbing her wet eyes with the other. Then she broke up again because it was just too funny, the pillow fight on the long pole that no one seemed to win. If you smote your opponent too lustily then you couldn't keep your seat, and if you didn't keep your seat there was the guckiest mud bath she'd ever seen a few feet beneath the pole. . . .

"It's the overhead light," Larue said. She switched it off but the light in the glass continued to shine forth powerfully, like the sun, striking Gillian full in the eyes.

Speechless, transfixed, Gillian began to whirl around, holding the frame at arms' length.

"What's happening?" Larue asked in a shrill voice.

"Look out, look out," Gillian said, blinded, her feet going frantically faster, her mouth falling open from the strain. Suddenly the outstretched frame shattered against a bed post. Shards of glass flew.

Gillian stopped, teetered, and fell backwards onto the soft carpet.

As if from the bottom of a well she stared at a wafer of blue sky, the no-longer-painful orb of the distant sun. She heard and felt the wind, it flowed coolingly over her flushed face as she was gently lifted and floated free, no longer burdened by the twenty-five pounds of dacron sail above her, no longer earthbound. . . .

Am I in the right place? she thought, as she looked down at her skimming shadow on the rocky slope of the mountain. A little gust of wind shook her; the tubular frame of the glider trembled uneasily. She moved the control bar to the left and shifted her horizontal weight to the right, banked effortlessly. Then, below, she saw the others waiting for her in the high alpine meadow. As she floated gradually down to the landing place, throat clogged from the exhilaration of her longest flight yet, she dropped her feet and pushed out on the control bar, raising the nose of the sky sail.

Her forward motion stopped just as she touched down, landing into the wind as she'd been taught. Perfect. No awkward nose dive this time. A couple of the other kids ran up to help her get out of the harness. She had flown fifteen hundred feet in half a minute. She was sputtering with wonder and delight.

Taking off her helmet, she turned to look at Mike way up there on the peak, just beginning his run to lift-off. An unexpected gust of wind snarled her hair, riffled the sleeve of her nylon jacket. It was much stronger than the gust which had momentarily caused her trouble not long after she became airborne.

If the tricky cross winds continued they would have to call it quits for the day, and she badly wanted to fly one more time . . . but Mike was aloft now, soaring higher than she had dared go, his yellow sail almost transparent against the burning blue. Little salutory winks of sun from the brightwork of his harness, the visor of his helmet: he was as beautiful as the stars of God.

She cheered and waved her arms, but then Mike seemed tempted by his power, he went so high it looked as if he would never come down; she was afraid that in a final demonstration of his freedom he would choose to soar above the peaks themselves and disappear over the great rim of the earth.

Two minutes, three minutes. Then, reluctantly, Mike drifted down toward the meadow.

It was as if he'd run into a wall up there.

He stopped, crazily, and for a few disastrous moments his legs thrashed as the delta sail, caught by wind-shear, ripped and puffed like a yellow burst of smoke from a cannon. Mike tried

to regain control of the damaged kite but it turned, sadly crippled, toward the cliff rising steeply at one end of the meadow.
He spun like a scrap of paper in the air, then was taken helplessly
by another bad gust which pushed him farther down—and faster
—and oh, suddenly much too fast, plummeting then with only
pennants of sail left streaming above him: down he went five
hundred feet or more, striking the naked rock a blow that put
out the sun, put out her eyes, left her writhing in thick meadow
grass, breathless in the ringing dark——

Sickened by disaster, Gillian struggled up from the comforter
which Larue had thrown over her as she lay on the floor, lay—
how long? She didn't know. Her only point of orientation in the
darkened bedroom was the night light of the ringing phone.

"Larue?"

She might have been deeply asleep on the bed, Gillian
couldn't tell. She reached the telephone before it could ring
again.

"Larue, I'm very sorry to call at this hour, it's Avery Bellaver
and I must speak——"

"Dad?"

"Gillian, is that—I'm so happy to hear your voice, I—I was
afraid——"

"Afraid of what?"

"Never mind that now. Gillian, you'll have to come home
tonight after all. I'll be at the door in about twenty minutes."

"What? Why?"

"Please give Larue my apologies."

"Apol—? Daddy, I don't have any idea what you're——"

"We can discuss it when I see you."

Her father rang off without saying goodbye, something he did
only when supremely distracted. Gillian sat holding the receiver
of the telephone, too surprised to think very clearly. So untypi-
cal, what had got into him?

"Larue," she whispered, "are you awake?"

Nothing from Larue. Gillian fumbled for the pull chain of a
lamp and filled the room with golden light. Larue was not in the
bed.

Gillian rose, turned, caught sight of herself in a free-standing
mirror.

Big drops of blood drying in, turning to rust on the front of
the blue nightgown.

Frantically Gillian went to her knees and pawed at the comforter. She uncovered more bloodstains, as if Larue had hemorrhaged suddenly while bending over to cover her up.

And blood had spilled nearby on the velvet pile carpet, not in drops but in ropes, a slaughterhouse trail to the dressing room and beyond, to the closed bathroom door.

There, bloody handprints on the white wood. A considerable spill on the floor.

Screaming, Gillian threw her weight against the door. It yielded, but not enough. Gillian screamed and screamed and fell back in a daze as Bjorn, the Swedish houseman, came running in.

—Terrible nosebleeds when I was a kid. I used to get so nauseated and dizzy I'd—

"She's fainted in there! She's bleeding to death! Get her out, get her *out.*"

Bjorn set his shoulder to the door and moved it a stubborn inch at a time. Larue was lying inside on the floor, face up, blocking entry. She looked as if someone had taken an ax to her. Bjorn wedged his way into the doorspace. He tried to find a pulse. He stayed hunkered over Larue for a long time, two fingers against her throat.

His wife Aase came in, glanced at Gillian, looked over Bjorn's shoulder. Then Aase looked away and took several deep breaths. She turned back and grasped Bjorn's shoulder with a hard hand. She said his name sharply. She had to shake him to rouse him. He came up weeping. He wiped his fingers on his pajama top. Soon it was red as the flag. His wife closed the bathroom door. They both looked at Gillian.

"Get her out of there!"

The woman shook her head.

"What is the *matter* with you people? She's bleeding to death!"

"Dead already," Aase said.

She didn't take her eyes off Gillian, even as her husband broke down and sobbed. Gillian was curiously dry-eyed. But something happened in her eyes, some dire shift toward madness.

"That's—she—you—"

"I'm sorry; dead," the woman said.

Gillian made a gagging sound. "But—how much do you think I can stand?" she said reasonably. She was standing against one

wall of the dressing room, hands pressed flat against the paneling. Her skin tone changed first, to a deep rose shade shadowed
with blue. As she grew more and more rigid almost every muscle
stood out beneath the skin, sinew and vessel and many bones
were delineated against white wood. It was a freakish and rivet-
ing exhibition. "How much, how much?" Her teeth were bared.
Her eyes looked like polished bone. There was so much tension
in her throat it seem impossible she could go on breathing. Her
eyes went from the man to the woman. And back again. And
faster. They were filled with such violence, violence in the face
of the inexplicable and unendurable, that the woman turned
cold. Aase was afraid that Gillian would spring at them, with a
psychotic strength that would ultimately destroy her. But not
before she did Bjorn and herself considerable harm.

Aase pulled Bjorn gently by the arm—led her distraught husband past the crouching Gillian, who watched them with a savage interest but didn't move. The woman's heart was beating
violently. She avoided the bloody places on the carpet and sat
Bjorn down and grabbed the telephone, keeping a wary eye on
the dressing room as she dialed for help.

Inside, Gillian made another small, critical sound of suffering.
But nothing happened. Nothing changed.

Sixteen

At two-thirty in the afternoon the temperature at Psi Faculty was three degrees above zero. The sky was so blue and clear it hurt to look at it. But another storm was moving down out of Canada, moving fast. It was thirty-six hours away, and it threatened to be a big one. Already they'd had two blizzards since Christmas, two and a half additional feet of snow, drifts to seven feet. Snowplows were still at work on the back roads between the campus and frozen Lake Celeste.

A security caravan stopped in front of the administration building. Childermass, wearing a black astrakhan coat and hat, got out of the middle car. Gwyneth Charles, muffled to the bridge of her nose, waited for him on the steps. Her head was bent in contemplation, or weariness.

"Hello, kiddo," Childermass said.

He had last seen his niece a month ago. Now all he could see of her was eyes. In thirty days her eyes seemed to have aged at least ten years. They were slow to react; they reflected the blue daylight but held no certain light of their own. He touched her. She was shivering inside her greatcoat.

"You've been working too hard," Childermass said.

"Hell, yes." Her voice was raspy, as if she had a bad throat. "We all have."

"And how's the Boy Wonder?"

Gwyneth didn't answer him. She stared for frigid seconds, eyes narrowed as if she suspected irreverence; then she turned abruptly and went into the Gothic building.

Childermass followed with his bodyguard and caught up to Gwyn in a windowless conference room. Granny Sig was there, fussing over the complicated sixteen-track audio and the color videotape equipment. Childermass, who loathed deviates because they usually meant trouble in his business, nodded perfunctorily. Granny Sig beamed at him and shut down the lights as Gwyneth was taking off her coat.

Childermass sat in an armchair facing a wall of ten television screens, the largest of which was nearly four feet square. In the semidarkness Gwyn lit a cigarette. He didn't miss the trembling of her hands.

"We thought you ought to see a rerun of his New Year's Eve performance before you see Robin himself. We'll show you Robin on the center screen. Relevant data will play back on the surrounding screens, and we've included full audio as well."

Gwyn looked at Granny Sig and dropped into a chair a few feet from Childermass. Granny Sig's fingers played over the console, punching buttons and turning knobs. Tapes rolled; pictures appeared with superimposed dates.

Childermass recognized the town square of Bradbury, Maryland, and the mesh-enclosed stock car. He smiled, imagining the discomfort—and, perhaps, the terror—of the VIPs locked inside. He cherished the memory of how his rival Byron Todfield had looked seconds after puking on himself; too bad there wasn't a record of their conversation as they waited in the dusk for the thrill of their lives.

Then he shifted his attention to an exterior view of a geodesic dome on the campus of Psi Faculty, the "cold lab" in which Robin Sandza did his extraordinary work. The dome was silvery in the waning light of the last day of December. Because of the power of the electromagnetic field which he generated when he was working, and its gory effects on the susceptible, Robin had been removed at least three hundred yards from everyone.

And there he was, on the big screen: four views. A closeup, with his face partly obscured by billowing breath; left and right profile; a full shot of him sitting in his padded pedestal chair, surrounded by equipment. Superimposed on the screen was the Fahrenheit temperature in the cold lab, just one degree above zero. Below that a light-emitting diode clock was splitting seconds almost faster than the eye could follow. For protection against the cold and for ease in monitoring vital signs, Robin wore a space-flight suit without the goldfish-bowl helmet. Lighting in the dome was subdued. On one of the sound tracks Childermass could hear the boy breathing, and the voices of technicians became audible.

—*Pulse 92, still dropping* . . .

—*Disturbance of the magnetic field during the PK trial was of a stochastical character with a parametrical resonance on a frequency of five cycles* . . .

—*We now have differentiation between the P and T waves; heart action remains slightly arrythmic* . . .

The pictures on the screen jumped as a cut was made. The clock advanced two and a half minutes.

Gwyn's voice: *Robin, we're putting the Bradbury circuits up on your screen. Do you want to give it a run now?*

Robin nodded. Childermass looked at the videotape of the stock car. He looked back at Robin, who was focused intently on the TV monitors in the cold lab, breathing clouds, suggesting the awesome power of a locomotive waiting in a train shed. Although he knew what the outcome was going to be, Childermass fidgeted impatiently in his seat. He looked curiously at an echoencephalogram of Robin's brain, wondering what it all meant to the experts.

—*Activity increasing in the occipital lobe and reticular formations* . . .

—*Pulse rising* . . .

—*We're detecting spin waves in the fluctuating force field* . . .

—*Pulse 180 and climbing rapidly* . . .

—*Gradient level 40 to 1* . . .

—*We have a very strong electrostatic field fluctuation* . . .

—*Heartbeat, brain waves and force field fluctuations are in ratio* . . .

—Pulse 240!

"He's there," Gwyneth murmured, reliving the event.

Robin was breathing explosively. On the Bradbury screen the stock car came to life, and Childermass laughed out loud. Gwyneth sat slumped in her own chair, fingers steepled. Childermass enjoyed the spectacle of the careening car for a few moments, and then he said:

"Do you know how he does it? From three hundred miles away? I mean, can you express it mathematically?"

"Not yet. But the distance involved is not important. Try thinking in terms of time and not of space. Time isn't propagated like light waves—it appears instantaneously everywhere. If you conceive of time as a form of primal energy coeffecting known mechanical and chemical activity, the theory, at least, is easy to grasp."

Childermass grimaced and watched the rest of the action, almost leaping out of his seat at the near-collision of the car with the train. As the stock car came softly to a stop the Bradbury screens went blank.

There were sounds of celebration and congratulation on the audio tape, but these faded swiftly; more screens darkened, leaving Robin alone and slumped in his chair, literally drunk: his eyes were wild but he laughed euphorically, pounding the console arm of his chair with a fist, turning lights on and off and on again in his freezing dome.

"What's the matter with him?" Childermass said, startled by the display of erratic behavior.

Robin giggled and gasped and moaned.

Granny Sig replied. "Euphoria; shock; pain. He's still fourteen years old. And he doesn't know how to handle it."

"Handle what?"

"Psychologically Robin is torn between the knowledge that he is both omnipotent and potentially lethal in the exercise of his powers. Then there's a more familiar dilemma. Our problems evolve quickly, but our bodies evolve slowly. And our emotions never change."

Gwyn, unable to look any longer at the spectacle of Robin on the screen, put her face in her hands. Granny Sig, taking pity on her, stopped all the machines and brought up the lights in the room.

"We'd better go now," Gwyn said. "I don't like leaving him by himself for too long at a time."

"I thought I was going to see some of the latest trials. Don't you have film?"

"Something always seems to be wrong with our film; it's a common phenomenon in cases of materialization. We've tried three experiments so far, exciting, but all failures. Here's a rough analogy. Water has a simple molecular structure. Boil it at 212 degrees Fahrenheit, it turns to vapor, or steam. Chill and condense the vapor, and you have water again. Any child can do it. Robin, by electromagnetically disturbing the cells of, say, a hamster, can change it into something inanimate: the only limitations are his creative concepts. He can produce a woodcarving, or a clay vase. But of course we don't get the hamster back. That's the part that defeats and frustrates him: composing a living entity from earth and wood. He succeeds in constructing facsimiles, actual fur and nails and skin on the outside. The insides are composed of amorphous squamous cells without genetic identity. The cells are idiot cells. Because they are unspecialized, without purpose, they're easily exhausted, and they quickly reach the Hayflick limit. After that——"

"I'd like to see one of his creations."

Gwyn shook her head. "No matter how carefully we preserve them, they dematerialize soon after dissection, like the entrails and tumors produced by the psychic surgeons of the Phillipines during their healing rituals."

"Robin keeps trying, though."

"Oh, yes. He keeps trying."

In winter those employed at Psi Faculty commonly got around campus on snowmobiles or touring skis. Granny despised the snarling racket of the machines and, because of her bulk, skis were not a practical alternative. To solve her transportation problem she had purchased an antique sleigh. It was pulled by two black Morgan geldings that stood dropping rich turds in the icy sunlight at the foot of the steps of the administration building.

Childermass looked unhappily at the sleigh and said, "Don't you have a car?"

"I'm just an old-fashioned girl," the transvestite replied, largely because she knew it would annoy him.

"If I thought your asshole was as nimble as your mouth I'd marry you," Childermass said. They let it go at that.

A security man drove the sleigh. The passengers sat bundled in lap robes facing each other in twos: Childermass and his bodyguard, Granny Sig and Gwyneth. All eyes were impenetrable behind dark glasses. No one attempted small talk. They were conveyed like fugitive czarists along a glazed road between walls of snow. The Morgans ran with taut high heads. The day echoed bells. They were pursued by a flickering shadow-show; trees dropped crackling showers of ice as the sleigh flew by.

When they arrived at the house where Robin lived with Gwyneth they saw him on the far side of the lake, sprinting around the swept ice on his racing blades. Robin took no notice of them. They went upstairs to Gwyn's second-floor study and observed him from the bow window. Childermass used a pair of 15X Vixen binoculars, which effectively placed Robin in the room with him.

Gwyn didn't make a sound when Robin took a nasty spill, but she reacted as if someone had jerked her up short with a noose around the neck. He went spinning clockwise toward a pile of snowy rock, hitting hard. Fortunately he was well-padded. Childermass, lowering the glasses, glanced at Gwyn. She turned away from him, a hand going involuntarily to her face; she hid her anxiety as if it were a sty.

Robin got up slowly. Childermass studied Robin's face as he clawed at the rough ice. Rarely had he seen such anger. When Robin was upright he attacked the ice again, arms scything across his body as he raced along.

"How long has he been skating like that?" Childermass asked Ken, who was passing drinks around.

"About an hour and a half, sir."

Robin fell again. They heard him howl, not in pain but in rage. He smote the ice with a fist before rising. He began to skate again, stiffly and doggedly, putting a great deal of effort behind his desire for speed.

"Can't you calm him down?"

Granny Sig sipped her Calvados and said, "Every day he has three hundred milligrams of phenobarbital and fifty milligrams of Prolixin. On trial days we double that dosage."

"What the hell are you saying? That's enough to kill him!"

Granny Sig smiled ruefully.

"Psychopharmacology is an empirical science, based on a number of assumptions, the most important being that drugs can affect the normal and pathological functions of the brain at the synaptic level. But in Robin's case the psychological parameters influenced by drugs are sharply limited. The problem seems to lie in his cerebral cortex, where most of the normal functions of the ego take place. Tranquilizers don't have the desired effect on the hypothalamic area. Therefore——"

"His ego is monstrous," Gwyn said. "And his normal drives are affected. Hunger, sex—he overindulges or he has no interest at all."

"Yet he often behaves like a laboratory cat whose cerebral cortex has been removed—he can fly into a rage over nothing. In Robin's case, as you know, that's indescribably dangerous."

For the moment Robin was motionless on the ice. He had his hands on his hips as he glared at something.

"What is he trying to prove out there?" Childermass asked, looking through the binoculars again.

"He feels he should be able to go from one triumph to another," Gwyn said. "From miracles in the lab to a three-minute mile or a world speed-skating average. Even though he's a better-than-average athlete, he's not up to the demands he makes on himself. When he fails his frustration is intolerable."

"How does he do in bed?"

Gwyn helped herself to another drink. There were two harsh spots of color on her cheeks. Granny Sig watched Robin as he resumed skating, making a wide loop on the ice. He seemed to have some spectacular feat in mind, and Granny Sig frowned.

"Robin," Gwyn said clinically, "has frequent ejaculations. He usually remains fully erect between orgasms. He gets very little relief or gratification from the act, whether we perform orally or genitally. But he—" She turned away so Childermass wouldn't see a glimmer of tears in her eyes. "He wants very much to please me. That's something still in our favor. He needs me because he is—potentially schizoid, as we've said, and often frightened. He trusts me to help him——"

"In his better moods," Granny Sig noted. "But at other. times——"

"We fight," Gwyn said. "It doesn't mean anything. Robin feels compelled to test my loyalty."

She had moved toward the window. What she saw startled her so badly some of the whiskey in her glass slopped onto her hand. Robin was skating directly at piled rocks that rose nearly four feet above the surface of the lake.

"Oh, God!"

Even as she prayed Robin leaped. Snow flew from one of the rocks as a skate blade nicked it, but he was up and over, a fraction of an inch from taking a serious head-first fall. He landed hard but with his skates under him, came to a wobbling spinning stop.

Childermass felt sick to his stomach.

"He'll kill himself with stunts like that; I don't care what his mental problems are, you two better get a grip on him if you know what's good for you!"

Gwyneth, deeply galled, closed her eyes.

"He's been working under enormous pressure for the past sixteen months. He needs to get away from here. We've planned a ski vacation, just the two of us——"

"No."

"But I promised!" Gwyn said, her insistence touching on terror.

"You should know better. I can't prove it, but I understand there's a price of at least a million on Robin's head. The Langley gang has the contract, they're checking around, but so far even a million bucks hasn't attracted a nonaffiliate good enough to penetrate Psi Faculty and do the job. It's just plain suicide. Todfield knows that. Sure, he could put together a team strong enough to overrun our defenses. But he doesn't want to go to war with me, and that's exactly what *will* happen if he gets provocative. I'll destroy the effete son of a bitch!"

Childermass tasted some of the Calvados that Granny Sig was drinking. "I don't know if this is piss or vinegar," he muttered, and set it aside. He wig-wagged his head at Gwyn. "No, no, as long as Robin is here I can be sure he's untouchable. But if he leaves with you, in twenty-four hours you'll both be dead."

"A bodyguard——"

"I'd have to use twenty men—an army!—to protect him. And that would only attract unwelcome attention to Robin. No ski trip, Gwyneth. Try to find another way to amuse him, and take his mind off the daily grind."

"All right then. But do this for me. Keep the girl in New York a while longer. Don't bring her up here, that could be disastrous for Robin."

"How so? He and Gillian are very close."

"Psychic twinship, yes——"

"He's been, what'd they call it, 'visiting' her——"

Gwyn nodded. "I know, I *know!* He doesn't often mention Gillian, though. He's jealous, I think. Call it sibling rivalry if you will."

Childermass chuckled; he found her diagnosis absurd. Granny Sig looked impassively at him, knowing her opinion was not desired.

"I'm warning you, uncle! Gillian's presence could cause big trouble. The competition might unhinge Robin completely——"

"I think you're jealous yourself. Of a fourteen-year-old girl."

"Oh, but that's idiotic. We just don't need her right now! Give me a week or two——"

"Because of what happened to her friend, Gillian is in a depressed state right now—in a frame of mind to accept our hospitality, to sever all connection with her family forever, so that she can't do them serious harm. Also she wants to be with her twin. She needs him, or thinks she does. No, I can't discuss it. The girl all but dropped in our laps. Now plans are in motion. We have to take full advantage of this opportunity."

Gwyneth bowed her head abjectly.

"If I disappoint him—and let Gillian take up my time—oh, don't make it *impossible* for me, there's so much more Robin and I can accomplish, uncle!"

"She'll be here before dawn tomorrow. Now not another word from you."

Gwyn bit her underlip. She was drawn to the window again. The amplified sun acted on her face like quicklime, melting it to bone and elemental terror. Around and around Robin skated, like a clockwork figure. Granny Sig drank, and studied Gwyn's anguished reflection, and drank some more.

In pale Virginia sunshine Peter Sandza methodically worked his
way around the combat pistol range at the Plantation, firing,
from fifty yards, three-shot bursts with a Smith and Wesson K-38
match revolver, using speed loaders following each six-round
position; sitting, prone, left and right hand barricades.

"Fantastic," Nick O'Hanna said, following Peter's progress
through the course. "Only three hits in the nine ring so far."
O'Hanna was an expert shotmaker himself, and it was his match
pistol Peter was using. "I doubt he's done much shooting in the
past couple of years, but his grand agg is going to be in the low
570's."

Todfield yawned; gunplay bored him.

Woolwine looked on patiently behind his mirror sunglasses.

"One of the many benefits of hypnotic hyperesthesia," he
said. "Peter's vision is keener than it ever was. All of his senses
are finely tuned. If he was efficient and deadly before, he is
virtually unstoppable now."

Peter fired his final six and went to collect his targets. He
brought them back to O'Hanna, smiling over them.

"Look at this cluster, Nick! Not a trace of the X-ring."

"Great shooting, Peter. You haven't lost your touch."

Peter didn't look at the other men; he hadn't been told they
were there, so in fact they didn't exist for him.

Peter handed over the K-38 to O'Hanna.

"You've done a lot of work on those contact surfaces," he
observed. "No resistance at all. Real easy trigger, but the firing
pin hit is solid every time."

"Well, you see, I didn't touch the mainspring, which is a
common mistake. What I did was——"

A helicopter circled the compound at the river half a mile
away. Todfield, who was standing only a few feet from Peter,
turned to Woolwine and said, "Almost three o'clock. Time for
Peter to be on his way."

Woolwine nodded, checking his own watch.

"He's ready."

Todfield shifted his stance uneasily and said, "We could still
change the game plan. We know the boy's exact location. We
could set Peter down within five miles of him."

"He would not survive," Woolwine said curtly.

"I don't think he has much chance of succeeding the other way."

"The odds are better than you think given his courage, his daring, his genius for improvisation in the face of extreme danger. During the last few days I have spent nearly forty years with Peter Sandza exploring the instinctual life, the mythos of his emotional dynamism. We are all creatures of myth, shadowed by archaic images of life and death. I quickly discovered, behind the systematic amnesias, the deep-seated hysteria that has ruled his life. At the age of ten Peter accidentally shot his father to death while on a hunting trip. A classic archetype chillingly come true. His life from that moment was shaped by an act of unwitting violence. Having slain the godhead, Peter sought to atone for his error by undertaking a painful quest against what are commonly held to be the evils of the world. But the quest was largely a delusion proposed by the archetypal Black Magician, Childermass; it served as a time of testing and preparation. Peter compensated for what might have become a pathological monomania by marrying and fathering a son of his own, leading a 'normal' life at those times when it was necessary for him to lay down the banner and quit the arena for a while. Is this too complicated for you?"

"Aww, shit."

Woolwine smiled thinly. "I'll be brief. As we know, Peter's true quest involves the taking back of his son from the arch-villain, the Magician who so treacherously manipulated him. Mythologically it's an apt conclusion. But to hasten the processes by which Peter is working out his destiny would be a fatal mistake. The fortress in which the boy is held is terrifically well-guarded. You would hesitate to send even your best men in there. Peter is certainly well-motivated to succeed; his hiatus here has in no way interfered with basic drive activity. But, symbolically and psychologically, it would be wrong for you to step in at this time and effectively end his quest. That comes under the heading of supernatural interference. It would throw him off stride, confuse him, make him vulnerable and prone to errors of judgment. He is not prepared for sudden success. In a way, he hasn't suffered enough yet."

"My God."

"Oh, true."

"Then why did he come looking for our help?"

"But it wasn't help he craved, it was betrayal."

Todfield shaded his eyes and looked hard at Peter, who stood talking obliviously with O'Hanna about gunsmithing. "Betrayal," Todfield repeated, perplexed and unsettled.

O'Hanna glanced at his boss, who nodded. O'Hanna touched Peter's arm.

"Peter, time for you to be going."

They walked past Todfield and Woolwine and got into a ranch wagon for the short drive to the helicopter.

In the wagon O'Hanna gave Peter a .357 magnum Colt Python revolver with a four-inch barrel, a silencer, a Bianchi holster and extra 210-grain loads.

"Your ETA at Westchester County airport is four thirty-seven," O'Hanna said.

Peter nodded. He took off his pigskin jacket and put the belt holster on.

"The car is a dark blue Cougar, New York license plate 776-WIH, registered to Richard Santry. It's in the second row of the parking lot as you walk out the door." O'Hanna pulled an envelope from his inside coat pocket. "Keys, credit cards, driver's license, two thousand dollars in fifties and twenties. I've packed a grip for you. Shaving gear, sweaters, shirts. Also tools of the trade: a Saber CM-300 Countermeasure System. That ought to come in handy."

"Right."

O'Hanna looked drearily out the window as they approached the helicopter.

"I—I wish there was more I could do, buddy."

"You've done a hell of a lot. I'll never forget it."

They shook hands just before Peter climbed into the Vought Gazelle.

"Well, I hope they keep biting for you," Peter said cheerfully.

"Yeh, hope so too."

Peter closed the copter door behind him. As soon as he fastened his lap strap he fell deeply asleep.

O'Hanna stood clear while the helicopter lifted off. There was a lump in his throat he couldn't swallow no matter how hard he worked at it. He felt a sense of outrage which he would never be able to express.

He felt dirty all over.

As the helicopter flew away Todfield said to Woolwine, "What's the operative word?"

" 'Commander.' "

"Where'd you get it?"

"Peter was a lieutenant commander in the Navy. He often referred—still refers—to his boy as 'Skipper,' and when he does so Robin invariably replies with 'Commander,' a term of both affection and respect."

"I see. And so, assuming we aren't putting our money on a dead horse——"

"Have a little confidence."

"Assuming that much, when Peter and Robin meet, God knows how, and Robin responds with the operative word——"

"Peter, if he happens to have a gun in his hand, will promptly shoot him through the head. If he has a knife, he will cut the boy's throat. If Peter has only his bare hands, then he will kill with a blow to the solar plexus or the back of the neck."

"Provided your conditioning works."

"Haven't we proved to your satisfaction, with other subjects, that it always works?" Woolwine said snappishly. "It's so much hogwash that a man can't be made to perform acts that go against certain instincts. You simply provide him with a rationale that supports an instinct more powerful than the one you wish to override. Peter loves his son, yes, but we should not forget that Robin has acquired mythological status in Peter's unconscious. The circle is closing. Peter slew his father, Peter's son will grow up to slay him. This primal fear will allow him to assume, temporarily, his own father's role; he will defend himself as the father could not."

"And when he comes to his senses and realizes what he's done——"

Woolwine shrugged. "The consequences for Peter will be unimaginably dreadful; shattering. Are you concerned?"

"No. Only the boy is my concern."

"You must tell me more about him sometime."

The suite which Gillian occupied was on the top floor of Paragon Institute. It was furnished comfortably but with no attempt at style. There was a park and river view. Gillian spent the better part of her days in the sitting room, in a rocking chair that faced the windows, while the heavy-set woman who was assigned to keep an eye on her, a Mrs. Cunningham, did needlepoint and crossword puzzles and seldom spoke unless she was spoken to.

Gillian was tranquil but lucid on a combination of hypnotic barbituates and antianxiety drugs. She was as tame as a bird in a jar. She thought about her parents but didn't miss them. She was able to talk calmly about Larue's death with Dr. Roth and his assistant Dr. Maylun Chan We. The thing that killed was in her mind, but they explained to her that the medicine quieted it; she couldn't hurt them nor anyone else. Gillian felt a subdued gratitude, but no emotion was very strong or persevered. The time passed comfortably for her. She listened to good music but was neither inspired nor compelled to play her flute.

There were two young women who spelled Mrs. Cunningham: a blonde whose hair was cropped as close as an alley cat's, another with coal-black and lustrous locks. Kristen and Hester —for a couple of days Gillian smilingly confused them. But then it was Hester, the dark-haired one, who began coming often, who always brought the medication and stayed to chat while Mrs. Cunningham took a long breather. Hester became a friend. Gillian was distantly aware of the danger of ever having a real friend again, but she just couldn't help liking someone as sweet-natured as Hester.

Twice each day, in the morning and again in the evening before dinner, Gillian left her rooms in the company of Mrs. Cunningham for the ten-minute in-house walk that, along with simple calisthenics and plenty of rocking, Dr. Roth had prescribed to maintain muscle tone. They went slowly along interminable hallways and down flights of stairs, meeting no one on the way. The first three days it was hard going for Gillian, but each time out they ended up in the kitchen where the cook, a black woman named Mayborn, had prepared a treat especially for Gillian. Mrs. Mayborn doted on Gillian and was expert at catering to the girl's pallid appetite.

For her part Gillian appreciated catching her breath and being fussed over in the kitchen, which was long and narrow and a few steps below ground level. The floors were maple and the brick walls had been painted a creamy yellow; a wealth of copper utensils dangled from the beamed ceiling.

Just outside there was a kind of courtyard or alley; sitting at the butcher-block table in a nook of the kitchen Gillian could gaze out at piles of snow turning dog-piss yellow on the cobbles. People walked briskly by and cars drove in and out. It was a busy troubling world out there, forbidden to her.

On Wednesday morning, as she stared at the door—the Way Out—she suffered such a case of nerves that she dropped a cup and saucer on the floor. Mrs. Mayborn was solicitous and wouldn't let her help clean up the mess; Mrs. Cunningham noted this deviation from her usual behavior and reported it to Dr. Roth.

The next time Roth saw Gillian he asked her if anything was bothering her. Gillian smiled placidly and said she didn't think so. He patted her shoulder and asked her to please try and eat a little more because she needed to increase her strength. Gillian promised to try.

Rock, rock.

The thing that killed was in her mind.

Then it was good to take the medicine, so the killing would never happen again.

She was aware of an emotion, a sense of suffocation and loss. It made her tense. She rocked patiently, certain that the emotion would drift away. But this time it didn't. It grew stronger, and tears seemed a possibility, although she scarcely remembered what it was like to cry.

But what happens to Gillian? she thought, rocking faster. *When I take the medicine, I stop being Gillian.*

Rock, rock.

The thing that kills is in the mind. It's in the mind. It's in the mind.

If I can't be Gillian, who can I be? What can I be?

Rock, rock.

The music on the stereo was *Slow Down*, a boogie number by Alvin Lee, which Hester had brought with her and asked Gillian to play. Hester liked it good and loud. Gillian looked on in mild astonishment as Hester, practically right under Gillian's nose, furtively but deftly emptied the capsules of diazepam and seco-barbital into a damp Kleenex she held in the hollow of one hand. At the same time she kept a sharp eye on the hall door, which was standing open.

"What are you doing?"

Hester put her mouth close to Gillian's ear in order to be heard.

"I'm cutting you off completely tonight."

"Why?"

"Because I have to get you out of here soon," Hester said, secreting the wadded tissue inside the ribbed sleeve of her sweater. She handed Gillian the empty capsules and a cup of water. "Swallow them," she said.

"Why do you want me to leave?" asked the baffled Gillian.

Hester looked frightened, which made Gillian feel apprehensive too.

"Because if you don't get out of here," Hester explained as she bent over the rocker, "you'll disappear just like Robin Sandza did. I know that's what they've got in mind for you."

"Who?"

"Oh, Gillian, you're too fucking dopey for me to get anything across tonight! God, how *am* I going to pull this off?"

"Hester, don't be upset."

"I've gradually been taking you off the tranquilizers for the last two days, but your system is jammed with junk. Tonight you go cold turkey. It'll be a shock. But you've got to keep pretending that you're still—just smile and act vague no matter what you feel. Don't make them suspicious! I'll talk to you again in the morning, by then I should have it worked out, I'll know how to get you out of this place." Hester saw the sheen of tears in Gillian's eyes. "Honey, no, don't start bawling! Everything will be all right. Trust me! And above all don't let on you're not stoned. I am in a *lot* of trouble if Dr. Roth finds out I've been shaving your medication. Do you understand? You don't want to get me in trouble, do you?"

Gillian shook her head excitedly.

"Steady—take it easy." Hester darted a look at the door. She snatched up a hairbrush and was smoothing Gillian's tresses over one ear when Mrs. Cunningham reappeared, wincing at the volume of the sound. Hester put the hairbrush in Gillian's own hand and tried to smile with real enthusiasm as she patted the girl's shoulder.

Gillian smiled whimsically back, and then a look of concern cut across her eyes like black thought, like a cat low on a fence.

"Be brave," Hester whispered, turning down the stereo. "Have a good night." And she got out of there, barely in time to make her futile seven o'clock telephone call from a windy toll station on York Avenue.

Okay. Two goddamn weeks without a word, and here she'd committed herself to a hasty course of action that was shaping up as a disaster. Peter had warned her often enough: *don't* be cute, don't play around with these people. If Peter was dead, then what good would it do to spring Gillian from Paragon Institute, provided she was dumb lucky enough not to bungle the job?

But dead—that was just too grim and awful and final. Hester refused to believe it. There was a very good reason why he'd let so much time go by without getting in touch. Peter had something clever up his sleeve.

If that was the case, then there was a good chance he didn't need Gillian any more.

Hester was ashamed of the relief she felt. The hell with what Peter needed or didn't need, what about poor little Gillian? What was going to happen to her in a matter of hours—a few days at the most?

Psi Faculty would happen to her. Whatever that was. Hester had risked her neck having another go at the computer. A number of cases—meaning, undoubtedly, real people—had been transferred from Paragon Institute to this other place. Hester knew no more than that about Psi Faculty; she knew it existed, somewhere, for the purpose of swallowing up gifted psychics like Robin Sandza and Gillian Bellaver.

So, all other motives aside, it was morally right for her to try to smuggle Gillian out of Paragon before she disappeared. Problems on top of problems: Hester didn't have the semblance of a workable plan, and supposing she eventually came up with something and succeeded, Gillian would be virtually helpless on her own. She couldn't be handed back to her parents; they'd put her in that place to begin with. Probably grateful to be rid of the unfortunate kid. Hester, with a conventional small-town, middle-class upbringing, had a low opinion of monied and prominent Americans. Being worshipers of the almighty dollar, they were all cold-blooded and essentially not very loving people. No, she couldn't risk returning Gillian to them with the hope they'd do the right thing.

But Hester knew she would be under considerable suspicion at the Institute: she would have to weather their suspicions while protecting and looking after Gillian until Peter showed up. And what would Gillian be like once she was off the tranquillizers? Half mad, therefore unreliable and potentially as dangerous (through no fault of her own) as Bubonic Plague. Hester might need some protection herself.

Nine o'clock. Music on. Rock, then mordant blues from a twenties cotton-chopper with a voice thin and bitter as Louisiana coffee.

> Oh, liver-rot me baby, treat me
> To your death's head pearly smile:
> Then you can ride me on down to your boneyard
> In a twelve-cylinder automobile.

Hester, wondering how Gillian was getting along at this moment, had the shakes. If Gillian acted badly, if she gave herself away, then Hester was doomed. Bummer time. Each vague voice in the hall outside her door, every footfall, caused her to freeze and sweat, freeze and sweat. Nine-thirty. When she heard her friends the Bundys go out singing an old Cole Porter song, happy as clams, she wanted to rush downstairs and be swept along for a random and light-minded evening: a few drinks here, a few laughs there. She got as far as the door, but she didn't open it. No good. No use trying to duck out. If MORG wanted her, they'd find her. If not——There was nothing else to do but prowl the neat three-room flat and get slowly potted on vintage woe, and dread the coming of morning when she would have to begin herding events already restlessly in motion toward the desired conclusion.

> *Turn down your sireen woman*
> *You like a ambulance on the street*

It was after two in the morning when she came up with her great idea: out of desperation, perhaps, because everything depended on Gillian's reactions once the escape began. But Hester liked the plan. It wasn't complicated; it depended for success on surprise and, hopefully, a half-minute of total confusion. Unfortunately, there was a potential stumbling block in Mrs. Cunningham. She didn't look like a woman who was easily confused, and she seldom strayed far from Gillian's side when Gillian was out of her rooms.

But Hester was all thought out; it was the very best she could do. All she needed now was a third party, a sweet dumb guy who would willingly do what he was asked to do without raising too many questions. She'd dated plenty of those, so Hester had already picked her man when she tottered off to bed and fell asleep in mid-yawn.

> *Casket-eyed baby*
> *Pull them shades down to the floor*
> *And hand me your blank check, honey*
> *For my final signature*

Gillian was restless after she went to bed, restless and vocal. Mrs. Cunningham looked in on her twice. She was thrashing and tugging at the covers, muttering through her teeth. The second time Mrs. Cunningham turned on the lamp by the door she saw Gillian's face glistening with sweat.

"This room. This bed. Robin's room. He——"

"What's that, dear?"

Gillian was suddenly quiet, gazing at her as if from a far corner of the mind.

"Would you be sick to your stomach, darlin'?"

"A little," Gillian croaked.

Mrs. Cunningham smiled to assure her that something would be done about it. She closed the bedroom door and, using the telephone in the sitting room, rang Maylun Chan We. Maylun prescribed an antinausea drug and a sleeping pill. Mrs. Cunningham then called the medical associate on night duty at Paragon; he brought the pills up from the dispensary.

When Mrs. Cunningham cracked the bedroom door again Gillian was lying on her side; she seemed peaceful at last. Mrs. Cunningham spoke softly to her. No response. Obviously Gillian's discomfort had eased. If she woke up later, the medicine was handy. Satisfied, Mrs. Cunningham went back to the sitting room and the bile, gall and bad blood of the nightly TV news, unaware that for the time being she was tending a shell instead of a sleeping girl——

Gillian had been lured elsewhere.

She has now a notion of horizon   and winter
Laid on with a trowel   snowfields   moon
Burning in blunt weather
Deflected by too much brilliance, all motion
Discontinued according to laws of time and
Distance
She waits for a confrontation with his psychic's
Mind waits with an eye for the precious past,
An expectancy he is bound to fulfill.

"Robin?"

Following the line of least resistance, they
Meet   with no great shock of recognition
Eyelocked   burning, in snowfields windless
as the grave.

Something quite formal between them,
a new development—she is taken silent
by the animus of his gaze.

"Come on," he says   is off again
highly combustible   like starflash
between the charring crosses. Sustained by
the narrow and merciless vision of her trust,
she follows in her skin of bridesmaid's tears
to the bed of his whore:

(Slash
eyed
bushed
baby
featly boned
and throbbing
luscious
to blood's
tame purr
ing posture
all strung out &
affording
a lewd
glimpse
of asshole)

Whore-
prancer   Robin showing off   riding her
sideways   upside down
or feet on the floor   You name it
Blood's a cataract
Nerves fine   black   beneath the skin
like waxed violin string's hum   here
he comes
His way of declaring himself
shooting off Roman candles of confession
creating galaxies of unrepented sins
How do you like her Gillian? Slow eyes
sink wounds

Her smile curling like flame blackens
the spirit, and he is (as he should be)
terrified as well as amused, having full
knowledge of the hereafter and heretofore

while his body, unequal to the strain
of living everywhere at once

Threatens to disintegrate.

"Now go away."

With a simple motion of his hand she is
swept, brief as a gnat, through time.

Excited by his cruelty   insatiable
he turns again to drowsy Gwyneth. He is
eager for accolades,
and the absolution that is sure to follow.

When Hester reported for work at eight on Thursday morning
Roth and Maylun were already there. Apparently they'd had a
long conference. Something was in the air, undoubtedly involv-
ing Gillian. Hester didn't have a clue. But at least the girl was
still at Paragon: she'd been afraid they might steal away with her
in the middle of the night.

At eight-twenty she accompanied both doctors upstairs. Gillian was awake and sitting up in bed, gazing out through frost-
stippled windows. There was a bland smile on her face, but her
eyes were puffy and humid and seemed, unless Hester was over-
empathizing, distressingly sad. Hester held her breath when
Gillian glanced her way, but Gillian's smile didn't change, and
her manner was indifferent. Hester couldn't decide if the indifference was studied or real. If real, then without a doubt sometime during the night they'd shot her full of shit, and that did
the trick, that just totally wrecked the plan right there.

Hester asked Gillian what she would like for breakfast, and
Gillian said, "I don't care," and then Dr. Roth examined her.
Gillian's blood pressure had climbed and her pulse was faster
than it had been twenty-four hours earlier. Roth seemed to feel
that was encouraging.

"I'd like to take a bath before I eat," Gillian said.

"Surely," Roth said.

"Could Hester stay and shampoo my hair?"

"Don't see why not. Hester?"

"I'd be happy to," Hester replied, trying not to study Gillian's mood. Maylun left medication and vitamins for Gillian and the doctors withdrew, heads together, talking in low tones.

"What sort of day is it?" Gillian asked, looking out the windows again.

"Cold." Hester shuddered for emphasis, then smiled at Mrs. Cunningham, who was laying out a dress for Gillian. "You could have your breakfast while I'm doing Gillian's hair."

"That's a fine idea."

"I'd like jeans today, Mrs. Cunningham," Gillian said.

"When you have all those lovely dresses?"

"I feel like jeans."

"Whatever you say, darlin'."

Hester went into the bathroom, leaving the door ajar. She ran Gillian's bath water, and when the big tub was half full Gillian came in. She didn't look at Hester. She took off her nightclothes in a corner, carelessly pinned up her hair, then stepped into the hot water and stood looking downcast at her body, which, though it needed replenishing right now, was elegantly structured and revealed modest curves that would round gloriously into womanhood. She was a ewe-necked beauty, five-feet nine with shady good looks and flaky lips—she'd probably never have a pimple, Hester thought wistfully. Gillian settled down to the breastbone, knees wide apart, and began to soap herself. Then, almost without warning, she went to pieces.

Hester stood rigid with anxiety as Gillian tried to smother big sobs in the washcloth. Then she used her head and switched on the noisy exhaust fan in the ceiling, hoping that the micro phones she knew had to be in the bathroom wouldn't pick up the sounds of grief which they'd drug-programmed Gillian not to feel.

That much accomplished, Hester, in a mothering twitch, knelt by the tub and put an arm around the slippery girl.

"Oh, Hester, it's the end of the world!"

"Gillian, Gillian."

"I want to get out of this place!"

"It's practically all set. Shh, shush, now. I'll take care of you."

Covering her mouth with her two hands, Gillian stared unbelievingly at her.

"But we *can* do it: I know we can."

"When?"

"This afternoon."

"H-how?"

Hester kneeled facing the door, watching in case Mrs. Cunningham appeared surreptitiously. She started Gillian's shampoo, and while she lathered she whispered in an ivory ear.

When she had finished laying out the plan all Gillian said was, "Mrs. Cunningham has a gun."

"Oh, God! Are you sure?"

"It's in a pocket of her cardigan sweater."

"But she wouldn't shoot you."

"She might shoot *you.*" Gillian couldn't control her tears, and her nose ran too.

"This will positively work, Gillian, and don't worry. Nobody will be hurt."

"I'm afraid, Hester; I know I'll do something really stupid and —where should I go again? *I forgot already!* My mind just gets blank."

"You'll be okay, I wrote it down for you."

When Gillian was out of the tub and robed Hester took a round Band-Aid from her pocket. She reached inside the robe, which startled Gillian, and pasted the Band-Aid high on the inside of one thigh.

"It's all written out. If you forget anything, just tear the Band-Aid open."

Gillian's teeth were clicking. Hester went to work on her wet head, rubbed until the scalp was a newborn pink. Gillian's head bobbed with the massage. She yawned and slowly went slack in Hester's capable hands.

"Hester, I can't stay with you, no matter what."

"We'll worry about that later."

"I'll have to be alone. *Alone!* For the rest of my life. Robin hates me, there's no place I can go now. He m-must hate me, to do what he did."

Hester was eager to ask questions about Robin. But the phone had rung in the bedroom, she had to answer it. Mrs. Cunningham. Gillian's breakfast had been prepared, and perhaps she'd like to eat in the Morning Room for a change. Hester promised to bring her right down.

She hung up, and remembered to pocket the medication that was on the little tray beside the bed. The vitamins she fed to Gillian.

Mrs. Cunningham should have walked upstairs to fetch Gillian herself; was she getting just a little lazy and careless? A good sign. Hester helped Gillian to dress warmly. Too much clothing for indoors, but she'd just have to endure it.

Further serious conversation was out at this point, so Hester prattled about movies and fashions and the difficulties a working girl had making ends meet in the Big Apple. Gillian listened without comment, her head fallen forward; she appeared to be in a rueful daze.

For Hester the remainder of the day was the meanest sort of torment. Trouble lay in her stomach like a small ticking bomb. It was Kristen's day off, so she had a heavy work load. Her mouth was constantly dry, no matter how much water or coffee she sipped. Her bowels quaked often, and that meant a lot of trips to the bathroom. She couldn't find items she had filed two days ago. She dialed wrong numbers and couldn't seem to handle simple sentences during dictation. Dr. Roth was hard-pressed to conceal his irritation.

Even with all these difficulties four-thirty arrived too soon. Suddenly there it was, on the clock in front of her. What had happened to three-thirty? Her lunch hour? *Four thirty-one.* Hester compensated for her panic with a mad rush. She gathered all the outgoing mail from the various offices; a lot of parcels today, almost enough to fill two shopping bags. Her coat, her hat, her gloves. Lugging the shopping bags, she all but ran down the stairs to the kitchen. Her face was bright red, her pulse too rapid to count. If it didn't happen *now,* she knew she would pass out.

Gillian, following her afternoon constitutional, was sitting at the butcher-block table a few feet from the door, nursing a cup of cocoa. Mrs. Cunningham and Mrs. Mayborn were smacking their lips over something that bubbled in a pot on the stove.

"Here comes the pony express," Hester said, breezing on through, not daring to look directly at Gillian. But out of the corner of her eye she saw that Gillian had raised her head.

"Running late, Hester," Mrs. Mayborn commented.

"It's just been one hell of a day, Felicia."

"I know; the boss almost snapped *my* head off over nothing."

Hester bolted up the short flight of steps—six in all—to the back door, which was secured by a Medeco lock. The ultrasecurity lock required a special key. Hester put down the shopping bags and got out her copy of the key and opened the door. The cold air felt good. She turned and kicked over one of the shopping bags.

Envelopes and brown paper packages cascaded down the steps.

"Oh, well, shit," Hester mumbled, scurrying down the steps after the mail. "Don't bother," she said, waving off Cunningham and the cook. All too soon she had the mail picked up, and Gillian hadn't budged. Hester looked frantically at her. Gillian seemed witless and paralyzed, as if her nerve had failed.

"For the love of God, Hester thought, *move your ass!*

And Gillian rose belatedly, creating no stir. She approached the steps mousy-meek and bent over.

"Here's one you missed," she said.

"Oh, thanks Gil——"

Then like a shot Gillian was out the door and running. She had remembered to give Hester enough of a shove so that Hester, rebounding, didn't have to fake a well-timed shoulder into the midsection of Mrs. Cunningham, who, for all her size, was fast on her feet in an emergency.

Mrs. Cunningham, speechless and winded, still had enough strength to pitch Hester like a toy against the nearest wall. She stumbled up the steps, fumbling in a pocket of her cableknit sweater.

The gun, Hester thought, horrified; but it wasn't a gun, it was a walkie-talkie.

"Security!" Mrs. Cunningham bawled as soon as she was on the sidewalk outside. "The girl is running. The girl is running. All units, 86th westbound. Redline it! Redline it! Topguy One and Topguy Two, get your glasses on her!"

Hester was just out the door when someone else, running hard from the house, bumped her in passing and almost knocked her down. It was Maylun Chan We. Hester had no idea where she'd come from. But she was the fastest woman Hester had ever seen: even before Hester recovered her balance Maylun had sprinted around the stalled Cunningham, who was still yelling into her walkie-talkie, and around the back end of a fuel truck that was parked across the mouth of the mews and pumping oil for the apartment building; she headed up the street after Gillian.

There was plenty of other activity around Paragon Institute. Two ordinary looking sedans parked at the other end of the mews erupted with hidden flashers and bold sirens. But the oil truck had the exit blocked. Hester ran for her life, pursuing the fleet Maylun.

Rush hour traffic had begun on 86th, which would slow down other chase cars trying to move west from positions beside the park on East End, but Hester realized in an instant that Gillian, fast as she was and with a twenty-second head start on the long block, could not elude Maylun. Heads turned, other eyes clocked the race. Who would have thought the demure Chinese doctor was a former track star? Hester, running, was a battle with herself. Behind her sirens screamed for clearance on the clogged street. A car jumped up on the sidewalk and jumped back again.

Just make it to the corner, Hester pleaded in silence. Her lungs, already, were roasting like chickens on a spit. Gillian turned half around and looked shocked when she saw Maylun barely fifty feet behind her, running with long dependable strides. *Go!* Hester demanded, but Gillian needed no warning. Jumping over a taut dog leash, she made York Avenue and ducked to her right around the corner. Moments later Dr. Maylun Chan We followed her.

Hester was a faltering third. She came to the corner limping and gasping and thoroughly frightened.

Gillian had made it into the back of the boxy Checker cab, but Maylun had one hand on the door and leaned in as if to pull her out of the seat. Gillian shrank into the opposite corner. Hester tried to scream at Maylun, to distract her, but she was too concerned with sucking wind to utter a clarifying sound.

Then Maylun stepped back, slammed the door and turned away as the cab pulled out from the curb and soon became anonymous in an uptown burst of traffic.

Maylun was obviously surprised to see Hester leaning on a lamppost observing, but she kept her poise.

"Your idea?" Maylun said.

Hester stared open-mouthed at the doctor, then astonished herself by nodding.

"Wha—Maylun, why did you——"

"Because there are things I just can't make myself accept," Maylun explained.

"I know wha——"

"Yes, well, do you also know what our lives are worth if you don't keep quiet?"

Hester managed a nod.

"Whoa—won't say a thing."

"Good," Maylun said, and she quickly pressed Hester's hand, sealing the conspiracy, just before they were caught up in a wave of MORG security teams.

When he heard Gillian retching in the back seat, Hester's friend Walter, the cab driver, said, "Use the Kraft paper sack to heave in."

Gillian put her head half in the sack and emptied her stomach. Walter turned on 91st and drove as far as Park Avenue before the lights changed. Then he uncapped a thermos and poured a styrofoam cup full of hot tea, which he handed back to Gillian. She was sitting upright and pale against the maroon seat back, pale with a strange luminescence; her skin was like neon. She accepted the tea.

"Hester said you might be sick from all the running," Walter said. He had prematurely gray hair curling over his ears, a kind and ugly face like a Disney dwarf's. "She told me about the bad situation you have with your boy friend. I can sympathize. Listen, don't worry about the sack. I'll throw it in the trash next red light. Like some music? How about QXR?"

"Okay."

Walter drove down Park, moving peaceably in the midst of the rush-hour madness so as not to jar Gillian's touchy stomach. She swallowed half the smoky tea, sipping slowly whenever a chill threatened to dislocate her bones and cause more retching.

"Here we are."

Gillian had been totally unaware of the blocks going by. The sun, too, had set: there were just a few windows alight in the fair open sky, high spots above the blur of the fast-paced lower city. Street levels were junked in shadow and the air was filled with gritty blowing things. Gillian's head roared at its own pace.

"Where?"

Walter indicated the theatre. They were on Thirty-Third, near Lexington. The theatre was called the Director's Chair. It showed revivals, double-and-triple-billed classics of the silver screen.

"Here," he said, smiling. He handed her a ticket of admission.

Gillian sat numbly holding it. She didn't know what to say or do.

"Goodbye and good luck," Walter told her. It seemed final. Gillian opened the door and got out. The wind traveled through her as if she were an empty cage.

"Don't forget your coat." Walter handed her a wool parka through the window. Then he drove off. The olive parka had a plaid lining. Gillian had never seen it before, but she put it on.

She looked uneasily up and down the street. She was nowhere she recognized. The wind climbed inside her coat, bit her earlobes and froze her neck before she did up the drawstrings of the hood. She turned round and around, eyes streaming neon. Gillian felt overcrowded by the occasional passerby, she was lashed to a sinking weight of the unfamiliar and the unasked-for. Simple to remember what Hester said, if only she put her mind to it. That would come. The tea she'd drunk had not fully satisfied her thirst, and her throat still rasped from vomiting, from breathing the wind in wrong. God oh God, my name is Gillian. A man with a mustache like a blackened bottle brush and dizzy tufted hair and a prop cigar regarded her with an indescribable passion from a poster in front of the movie house.

Her ticket was accepted at the door. It might be all right with Hester if she sat down for a little while; maybe, for all Gillian knew, she was supposed to do just that. An old-fashioned

popcorn machine stood in the lobby and, watching the crisp
white stuff spill from the kettle, she hungered. But she had no
money. She promptly put her hands in the pockets of the
parka and found a new five-dollar bill in each pocket. Hester
made miracles. Breaking one of the fives, Gillian bought
popcorn and chewing gum to clean her teeth after the popcorn. They didn't sell soda. She had a long drink of tepid
water at the fountain, then went down into the cubbyhole
dark toward the lisping center of the screen. Pandemonium.
Three fey clowns. Gags whizzing by almost faster than the
ear could follow. *Cocoanuts.* There were perhaps a dozen dedi-
cated old-movie buffs in the small theatre lapping it all up.
Gillian sat right in the middle of the house, three seats in from
the left-hand aisle.

Groucho said: *Now over here—on this site we're going to build an
eye and ear hospital. This is going to be a site for sore eyes.*

Then he said: *Love flies out the door when money comes innuendo.*
And later he said:

But by then Gillian had finished most of her popcorn, and she
had settled down half asleep inside her warm and hooded coat.
To wait. Wait for Hester to produce more of her miracles. God
oh God I am Gillian. I *was* Gillian. It was almost the end of the
world, but perhaps not too late for miracles. If not, then nothing
left to do but die: die.

If only she knew how.

Hester had decided before she set foot in Roth's office that the
best defense was a whopping case of hysterics, which Roth unexpectedly touched off himself—there was a look in his own eyes
that could only have been inspired by the nearness of the heads-
man's ax. Dr. Irving Roth was in deep shit. So were they all, in
a sense, but the ultimate responsibility for Gillian's escape was
his.

"Hester, Hester—stop it now, we're not blaming you."

"If you blame anyone," Maylun said fearlessly, "blame me. I
prescribed for Gillian. She shouldn't have been able to run like
that. Shouldn't have occurred to her."

"She's a very unusual girl," Roth said bleakly. "But we'll find her. Could you for God's sake do something about——?"

Maylun bathed Hester's face in ice water. The phone on Roth's desk was ringing. Phones were ringing all over Paragon Institute. Roth selected a line at random. It was Avery Bellaver returning an urgent call.

"I wonder if you could come over here right away?" Roth said.

In the MORG helicopter flying south over the Hudson River valley one of Childermass's executives put the receiver of the scrambler phone on the hook and said to his boss, "No trace of the girl yet."

It was not a thing easily said to a man infamous for the way he took bad news; but Childermass, in his shirt sleeves, just leaned way back in the lounge chair, his one hand lax behind his head. He looked out at the dark of night seeking rumors of the moon.

"Inside job."

"Yes, sir."

"Solve it, we'll know where Gillian is."

"I think so."

"Tell them it sounds like the Chink to me. Tell them not to be subtle down there. Tell them no time for fucking subtleties, put her yellow tit in the old cider press."

"What about the other one, Hester?"

Childermass didn't like being presented with an alternative.

"Here I am giving you a million dollars' worth of advice, and you're listening less than a nickel's worth." He turned his thumb down decisively. "I met her. Not a brain in her head. Know your enemy. It's the Yellow Peril every time. Somebody give me a smoke."

He sat languidly with his cigarette, toe-tapping, thinking, whistling. Other men in the helicopter sent ugly coded messages, and were terrifying on the phone.

"Finny, fanny," Childermass said under his breath. "Double whammy. Stars are falling on Alabamy." His forehead creased deeply. He spat out a mouthful of smoke.

"And falling. And falling."

Gillian awoke in the movie house feeling stuffy, and there was perspiration on her upper lip; she was too hot in the parka. She fumbled with the drawstrings of the hood and unzipped the coat. When she laid the hood back she discovered that someone was sitting in the seat next to her.

"You almost dropped your popcorn," he said. "I saved it for you." He handed her the container. By now the popcorn wasn't any good, but Gillian smiled anyway.

"Thank you." On the screen a bum had accosted Harpo. *Could you help me out?* he said. *I'd like to get a cup of coffee.* Whereupon Harpo reached into a pocket of his commodious trousers and handed the bum a cup of piping-hot coffee. The young man next to her laughed and laughed. Gillian, benumbed, wondered what movie she was watching.

"I don't know how many times I've seen Harpo do that," the young man commented, "but I always find it funny."

Gillian looked politely at him, but he was already familiar. She'd spent her life around young men just like him. Given two guesses, she could have named his prep. Then—Princeton, of course, wasn't he wearing a Princeton ring? Hands folded on top of the expensive cashmere topcoat in his lap. His nails were manicured and gleaming. His hair had been modishly styled to give dimension to a rather small but handsomely boned face. Even his choice of shaving lotion was predictable. He was trying to raise a mustache. He had to be older, but he looked about nineteen.

"My name is Bradford," he said.

"Gillian."

"Hello, Gillian."

He laughed again as Groucho swindled a bartender. Gillian stirred in her hard seat and sighed. Bradford looked at her patiently for a long time. Gillian slowly crushed the popcorn container and picked part of her lower lip raw and then acknowledged him again by raising her eyes.

"Would you like to go home with me now?" he asked.

She felt a shiver of excitement, pleased that she didn't have to sit there any longer in league with ghosts whose jokes were dated and whose humor seemed irrelevant, reflecting a life style as remote as the *chanson de geste*. Still she was inclined to be cautious.

"Hester sent you?"

Bradford's smile was fully reassuring.

"Of course," he said.

Hester, after her ordeal, couldn't bear riding the bus home, so she took a cab to the corner near her flat and did some necessary shopping at the superette. Then she picked up something for her head and something for her stomach at the drugstore, called for a package of laundry and fought the bitter wind to her doorstep. By that time she was starey-eyed and unsteady on her feet.

It was already after seven and she was damned worried about Gillian, but Gillian would be safe where she was for hours longer —until shortly after midnight, according to the theatre schedule. Meanwhile Hester had other worries. Even though the men from MORG had been surprisingly gentle with her, asking only a few questions, it was not unlikely they'd followed her home. And why had Maylun disappeared so suddenly, leaving Roth to dissolve in his own grease? She'd never seen a man so shaken. Hester was suspicious and frightened. MORG was the enemy now, and MORG was powerful.

A note on her door from Meg Bundy: *Scrabble tonight? Give us a buzz.* Hester felt badly. She'd turned down their invitations so often of late they were going to think she was standoffish. As she unlocked her door she tried to frame a reasonable excuse. *Can't make it tonight, I'm harboring a fugitive.* But thanks anyway.

Hester opened the door an inch, blocked it open with a foot, stooped for an armload of packages. She backed into her apartment, finding the wall switch by the door with a free finger. A lamp went on next to the sofa in the living room. The door slammed shut.

Hester turned around and all but died; groceries and laundry thudded to the floor.

Peter Sandza was standing in the middle of her living room, holding up a hand-printed sign. Printed with her lipstick.

DON'T TALK, the sign said. THEY ARE LISTENING.

Seventeen

Peter wouldn't let her say a word but he held her lovingly, putting a hand over her mouth so she couldn't weep aloud. With a remote control unit he turned on the television. Then he unbuttoned her coat, unzipped her skirt, skimmed her pantyhose down to her boot tops. Hester had never been screwed so urgently in her life. It was a fun rape. She came, either on the shag rug, or on the way down; afterward she couldn't remember which.

No more headache; no more sour stomach and nerves; Hester had been purged. They did blissful erotic things to each other. In conjugation his strength had her glowing with vitality. Hester held Peter's face in her steady hands, tongue flicking out to touch the tip of his nose, his salty eyelids.

"You're so brown. Where've you been?"

"Florida."

"Oh, Florida. And what were you doing in Florida?"

"Fishing, mostly."

"Fishing! Well, well. Any luck?"

"I threw them back by the carload."

"I don't suppose it occurred to you that while you were down there fishing I was up here going berserk every night at seven sharp."

"Hester, I'm sorry."

"Sorry doesn't get it. Mmmm. *Oh.* Okay, I'm not mad any more. Darling. Are you about to come again?"

"With just a little help——"

"Help like this? First we *peel* the apple, then we *core* it—ah! God. Babybabybaby."

In repose Peter told her the story of his arduous escape from the hospital, and the long killing pursuit.

"I almost bought it in the river, Hester. Hit my head on something while I was swimming under water. I lost my bearings. The current carried me at least a mile from where I'd planned to go ashore. I stayed in too long. My body core temperature was falling fast; another minute of that cold water and I couldn't have done the right thing even if I'd been able to think of it. Thank God it was New Year's Eve. Some long-haul truckers were having a party in a private place, and they'd left their rigs on the river bank. I crawled into a bunk behind one of the cabs, wrapped myself in wool blankets and sucked on a box of sugar cubes I found. I needed the fuel; just a six-degree loss of body core heat is fatal.

"Woke up at dawn at a truck stop somewhere south of Wilmington, Deleware. I still couldn't think very clearly. Borrowed some clothes and took off. I was sick and I knew I needed help. Washington was closer than New York. I took a big chance and looked up an old friend named Nick O'Hanna. We were in the Navy together. I told Nick everything. He got me a doctor and then he flew me south to his place in the Keys for R and R. I sweated out the flu, or whatever it was. Nick brought me back to Washington; this afternoon I hopped a commercial jet to the Westchester airport and drove straight here. Nick and his boss, a man named Todfield, are trying to get a line on Robin for me. No luck so far."

Hester sat up and traced the outline of Peter's mouth with a finger.

"I want to talk to you about that. But first why don't we take our clothes off and *really* make out?"

Peter smiled but shook his head sternly. Play time was over. Hester made a face that accused him of pooping out too soon, but she stripped anyway because she was rumpled and sticky.

"Right back," she said.

In the bathroom, taped to the mirror, was another of Peter's signs, warning of a planted listening device. Hester shuddered at the thought of her apartment crawling with MORG's obscene little bugs and kept her mouth shut while she washed herself. She put on a plushy jump suit and sprayed the root of her throat with something beguiling and then, just because she felt like it, she added rococo earrings, filigreed Mexican silver set with big opals: a "thank you" from the Bundys for helping them paint their apartment.

In the living room she lay with her head in Peter's lap where they could talk all they wanted, protected by the blaring TV.

"How many of their teeny little microphones did you find?"

"Six."

"Six! How did you know where to look? I wouldn't have known where to look."

"The placements were strictly routine. I used a detection system called a Saber kit. It took about twenty minutes."

"Couldn't you rip them out of the walls?"

"I could also stand naked in the window with a lampshade on my head."

"Oh. Uh-huh, I see what you mean. Are you sure you didn't miss any?"

"I'm sure."

Hester looked around with loathing. "How'd the buggers get in here? I have some damn good locks——"

"And they have the people who make the locks for people like you."

"Yah! I can't stand it. They've been eavesdropping. On me! Somehow I don't feel like a person any more. They've taken away my citizenship. They can tune in whenever they're in the mood. They hear me chew and gargle and shit and whip my beaver when I'm blue and lonely and, and they, they drilled holes in my walls! They drilled holes in *me!*"

"Almost," Peter said calmingly, a hand on her arm.

"How long do you think I've been bugged?"

"At least two weeks. Some of the placements, the telephone, for instance, must have been made when you started working at Paragon Institute."

"And that's why you've always stayed away from here."

"One of the reasons."

"Where are they listening?"

"Somewhere on the block."

"In this building?"

"It would be convenient."

Hester's breath hissed between her teeth. She hunched her shoulders uneasily.

"Well—that really complicates things. I've got her, but now I don't know what to do with her."

"Got who, Hester?"

She smiled proudly at him.

"Gillian Bellaver," she said.

Bradford lived a few blocks from the Director's Chair Theatre, in a co-op at Park and 38th. Bradford's last name was Whitlock. There were a lot of Whitlocks around, and they all had money. He didn't ask, so Gillian didn't tell him she was a Bellaver. He was, however, curious about where she went to school. Bordendale, Gillian told him. Bradford seemed surprised and then flustered. I thought you were older, he said. His smile revealed the gum line. You *look* older, he said. They paused in front of his building and Bradford asked her if she would like something to eat. He praised the candlelight restaurant on the corner. Gillian was cold but not hungry. No, she said. Let's go on up. Bradford's smile was antsy. His blue eyes had a sparkly unreal quality, but Gillian didn't think he was high on anything: some people just had baby-doll eyes. Cute if you were a girl. Bradford held her elbow awkwardly and they went in. The doorman was deferential, and the elevator operator was delighted to have Bradford's company. He called Bradford "sir" five times on the way to the penthouse.

The front door was opened by a huge man with white hair and a mass of liver spots on his aged face. He wore gray trousers with sharp creases, a white shirt and a charcoal vest with a subtle blue stripe. He spoke softly and never once looked directly at Gillian. Still he seemed to regret the fact of her presence.

"Good evening, sir."

"Good evening, Elias."

They took off their wraps and handed them to Elias. There were framed sketches in the entrance hall that looked to be the work of Old Masters, and one massive fifteenth-century oil of a king posing on a balcony too snug for his full-grown frame. The furniture was French, all of it at least two hundred years old, and also of exhibition quality.

"May I fix you something to eat, sir?"

"I don't think so. Later."

Elias nodded a fraction of an inch and departed arthritically, his feet shuffling in slippers. Bradford took Gillian's elbow again and escorted her into the living room. More antique furniture. Two lamps were lit in opposite corners. Beyond the terrace the view was dominated by the lights of the United Nations Plaza on the river.

"Do you live here by yourself?" Gillian asked.

"Yes." Bradford played with the buttons of a lighting-control system concealed in a game table, illuminating great numbers of old paintings and drawings on the walls. He called her attention to one after another.

"Here's a favorite of mine, by Giordano. It's just a little sketch. She looks a lot like you, Gillian."

Gillian studied the drawing politely; she didn't get the resemblance. Still, she couldn't be all that certain any more. Cornered there with after-effects, she glanced hopefully at an old mirror, but it was far enough away so that she couldn't make herself out.

Bradford lowered most of the lights and joined her; he put a hand lightly on her shoulder. Gillian looked into the baby-doll eyes.

"How long have you known Hester?"

"Oh—two years."

"Will she be coming soon?"

"Don't worry. How about something to drink?"

"No, I don't drink."

"I don't either. Wine with meals. You couldn't call that drinking. Are you into grass?"

"No."

"That makes two of us. Oh, once in a while I'll have a joint, just——"

"—To be sociable. I'd like to use the bathroom," Gillian said. "Surely."

He took her through his bedroom, which was monastic in its simplicity: a single hanging fixture, chains and crudely hammered brass, a low wide bed with a heavy superstructure, raw beams stained dark. The floor was of faded red tiles like firebrick. White walls. The bathroom was conventional and had some color: stained glass, walnut paneling. Gillian locked the door and looked into a mirror that made her eyes water blindingly. A rheostat controlled the lighting around the mirror, and she dialed it low. The bathroom smelled of the shaving lotion he fancied.

Gillian knew she had made a mistake: Bradford was no friend of Hester's. He'd lied to her. What did he want, then? —What else? Gillian swallowed hard and shook. She ran water to bathe her face and calm herself. She suffered a cramp like a menstrual cramp; it left her ashen. She unbuttoned her jeans and sat hunched on the john with head in hands. Moving her bowels was some relief, but the movement happened with difficulty and it hurt. Probably she'd missed Hester by being stupid. What was she going to do now?

Her fingers touched the round Band-Aid near her groin and something stirred in her memory. She peeled the elastic from tender skin and held it in her hand. Now she remembered the Band-Aid's purpose. Hester had put it there for her in case she got lost or drew a blank somewhere along the way. Shrewd Hester: there'd been plenty of blanks. Gillian pried the gauze loose from the elastic. A note under the pad, in characters so tiny Gillian had to turn the lights up to full again in order to read it. There seemed to be nothing to the message but an address on east Thirty-Sixth Street. Hester's apartment? Gillian pressed the pad back into place and stuck the Band-Aid in a more convenient location, on the inside of one wrist. She knew she might turn forgetful again, although her mind seemed clearer now than it had for hours.

When she left the bathroom buttoning her jeans she encountered Bradford. He had taken off his clothes and was bending over with his backside exposed to her, hands grasping his ankles. He had laid out a wicked-looking assortment of flagellants' tools on the bed.

"Punish me, Gillian," he panted.

Gillian was startled, but not fightened; it wasn't exactly an assault. She looked at his upside-down and reddening face.

"You lied to me about Hester."

"I had to. Otherwise you wouldn't have come. Now you can get even. Hit me. Make me scream."

His buttocks were a nightmare. Scars and welts the color of earthworms. Gillian looked away.

"Let me go," she said. "I have to find Hester."

"The door's locked. You'll have to whip me if you want the key!"

"I'll scream. That's a promise. Elias will hear me."

"He's heard your kind scream before. I want the black one with all the little knots. Get it for me, Gillian. Use all your strength. Hurt me."

Genitally he was undeveloped, childlike, his scrotum hairless, puny as an out-of-breath balloon. His half-aroused cock was in proportion. Bradford would never grow up. He lived luxuriously in hell. For the first time since morning Gillian thought about Robin, as she had last seen him, in bed with his whore. Trying to mock her. But living in hell. She pitied him, but she realized now he would never grow up either; Robin was doomed. A flash of insight that was worse than a cramp; she wondered where that left her.

Gillian approached Bradford and stood looking calmly at him. He was filmy with perspiration. He trembled all over.

"Do it, do it."

"Stand *up*, Bradford," Gillian said. When he didn't obey her she lifted him by the hair of his head. He jittered with expectations. Gillian stared into his evasive eyes, brilliant now in the blushing face.

"*Is* it the end of the world, Bradford? What do you think?"

"Are you into one of those nutball religions?"

"No," Gillian said, and she kissed him softly on the cheek. Bradford flinched, drawing away in confusion and dread.

"I don't like being kissed," he said. "And don't *look* at me. Just beat me the way I deserve." He covered his inadequate sexual equipment with one hand, resembling a flighty nymph in one of the old paintings that filled his rooms.

"I can't do that," Gillian explained. "I'm sorry you're in such a mess. I'm in kind of a mess myself. But the difference is—the difference is—I can't just give in. I have to do something about it. If you'll unlock the door I'd really like to go now."

Bradford began to cry, in such agony that Gillian couldn't watch him; the tears were worse than his pathetic scars. He spared her by running into the bathroom and slamming the door.

After walking around the austere bedroom a couple of times she decided to try the door. It wasn't locked after all. Bradford had told another lie. Gillian looked sympathetically at the bathroom door, then walked through the quiet flat. Elias was nowhere around. She found her coat in a closet and put it on. Her footsteps echoed in the entrance hall. Three minutes later she was on the street, walking sadly toward the river.

Even before they left the little mom-and-pop restaurant on First Avenue Miles Bundy knew he was in for a rough evening. It was all he could do to keep from belching as he shook hands with the proprietor on their way out, but his expression must have been something to see: Meg looked as if she were biting on a nail to keep from laughing.

On the street he let it roll out profoundly, not caring how many windows he shattered.

"Oh, my," Meg said. "Don't point that thing at me."

"So much for those charming little places nobody knows about yet."

"You insisted on eating Hungarian. I warned you."

"I can handle Hungarian cooking. When it's good. Those two must be gypsies. Straight from the campfire. They'll throw anything in the communal pot. Hair, hide and all." Miles was sourly incredulous. *"That's* what it feels like. It feels like I just ate a scalp."

"I liked the sobbing violin, though."

"And the violinist?"

Meg nodded dreamily. "He's the sort I'd like to take home with me for a few hours. In chains."

"He was getting a pot belly. He uses shoe polish on his hair."

"He has eyes like homemade sin. I couldn't help noticing how charming you found our dusky serving wench. Do you suppose those were really toothmarks on her breast?"

"Once-bitten, like a poisoned apple. Do we have any Maalox at home?"

"Martians," Meg said.

"What?"

"All Hungarians are supposed to be descendants of a lost tribe of Martians who came to colonize the earth. That's why their language has nothing in common with other European languages." Miles was staring at her. "Hungarian is a *very* difficult language to master. And, personality-wise, they're a breed apart. They have this other-worldly, spaced-out quality. A vale of mystery lies behind every smile."

"Urrrp. Goddamn it."

They walked silently the rest of the way home. Meg let them into the building with her key, and they continued upstairs.

"Aren't we on the Late Show tonight?" Miles said.

"Thursday? Uh-huh, Channel 9 at eleven."

"That one we did with Cyd and Frank and Ann Miller? *Texas Red?*"

"The 'Billy the Kid' fantasy number," Meg said. "Terrific. Can't wait to see it again." Hester's television was blasting game-show banalities which were clearly audible in the hall. Meg glanced at the door as they went by. "Hester got our note."

"It was Gene and not Frank," Miles said. "And it wasn't Ann Miller, it was Betty Garrett."

"You know, you're right? Betty Garrett. We wrapped just a couple of weeks before Larry got nailed. I always confuse that flick with *Holiday in San Antone.*"

"The 'Fall of the Alamo' ballet."

"Only one of the all-time greats——"

"Academy!" Miles said, leaping gracefully and clicking his heels, still spry as a pup. Then he farted. Meg wrinkled her nose and opened their apartment, turned on lamps inside. The painting had been completed, and all the furnishings were in place.

"Maalox you said?" Meg asked, going to the kitchen.

"And a glass of milk to wash it down." Miles piled his loden coat on the awning-striped sofa, then sat in a leather chair in his favorite corner and exchanged low-top boots for slippers.

"Holiday in San Antone," he said. "Didn't I slip on some wet tiles and sprain my back?"

Meg was busy and didn't reply. Miles got up and unlocked an armoire with heavy carved doors. There were drawers inside, also with locks. He pulled out two deep drawers. One contained a bulky UHF receiver, the other a voice-activated tape deck. A glance at the take-up reel assured him that nothing had been transcribed in their absence. He warmed up the radio, a relic of the fifties, and from another drawer removed two pairs of headphones.

"I don't suppose you remember the name of that Commie rat bastard who played the tent show impressario?"

Meg returned to the living room with a silver tray. Maalox and milk for him, tea and lemon for her. She put the tray on a low copper-clad table. A replica of an Aztec calendar stone was stamped in the copper.

"Was it Lawrence Keats?"

"Lawrence Keats! Yeh. We fixed him pretty good, didn't we?" Meg said affectionately, "We fixed a lot of them, hon."

Miles locked in the frequency he wanted. A red light glowed. He incautiously dialed the volume too high and tried the number three microphone. Rock music nearly burst his eardrums and he yanked the headphones off.

"Owwww, Jesus, what is that?"

"Grand Funk?"

"No, I mean she's got the fucking TV going in the living room, and the fucking stereo is on in the bedroom—a party? Would she have thrown a party without inviting us?"

"No. Try the bathroom," Meg suggested, feeding him a spoonful of Maalox. Miles gulped it down and reached for his milk. He drained the glass and went back to work, carefully adjusting all the dials.

"Water dripping," he said. "She really should have a plumber in." Bored, he did Ronald Coleman for Meg. "Hester, my darling, where are you? You can't be asleep, not with all the racket." He lapsed back into his own voice, and sulked. "Hester's being impossible tonight."

"She must have the lonelies."

"Could be. Well. Kitchen." Miles tuned in another bug. An unidentifiable sound issued from the headphones. Miles frowned, holding the phones so Meg could hear too.

"It might be an FM radio between stations," Meg guessed.

"And it might be our lousy cold war equipment," he muttered. "I mean this stuff is so *dated*. This is simply not my idea of sophisticated snooping."

"Always been reliable."

"We could use a thermal-imager and a people-sniffer, just for openers."

"Probably there's only so much gear to go around."

"And we're low priority. Very low priority."

"Well—MORG wanted us back. That's something." She put her arms around him and rested her cheek against his shoulder.

"There's one thing that still galls me, Meg."

"I know . . ."

"After all we did for the Industry—rooting out all those goddam Reds and Comsymps . . ."

"I know. I know."

"The Duke wouldn't shake hands with me. I went up to him at the benefit and introduced myself—'Mr. Wayne,' I said, 'I'm Miles Bundy, and I think we have a lot in common.' I wasn't expecting all that much—maybe a 'Well done, fella.' Hell, he hated Commies as much as I did! But the Big Guy just turned away. He snubbed me."

Meg nuzzled the back of his neck.

Miles, listening, said, "There's too much noise. Know what I mean?"

"Strategic noise. I was thinking the same thing. I wonder if it's possible—why don't we see if Hester is wearing our little present?"

Miles tried a different frequency, and suddenly they both could hear Hester quite clearly.

"**S**ooner or later," Peter said, "Maylun will talk. So consider yourself unemployed. You'll have to go with Gillian and me."

"You bet I'm going." Hester beamed and dropped two more pieces of floured plump chicken into the pot of boiling fat on the stove. The fat crackled loudly, another satisfying increment of sound to defeat the microphone aimed straight down at them from inside the light fixture on the ceiling. She'd placed a churning blender on top of the fridge and tied a transistor radio tuned to static within a few inches of the bug. They spoke in normal tones with the confidence that even the best filtering equipment available couldn't isolate their voices in all this interference.

Peter had already eaten half of the chicken and was working over the bones of the last piece on his plate. Hester was pleased with his robust appetite.

"When was the last time you had something to eat?"

"I don't remember." Peter frowned and put down the bones and sat back in his chair, staring at the wall. "I don't remember," he said again, as if that lapse annoyed him.

"Hey, don't quit on me now. This batch will be cooked in a minute." Hester looked at her watch. "Do I have time to pack a few things?"

"We've hung around too long already," Peter said.

"It's only five past eight."

"Shall I tell you what's happening to Maylun about now?"

Hester turned cold. "No. No. Don't. I can stuff an overnight bag quick as a wink. Are we taking my car?"

"No, you'll be hot. O'Hanna fixed me up with wheels. I'm in a lot on Forty-seventh just off Third. Dark blue Cougar, this year's model. We'll leave here separately. I have to check you for loose tags. I'll give you a pay phone number to call after you've walked around for a bit. If I'm satisfied, I'll babysit while you pick up the car. Then we'll find out just how useful Miss Gillian will be."

"Peter, she knows where to find Robin. She *must* know. I think those birth charts I saw in Roth's office belonged to Robin and Gillian. Otherwise why should he be so secretive about them? If they were born so close together, almost to the second, then it's possible they're, they could be like twins, you know? Astrological and psychic twins."

Peter smiled painfully. "I don't put much faith in astrology."

"Never mind; I'm convinced Gillian's on his wavelength. And she'll take us right to him."

The oil on the stove was smoking. Hester turned down the gas jet and turned on the stove exhaust fan. She fished out the pieces of deep-fried, crusty chicken. Her own stomach was hollow, and her mouth watered. She sat down quickly opposite Peter to eat.

Meg poured another half-cup of lukewarm tea, added a squeeze of lemon and sat on an arm of the sofa, looking across the room at her husband.

"We were given carte blanche in this matter," she said.

"They never expected us to come up with the big fish."

"If we don't exercise our privilege, then we won't be granted any more privileges."

Miles toyed with the headphones in his lap and said nothing.

"In our line of work, even one step backward is a step into oblivion." They both thought about that. Meg sipped her tea. "I'm not ready to self-destruct, babes," she said softly.

Miles looked up. "I was only feeling a little sorry about Hester."

Meg nodded, but she was firm with him and wouldn't smile. "Yes. There's that. But Hester's not what you would call innocent, is she?"

Meg set the teacup aside and picked up the receiver of the telephone. She held it without dialing, eyes steady. Thirty-three years as a team. She liked the final word to come from Miles. It was one of the courtesies that had kept their marriage solid.

Hester, wincing, detached the silver-and-opal earrings.

"I'm not used to wearing these things," she said. "They each weigh a ton." She held them out for inspection in the palm of her hand. "Do you like them?"

"Pretty," Peter commented, his mind elsewhere.

"The Bundys gave them to me." She waited for him to be impressed. "Meg and Miles *Bundy*. They were in all those movie musicals back in the forties and fifties. I gave them a hand when they were moving in upstairs, so—a couple of days later they gifted me."

The phone rang on the wall behind Hester.

She looked wide-eyed at Peter, who said, "Maybe you should." Hester put the earrings on the table, leaned back and snagged the receiver.

" 'Lo. Oh, hi! I was just ta—thinking about you. No, no. Listen, I meant to call about the scrabble, okay if I beg off? Oh. Oh, he is? Serious? What are you doing for him? Hmmm, well, I bet he'll like *that*. Uh-huh. You're in luck, I didn't throw it out, it's still in the bedroom. The whole paper or just the crossword? No, you don't have to bother, Meg—well, okay."

Hester hung up smiling.

"That was Meg. Miles is sweating out a cold and wants the crossword from Sunday's *Times*——"

"She's coming down?"

"Just to the door, I'll get rid of her super-quick."

Hester had pushed open the swinging door of the kitchen before Peter thought to ask, "When did they move in?"

"Oh, like, three weeks ago. And you should see what they've done with their place already."

"Love to," Peter murmured, as the door swung shut in his face.

In the living room Hester turned the volume of the TV down. She saw Peter's Colt Python on a corner of the coffee table—he'd put it there after it slipped from his belt during their love-making. She picked up the Colt and carried it to the bedroom. There she stuffed it into her purse, which was lying at the foot of the bed. She turned off Grand Funk. The sudden quiet was a blessing. Hester leafed through the sections of last Sunday's *Times* looking for the magazine.

Peter, hands locked behind his head, stared at the light fixture from which the transistor radio was dangling. Then he looked at the telephone on the wall. Something crawled uneasily in the back of his mind; lay down to rest; crawled again. He shifted his attention to the earrings lying on the table.

The front door buzzer sounded.

Hester, carrying the *Times* magazine section, left the bedroom. She paused to shut the door behind her, looked around the living room.

The shag carpet was well-trampled where they'd made out, but who else would notice? She hurried to meet Meg.

Peter picked up the earrings, one in each hand. He weighed them. Perhaps there was a difference in weight, but he wasn't sure. He put both earrings down, lifted a glass salt shaker with a thick bottom and brought it down hard. One of the "opals" cracked into a dozen pieces. He picked it apart, found a small radio transmitter known in the trade as a "sugar cube," and a subminiature surveillance microphone small enough to fit into a tooth cavity. The sugar cube was powerful enough to broadcast their voices more than two hundred yards.

He shot straight up out of his chair.

"Hester! No!"

As Peter cried out Hester opened the front door on its chain. She caught just a glimpse of Meg standing outside. Shocked at hearing Peter's voice, Hester turned her head toward the kitchen.

The shot from the silenced revolver in Meg's hand struck Hester behind the left eye and two inches below the temple. The flat-nosed bullet blew most of her brains out and broke her neck and the impact hurled her half way across the room. Miles stepped forward with bolt cutters in his gloved hands and chopped through the door chain. Meg kicked the door open and they rushed inside, nimbly jumping over Hester's twisted body. The front door slammed shut. Miles had his own revolver in his hand. They bracketed the kitchen door. All of it—the shooting, the forced entry, the stake-out—was beautifully choreographed. It took them four seconds.

"Peter!" Meg called.

"Peter, it's over," Miles said. "We're familiar with the layout of the kitchen. There's no other door, and no place you can hide. If you're armed, you don't have a hope of hitting us. We'll shoot through this door if we have to."

Seconds wound down with the slow pressure of thumbscrews. Meg and Miles were too well disciplined to look at each other. Even a momentary distraction could be fatal for them. They waited, tense but confident.

A muffled, indecipherable sound from inside the kitchen.

"Say again, Peter?"

"H-Hester?"

Meg said calmly, "Hester is done for, Peter."

Another pause, and then they heard him sobbing.

"Oh God, oh God I'm so tired—can't make it any more. I just can't——"

Meg couldn't help herself, she had to glance at Miles. He was every bit as surprised as she was.

Peter's breakdown quickly verged on hysteria.

"We sympathize, Peter," Miles said, his mouth twisted in contempt. "Now you simply must do this our way, and the sooner the better."

"I don't want to die!" Peter wailed.

"But we won't shoot. You have our solemn word."

They heard him shuffling and sniffing in there. A chair scraped on the tile floor.

"Come out, Peter. Hands where we can see them."

The swinging door creaked open a bit. Peter had his back against it. He peered through the thin crack at Miles. Tears ran down his cheeks. Meg moved a full step to her left so the door wouldn't be in the way when Peter came out. Miles nodded almost imperceptibly at her. She was the marksman of the team. She would be only about eight feet from Peter. She would shoot again for the head to end his charmed life in a gusher millisecond.

Miles smelled fried chicken and hot cooking fat; his gassy stomach rumbled.

"Don't shoot!" Peter begged them. "I, I, I'm COMM-MINNNGGGG!"

As he screamed he threw the door wide open, swinging around with the pot from the stove held head-high; insulated mittens protected his hands. Meg's quick shot glanced off the iron pot an instant before she and Miles were drenched with a gallon of scalding fat.

Miles caught the worst of it, full in the face, but Meg was sufficiently splattered to ruin her aim. Her second shot was a clear miss as Peter swung all the way around and smashed in the left side of her face with the pot. Miles, rooting in the carpet, made ghastly pigyard noises. His eyes were poaching in their sockets from the heat of seared-shut lids; half his head had been flash-cooked to the bone.

Peter wrenched Meg's revolver from her outstretched hand, stepped over the still-smoking Miles and kneeled beside Hester. She was all but unrecognizable. Peter bared his teeth in a terrible grimace. He got up and turned on the TV to cover the sounds Miles was making.

"Mercy! Mercy!" Miles cried, curving around and around his his agony like bait on a hook.

Peter took aim and shot him twice in the head. Then he returned to Meg. She was still conscious; her mouth hung open and her eyes had backed up in her head. Her fingers plodded nowhere in the carpet. She was blistering the length of her fine body. Her left jawbone was crushed and her nose had been spectacularly displaced.

Peter shot her too.

For a while after he lowered the gun Peter stood staring down at Meg, feeling a balloon-spot on his cheek where he'd been scalded by a drop of oil. The air he breathed was burnt, atrocious. It would have taken a stronger stomach than his to stand it. He turned and vomited.

When he looked up someone else was there.

Gillian stood just inside the front door, holding it open behind her back. She was looking at Hester's warped remains, engrossed, her face just beginning to twitch out of control. Peter wiped his mouth with one hand. Gillian's head flew up at this gesture, but she continued to stand stock-still, hands behind her back, as if they concealed a surprise. She gave him a look through stinking blue haze.

Madcap laughter on TV. Gillian's eyelids fluttery as bats. Gillian, taking in this repository of hell.

"I knocked," she said.

"Gillian."

"I knocked but——"

She slid back through the door fast but without panic and was gone.

Peter let the revolver drop from his hand and went after her. Down two flights of rubber-treaded stairs. Through the inside door and the outside door. Gillian, running in the street, confronted a speeding cab. She missed it with a dazzled change of direction and by the length of her outstretched arm and leaped to the sidewalk. Peter hung back until the cab screeched on. She was a good runner but the parka had to be heavy as an anchor.

Gillian came to an excavation that had eaten away half of the block on the north side of the street. It was surrounded by a high board fence and a long boardwalk with a roof over it. She balked at entering this tunnel and turned back to the street. As she tried to climb between two sports cars jammed bumper-to-bumper at the curb Peter caught up, snatched her back by the hood and threw her ruthlessly against the fence. Gillian yelled but there was only surprise in her voice, not terror. It sounded like kids playing, and anyone looking their way would have had trouble locating them in that dark and cluttered pocket of the street.

When her chin came up Peter jammed a thumb under the angle of her jaw. Gillian blacked out instantly, before she felt pain, and swayed drunkenly into his arms.

He lugged her down the cellar steps of a gutted brownstone beside the excavation. Out of sight of the street, he sat Gillian on an over-turned trash can and held her head up so she would come around faster. When she moaned he used the wide belt from her parka as a gag, holding it tight-fisted behind her head.

Peter was shaking; he wasn't wearing a jacket, only a lightweight turtleneck sweater. His breath echoed back through window-sized gaps in the facade of the old house.

When Gillian opened her eyes and focused on him her instinctive reaction was to fight. She kicked and grappled wildly and slid off the trash can, which made a rolling racket in that narrow place. But he held her head steady and made her look at him in the light reflected from a sill of polished ice directly above them.

"Gillian, it's Peter. Don't you remember? The hospital. I helped you there. I said I'd be back. *Remember*, Gillian!"

A wind whipped along the street, singing its eerie cold tune. A car swished by, Hispanic radio loud and gay. Gillian still struggled, but more deliberately, eyes crossing and recrossing his face until, in a moment of startled comprehension, they froze full upon him.

"I didn't kill Hester. She was my friend. The man and the woman were spying on her. One of them shot her, just a few minutes ago. And I . . . I killed them both."

Gillian's eyes closed; she made small sickened sounds behind the chewed gag but her hands, which had pounded him, were now quiet and clinging.

"I'm Robin's father," Peter told her.

He loosened the ties of the hood and put a hand inside, stroking one side of her face. Her breathing had quieted. He loosened the gag too.

"I have to find my son. Hester thought you could help me. That's all I want from you, Gillian. Help."

Gillian looked up sharply but he missed the trouble in her

eyes, the warning: his attention had been diverted by another car on the street.

This car stopped abruptly. When the curbside doors opened Peter heard the unmistakable blast of static from a police radio, followed by a droning voice that cut in and out. The radio was turned down, or off. Footsteps. Two, no, three men running up the steps of a brownstone. A second official car went by above their heads, traveling the wrong way on the one-way street. The driver rode the brakes too hard.

Peter put a cautionary hand on Gillian's shoulder and eased up two steps, stretching out like a cat. He looked past the yellow flashers that marked the construction site. The cars parked diagonally across the street in front of Hester's building weren't NYPD. All the men wore dark gray trench coats. The street was filling up with Homefolks. Maylun Chan We had sprung a leak, after an hour or so of inspired persuasion.

Peter returned to Gillian. His eyes stifled like a snake's, they set a pulse to hammering in her throat and numbed the corners of her mouth.

"It's MORG. There's a lot of them, and they'll kill me on sight. Tell me where I have to go, Gillian. Tell me where I can find him."

She shook her head.

"I don't know."

"How can you lie to me? Don't you know what it means?"

"Yes, but I——"

His hands went around her throat; his thumbs pressed the darkness home a little at a time. Then as quick as it had come the fury left his face, and he let her go. She sagged in a corner gasping for breath.

"Oh, Jesus," he mumbled. "Oh, no. I'm sorry. Forgive me, Gillian."

Peter touched her awkwardly; she shook her head again and crossed her arms and rocked, not making any more sounds.

Gillian was unaware that he'd left her. Then the voices of the men in the street sounded closer and she looked up, stunned. It took her a few moments to realize where Peter had gone. She crawled frantically through the window space into the wrecked house. She took three steps and stopped, paralyzed by pitch blackness.

"Peter!" she whispered.

He didn't answer. Gillian went on, groping, ran painfully into a post and rebounded to the concrete floor. Looking back, she could see the clear rectangle of the window. She fought the urge to give in and retreat.

"Peter," she sobbed. "Don't leave me!"

She got up and went hesitantly forward, hands outstretched. A match was struck inches from her face. She flinched, filthy hands pressed against her mouth.

"Gillian, go back."

"No, I can't! I don't have any place to go. Peter, I did see Robin. Last night, or the night before. I know I can find him again. It'll take a little time. Just let me go with you. I promise I'll find him for you."

Peter blew out the flame. For a while Gillian stood there shuddering, hearing him move around in the dark. Then she felt him next to her; his hand gripped her elbow.

"I saw a flight of stairs. This way. Walk carefully with me, there are holes in the floor."

Peter couldn't risk another match, but he guided them with shuffling slowness to the stairs he had picked out by the glow of the first match. On the floor above there was enough cast-off light from the city to show them a back way out through a rubbled lot. One block north they climbed over a chain-link fence and continued, arm in arm, toward Forty-Seventh Street, where Peter had parked his car.

For the moment they were free.

Eighteen

After looking briefly into Hester's apartment, which still smelled oppressively of cooked flesh and spilled blood despite the fact that all the bodies had been removed, Childermass went upstairs to the Bundys'. He settled down on the sunny Mexican sofa and asked for a neat Scotch. This was brought to him. The time was twenty minutes past nine. For several more minutes Childermass listened to the tape recording which Miles Bundy had made earlier that evening.

It had been longer than a year since Childermass had heard Peter Sandza's voice. He listened with an expression of pained fascination. So near in time, and so elusive. Twice he put down his glass to fondle the stump of his left arm. The other men in the room, embarrassed, stared out the windows or at the tips of their shoes.

"I'll miss the Bundys," Childermass said when the tape had ended. "I was really fond of those dancing fools. We were together in the bad old days, when all there was to MORG was a row of crummy offices in a warehouse across from the Navy yard. Nineteen hundred and forty-six. Did you know that, Richard? Meg and Miles Bundy were among my first recruits."

"I didn't know that, sir," Richard Kanner said. He was the senior executive on hand, chief of Homefolks, MORG's domestic division. "If only they'd called for backup——"

"I can't fault them for taking the action they did. I know they didn't realize they just weren't good enough any more. Time is a thief, and Peter Sandza is inhumanly difficult to trap. You can't believe how good he is until you've actually been up against him. And how many men have survived that interesting experience?"

"Sir, I think we should get out an APB on that blue Cougar."

"Why bother? Peter has had an hour, he's well rid of it by now. We could put their descriptions on the police networks, but that's a long shot. Even if they're picked up we'd be fortunate if we could move fast enough to keep the girl off the front pages: the Bellaver name makes her hot copy."

"He might not have Gillian with him."

"I think he does. Therefore we can be one hundred percent sure where our man is going. Hester said it best: Gillian is on Robin's wavelength. We'll fall back and wait for them at Psi Faculty."

"There's that other problem. How does Nick O'Hanna fit into this?"

"I'm listening," Childermass said, and he winked at a subordinate nearby.

Kanner clasped his hands between his knees.

"Well—obviously Peter went to them looking for help. Because of the weapon, the articles of clothing and the electronic devices which we found in Hester's apartment we can assume that O'Hanna agreed to supply Peter's material needs. Let's also assume he's backed by the full faith and credit of the Langley gang. But they're under edict. They want the boy killed, not liberated by his father."

"How many ways can you skin an old cat, Richard?"

"They plan to double-cross Peter?"

"Why, sure. Leave it to Todfield. Should Peter succeed in taking back his son, they step in at their leisure and do the dirty. But, because we're not going to let Peter anywhere near the boy, not even for old time's sake, it's a losing proposition. Don't be concerned about the Langley gang. Things are working out our way."

Childermass stood and was helped into his suitcoat, then his long black astrakhan.

"Well, he's out there," Childermass said, smiling. "The existential fugitive, holed up with a girl who has been under such a severe strain she could go raving mad at any moment. She has the unpredictable power to destroy him. Even if he survives Gillian Bellaver, Peter's on his last lap. Very nearly a burnt-out case, but does he know it yet? Oh, no, there's still that last stubborn spark of hope. For a long, long time I thought he was enchanted. I really did. I doubted I would face him again long enough to see that ineffable spark die out before my eyes. Leaving nothing. A heap of human wreckage. But it *will* happen. It's academic now. I'm paid in full and guaranteed. What a hell of a thrill. I'll be having dinner tonight at Twenty-One with friends. After that I'm going to suck on a pair of thousand-dollar tits and cakewalk on the ceiling of the fanciest suite at the Waldorf. If you need me, Richard, I'll be at Psi Faculty by sunrise. Try not to need me."

We have to close in five minutes," said the woman in the Port Chester library. "Have you found what you were looking for?"

She smiled at Gillian, who was leafing through a thick reference work entitled *Catholic Colleges and Universities in North America.* Gillian replied with a tight-lipped shake of her head. She had looked at every page at least twice, and now she was concerned. There were hundreds of photos of campuses in the book, but none of the schools were familiar. Anxiety caused her vision to swim and blur.

"Gail, honey."

Gillian, unused to her new name, glanced guiltily at Peter, who stared calmly back at her from across the table.

"You're sure it was a Catholic college?"

"Yes. Because of the chapel."

"Tell me about the chapel again."

"It wasn't like the other buildings." Gillian used her hands descriptively. "The chapel was on a knoll, or a hill, all by itself. Mostly stained glass and—a lot of angles, you know, very futuristic, tent-shaped. The roof angles rose to make crosses and the crosses became three open spires. And everywhere the moon was shining there were long black crosses on the snow. It was really very beautiful."

The librarian nodded. "How long ago did you visit the college?"

"Years and years," Peter said, chuckling.

"I was just a little girl," Gillian explained.

"You have a wonderful memory for places," the librarian said. "Well, we're really getting awfully close to the witching hour around here."

Peter struck his forehead lightly with the heel of his hand. "Am I dumb," he said. He reached across the table and lifted the book, read the date on the cover. "This year's edition."

"Yes, sir, the very latest——"

"But the college is closed. Out of business."

"How do you know that, sir?"

"If it wasn't, then it would be pictured in this book. Do you have an earlier edition? Three or four years back?"

"I don't know. We're constantly updating our reference shelves. The older volume might well be in a carton downstairs awaiting disposal. If you could come back in the morning——"

"There's just no way," Peter said dejectedly. "Gail and I are passing though, and I'm pinched for time. I'm an architect by profession, and I've been commissioned to redesign a college campus in West Virginia. We're touring campuses in the east looking for ideas. Gail remembered this Catholic school, and it sounds like an impressive place. I'd sure like to see it before we head home. Are there many cartons?"

"Quite a few . . ."

"I'll be glad to help you look. It shouldn't take long."

Woodlawn College for Women. Lake Celeste, New York.

When they had a room for the night, Peter located the town on an oil company road map. Lake Celeste was on a state road in the eastern Adirondacks, an area dotted with lakes and medium-sized mountains that supported three ski centers. Population 350. The nearest railroad was thirty-five miles southeast. No airport closer than Glens Falls. There was one way in and one way out, a plowed road which easily could be blockaded.

The surrounding countryside and the campus of what had been Woodlawn College lay under four feet of snow, and more was on the way. Peter had phoned the weather bureau at JFK to get an accurate forecast. Up to eight inches of fresh snow were predicted for Friday night; near blizzard conditions would prevail. Either that made things impossible for him, or it was just what he wanted. He couldn't tell yet. He needed better maps of the Lake Celeste region; government geological survey maps which would show him the location of every building on the campus.

Up to a point Gillian had been helpful, describing the large house in which Robin lived. But when he asked her to Visit again, to go back for a closer look at the inside of the house, she flatly refused. Soon after she wept bitterly; eventually she cried herself to sleep on the double bed in their shared room.

Peter was surprised that Gillian had held up this long. She had to be a mass of raw nerve endings, tormented by each new horror thrust upon her. Gillian's good life had been blasted nearly off the tracks; it ran crazily now, wobbling and screeching into a future that looked like Hell. Yet she had the iron will of those survivors who had walked out of Nazi concentration camps at the end of World War II, wounded, diminished, but never beaten.

Her reluctance to re-Visit the Woodlawn College house was Robin's fault. Peter guessed that much, but their strange, otherwordly relationship baffled him. Robin had done something to hurt her deeply. Almost overcome by fatigue and tears, Gillian tried to explain: after eighteen months in that place, Robin was very different from the image of the boy Peter still cherished. But her thoughts became disconnected. She rambled about childhood things that mysteriously involved Robin, then she simply cried over what was lost or irretrievable. He understood very little of what she meant to say.

From the bedroom windows of the inn in which they were staying Peter read the illuminated face of the clock in the pre-Revolutionary Congregational church. It was six minutes to eleven. At this early hour the historic village of Mt. Carmel, Connecticut, was utterly still. He hadn't seen a moving car for ten minutes. Mt. Carmel was in the southwest corner of the

state, off the main roads and a little too far from New York City
to serve as a bedroom community: backwater status had enabled
the village to retain most of its Colonial character. Moonlight
glistened on polished snow and the tall bare trees that lined the
common.

On the bed Gillian breathed huskily and worried in her sleep.
She was fully clothed but the room was draughty: Peter threw
a blanket over her. There was a smudge of dirt, blending into
one eyebrow, which he hadn't noticed before. She had a nail-
biting habit. Her hair was a welter on the pillow and she was
pathetically pale. But Gillian had an undeniable, visceral impact
on him; it wasn't lust, he thought, but foreknowledge of the
marvellous woman she could be, given any kind of chance.

Considering the company she'd chosen to keep, he wondered
what her chances were of living beyond tomorrow. . . .

In a remarkably vivid and ugly transposition Peter saw Hester's blown-apart head on the pillow. He jerked away from the
bed and sought the bottle of gin he'd bought immediately after
leaving the Port Chester library. He poured a stiff shot, knowing
that tonight he could absorb the full fifth and remain very nearly
sober. No, he was not going to dwell on Hester. He'd always
known it could happen, despite all their precautions. And so
they'd killed her. Probably she didn't have an inkling that her life
was over, certainly she hadn't suffered, there was no use snivel-
ing about it. Hester didn't need an hour of teeth-chattering
soggy remorse in place of a eulogy, that would serve only to
make him less effective, reduce critical focus at the worst of
times.

Peter drank the gin in his glass in measured sips and forced
his thoughts to the problem at hand.

He had taken with him to Hester's the expendable electronics
gear, his Python revolver, which he wished he had, and a topcoat
and sports jacket which he could easily replace. Most of his
clothing, all of the two thousand in cash and the false identifica-
tion he'd prudently left locked in the trunk of the Cougar. He
was now driving a rented Volaré Wagon, but he had no intention
of driving it as far as Lake Celeste. MORG would have every inch
of the town under its control, they'd be picked up in a minute.

Leave Gillian behind? He considered this option again, but he
realized he wasn't going to be less conspicuous traveling alone,

and she had a talent he might still make use of, the ability to telepathically communicate with Robin.

There was another, emotional factor in his final decision to take Gillian along. He had a poignant feeling of responsibility for her life that overwhelmed common sense; it had started that night at the hospital and was now more powerful than ever. Peter had no doubt that Gillian was strongly attracted to and dependent on him. No, he wasn't going to abandon her. He'd thrown Hester away, but possibly there was something he could still do for this one.

The next time he went to the windows to look at the clock it was ten minutes to two in the morning, and the bottle in his hand was nearly empty.

Peter yawned. He had come up with some workable ideas, a way of using the coming snowstorm to advantage. At the same time he was realistic about the probability of success. He yawned again, nerveless but not yet sleepy. Gillian lay peacefully on the bed. As he turned out the single lamp in the room he wondered if she was all there, or if she had gone wandering. In the bathroom he relieved himself of a good part of the gin he'd drunk, brushed his teeth and went to bed beside Gillian.

As soon as he stretched out she turned over and put a loose arm across him, burrowed close and warm with a long exhalation of pleasure, or a release of deep tension. Peter held her head against his chest, kissed an exposed ear and closed his own eyes.

Shortly before dawn he woke up feeling panicked, certain that, in the course of a dream he couldn't recall, he had died.

In sleep Peter had retained a tentative grip on Gillian, but her back was to him now; she was half in and half out of the blanket, warm enough and still fast asleep. The moon had set but there was outside light in the room, a faint morning sheen. You never died in dreams, he thought. You could suffer but not die. Was it simply the cold weight of Hester on his conscience?

The panic was a momentary thing, lying on his back he breathed it all away. But now that he was clearly awake he was obsessed by something not a part of any dream. A catastrophic event had taken place, a gross insult to his mind—palpable fingers had probed his precious gray matter like a small boy grubbing in earth for night crawlers. He was shocked by the image; he quivered childishly and groaned aloud.

Gillian sat up still immersed in sleep and gave him a puzzled look; then she gasped and scrambled away from him. She fell off the bed and rebounded tall holding her head in her hands, making thin sounds of distress.

"Gillian, it's Peter. Don't yell. Easy, girl. You're all right."

She needed another full minute to get her bearings.

"Bathroom," she mumbled.

He got up and guided her in and closed the door. It was then he realized something was wrong with his left hand. The last two fingers had no feeling. They were inert, dead twigs on the surviving limb. The edge of his palm was numb to the wrist. The very tip of his middle finger also was numb. He had control of only about half of his left hand.

So he'd slept on it wrong. Feeling would return. But even as he tried to assure himself that the condition was temporary he realized the truth. It wasn't a circulatory problem or a pinched nerve.

Stroke, Peter thought, more amazed than afraid. The quietest kind of death. A threadlike vessel had ruptured somewhere deep in the right hemisphere or basal ganglia of the brain. The seepage of blood had painlessly destroyed a little patch of neurons. Result, two fingers dead. There was some chance he would regain the use of those fingers. He knew how fortunate he was: he could function with a hand and a half. He might have been lying there on the bed unable to move or speak. He might have been stricken in a thousand bizarre and crippling ways.

Oh, God, if only it doesn't get worse. Don't let me die a creeping death, he prayed.

Gillian came out of the bathroom.

Peter, standing by the windows with his left hand in his right, looked at her in awe. It hadn't occurred to him that he might be affected, waking or sleeping, by the immense power that had killed the woman in the hospital. He had no idea of how it worked or why it worked, why some were immune and others susceptible. He wondered if Gillian knew.

"You slept with me," she said.

"Not in the Biblical sense."

"I know that. I should have told you—there's something—well, I think you already know how weird I am. But it's worse than that. Do you know what a poltergeist is?"

"German word meaning 'noisy spirit.' It involves psychokinesis—furniture moving, objects flying around, pictures falling off walls without a hand touching them. I read somewhere that this sort of psychokinetic activity depends on energies generated by the repressed angers or sexual frustration of certain adolescents. There usually seems to be a child around when there's a poltergeist."

Gillian turned on her side and looked at him.

"I can read people, you know? Like a clairvoyant." Peter nodded. "I don't remember much of what they told me at Paragon Institute. They had me on junk to keep me from thinking too much, and—remembering." Her voice quavered. "I was somebody else there, the mousiest little——"

"Gillian, honey."

Her teeth were clenched, but she wouldn't cry.

"I'm sorry. What I'm trying to tell you—when I'm into clairvoyance, having visions, I become some sort of awful generator. Like a poltergeist, but I don't smash dishes. I bleed people out. Kill them. I killed my b-best friend."

"But you're not to blame."

"How can you say that?"

"You're no more guilty than if you'd carried a rare virus around for years, then inadvertently handed it off to a few people who are particularly susceptible."

"For a virus there are antiviruses. The only cure for me is——"

Gillian didn't finish the thought, but her meaning was clear. Peter came to keep her company on the bed.

"Did you hurt your hand?" she asked.

Peter hadn't been aware that he was massaging the unresponsive fingers.

"It's a little sore; nothing to worry about. Gillian, while we were next to each other, asleep or half asleep, did you read me in some way?"

"Yes."

"Can you tell me about it?"

"Not much to tell. I just had an impression of someone . . . who you're very close to."

"Do you mean Hester?"

"No; it was a man. You'd do anything for him—I think you must love him, more than anyone you've ever loved. Even more than Robin. You cried when you had to tell him all about your father. It hurt so bad, talking about those things in your life you've tried to forget."

Peter stared at the windows. The dark diamonds in the curtains were becoming visible as the sky lightened.

"What does he look like?" Peter said, his voice strained.

"He's small. Old. Not much hair. Just a very ordinary looking person. But he wears reflecting sunglasses; you can't see his eyes."

"I've had very few friends in my life, Gillian. I don't know the man you described. You must have dreamed it."

"Dreams and visions are different," she said. "He's real. What happened to your father?"

"I don't know," Peter said remotely. Then, "Yes. I do. It was his heart. I was only about ten. Fathers die. And are buried. And you try not to think very much about them after that."

Peter got up and walked the floor.

"Robin thinks I'm dead. They've convinced him of that. Otherwise he wouldn't have cooperated with them. It'll be a hell of a shock when he—well, that's just one more problem. Getting to Robin: that's all I'm concerned with now. I have to find Robin. Find Robin. Find Robin."

He pounded a wall with his right fist, hard enough to rouse everyone in the inn. Gillian sat up on the bed.

"Peter!"

He turned slowly, fist poised.

"What's the matter?"

"*You.* You're scaring me."

Peter sat at the foot of the bed. He made no comment about his wall-banging, but he opened and closed his right hand several times, his head bent in concentration.

"I know very little about the human brain. But I think there may be a way of helping you, Gillian."

She shook her head. "I'm harmless when I'm doped. Or, I suppose they could do an operation; plant electrodes in my brain and just—turn me off forever. But I refuse to end up like that. I would rather be dead."

"What affects you might be described as a rare form of epilepsy—"

"Oh, God," she said listlessly.

"But there's nothing to be afraid of. Many epileptics are learning, through biofeedback training, to cut off potential seizures by regulating their own brain waves. You may be able to fully control your clairvoyance, and the side effects, the storm of magnetic energy that does the damage."

"I can't believe that."

"A handful of people have extraordinary bodies, which they train to perform feats which are literally beyond duplication. Houdini, the escape artist—or those marathon runners who like to go up and down mountains all day. Not too many years ago I was a member of an elite Navy assault team. I trained myself to swim, twelve, fourteen hours a day. I thought that was pretty good, but there was a little guy in my outfit who could outswim me, and do a thousand situps afterward."

"What does all that prove?" Gillian said.

"You're bright and intelligent, not a freak or an idiot-savant, capable of only a single, bizarre mental feat. You and Robin absolutely prove what we've always known, that the mind of man is capable of anything. Mentally, you've split the atom. All you can think of now is the holocaust, the potential tragedy. But your power is basically more useful than the power of the atom, once you've made the effort and acquired the necessary controls. Maybe no one can help you, Gillian. You may have to do it all by yourself. But I think you're tough enough to give it a hell of a try. If I didn't think so, I wouldn't waste my time on you."

He wasn't surprised to see Gillian crying, but the change in her was remarkable; her head was up, face coming clear as a cameo as she turned it toward the dawn windows. She was, just then, as beautiful as ever he'd wished her to be. He watched her come of age and held his breath, afraid that any move on his part, the faintest gesture, might annul the new growth.

"It's just—too much to hope for; I don't dare believe it."

Peter pressed his advantage. "I only said there was a chance, Gillian. But I think it's a damned good chance, for you and for Robin."

"Robin, yes; oh, he needs help! And soon, before he——"

"If you believe *that*, then try to communicate with him. It's vital."

Gillian sat back and dried up; her eyes were alert.

"I'll try," she said. "You mean now?"

"No. Let's move in closer. We've got some hard traveling to do."

Peter rose and took Gillian by the hand, helping her off the bed. For a long moment she leaned gratefully against him. Then she tensed, but tried to be casual as she stepped away. Now her death-bringing fear was instinctive, but at least she had an alternative to hopelessness. Peter smiled thinly. The middle finger of his left hand, which he tried not to let her see, was numb to the first joint. And the dead fingers had begun to curl toward the palm. The small cerebral vascular accident she had precipitated in his brain was still in progress. He could be detached about his accident, fatalistic. But he worried that the time left would not be enough time.

"I guess you'd like to have a toothbrush," Peter said.

"And a hairbrush. And—these jeans are so raunchy. And if I had about nine thousand pancakes and plates and plates of sausage I could eat every bite!"

"Amen. We ought to be able to find a place over on Route Seven that's serving early breakfast. I'll provide you with a wardrobe when we get to Poughkeepsie."

"Poughkeepsie?" Gillian said, with a humorous perplexed tilt of her head.

The travel agent Peter found near the Vassar College campus was every bit as helpful as Peter hoped she'd be.

"It's the height of the season, and accommodations are *very* scarce in the Lake Celeste area. How about Vermont? No, forget I said that. Vermont is worse."

"I thought the snowstorm might keep people away from Lake Celeste."

"That'll be over by tomorrow morning; forecast is clear and sunny for the weekend. Let me think. You want to be near Lake Celeste. That limits us to Shadowdown, Great Spirit Mountain or Purviance. Two rooms—impossible. How old's your daughter?"

"Fourteen."

"Would she be embarrassed, sharing with her old man?"

"It's the skiing that counts."

The agent reached for her telephone. "The manager of Shadowdown is a very dear friend, but I'm going to try this once too often." She consulted a rolodex, dialed long distance, whistled through her teeth, studied Peter.

You are a *lot* of trouble, you know that?" She beamed at him. "Don't worry, I'll get you into Shadowdown. I know how it is. I'm raising two kids alone. You make promises, you break promises. Comes a time when you just can't let them down. Right now skiing with her dad is the most important thing in your daughter's life. You gotta be a hero to your kids once in a while."

After making a couple of purchases, Peter met Gillian in front of the Vassar College library. She looked pleased with herself.

"They had the maps. I Xeroxed two copies."

It was a bright cloudless day. The snow was melting, and water ran in freshets in the street. Peter took Gillian's arm as they strolled together. He wore a tweed jacket over a wool turtleneck sweater, and when the sun was shining directly on him he felt a little too warm. He kept his left hand in the jacket pocket. Gillian carried her parka. Her cheeks were reddening in the crisp air. She looked like any other pretty student to him; prettier than most. They were just a part of the crowd on campus, and no one paid much attention to them.

Peter said, "We're booked into a resort called Shadowdown. It's seventeen miles and on the other side of a mountain from Woodlawn College. Our train leaves at one-forty. On Fridays the railroad puts on extra sections for ski buffs. There's always a big local contingent bound for the Adirondacks, including a lot of unattached college kids."

"Will MORG be looking for us up there, Peter?"

"Yes."

"Are we going to disguise ourselves?"

"We'll take on the coloration of the group. It's much more effective than you might think."

"Something's been nagging me. If they expect you—us—to come, why wouldn't they take Robin somewhere else? Wouldn't that make sense?"

"Moving an individual under guard greatly increases the risk factor. I don't think they're all that worried. If anything, Childermass may be over-confident. There's a ski shop a few blocks from here. Do you feel up to walking?"

"I feel fine," Gillian replied.

At the edge of the campus in the shade of a wall she hung back for a moment, bothered, frankly wistful. So close to the reality and routine of classes, friends, weekend dates, she felt just a step out of her proper life. But what a step, Peter thought, and probably the same thought occurred to Gillian: she turned quickly and walked on, the hard sun flash through trees taming her blindly, melting down her eyes.

"Friends of mine," she said, "were going off one deep end after another. Sex, breakdowns. Pressure got to them. I was sorry. But I felt kind of above it all, you know? Insulated. I knew who I was. I knew what *I* was all about."

"Are you feeling sorry for yourself now?" Peter asked unkindly.

". . . Desperate," Gillian said, just getting it out.

"That's okay," he said, taking her arm again with his workable hand. "That we can use."

In the ski shop Peter spent nearly seven hundred and fifty dollars to outfit them. He bought, in addition to equipment and clothing for the slopes and for après-ski, a dark two-piece snowmobile outfit, a helmet and appropriate boots. They left the store loaded down with gear, wearing Scandinavian sweaters and ski pants. Gillian had pinned up her hair, which she wore under a knit cap. She was also wearing pink-tinted glasses with heavy French frames. Peter doubted that her own mother would have recognized her from more than six feet away.

"Snowmobiles are usually banned from ski areas," Gillian said on the street.

"Shadowdown ought to have quite a few of them for staff use. I'll find what I need."

"Is that how you intend to get to Robin? By snowmobile? Even the new ones make a lot of noise—around seventy-three decibels."

"Under the right snow and wind conditions the sound won't carry fifty feet."

"But you're taking a terrible chance going out in a blizzard——"

"Gillian, it's the only chance. If things are lousy for me, then they'll be lousy for MORG. Now let's cool the questions. What you don't know can't hurt either of us."

They stopped at a luggage shop and purchased a big shoulder tote for Gillian. Back in the car Peter unwrapped the cassette tape recorder he'd picked up earlier. He put in a blank tape and talked for fifteen minutes about himself, about Robin, about MORG.

Then Gillian took her turn. She spoke haltingly to her parents, broke down, recovered and told them exactly where she could be found.

"But what good is this going to do?" she said, while Peter sealed the cassette in a double thickness of manila envelopes.

"Your family—I mean all of the Bellavers—has tremendous power, Gillian. They have access to all the power there is in Washington. But even with MORG in a predicament they'll have to move quickly along the lines I suggested, in order to protect us."

"Couldn't we just call them and tell—"

"MORG will have a tap on their line. But they won't intercept the mail."

Gillian addressed the envelope to her parents and marked it for special delivery while Peter asked a cop for directions to the Poughkeepsie post office.

When he was back in the car she said, "Why will MORG be in a predicament?"

"There's no clear line of succession; Childermass has always been afraid to put too much power in the hands of his subordinates. Cut off the head and MORG's enemies will devour the body. Then the skeleton should crumble slowly away on the banks of the Potomac."

"That's what you're going to do? Kill Childermass?"

"Yes, if it's the last thing I ever do," Peter said.

Gillian blinked several times. She put her head back against the seat, face turned to him. She looked depressed. Peter didn't question her mood. Neither of them spoke for quite a while.

They arrived at the Penn Central terminal across the river from Poughkeepsie fifteen minutes before train time.

Everything that wasn't essential, including the clothes Gillian had been wearing, was left in the rented wagon. Even so Peter found himself burdened.

"Is your hand worse?" Gillian asked. "You haven't been using it."

"About the same."

"I can carry both pairs of skis," she said, and proved it, balancing them on one shoulder. They joined a crowd of about one hundred weekenders on the station platform. It was a young crowd, but there were several family groups; Peter saw three men about his age with half-grown children.

He had explained to Gillian that it would be a good idea if they didn't spend much time together until they were safely in their room at Shadowdown. He anticipated a MORG watch on all the resorts, but with upwards of four thousand skiers arriving in the area for the weekend, it was unlikely MORG could pick Peter or Gillian out of the crowd.

Gillian left him with the skis and strolled along the platform. By the time the train was there she had a boy at her heels, whom she introduced as Cary. Cary was on the chubby side but looked like a lot of fun. Peter smiled benevolently.

Thirty-seven minutes later, as the train pulled into Hudson, New York, Gillian said in his ear, "Dad, this is Francis."

Peter looked up. Francis was tall and wore glasses and braces. He had hair like a caveman. Peter shook his hand and spoke privately to Gillian.

"What happened to Cary?"

"Oh, he's with us. He's——" She waved a hand airily toward the coach behind them. "Do you think I should try for three?" she said, flushed with accomplishment.

"Gail, honey, aren't you overdoing the protective coloration?"

"This is *fun*. I never picked up boys before."

Peter's protection was a man named Galleher. He had three boys with him who were ten, eleven and twelve years old. They were going to Shadowdown. Galleher was an insurance man. Peter lamented the fact that he'd never owned enough life insurance. Peter and Galleher became fast friends at that instant. Peter won his sons over by letting the two oldest beat him at chess. By four thirty-nine, when the train stopped at Ft. Edward to let off most of the skiers, Peter, Galleher and the boys were inseparable.

The resorts had sent yellow school buses, leased for the weekend, to pick up their guests for the forty-minute trip into the mountains. Peter got aboard one of the two buses going to Shadowdown, Gillian on the other with Cary and Francis.

At Ft. Edward snow was already falling, but lightly; far to the west the setting sun was red and smoky like a fire in a tunnel. By the time they reached Shadowdown it was dark and ten degrees colder; the snow had quickened to a lash.

Shadowdown consisted of a chalet-style main lodge and three gingerbread wings built one above the other on the mountainside. They were connected by a funicular elevator and two enclosed stairways. There was a slope for night skiing, an outdoor skating rink and a bubble-top pool just behind the lodge. Accommodations for three hundred people ranged from deluxe, with private sauna, to dormitory-style living, which was one reason the Gallehers liked Shadowdown. For food, guests had a choice of a smart intimate restaurant, a cafeteria open twenty-four hours and a beerhall that served authentic German specialities.

Peter and Gillian had been booked into the second tier of rooms on the mountain. Their room was overheated. They had twin beds with blue spreads, dark Weldwood paneling, snow scenes on the walls, and sliding glass doors to a balcony that overlooked the bright pool bubble and the immense sloped roof of the chalet below. After a minute on the exposed balcony the flying snow, thick as pablum, drove Peter inside.

He sat down on one bed and consulted his left hand. Three fingers gone now, the palm almost without feeling. But a greater worry was a numbed spot about the size of a half dollar he'd found on his forearm just below the elbow. He went into the bathroom for a plastic glass, stripped off the paper and poured two ounces of gin from a new bottle he'd bought.

In the bedroom Peter unfolded the Geological Survey maps of the region which Gillian had xeroxed for him. He located Shadowdown, then found what he was looking for. The river was called the Breed. It began as a trickle half way up Shadowdown Mountain, broadened in the valley below and eventually wound through the middle of Woodlawn College, where, on the eastern boundary of the campus, it had been dammed for a swimming lake. There was a house or a building, unidentified, beside the lake.

The Breed was less than thirty feet wide in places. Probably five or six feet deep at full flood in the late spring, with deeper coves here and there.

Peter dialed for the recorded weather, courtesy of Shadowdown Lodge. The temperature at 6 P.M. was fourteen degrees and falling. Wind northwest at thirty-one miles an hour. There was a heavy snow warning for the twelve-hour period ending at seven Saturday morning. Eight more inches of snow expected on top of the four feet already on the ground.

Peter sipped his gin and thought about the route he would take to Woodlawn.

Counting all the twists and turns in the river, the distance was more than twenty miles. Visibility at all times would be only a few feet. The wind-chill factor might reach forty below. Those were the least of his problems. He didn't know the river. Depending on the weight of the machine he chose, he needed at least six inches of ice at all times. But snow acted as an insulator over ice, and kept the ice from building up from below. Even in the middle of winter he might, without warning, hit a stretch where ice was only a brittle shell. Ice-fishing holes were a possible hazard. A small spring in a cove could produce a breach in the ice. If the river had any kind of current, then the ice would be very dangerous in places.

But there was no other way to do it. If he tried going overland in the blizzard he would quickly be lost even with a compass, or else he'd bog down in drifts as high as his head. With luck and care the frozen Breed River would take him where he wanted to go—if his left arm and hand didn't give out completely. Driving a snowmobile over ice for mile after mile was a chore that required a great deal of strength.

He'd been in the room for fifteen minutes; Gillian hadn't shown up but he wasn't worried about her. He put on a feather-light, down-filled parka and amber-tinted glasses and went out again.

Shadowdown was filled to capacity and the storm had pushed everyone indoors. Already there was a lot of partying going on. Shadowdown's security people were easy to spot. He tried to put MORG out of his mind. Even if they were there, doing their quiet work behind the scenes, checking all registrations, he wouldn't know until it was too late.

Without going to any real trouble Peter discovered four snow-mobiles parked in a basement storage area beneath the kitchen; it was accessible by ramp. There were double doors no one had bothered to lock, but he could have picked the lock with a hangnail. The overhead lights were on. Keys were in the igni-tions of the snowmobiles. He looked the machines over carefully and found one with a studded track, ideal for running on ice. The two-place snowmobile had a 35-horsepower rotary engine, which was quieter than the customary two-stroke Japanese en-gine, new wear rods, drive belt and springs. It was fully fueled.

When he returned to the room the door was standing open. Gillian was having open house: Cary, Francis, and a young cou-ple from Hamilton College who were friends of Cary's. After introductions Peter leaned against a wall with folded arms and smiled and said nothing. In about five minutes the other kids left, and he closed the door.

"I had a sandwich already with the boys, do you want to get something to eat? Cary's pre-law at SUNY in New Paltz and Francis is a funny-car freak. Tomorrow they——"

"Gillian, we have work to do."

The reminder was enough to sober her up, and cause an attack of despondency.

"I know."

"I want to leave in an hour," Peter said.

"I don't see how you'll get anywhere. It's a total white-out."

"Try to get in touch with Robin now."

Gillian's eyes flicked down, and up, and across the room, finally lit into him with a remorseful fury. Peter had no trouble standing his ground. His preternaturally calm eye wore her down.

"I'm not sure if——"

"Now."

She turned away helplessly and sagged on the edge of a bed.

"All right."

Peter didn't move. Gillian said, "I think you should be somewhere else. I'm afraid of what might happen if you're in the room."

"Do you go there, or what?"

"No, it isn't like that. Robin can travel anytime, but I have to be asleep or unconscious to Visit. I just try to reach out and find him. Robin says you make a thought-form, and then you throw it. Our minds come together, they interlock." She held up her joined clenched hands. "He's much better at it than I am. But this close to him I think I can do it. If it's quiet and I can concentrate." There was boisterous laughter in the hall outside their door, and Gillian smiled tensely.

"I'll put cotton in my ears," she said.

"There's a building or a large house at the edge of an artificial lake on campus. That may be the house you told me about. If Robin's in the house, I want him to stay there. And I need to know a safe way in."

"Okay."

"I'll have dinner now. I'm not hungry, but I'll need the fuel later. Forty minutes?"

Gillian shrugged.

"If it's going to work, it'll work by then."

Nineteen

It seemed to Gwyneth Charles that she had just settled into the steaming bath and briefly closed her eyes. When she opened them again Robin was there. In *her* bathroom, looking starkly down at her. She trembled involuntarily; his stealth was unsettling. For several moments she thought she might be dreaming him. She really didn't know if she was awake or asleep.

Just a few minutes alone, she thought. Is that asking too much?

"What do you want, Robin?" she said tonelessly.

"I got tired of waiting. What's taking so long?"

"Robin I need—a good soak, and a little goddamn privacy." The ice rattled in Gwyn's glass as she drank, swallowed the firebolt of whiskey in one lump. She waited nervously for it to do some good. The Wild Turkey bourbon quieted her muscles but not her nerves.

Robin hung on, she wasn't rid of him. Gwyn handed up the glass.

"Make me another while you're here? The bottle's on the drink cart. Wild Turkey."

Robin took the glass from her. He looked at it, then ran his tongue around the inside. He was so handsome tonight, Gwyn thought, in his dark blue suede shirt-jac, gray slacks, Gucci loafers. He licked and licked the glass. Ummmmmm-ummmmmm. As usual Gwyn couldn't take her eyes off him even when she most wanted to. The dark look of hazard around his own eyes could hypnotize her.

Robin put a lump of ice in his mouth and knelt beside her. He kissed her, then passed the ice into her mouth.

Gwyn shuddered and drew away and spat out the ice. He sat back on his heels, frowning.

"I thought you liked to do that."

"I *do* enjoy it, in bed when we're f—" She quickly covered her face with wet hands: loathing was there for him to see, and make use of, in his incredibly complex, scheming way.

"Please, Robin," she said, in a voice that was squeaky tight, "get me a drink?"

The next thing Gwyn knew—it had begun to really frighten her, all the gaps in her attention span—he had the cap off the bottle and was pouring the expensive bourbon into the toilet.

"Robin!" She foundered but didn't climb out of the marble tub, which was nearly flush with the floor.

"I don't like it when you smell like this stuff," he said, eyes on the flowing amber tail.

"I won't drink any more tonight! Don't waste it!"

Robin turned the bottle rightside up before all the Wild Turkey gurgled away.

"Would you like me to do your back?" he asked pleasantly.

"I merely want—we've been together for days and days—you never give me—all right. Yes. Please do my back, lover."

He brought the bottle with him, placed it on the flat edge of the tub. Gwyneth glanced at the bottle with badly concealed longing. He'd put it well within reach to tempt her. But if she tried to steal a nip Robin would be infuriated, and she just couldn't stomach another of his man-child rages. So she straightened up and handed him a soapy loofah.

Robin peeled back his sleeves and scrubbed along her spine.

"I enjoy a drink once in a while," Gwyn explained. "I need it to relax. As you know I'm highly allergic to barbituates, and I, I haven't been sleeping. Not well at all."

"You can't sleep?" he said, as if it was news to him.

"Not when *you* don't sleep. And you haven't closed your eyes for, it's been almost five days. I don't know how you can stay on your feet."

"I feel okay."

"Oh, Robin! You're in another world. You've pushed yourself almost beyond mortal limits. You don't seem to be aware that there *are* limits, but *I* know what's happened to you."

He shook his head, seeming puzzled—or was he taunting her? Gwyn felt too bleary to make a rational judgment.

"Nothing's happened to me, Gwyn." He put the loofah down and stood, towered over Gwyn in her sunken tub. Six-two and still growing. Youthful-sulky good looks that fascinated her so. Gwyn's fuddled desire for him seemed a monstrous thing, but imperishable: it grated inside her like broken bones. She slunk to the chin in her bath, eyes smarting.

Robin picked up the Wild Turkey bottle. He uncapped it again and sipped some bourbon. The taste was mildly disagreeable, but the after taste and expanding warmth obviously intrigued him.

"I've wondered why you drink this." He had another deep swallow, and savored it. "Okay, I guess."

"Robin, easy. That doesn't mix with your medication."

He drank again, ignoring her. There'd been a third of a quart left when she persuaded him not to consign it all to the toilet.

"You *have* been taking your medication?"

"Snowing hard now," Robin observed through a glass port above the bathtub. "Maybe later we could go out and play. We could have a real snowball fight."

"Robin, if you won't follow your schedule of medication, then we can't—you're caught up in a very destructive cycle, whether you realize it or not. You burn six thousand calories a day! You're on the verge of consuming yourself."

"Are you through with your bath?"

". . . Yes. What time is it?"

Robin looked at the solid gold, Rolex Oyster wrist watch she had given him for his fourteenth birthday.

"Ten after seven."

Gwyn sighed. "I need to dress. We're having company for dinner." She attempted a lighter tone. "Now don't drink any more of that; we don't want you turning into a teen-age alcoholic."

"Who's coming?" Robin asked, lowering the bottle after another belt.

"Granny Sig. And—my uncle."

"I don't like him."

"I know," Gwyn said, stepping out of the tub and draping
herself in a towel. "I can't help it. Anyway he's company. We
never have company."

"Who else?"

"No one else. *Robin, will you put that shitting bottle down?*"

He wiped his lips on a corner of her towel. "Tongue gets
numb," he said.

Warm and wet as she was from the bath, Gwyn could feel the
heat Robin gave off. He was burning like a furnace. He helped
her dry her body. A blue-eyed bruise peeked at him from beneath one breast.

"How did you get that?" Robin asked.

"Your fist."

"Hit you? When did I ever hit you, Gwyn?" His voice, still
changing, unexpectedly climbed high. If she hadn't felt so badly
she might have smiled.

"Quite often when we—let's not discuss it. May I have the
towel?"

"Don't you want me to dry between your legs?"

"No." She was sure it would lead to sex. Four times today;
a week of harrowing circus. The body in which she took so
much pride had no resiliency any more. Robin had lost all
control. When he thought of sex he had to do it, no matter
where he was, or who else might be around. Two nights ago
he had raped her in front of Granny Sig. A low point in
Gwyn's life, by far.

Robin stepped back and, despite the disapproving expression
on her face, he drained the bottle of bourbon, sucking out the
last slow drops.

"It won't hurt me," he assured Gwyn. "Nothing hurts me."
He was puffed up with boasting; his eyes, looking at her, were
busy and clever. "Nothing hurts me. You could put poison in it,
and it wouldn't hurt me." But he was sweating now. He nursed
the empty bottle, turning the mouth of it around and around
between his lips.

"Is that what you'd like to do?"

"What?" Gwyn said, drifting and vacant again. She reached for a dry towel.

"Poison me. Get me out of the way."

Something flared dangerously in Gwyn's head.

"For God's sake, what a miserable, stupid thing to say to me!"

"You wouldn't do it?"

"No. No!"

"But you lie to me. That's a kind of poison."

"I do *not* lie to you, Robin. And I'm tired of—accusations! Your sick demeaning possessiveness! Your taunts and brutality and——"

He turned smoothly and threw the empty bottle against a marble wall of the bath. Gwyn jumped and got gooseflesh.

"Smash," Robin said, without emphasis. He turned back to her and clamped a hand under her cunt. It was not a loving gesture. He showed a butcher's indifference to her crawling flesh. He thrust a fingertip against the nub of her uterus.

"GET YOUR HANDS OFF ME!" she screamed, finally past all endurance; and she spat in his face.

Robin's reaction was, weirdly, boyish shame. Tears welled up in his eyes. He let go of Gwyneth. His lips quivered.

"Because it isn't kind. It isn't loving. It's humiliating!" Gwyn's voice became a groan. She was weeping too. She used the towel to wipe away the slash of spit that divided his freckled nose. "Oh, God, Robin. Sweet, sweet Robin, what's happened? I loved you so. I want my boy back. I want my beautiful, loving boy." She put her hands on his head, groping blindly. He ducked and ran. He slammed the bathroom door. Gwyn stood there and shook from terror and passion.

When she went to look for him Robin wasn't in the bedroom of her spacious apartment, which took up nearly all of the third floor in the south wing of the house. The door to the living room stood open an inch. Gwyn heard soft music and Ken's murmuring voice. She smelled heavenly hot hors d'ouevres on the serving cart. Ken had come in and fixed a big log fire for her. Gwyneth sat naked and almost close enough to singe her hide, mentally immersing herself in the liquid-looking flames. For a few precious minutes she drew on the fire's heat for the strength to dress herself.

With her cheeks naturally reddened Gwyn added only a touch

of lipstick, then shadowed her eyes in bosky green. She gave her hair a few swirling touches with the brush. She put on an ankle-length white wool skirt, white kid boots, a long-sleeved white blouse with a high, Gibson-girl collar, and a white wool bolero vest. She added no ornamentation, not even finger rings.

Ken knocked at the bedroom door and when she opened it he handed her a drink, Wild Turkey on the rocks. Gwyn gasped with pleasure and drank deep.

"Robin said he broke your bottle."

"Oh." Gwyn peered anxiously past Ken's shoulder but couldn't find Robin in the forty-foot living room. Ken pointed to a grouping of high-backed leather chairs near undraped windows; the storm outside was whirling against the leaded glass.

"How is he?" Gwyn whispered.

Ken held praying hands at the level of his breastbone; his hands flew apart in a mime which she was too brainless to interpret. Perhaps he meant that Robin's mood was acceptable; perhaps it was a warning. *Do not touch.*

"I see." Gwyn drank more whiskey. "Could you leave us alone for a few minutes? We, we had a little spat." The muscles on one side of her face jerked, telegraphing a wild laugh which she never uttered.

"Right."

"Hold—hold the others when they get here. I'll ring."

"Sure you'll be okay?"

"Why shouldn't I be?"

Ken smiled comfortingly and walked away across the living room, closing the outside door behind him.

"Robin?"

He didn't answer her. Gwyn couldn't tell, from where she was standing, which one of the deep chairs he occupied. She walked slowly toward the chairs, swaying slightly from fatigue, from the effects of the whiskey. It would be nice to pass out, she thought, and let somebody else worry about him for awhile. But she was possessed by an unreasonable fear: if she lost touch with Robin, even for an hour, she would never see him again.

"Robin, wouldn't you like something to eat?"

Gwyn saw him slumped, glowering, in the cold well around the exposed windows. His fingernails dug at the tough leather of the armchair. He still wouldn't speak or look at her. She heard

the wind scream, and breathed raggedly in response. An unpleasant episode was definitely on the way. In the past when
Robin had overloaded his circuits, narcolepsy resulted. During
a narcoleptic phase, when he wasn't sleeping he was beautifully
docile. She recalled weeks of bathing him, feeding him with a
spoon, acts which she found enjoyable, soothing to both of
them. Now he couldn't rest, and outbursts of violence were the
norm. After the squalid rape episode, Granny Sig had recommended locking him up in a straitjacket. But Gwyn couldn't
make herself believe it had come to that. Despite his tantrums
and gross behavior, she couldn't betray their relationship so
coldly. Robin would calm down; she'd find a way to appease him.

Gwyn leaned against the back of his chair and stared at his
raking nails.

"Get away from me."

"Can't we make up?" Gwyn wheedled.

"You spit on me!"

"That was—I'm very sorry, won't you just try to understand
the strain I'm under? I'm so worried about you."

Scratch, scratch. The sound of his nails gave her fits. Gwyn
leaned over Robin, hair hanging against the side of his face.

"Stop," she pleaded, her voice low.

His hands froze into claws.

"Thank you, darling. Now please forgive me. Please, please—
Gwyn wants you to forgive her. Gwyn's sorry she acted so terrible." She drew the long curtain of her hair back and forth across
his face, stealing stage-struck glimpses of his precarious mood.

"You said we could get out of here. Go skiing, just the two of
us. Now we *can't* go."

"My plans were changed. By a higher authority."

Gwyn was motionless, listening to him breathe. Lips pursed,
she waited with a ripening, not unpleasurable apprehension for
Robin to do his thing.

He surprised her by not commenting at all. She dared to touch
him, and found him less rigid than she'd expected.

"Could we go some other time?" he asked, resigned and
withdrawn.

"Well—I'm sure I could arrange it."

"Okay."

"Kiss?"

He allowed himself to be kissed. His nose was cold from sitting in the draft. Gwyn straightened up smiling, so relieved she thought she might float away. Robin put his hands in his lap. He was mercifully quiet: calmer than he'd been for days. His eyes were half closed.

"I just have to have something to eat," Gwyn said. And drink. She poured the shot of bourbon first, then approached the stainless steel serving cart Ken had parked a few feet in front of the fireplace. She was ravenous. She all but gobbled six large Swedish meatballs, using her fingers, then greedily uncovered the seafood au gratin.

Meanwhile Robin was up and around on little cat feet. Gwyn paid no attention to him until he locked the door.

"Why'd you do that?"

"So nobody can get in."

"But why don't you—Robin, what's the matter?"

"You know what's the matter."

"I honestly don't."

"It's Gillian."

"Gillian?"

"I told you I was all through with her, I don't want to see her ever again. I told her to stay away from here."

"When did you——"

Robin looked around the room, slow and watchful.

"But she's here," he said.

"That isn't possible. Gillian is somewhere in New York. She ran away from——"

Robin stared her into silence.

" 'Robin, Robin,' " he mimicked. "Don't you think I know her voice? Oh, she's here. Where did you hide her?"

"I don't know anything about Gillian."

Robin stopped prowling and stood on the other side of the serving cart. He leaned across it, staring at Gwyn.

"That's a lie."

"No, it isn't."

"She'll do all the things I can do. You won't miss me at all."

"Robin, what are you saying?"

He pointed at the round dining table.

"Company's coming."

"That's right."

Robin counted on his fingers.

"You. Me. Granny Sig. Childermass. Gillian. That makes five."

"But you can see we're not expecting anyone else. There are just *four* place settings."

"Four for dinner. I won't be here. I'll be dead. Gillian's taking *my* place after you poison me."

"That's rid——"

Robin erupted. He pushed the wheeled cart past Gwyneth and ran it into the fireplace. Logs blew up in fountains of sparks. The cart overturned and the stink of spilled and charred food quickly filled the room. Smoke rolled over Gwyn and she backed away, choking. Robin followed her. Gwyn, bending double as she coughed, fell into a chair. There was a scalding pain low in the back of her head, it felt as if she'd torn a muscle with her coughing fit.

Clasping her head tightly with both hands, she looked helplessly up at Robin. Her mouth creaked open, but she couldn't speak. The pain was very bad, and worsening. Her brains were coming to a boil.

"Remember?" he said, "I told you I don't have to touch you to hurt you. I'm hurting you now. Because I don't love you any more. I'm tired of you."

The heat from the fire seemed more intense. Thick tears welled from the corners of Gwyneth's eyes; her face had broken out with what she thought were beads of perspiration. Gwyn was stifling. She tore apart the high collar of the blouse, got up and snatched a napkin from the dining table. Shaking dreadfully, she pressed the linen napkin to her face. It came away crimson.

Gwyn screamed. Through a heat haze she saw Robin turn and walk idly away from her. His mind seemed to be on other things. Gwyn stared at the backs of her hands. She was bleeding from almost every pore, tiny perfect bubbles of blood merging, flowing. She smelled of wrack and weed, of the strong salty sea; she felt the running of a fatal tide through her disappearing skin.

Gwyn stumbled after Robin, coughing, no longer able to see him clearly. The tears she wept were tears of blood binding her lashes like glue. Gwyn flowed weightlessly on a rolling wave, spilled on the carpet. She got up gagging and lifted one slow foot, coughed another billowing wave and caught it perfectly, rode sensationally but without effort toward an unforeseen shore.

Robin looked up from his reverie when he heard pounding at the door.

"*Gwyn!*"

"Go away," he said, but not loudly enough to be heard through the thick door.

The room was stinking. He needed air.

The windows were casement-type, twenty inches wide. He opened three of them. Snow blew in, stinging his face.

Better.

All the doors in the house were solid oak and two inches thick. They'd had to get an ax. They were chopping now.

No place for him to go except into the bedroom, and from there into the bathroom. Two more doors. But they had their ax. It wouldn't take them long. Then what?

Robin shivered and breathed deeply. Night and cold and wind-driven snow. Snow was piling up on the inside ledge, flickering across the carpet. He saw big flakes melting on Gwyneth. She was all red where the white had been.

Chopping. The iron-hard wood. Resisting the blade of the ax. They couldn't hurt him. Nothing could ever hurt him.

Little by little the ax winning.

In another half minute the door would be split in two, and he just didn't want to talk to them about Gwyneth. That was over with. What was there to tell? It would be boring.

But he found the snow exhilarating. The frigid night challenged him.

Robin moved quickly to the bar and picked up an almost full quart of Wild Turkey bourbon. He put it inside his jacket for safekeeping. Then he walked to the windows past Gwyneth. The bog in which she lay, limbs twitching in crisis, was spreading hugely on the gold carpet.

He climbed sideways through a window frame, tucking his face below the shoulder to protect it from the brunt of the wind.

The limestone ledge outside was six inches deep, with an icy edge. This side of the house was very close to the swimming lake. He had wondered, last summer, if he could dive from the ledge into the lake. But the water wasn't deep close to shore, and there were all those rocks at the edge of the veranda to think about. He knew he could have made it, but he let Gwyneth talk him back inside. Robin smiled now, remembering the expression on her face, the little drops of sweat that fell from her nose and chin.

Back then it was a lot more fun, being with her.

Robin looked down. He could see a faint glow from lighted windows. Otherwise nothing but the whirl wind, like a spectral white dog chasing its own tail. Sheer stone wall going down, thirty feet or more to the ground.

Going up would be easier. There was a fourth floor, little used, then an attic floor, slate roof not too steep, gables set in all along the roof line, and chimneys: five big chimneys in all. To his left, near the windows, was a well-anchored drain pipe. Little out-croppings of the stone wall went up as far as the copper roof gutter: an inch here, two inches there. Handholds. Everything was very slippery, of course.

But the door had broken at last. Looking in through the windows, Robin saw a gash in the oak panels half as wide as a man, saw a hand reaching to release the lock. Gwyn was almost still, just faintly twitching now, frail as a starved child on all that blotted carpet.

He wondered if he could galvanize her, as he'd galvanized dead animals in the lab, making them jump around. Maybe he could get Gwyn on her feet one last time to greet the door crashers. But it wouldn't fool anybody, even if he succeeded in getting her to do a flipflop kind of dance. Dead was dead. So let her lie there.

Robin took a deep breath and started climbing up the side of the house, the wind clawing at his back.

When Peter returned to the room at Shadowdown he found the balcony door wide open. The drapes were whipping wildly in the dark, and the room temperature had plummeted.

Gillian was outside clutching the railing, shivering uncontrollably.

She hadn't worn a coat out there. Her hair had frosted. Her eyebrows were a ridge of freezing snow. Peter pried her loose from the railing and carried her in, closed the thermopane door, kicked the heat high, wrapped her in blankets from both beds. She had vomited outside, and some of the mess was frozen like sequins on her sweater.

Gillian clung to him, chattering. He examined her fingers for patches of frostbite and didn't find any, but he knew when her circulation returned to normal she would be in pain. As he held her close one of her ears felt hard as porcelain against his cheek.

"What happened to you, Gil?"

She tried, but she couldn't sound her words. A free hand drummed helplessly against his back. Mindful of hypothermia, Peter laid her down and wrapped her more snugly. In the bathroom he plugged in the courtesy coffee maker. When coffee was ready he supported Gillian with an arm around her waist and made her drink half a cup. Her violent shaking dwindled to random jitters.

"Owwww, my hands, my hands!"

"You could have lost a couple of fingers. How long were you on the balcony? And what the hell were you doing out there without a coat?"

"I lost track of time. I went outside because—cold makes it easier for us to get in touch."

Someone thumped the door of their room and Peter looked around, but it was just another impromptu party traveling up and down the halls.

"Come out, come out, whoever you are," a jolly girl said, and someone else laughed. Then the voices faded.

"Did you get through to Robin?" Peter asked Gillian.

Gillian's eyes looked as if she might fly to pieces again.

"Robin's in trouble. He k-killed her, I think."

"*What?* Killed who?"

"The woman. I don't know who she is. Robin lives with her. Robin bled her out. He did it deliberately. My God. *He did it deliberately.* Can you get to him? I think he'll die if you don't. I feel him freezing—freezing."

Gillian bent at the waist, hugging herself tightly, crying from the pain in her cold hands, or from the pain she felt for Robin.

"Where is he now?"

"At the house on the lake."

Peter left Gillian crying on the bed. He changed into his

snowmobile boots and took the helmet down from a shelf.

"Take me!"

"It's too dangerous, Gillian. Frostbite would be the least of your problems. Lock the door and don't leave this room. I'll be back. If I don't come back stay put until you hear from your father."

"Peter!"

Someone passing by in the hall was trying to sing a lusty German *brauhaus* song. Another voice picked it up. Peter paused with his hand on the knob for a last look at Gillian. Then he let himself out of the room.

Three revelers were propping up the wall opposite his door, passing a bottle back and forth and trying to sing three-part harmony. They were hairy, husky young men in striped ski sweaters. With them was a snow bunny who wore a bright yellow band on her dark head. She'd made a mistake with the head-band, it caught Peter's eye just when she needed an unobserved moment to dip into her shoulder-strap bag. The skiers were not skiers at all, and the party was for him.

Peter didn't hesitate, although he knew it was near to hope-less. The first man off the wall intercepted the arc of the heavy, high-impact plastic helmet with his chin, and his jawbone snapped in two places. Peter pivoted in the unfamiliar, awkward boots and kicked Hairy Two full in his bulging groin. He had to get to the snow bunny, but she was backing off coolly, some sort of weapon in her hand.

"Jerry!" she barked at Hairy Three, who had come between her and Peter. He dived for the carpet, leaving Peter wide open. Snow bunny fired. Her aim was accurate. The barbs from the Taser struck him in the face. With the circuit closed, a rocketing high-voltage shock pitched him blind against the wall. The elec-trical current, which could climb rapidly to fifty thousand volts, had disrupted his nervous system and he had no muscular con-trol. As he slumped on to the floor, twitching and jumping, he saw her coming closer, thin wires dangling between them. The pain was unendurable.

Turn it off, Peter thought. Off, off! But he was aware of how much she was enjoying it.

Sometimes Robin could hear voices, up there where the snow and wind were wild and haunting. He knew he'd caused a lot of excitement tonight. They'd turned on all the outside floodlights. Dark where he stood above them all, but it was like looking down into a shifting, eerie, golden sea. When the wind slackened briefly and the snow curtains parted he could see bundled figures on the ground. They were still trying to find him with binoculars and hand-held spotlights that flickered across the many dormers, parapets and chimneys. But the light never touched him. He was too quick and agile.

For a while the powerful bullhorn voice had pleaded with him. He ignored it. Then two men had come out from the attic to try to bring him in. The roof was narrowly flat at chimney level, like a catwalk but roughly slated. And always there was the treacherous ice. The men moved nervously and with great caution, not like him. Robin, mildly contemptuous, wasn't in a sporting mood. From his best hiding place within the waist of a figure-eight chimney Robin got around behind a tall man in a blowing trench coat and gave him a shove.

The tall man took the other man with him, a long flailing slide down. One of them, lucky or quick witted, grabbed and hung on to a copper gutter for a time. Others tried to rescue him, but he was virtually inaccessible and scared stiff. Finally fear got the best of him, or else his fingers froze in their gloves, and he dropped off too. After that the bullhorn voice was angry. Robin laughed quietly to himself, threw down snowballs and dodged the sizzling beams they threw back up at him.

Probably they thought he would get tired, or freeze or something. But the high chimneys provided warmth and adequate shelter. When his fingers became numb he climbed up and thawed them in hot wood smoke. For serious chills the bottle of bourbon he'd brought along was just the thing. It stopped the head-to-toe shakes right away. Unfortunately he'd drunk most of it. There was only a swallow or two left. When the bourbon was gone he sensed that all the fun would be gone too.

Granny Sig helped herself to another glass of Calvados and looked across the second-floor study at Childermass. He was using a walkie-talkie, communicating imperiously with MORG's forward observation post high in the attic. Granny Sig glanced at her watch. It was twenty minutes past nine: Robin had been on the roof for nearly two hours. Outside the temperature had dropped to three degrees below zero, and the wind-chill factor might very well be incalculable.

As Granny Sig saw it, Robin had two choices. He could come in and take his medicine. Or he could stay out there and, inevitably, cavort beyond his means, tumble down and break his neck. All the attention was a blissful narcotic: it inspired him to attempt feats of daring that would confirm his belief in a super-human prowess. Granny Sig had tried to persuade Childermass to damp all fires, turn off the lights and go to bed. After a while cold and boredom and curiosity might prompt Robin to crawl back inside to find out why he was not the center of attention any more.

Childermass thought that was a lousy idea. Considering the source it had to be lousy. Granny Sig sipped her potent brandy and smiled wryly at Childermass's back.

Well, honey, I'm all you've got right now. But her bravado was, God knows, pathetically hollow. She began to shudder and shake as if in the familiar act of laughter. Instead she produced two large tears, at the outer corner of each eye. They hung there like second sight. Now that Gwyn, Granny Sig's champion and protector, was gone, she had again become unemployable in her profession. If Robin—the wretch—died as well, very likely her life was in real danger. Something had to be done about that, but Granny Sig was at a loss to know what.

She produced more tears, a raining volume. They splashed into her glass.

"What the hell is the matter with you?" Childermass said, walking toward her.

"Just crying the blues, I guess."

"You goddamn flippy queen. We've got a problem here. Get yourself together."

Granny Sig nodded, then sniveled and sniffed until control and tranquility were restored.

Childermass lifted up his eyes.

"He's like a young goat up there. Fifty feet off the ground in a howling blizzard. Can anyone get through to him? I'd like a professional opinion, care to take a hack at it? What's his mental condition? Is he stable or deteriorating?"

"He's quite insane."

"Don't give me the bad news all at once. What do you mean, insane?"

"Haven't you had a close look at Gwyneth?" Granny Sig said in a fulminating rage. "Don't you realize what he did to her? Given his disposition and unique abilities, still it took concentration. It was an act of premeditated murder. Those two smashed men were *pushed* off the roof. He's turned into a homicidal maniac."

"Is that treatable? Well, what the hell am I supposed to know! I'm not a psychiatrist. Sane or insane, Robin is still incredibly valuable. I'll leave it to you to deal with him once we get him in."

Ken entered the study. "The cars from Shadowdown are here."

"Where the devil have they been, on the scenic route?"

"Bad roads tonight," Ken said.

"Get 'em up here," Childermass said, and Ken withdrew.

On Childermass's face there was a naked look of anticipation and savage hunger that made Granny Sig feel squeamish and vulnerable, and, when he went all glassy-eyed and groped his aching stump, she wanted to vomit. Didn't, quite. Childermass's breath whistled like doom through his teeth.

"Get me a neat Scotch," he said, eyes on the open door.

He didn't move or speak after that, just stared at the door, waiting. Granny Sig had to put the glass in his hand. They both heard voices. Then Peter Sandza and Gillian Bellaver were brought into the study by a cadre of tough young MORGs.

Peter wasn't standing too well on his own. He looked to be in mild shock. One side of his jaw had been burned by the Taser current. His left arm hung badly. But his eyes were steady as he faced Childermass, and he had his other arm protectively around the frightened girl.

Childermass approached them. For the moment all his attention focused on Gillian. He had a smile for her. That was a kindness she hadn't anticipated; she bit her lip and bowed her head.

Then his eyes slid past her to Peter.

No one else in the room moved or spoke. It was like a wake, for someone who wasn't quite dead yet. Premature feasting would have been tacky. They all watched Childermass for a clue as to how to behave.

Childermass smiled at Peter too: because his smile was so unexpected it seemed ghastly as a gunshot.

"Welcome back, Ace," Childermass said. "Maybe you could give us a hand with something."

Robin was disgruntled. It had all begun to seem pointless to him.

Apparently they didn't want to play any more. He hadn't heard the bullhorn's urgings for a long time. They'd stopped beaming lights at the roof, trying to illuminate his hideaways. No matter how boldly he exposed himself now, he just couldn't get anyone's attention.

And his feet were cold. He hadn't wanted to think about it, but they were really cold. He couldn't remember when he'd last felt his toes. Toelessness made him a little clumsy, and clumsiness upset him.

"Rob-in!"

Oh, shit. Now who was that?

He had to do something to keep from being bored, so he conceived the idea of racing from one end of the long L-shaped roof to the other, just to see how fast he could get there. Skipping over dormers and running that risky high pitch, the icy spine of the roof—probably even a squirrel couldn't do it at night without falling.

Might be fun at that, to fall and fall, float down into a drift for a deep tidy nap. He felt as if he could sleep now, oh really sleep if he——

Later. First he would run. But he had to do something about his feet.

He uncorked the Wild Turkey bottle and drank the last

mouthful of bourbon, leaning against a chimney that had been hot earlier, but which now had cooled off. He imagined fires going out one by one down below. They'd had the brilliant idea of trying to freeze him into submission. They wanted him begging at the attic window where he'd had glimpses of faces watching. Let me in, let me in. Like a little kid. *I'm thorry.* Bullshit. He wasn't going in yet, and when he did he would pick his own window.

"Robin! Robin!"

Fuck *off*, mister. Or fall off.

No feeling in his feet, the strangest feeling of all. Robin supressed a giggle and belched instead.

Probably he shouldn't have thrown his shoes away, but he never could have made the vertical climb to the roof in a pair of Guccis. The wool socks had protected his feet for a while, even when they became wet and then stiff as chainmail. Now he had to find another way to warm his turned-off toes.

"Robbbbinnnnnn!"

The man's voice was nearer still, and spookily familiar though distorted by the wind. Wind, shut up! Robin listened. He didn't hear the man again. Well, right now he didn't care to be bothered. Keep coming, Robin thought; see what you get. Walk right on by this chimney and step down. Way down.

Robin set the bottle carefully on the slate behind him (might have missed a drop or two), and laboriously peeled the frozen socks from his feet. He unzipped his pants. He pissed jerkily at first, then produced a satisfying flood backed by the nearly full quart of bourbon he'd drunk during the last two hours. Pissed hard on his frozen feet, which he couldn't distinguish from the pieces of slate he was standing on.

Flashlight, its snow-crazed beam just touching him.

When the beam flicked away Robin wedged himself deeper in the waist of the chimney.

"Robin? Where are you? Please answer me!"

I'll kill you, Robin thought. Don't think I can't do it.

The room to which Gillian had been escorted by Granny Sig and Lana, the black-haired girl with the yellow headband and the deadly Taser, was a spacious end bedroom on the third floor. East-west windows and a big north fireplace wall. A fire on the hearth was burning low. Granny Sig turned on lights. Gillian stood shivering.

"O-open the windows," she begged.

"Lamb, you're shaking to pieces already," said Granny Sig.

"He's up there! Right up there!" Gillian pointed to a corner of the ceiling. "Please open the——"

Granny Sig looked at Lana, who moved her tough little jaw over a wad of gum. Lana shrugged.

"It's only your ass," she said. "Freeze it off if you want to."

Gillian snatched at the drapes of the east-facing windows.

Peter slipped and fell to his hands and knees. The steel flashlight he'd tied to his right wrist banged against the slate roof, but the faceplate was unbreakable glass and the light didn't go out.

Jesus, he thought, sweating inside his clothes despite the cold.

He stood up cautiously, a hand going to the nylon cord looped around his chest and waist. The line to the attic window he had climbed out of minutes ago was taut. He signaled curtly for slack. Just as he got it the wind, reversing abruptly, almost picked him off again. Snow felt like ground glass on his face. He crooked his left arm with difficulty and cleaned his lashes with the gloved back of one hand.

"Robin?"

But maybe the watchers had been mistaken, and hadn't seen him on this end of the roof after all. Robin could be a hundred and ninety feet away on the other side of the house, crouched in the lee of another chimney, unable to hear him. Certainly he wouldn't be able to see much better than Peter, and Peter felt nearly blind up here.

Or Robin might have fallen, soundless and unseen, some time

ago. In the morning, sun breaking orange over the vast white fields, they'd find him half-buried in a drift gone hard as rock during the subzero night.

The wind changed again and Peter smelled something unmistakably human: urine.

He brought his light to bear on the big chimney ahead. There was nothing beyond it but the dark and the streaming snow. Nothing in front of the chimney, either. But he moved closer, playing the light back and forth over the several facings of the double-octagon chimney.

Something was reflecting light in the deep dividing niche—it reflected high as lurking eyes. Oh God. He took another step.

Another.

"R-Robin?"

A face emerged warily from deep shadow. He was wedged in there sideways, although the niche scarcely afforded room for an average-sized boy. Peter could see that Robin was far from average. He'd grown tall, taller than his father. Peter doted on the red, snow-encrusted sprawl of curls on the manly forehead. *Oh beautiful!* Peter sobbed aloud. So familiar a face, yet dauntingly strange. He lowered the light so it wouldn't blind his son.

"Robin—Robin!"

Robin bared his teeth like a dog. Peter came up short and signaled impatiently for slack in the nylon line. They gave him another two feet.

"It's Dad, Robin."

Robin remained very still, but his eyes narrowed.

"I know—they told you I was dead. They lied! I've spent the last eighteen months looking for you. I never gave up, I—what's the trouble, Skipper? Don't you recognize me? Can't you say hello to your old man?"

He realized, belatedly, how stupid that sounded. Because he was standing behind the flashlight, Robin couldn't possibly make him out. To Robin's dazzled eyes he was just a vague shape in the near-dark.

Smiling, Peter turned the light on himself.

"Here I am, Skipper. It's no joke. I'm not a——"

Robin's charge took him completely by surprise, but at the perimeter of light he was casting on himself he saw the flash of a bottle aimed at his head and jerked his left shoulder high to take the crippling blow. It ended what little feeling he still had in the length of his arm. Slipping, falling, he clutched at Robin with his right hand and pulled the boy off balance. Then they both stepped off the flat of the roof and onto the slant, which was twelve feet of greased lightning.

They plummeted in a tangle to the gutter shelf and hung there. The two men at the other end of the nylon rope were jerked up against the inside of the attic window by the combined weight of Peter and Robin, and they lost valuable line, which branded their hands smoking hot and deep as the bone.

Outside, Robin went over the edge, hand in hand with Peter. He dangled face-up in the biting wind, eyes wide and a clean, celestial blue in the light from the dangling flashlight, his mouth almost a perfect O of surprise. Peter, with the lower half of his body on the roof and the looped cord strangling him at the waist, tried to reach out with his left hand to reinforce the precarious hold he had on his son.

There was no response at all. His left hand lay cramped and useless beneath him.

"PULL US UP! FOR GOD'S SAKE PULL US UP!" It took all the breath he had, but the wind shrieked louder.

Peter felt a sawing on the line; they slipped another two inches. Robin, still gazing at him in rapt attention, gasped but didn't struggle.

"Reach up," Peter said. "With your other hand. Get hold of the shoulder of my parka. Climb up over me. I'm—*God*—tied down, I can't fall. Come on, now. Do it. Before I pass out."

Robin reached up slowly, very slowly. His left hand touched the down-filled parka. He looked deeply into Peter's eyes. His hand moved on, touched Peter's face. Tears fell on the back of his hand.

"Oh, Skipper," Peter mumbled. "Come on; just come on. Grab hold."

Something joyous broke through the rigidly neutral expression on Robin's face.

"Ahhhhh—" he said, secure in that moment of vital recognition. "Help me, Commander!"

He smiled.

Then he fell, released by Peter.

Fell down and down, and smashed into the rocks at the edge of the lake.

The wind prowled over him. Men ran and lifted his body, and

there was a dark blot where his head had split open. Peter, hanging head down from the edge of the roof, looked on with somber inquiring eyes, betraying no understanding of the sudden tragedy. His expression of earnest inquiry didn't change when the one-armed man appeared in the snow to rant and curse him. It didn't change when the rope squeaked and slackened and he was lowered off the roof. Easier for him to go down than up. He momentarily lost consciousness when his legs swung down and the blood rushed from his head.

Peter was lowered another ten feet. When he lifted his head he saw Gillian's stunned face at a window. Grief took him by the throat.

"Oh, girl," he said—or thought he said. "How did it go so wrong?"

Peter wondered if she'd heard him. But he couldn't bear to go on looking at her. His eyes filmed over and he slumped, his head nodding forward. He swayed in the wind at the end of the crushing rope.

Childermass ran through the bedroom and pulled Gillian away from the window. He leaned out, batting the snow from his eyes.

"Peter! Peter, you son of a bitch!"

Peter's head was caked with snow. It drifted down his silent, closed face.

"You let him go! I saw it! You killed your own son! *Why!* Goddamn you, Peter, I know you're not dead! Give me an answer!"

He seemed to have seriously misjudged Peter for the last time. But then slowly, very slowly, Peter lifted his head until he was staring into Childermass's furious eyes. Granny Sig, looking on, thought she saw Peter smile. Perhaps not. But the gesture he made was unmistakable. Right hand lifted, rigid index finger extended.

Childermass turned away from the window, seized the nearest MORG agent and said, "Give me your piece."

"No!" Gillian screamed. She was dragged to the floor before she could place herself between Childermass and Peter.

Childermass was handed a .44 Magnum revolver. Six rounds of high-velocity, hollow-nosed ammunition. Taking up his shooting stance at the window, Childermass blew a great deal of

Peter away with the six shots. Set him twirling fiercely in a lull.
He had the decency to pull the drapes immediately after.

Lana was sitting on Gillian in order to keep her under control.
Gillian's eyes rolled hysterically as Childermass kneeled beside
her.

"Well, I don't have Robin any more," he said. "You'll have to
do."

He threw the hot revolver on the bed and left the room.

Twenty

The thing that killed was in the mind.

In her dream Gillian opened windows wide as the world and looked out at Peter, who was suspended in a void on a child's swing. Feet together, pumping rhythmically—successive arcs carried Peter higher and higher. He laughed and waved at her as he swung past the windows. Such good spirits.

/The doll, he called.

Gillian looked reluctantly at the Skipper doll in her hands. She'd always had Skipper, and she didn't want to share him. But Peter insisted. He had a right to Skipper too.

/Give him to me, Gillian, Peter said on his next slow pass at the windows. /Hand him over. His mood had changed. He wasn't laughing any more. She knew she'd better do what he said.

All she needed to do was lean out and Peter would swoopingly gather Skipper in his arms. But she couldn't be brave about the void she faced. Nothingness terrified her. She wanted to close her eyes and hold Skipper at arm's length for Peter to snatch away. But she had no eyelids. No matter which way she turned her head she was forced to see. Endlessly she went on seeing.

Skipper's head was in her hands. Skipper hung down dancing within reach of Peter, but Peter missed him. When Peter stretched out backwards, making a second effort to get his hands on Skipper, he lost his seat. He took Skipper down with him, they dwindled in the lonesome void. Gillian at the windows, hands outstretched, seeing, seeing. She was cursed with eternal vision. The eye dictated to the mind. It was a strange form of insanity, and the horrors had just begun.

She was still holding Skipper's head.

It rolled woodenly on her flattened palms, winking and giggling, sticking its tongue out at her. The head rolled up one arm and perched on her shoulder. There it turned into a toucan, a bird with a tyrannical eye and a fierce horn beak that gleamed like polished boots. The toucan picked up an ear and ate it. Gillian tolerated this. Peckishly it dismantled the bones of her head. Then it paused, gloating over the throb of blue uncovered brains. Now this is too much, Gillian thought tearfully. What's mine is mine. You miserable bird!

She awoke with a quiet shudder, blinking, instantly reassured that she was not doomed to a lidless existence. The mind despised the all-seeing eye, and did its best to shroud reality for the sake of the vulnerable organism. Her dream dissolved slowly. There was a glaze of firelight on the ceiling of the cold room in which she was bedded. She heard someone else breathing, through a stuffy nose, heard the pages of a magazine turning. Gillian moved her head carefully on the pillow, not wanting to rustle the crisp sheets.

The girl with the yellow headband was sitting in a chair near the fire with a magazine in her lap, rubbing her nose on the back of one hand. A high-intensity lamp beamed down on her. Gillian heard a clock ticking and wondered what time it was, and why she wasn't sleeping. Granny Sig had insisted that she take the capsules that would bomb her out for a day or more. Granny Sig had been kind of tough about it.

But her mind, despite the awful dreams, was sharp and clear. She was wide awake and, she hoped, able to think rationally. She even remembered the name of the girl with the yellow headband. Lana had been a constant companion since Shadowdown.

So if she wasn't sleeping, then the pills she had swallowed were nothing but sugar.

There was a point to that.

Granny Sig was the only one who seemed to care about her. As far as she knew, Gillian had never met a real transvestite before, although some of her mother's acquaintances. . . . She'd always considered transvestites to be woebegone, ridiculous creatures, but Granny Sig was forthright and intelligent and very easy to talk to. They'd spent nearly two hours discussing the tragedy, talking over Robin's many accomplishments and his ultimate failure to cope with his powers: The powers which she and Robin had in common. It was not difficult then for Gillian to unburden herself. Granny Sig understood.

A phone beside Lana rang. She glanced at Gillian, who was studying her through slitted eyes, and picked up the receiver. She listened for a few moments without speaking, then turned her head again.

"Totally knocked out," Lana said. She listened a while longer, then put down the receiver and approached the bed. Gillian feigned sound sleep. Lana put a hand on one shoulder and shook her gently. Gillian sensed that wouldn't be all, and willed herself to be a rock. Lana pinched her earlobe with sharp fingernails. Gillian didn't bat an eye.

Satisfied, Lana left her, murmured into the phone again, hung up and left the room.

Gillian waited, counted off two minutes. Then she sat up. She was alone. She got out of bed and, shivering, put on her clothes. She was thinking about Peter and the talk they'd had less than twenty-four hours ago. She wept for Peter, but her tears didn't last long. It wasn't what he would have wanted.

Her room was on the third floor. Granny Sig had made sure, during their whispered colloquy, that she had full knowledge of how the house was laid out.

The staircase down to the little-used servants' quarters was cold and poorly lighted; Gillian stumbled once and made some noise, then froze to the railing until she could get her heart out of her mouth.

When she reached the second floor the door, as Granny Sig had promised, was unlocked. A cabinet clock ticked loudly as she walked down the hall to the south wing. It was ten minutes past four in the morning.

But what about dogs? she had said, and Granny Sig said,

Childermass hates vicious dogs. He won't have them in the house.

All the bedroom doors in the south wing of the house were closed. Gillian was momentarily confused. She counted and recounted, then put her ear to one door and heard nothing. Listening at the next door she heard Lana, faintly, talking inside. She waited, poised to run. Nobody came near the door. Gillian continued to listen, but she didn't hear Lana speak again.

/What you do accidentally, Granny Sig said, you can do on purpose. By willing it.

No, it's horrible, I can't!

/Then you will surely end up like Robin. As mad and monstrous as Robin.

(The thing that killed was in the mind)

Gillian turned the knob and eased the door open. She entered the sitting room of Childermass's suite.

A single lamp was lit. Beyond the lamp, in the bedroom, Childermass sat naked on the side of his bed. Lana, still wearing her yellow headband but nothing else, was down on one knee between his legs, face close to his groin. She nuzzled and nursed. For all the reaction she was getting she might as well not have been there.

Gillian singled out a closet door near the bedroom door. Then, without much interest, she watched the sexual dumbshow as long as it lasted. Very tiring for Lana, but she brought him off.

As soon as Lana was finished, Gillian popped into the closet.

She heard them talking again. Apparently Childermass was an insomniac. He thought a hot bath might help. Gillian heard Lana in the bathroom filling the tub. When she came out Childermass complained that he was hungry. He wanted steak and eggs and a shot of brandy. Lana put her clothes on. From deep inside the closet Gillian watched her leave the bedroom. A few moments later the outside door clicked shut behind Lana.

Cut off the head, Peter had told her, and MORG's enemies will devour the body.

Gillian opened the closet door and started into the bedroom. Then she doubled back to lock the outside door.

Up to now she had stayed reasonably calm, but the act of locking herself in with Childermass almost snapped her nerve.

Her mind seemed to slip out of gear, because the next thing she knew she was standing agape in the bedroom just a few feet from his bath, hearing him sigh and splash lethargically in the deep tub. Childermass's back was to the door.

/What affects you might be described as rare form of epilepsy.
Oh, God, how can I do this?
I'm like a generator. Turn me on, turn me off.
/Robin could do it, said Granny Sig.
(What I can do you can do, Gillian. You're my sister)
But what turns the generator on, Granny Sig?
/Hate. Anger. Any powerful emotion.
I can't. I'm too afraid.
/Yes, fear. Fear will do. Use it.
/Use it, Gillian!

Keeping an eye on the bathroom door, Gillian quietly stripped the coverlet and blankets from the bed. She moved deliberately, but her pulse was hammering incredibly fast, at well over two hundred beats a minute. Her skin was flushed. She pulled the top sheet off and folded it twice.

When the bathroom door opened on a squeaking hinge Childermass trembled all over, startled out of a nodding doze.

"Lana?" he said. "Run some more hot water. And I could use a smoke."

"Go to hell," Gillian said.

With a mighty splash he sat up straight, craning his head. He had only a glimpse of Gillian's furious face before she threw the doubled sheet over him and followed with an armlock on his stubby body, bearing him down, holding him in the tub with all her strength. His scream was muffled by the sheet and cut off by a gush of water down his throat, although he managed immediately to get his face above the water line. He fought with his one arm, but the wet sheet clung suffocatingly. When he kicked his feet his head slipped far under water and Gillian pressed down again, snorting, her arms wet to the shoulders, her face dripping.

Then his blood began to flow beneath the sheet. Childermass, gasping and sobbing, thrust his head up yet another time before he sank again. Gillian looked away. It was terrible, yet better than her dreams. Here she could close her eyes and not watch the sheet turn red, the water turn vilely dark.

With her eyes tightly closed she remembered the expression on Childermass's face as he murdered Peter; she wondered what he looked like now. Gillian didn't really care. Her fury had ebbed almost immediately after she laid hands on him. She had fed it all to Childermass and now there was nothing to do but hang on while his strength flowed out of him.

It might have taken a minute, or an hour.

Cleaning up afterward was difficult; Gillian gagged and almost fainted. She had to strip herself to the waist. Fortunately the ski pants were a dark blue color, and she didn't mind the few spots on them.

In the bedroom she pulled a blanket around herself and opened windows. The snow had faded to isolated flakes and there was delicate color in the sky that became wave after wave of welcome light across the dumpy snowfields.

She didn't know what would happen now. There was no use trying to run. Her parents would know where to look for her, and they'd come soon. No one would stand in their way for long.

Lana was outside in the hall, rattling the knob, alarmed by the lock. Gillian was in no hurry to let her in. Something she had to do first.

She left the windows and found a mirror in which to see herself steadily, see herself true; redirected winter light struck her forehead like fire through a lens.

Maybe they'd lock her up for a while. She was dangerous, no doubt of that.

Dangerous—but not guilty.

Thank you, Peter, for telling me. I think I believe it now. There must be ways to control it. The thing that kills is in the mind. . . . But it's *my* mind. I'll find a way. No matter how long it takes.

She touched her face, and found that touch comforting.

"Okay," she said, "you're somebody I can live with."

Gillian smiled.

70 SUTTON PLACE

Joseph DiMona

A searing novel about the private lives of the beautiful
people – by the author of LAST MAN AT ARLINGTON.

70 Sutton Place is the most exclusive apartment block
in New York – a palace for the very rich and the very
famous. People like Pamela Morrow, the film star every
man wanted; John MacArthur, the glamorous senator
with a roving eye; Madame White, the legendary black
blues singer; Harley Widener, the theatre producer;
Jay Kohner, the magazine publisher; Bob Taylor, the
advertising executive.

But New York is a jungle, and even the very rich can't
stay isolated for ever. When both the Mafia and a Black
Power group decide to infiltrate the block, the sensuous
calm and glitter of 70 Sutton Place is shattered, and its
residents find themselves trapped in a web of terror and
violence that threatens not only their guilty secrets, but
also their lives.

LAST MAN AT ARLINGTON

Joseph DiMona

A knife-edged thriller that outpaces Forsyth in its
exposure of the ruthlessness and paranoia of
contemporary American politics – by the author of
70 SUTTON PLACE.

It begins with a death-threat. Six people who held minor
posts in the Kennedy administration are informed that
they will be killed to mark the tenth anniversary of his
assassination. The last name on this seemingly
arbitrary death-list is that of George Williams of the US
Justice Department. It looks like an insane hoax until
the first, Congressman Thomas Medwick, dies in a
dubious accident. Then the second is murdered with a
weapon used by the CIA. Aware his own time is running
out, Williams sets off on a one-man hunt for the
anonymous assassin. The trail takes him from
Washington to the jungle of Guatemala, but the closer
he gets to recognising the grim logic of the death-list
the deeper he finds himself in a terrifying battle for
survival.

'The American DAY OF THE JACKAL'
New York Magazine

'I read it from cover to cover without interruption and
remained under its spell for hours afterwards. It is a
superb thriller which has the rare distinction of being as
thought-provoking as it is exciting . . . At times the
tension is almost unbearable. In Joseph DiMona,
Frederick Forsyth has met more than his match.'
Irish Times

All Futura Books are available at your bookshop or newsagent, or can be ordered from the following address:
Futura Books, Cash Sales Department,
P.O. Box 11, Falmouth, Cornwall.

Please send cheque or postal order (no currency), and allow 22p for postage and packing for the first book plus 10p per copy for each additional book ordered up to a maximum charge of 92p in U.K.

Customers in Eire and B.F.P.O. please allow 22p for postage and packing for the first book plus 10p per copy for the next six books, thereafter 4p per book.

Overseas customers please allow 30p for postage and packing for the first book and 10p per copy for each additional book.